Acknowledgments

I'd like to thank my husband for his constant encouragement, and my daughter, Faith, for sleeping through the night, or this would not have been possible. Thanks to my sister Karen who forced me to take chances and financed a lot of them. Thanks to Tom Carson, David Chase, Bob Girardi, and Dave Marsh for their own work, which has been such an inspiration to me. An all-purpose thanks for everything to Lyla Oliver and Yossi Sharon, and especially to my agent, Cynthia Manson. Finally I'd like to thank my editor, Chuck Adams, for helping me find my way home.

For Nick, who would not let me quit

"Many—far too many—aspects of life which should also have been experienced lie in the lumber-room among dusty memories; but sometimes, too, they are glowing coals under grey ashes."
—C. G. Jung

"God's anger broke through the clouds,
And he spilt the cargo for all to see—
The fault of the sailor, the fault of he
Who asks no questions about the cargo he is carrying."
—Daniel Lanois

Part One

1

Valerie's marriage died one insignificant evening in early September. It was four years old and had been ailing for some time. The decision to end its life came to her suddenly. She was standing in the den, wondering if she should go for a power walk or collapse in front of the evening game shows. Out of nowhere she became acutely aware that her life was ridiculous, and the effort to deny it had finally exhausted her.

The notion itself was not new. She had suspected the absurdity of her circumstances for a long time. Years, perhaps. But it had never occurred to her with such undeniable clarity. She had never really felt, with such intensity, that slipping into her spandex shorts or hearing the theme music of *Jeopardy* might actually provoke a mental breakdown.

Still, it was important to be sure that she wasn't overreacting. She walked through the house, checking for things she might miss. To call the place a house was an optimistic exaggeration. It was a tiny, thin-walled bungalow in the hills above Malibu. There was something often described as a breathtaking view from the front of the house—which meant that the Pacific Ocean could be spotted over the roofs of other bungalows. In the early days, this view had enchanted Valerie. It was Malibu, after all, with its spectacular hills and its dramatic fog cradling the rocks against the shoreline. But lately, the view depressed her. The ocean had no calming effect. It looked angry, pitching relentlessly against the bluffs. The surfers bobbed in the waves like shipwreck survivors. The water spit gobs of chemical-infested seaweed onto the dingy sand. Carcinogenic rays of sunlight beat down onto the women in French-cut bikinis. A few yards away, traffic screamed past on the Pacific Coast Highway. It was hard to call Malibu paradise.

The rooms of the house were small and musty-smelling. Their bedroom, which should have been in the front facing the ocean, was in the back next to the kitchen. Her husband had taken the ocean-view master suite as his office. She had not argued at the time. She had confidence in his ability to compose great screenplays in that room, and the sacrifice seemed a noble one.

The third bedroom, a glorified closet, was referred to as Valerie's office. But Valerie had no business to conduct in it, as an actress's life really consisted of sitting next to the phone in any given location. She occasionally allowed herself to think of this room as a nursery, but lately that had depressed her even more. The odds of its being used as such were so remote that neither of them had seriously considered the impracticality of its location—downstairs, next to the laundry room. Even Valerie, whose maternal instincts were anything but well developed, knew that no one would stick their kid in a dank basement. So the sight of that room, littered with all the things they didn't know what to do with, convinced her that her decision was valid. All that remained was the task of telling her husband.

Jason was hunched over the desk in his study, late sunlight spilling across the room, turning it the color of golden ale. He was writing, as he always did, like a sixth-grader, one arm covering his paper to ward off roving eyes. He looked petulant and impish when he wrote, which was one of the reasons Valerie had trouble taking his work seriously. She hadn't been allowed to read anything since his first screenplay, the one which was actually made into a movie. All she really knew of his work was the process. For months he scribbled this way, then suddenly he began tapping on his computer, and finally, without much warning, he was finished.

Pieces of paper were scattered around his feet. Discarded nubs of pencils collected by his elbow like twigs. Jazz music came from some indistinct location, sporadic bleats of a trumpet. Valerie disliked jazz. In fact, she shared few of her husband's interests, which was one of the reasons she found herself in her current predicament.

"Jason," she said with a jolt, realizing why she had always disliked his name. There was no dignity to it. It was a teenager's name—the first guy on the block to have a ten-speed. It was difficult to approach someone named Jason with a subject such as this and expect it to sustain its importance. But she had no choice. "Jason, I've made a decision."

He held up a forefinger and continued writing.

"I am leaving you."

He put a period at the end of a sentence, covered the legal pad with a sheet of typing paper, and looked at her.

"Where are you going?"

"Home."

"You are home," he said with flat impatience, as if speaking to an Alzheimer's victim.

"Home to Maddock."

"Oh, here we go. Maddock, Virginia. I don't understand your fascination with that place, Valerie. You've turned it into some Faulkneresque hamlet. It's a backwater. You'll be bored in two days."

She stared at him for a moment, unsure how to proceed. Jason had a talent for making a conversation take a sudden, irrelevant swerve.

"I don't think you understand. I am *leaving* you."

There was an uncomfortable silence. She thought about walking out then, but she wasn't sure the scene was over. As Jason would say, it had no closure.

Finally he threw his hands up in a gesture of exasperation.

"What do you want me to say? 'Please don't go'?"

Valerie hesitated. This was precisely what she had expected him to say.

"I'll call you from home," she said.

"Why do you keep calling it home?"

"Because it is."

"You've lived in L.A. for fourteen years. You haven't spent more than a long weekend in Maddock in all that time. Yet you're sitting here talking about going home. You're like Scarlett going back to Tara or something. Jesus, it's like Thomas Wolfe time. I can't grasp it."

Valerie felt confused, as usual, wondering how he had managed to steer her miles away from the point. Furthermore, shouldn't he be concerned?

He was staring languidly at her with those tepid brown eyes, the fullness of his lashes making him look dreamy, purposeless. She knew there was an intensity to him—it was one of the first things that attracted her to him, in fact—but it did not reside in his eyes. Surely there was a slow-burning fire of angst or vision or something . . . for how else was it possible to explain his behavior? He sat in his study churning out one screenplay after another, which, though they often sold, were never produced. Yet he would not give up. She supposed she should admire his tenacity, but it was starting to look like childish willfulness. A kid who did not understand that the party had ended and everyone wanted him to go home.

"Well, I hope to God he is a genius," Valerie's mother had once remarked. "Otherwise, there is no excuse for him."

Looking at her husband now, she knew it was unlikely that Jason would ever prove himself a genius, and that this was finally the problem. He was a thirty-five-year-old man who made up stories for a living. Who sometimes wore the same shirt for days. Who drank scotch before dark. Who didn't own a suit. Who got lost on his own street. Who occasionally looked at his wife as if she were a complete stranger, some transient who had strayed into his existence. And these things were not indications of a great mind at work but of an average mind that was not working particularly well.

Through the window she could see a patch of ocean, the waves curling and crashing onto the pale sand. Jason's desk was situated so that he had his back to the view, as if he didn't want to know about it. This always raised the question in Valerie's mind as to why he so desperately needed to create in this room. But if she asked, she knew he would be ready with an answer that would make her feel small and incapable of understanding "the process." So she didn't ask. It no longer mattered.

Valerie finally walked away, feeling defeated. Pausing at the door she said, "Don't you even want to know why?"

Jason crossed his arms and shook the hair away from his forehead. It was dark and thick and perfectly straight but for a couple of rebellious curls. His jaw was square and austere. He should have scared her and had at one time.

But no more, she thought sadly.

"I'll tell you why," he said. "You're leaving because you're disappointed. Being married to a screenwriter has not lived up to its promise. You expected to be going to screenings and traveling to exotic locations and eating at Morton's every Monday night. You had no concept of the difficulty of this life. You didn't count on the struggle. Valerie, you're not cut out for hard times."

"And you," she said, "are not cut out for anything else."

She walked away then, with the image of him sitting behind his desk in the brassy sunlight, the smallness of him looming large in her mind.

2

Valerie did not watch the movie on the plane. Her faith in movies had been demolished by Hollywood. Her own brief excursions into extra work had allowed her to see the wires in film-making. She knew how many takes had gone into getting those earnest performances. She knew how childish and demanding the stars could be, how they cried on the set or locked themselves in their trailers because of a bad hair day. She knew from experience how tired the extras were, how they were herded around like cattle—their names never learned. Many was the time she'd been referred to as "female atmosphere."

Looking around, Valerie saw the passengers hooked up to their headphones, mesmerized by the images projected in front of them, mouths twitching with smiles of surprise. Not believing in movies made Valerie feel disconnected from the human race.

There was a time when nothing had mattered more to her than movies and the possibility of being in them. There was a time when she had not valued her uncomplicated existence in Maddock, Virginia. Growing up there, she always felt she was being excluded from some exciting social occasion. She was afraid that people in better places might be looking for her, and they would never find her, tucked away in a forgotten corner of the universe.

She had begun in the first grade telling her friends, her teachers, her neighbors, anyone who would listen, that she intended to leave Maddock in search of stardom. No one had laughed it off. It was a serious claim. Her mother even entertained the idea of taking her to see a child psychologist but finally decided against it, as that would have been more problematic in the long run than Valerie's outrageous proclamations. So her parents waited for it to go away. To keep peace, Valerie made her plans in secret. Her insouciance was a result of the private knowledge that nothing she did in Maddock could have lasting consequences. As a result, she spent a charmed and idyllic youth surrounded by people who wanted her or wanted to be like her.

When she got older, she began to notice that most, if not all, the people around her were perfectly content to stay in Maddock. They rarely envisioned vacations farther away than Myrtle Beach, South Carolina. Her best friends, Tess and Mary Grace, occasionally fantasized about Florida as if it were some distant, exotic location, where they might, if they played their cards right or married well, be allowed to visit. Valerie sometimes shared with them her dreams of living in a penthouse on the Upper East Side of Manhattan, or a waterfront property in Malibu. She spelled out her plans to become famous (starting out as a model, segueing into acting) and they stared at her in awe, as if it took courage just to imagine such things.

Valerie's desire for such a life stayed with her all through high school, and only began to diminish slightly when she fell in love. Joe Deacon, a tall, dark character of Irish extraction with lazy blue eyes, had captured her attention in her senior year in high school. He was raised in Richmond in a background of old money and had inherited a slow and easy aristocratic manner, even though the family fortune had long since disappeared. Joe was a boarding student at Millburn Academy, the military school three blocks from Valerie's house. The school was Maddock's only claim to fame, and its most direct connection to the outside world. Because of Valerie's great curiosity for anything outside of her hometown, she was naturally drawn to Millburn Academy and to the boys who attended. Joe was not the first Millburn student she had dated, but he was the most shining example of what the institution had to offer. He was the personification of Southern aristocracy, down to the fortune that had been frittered away.

Valerie was taken with him. He was handsome and smart and sophisticated. Only his lack of ambition concerned her. He gave lip service to the idea of moving away with her, but she knew his heart wasn't in it.

She had, however, managed to talk him into attending the University of Richmond, the only college of any repute that had accepted her. Their romance endured various temptations, because Valerie was no less noticed at college than she had been in high school. Somehow, Joe's phlegmatic manner, the confidence derived of breeding, had kept her interested and forced her to resist all other advances. Soon she became intrigued with her own feelings. She loved this man enough to question her ambitions.

What do you think you're going to do in Los Angeles? she'd ask herself, lying awake night after night in her dorm room, listening to the distant roar of parties on frat row. To make matters worse, Joe proposed during their junior year. He was an excellent student and, at her urging, was going to apply to law school. Their future together, by comparison, was easy to imagine. He would set up a practice in Richmond, or Maddock if she preferred. They would have money. She wouldn't have to work. They could take as many trips as she wanted to New York or L.A. or Europe. He promised her a honeymoon in Paris.

Her mother was eager to see this match take place. She came to Richmond and took Valerie shopping for wedding dresses. No expense would be spared. They would give her the biggest wedding Maddock had ever seen. Valerie found her resolve weakening at such a pace that her dreams of escape became shadowy, unfocused. She began to regard them as something belonging to her childhood. Los Angeles offered nothing but an enormous question mark, and the only thing it promised was anonymity.

Then, in her senior year, she signed up for Advanced Drama, where she encountered Phil Saxon, the head of the department. He was one of those teachers who collected admirers and inspired an irrational desire to please. He convinced Valerie she was destined for great things. She had a presence, he told her. A room went silent when she began to speak, he said. She became his project. She played Blanche DuBois and Lady Macbeth. Phil Saxon told her no one had ever brought those characters to life as she had, in his entire experience as a teacher.

She did not believe him. But she did believe that there were other places to go, other things to be than a small town lawyer's wife. And Joe helped to reinforce that idea when he started to discuss Myrtle Beach rather than Paris for their honeymoon.

"I'll have a lot of law school bills to pay. We'll need to start saving for a house. And besides, Paris isn't going anywhere. It's survived two world wars."

So Valerie had gone to Los Angeles, and Joe had married someone else. Shortly after, Phil Saxon had fallen asleep in bed with a lit cigarette and died in the fire. A gifted female drama student had narrowly escaped.

•   •   •

Valerie ordered another Bloody Mary when the stewardess came around because the first two had not eradicated these memories, nor those of Jason. She kept picturing him at the screening, the first time she ever laid eyes on him. In those days she was working as a temporary secretary, taking acting classes, looking for a commercial agent, getting occasional extra work and doing modeling for local department stores. It had seemed like a full life at the time.

The screening was of a movie that she had never heard of, a lesser-known offering whose main selling point was that its writer was a fabulous discovery, one of those young talents turned up from the slush pile and currently being courted by every agent and studio in town. The movie was a slick murder mystery, all about a lawyer who is thrown into some netherworld and emerges a better person because of his various brushes with death. It was full of smart twists and clever comebacks, which inspired the audience to whoop and applaud mid-scene. By the end, Valerie was equally convinced of the writer's genius.

Perhaps she had just gotten caught up in the moment. Screenings had a way of encouraging that. The milling around and kissing of cheeks, the kudos in the lobby, the backslapping at the banquet. It was contagious, the feeling of importance. And on that particular night, Jason had been at the center of it. The most photographed, the most touched, the most surrounded by well-wishers and gushers of every type.

Valerie had hovered by the seafood bar at the banquet, watching him and concluding that he was in fact a genius—his hair was so wild, his jaw so imposing, his manner so unconcerned. He was leaking things—bits of paper from his pockets, splashes of champagne from his glass, edges of his shirttail from his trousers. He wore jeans and a Weavers T-shirt and a raw silk jacket at least one size too big for him. He regarded his surroundings as if they simultaneously fascinated and bored him beyond measure.

Valerie waited by the shrimp until she saw him go to the bathroom. Then she followed him in.

He was zipping his fly when she came in. The surprise on his face gave her courage, so she introduced herself and asked him if he was doing anything after the banquet.

"Do you always follow men into bathrooms?" was his reply.

"No, it's my first time."

He stared at her for a moment, but not the way men usually did, the slow vertical cruise, adding figures in their heads. Instead he was studying her face, or more specifically her eyes. He was trying to see something in her rather than on her.

"You're from the South?" he questioned.

"Virginia."

He nodded slowly.

" 'Bright and fierce and fickle is the South,' " he said.

"Oh yes," she said, laughing, hoping he wouldn't ask her to identify the quote. It was the first of many times she would hope that.

He smiled, and that was the beginning.

Away from the spotlight of the event, Jason lost some of his initial appeal. He chose Musso and Frank's without consulting her. There he proceeded to spill change from his pocket, order before she did, and drink much too fast, leaving droplets of scotch on his lapel. But unlike the actors Valerie usually went out with, he seemed genuinely interested in something other than himself. He asked questions about her and listened with his eyes.

It was then that she told him about Maddock. In the time she had been in Los Angeles, she had begun to see her hometown in poetic terms. When she talked of it, she felt she was narrating some PBS documentary. At the same time, it all sounded quite accurate to her.

It was a small town on the North Carolina border, full of tree-lined streets and Victorian houses, with front porches that went on forever, where neighbors sat drinking iced tea with mint, discussing at leisure the events of their day. Magnolia blossoms bowed in the breeze. Dogs wandered by, unfettered. Cars passed slowly, when they passed at all, and front lawns exploded with the colors of the season: red and gold leaves in autumn, daffodils and dogwood in the spring, roses and morning glories in the summer, evergreens laced with snow in the winter.

Town was a two-block stretch of shops with colonial brick facades and muted awnings. The sidewalks were full during the day, and everyone knew each other and spoke or stopped to chat, and nobody ignored anybody or was in any special hurry. It was a gentle, civilized way to live.

"A regular Bedford Falls," Jason had replied when she finished her discourse.

"Sort of," she agreed, her mind racing to identify the reference. But Jason went on talking.

She listened to the story of his upbringing—son of a telephone repairman in a New Jersey suburb—and was grateful when he tired of it and moved on to another subject. She didn't want to know too much about Jason's background. She wanted to remember him as she had first seen him—an aloof intellectual, courted by the industry, flashbulbs popping around him, pencils scurrying whenever he spoke.

He was not the most handsome man she had ever gone out with. Nor was he the best dressed or the most charming. But he seemed to be the smartest. He seemed to know something that he refused to share with the world, mainly because he despaired of the world's capacity to comprehend it.

Jason was the first man who could make her envision things. She saw a future for them—all breathless and chaotic—movie offers and sudden plane flights and famous actors dropping by or phoning at all hours of the night. A life with him would be full, leaving no room for restlessness or inertia or questions of her own purpose.

But did this mean she loved him? She must have, she often told herself, because she married him against her mother's wishes. Helen had missed these nuances in Jason's personality, and focused instead on the fact that he always needed a shave and never wore socks. Valerie couldn't convince her mother that this man was destined for greatness. And as the years went by and his screenplays did not become movies, she could feel her mother's satisfaction hanging over her like a fog.

Valerie had forfeited the biggest wedding in Maddock. Instead they had a civil ceremony, and she wore a cream-colored cocktail dress that she had bought to wear as a seat filler at the Academy Awards. "Tawdry" was a word she tried to put out of her mind when she recalled the affair. "Congratulations, Veronica," the justice of the peace had said to her as he hugged her a little too tightly. Jason's agent and his common-law wife were the witnesses.

"Would you like another Bloody Mary?" the stewardess asked.

Valerie hesitated. She never had more than three drinks at a sitting, but these rules didn't seem to apply in the air.

"All right."

She started to feel drowsy. She closed her eyes and drove herself down the main street of Maddock, placing all the shops where they belonged. The post office on the left, next to the stoplight. The five-and-dime across from that, then Bill's diner, where it was appropriate to buy a hot dog from the window but never to go inside and sit down. She passed the drugstore with its antique apothecary sign, the bank, the jewelry store, and the courthouse where she and Tess and Mary Grace used to ride the elevators for recreation.

She hurried her journey, leaving gaps along the street, in an effort to get to Military Drive. There she made a left and at the bottom of the hill she saw the brick-and-marble sign under a pale golden light: Millburn Academy, Established 1908.

She knew those grounds well. She could place the soccer field and the chapel and the old gymnasium and the barracks. And she could see the boys in their crisp gray uniforms, their angular faces and perfect posture, the light reflecting off their polished shoes and belt buckles.

She had been infatuated with so many of those boys, always finding them superior to the local ones who by comparison seemed crass and lazy. The Millburn boys had substance. Their lives had story and scope. The Millburn boys had journeyed far to come there, some geographically, all of them emotionally. The Maddock boys had not journeyed at all, nor did they ever plan to.

She and Tess and Mary Grace had dated Millburn boys exclusively. Mary Grace was perpetually overweight, so she had no choice. (The cadets, often lonely and in desperate need of female companionship, were willing to sacrifice their standards in a way that local boys weren't.) Tess was painfully shy, and appreciated the polite and unassuming manner of the Millburn boys. They always behaved like gentlemen; they never swore in front of ladies, stood up when one came into the room, and were respectful when suggesting anything in the area of romance. Whether this was beaten or bred into them was unknown and unimportant.

"Send us a boy," promised the brochure, "and we'll give you a man."

Joe Deacon had actually posed for the photograph on the brochure, his tall, straight figure in full-dress uniform, outlined against a color-treated sunset. It was this image of Joe that remained with Valerie, though she knew both the brochure and the man had changed.

He was married now. He had married Tess. She knew it but couldn't get it to crystallize in her mind.

She had not been invited to the wedding. She supposed that made a certain amount of sense. She was in L.A. by then, and she and Joe had not parted on amicable terms. But Tess had been her very best friend. The exclusion still hurt Valerie a bit, even after all these years.

How many years? she wondered. At least a dozen. She'd been in L.A. for fourteen. All those years, all those miles, and where had she gotten? To this particular limbo so indistinct that it couldn't support an epithet such as middle age. She was just thirty-four. Thirty-four and on the edge of divorce, her first clear failure. Mistakes she had made. Mistakes were what everyone made when they were young. After that came failure.

It occurred to her, as she sucked the last traces of tomato juice out of the chunks of ice, that going home might well be her second failure. But that wasn't necessarily so. Surely greater people than she went home from time to time, looking for something they had neglected to take on their journey.

3

Every morning when he got up, Joe Deacon felt like the luckiest man alive. He had a wife he loved and respected, a good home in a quiet town, a job that offered moderate challenges and mobility. He went through his morning routine with the wide-eyed optimism of a child, certain that nothing but good things lay in store for him. He whistled as he shaved, admiring his full hairline, which showed no signs of deserting him. He sniffed his shirts appreciatively, savoring the clean, starched aroma for which Tess was responsible. He pictured her ironing them lovingly, maybe smiling as she did it, and a current of fondness passed through him.

Sometimes he sat on the edge of the bed, listening to the sounds of the kitchen, Tess moving around energetically, fixing breakfast or unloading the dishwasher, occasionally singing to herself, or swearing as she banged a knee or caught her finger in a drawer. She was mildly accident prone, and in the mornings, even that trait struck a chord of affection in him.

He loved his mornings, and it only depressed him a little to confront the knowledge that this perfect bliss tended to ebb considerably as the day went on. By lunchtime he had moved into a state of moderate satisfaction. In the afternoons he felt tired and remote. By evening, especially after a hectic day, he walked home with a sense of something bordering on despondency. The day had not surprised him. His days never did, and that awareness made him feel heavy and lethargic.

But he was never depressed for long, because he knew morning was coming, and with it would come that rush of near euphoria.

This particular morning Joe was optimistic but unsettled. As he shaved and dressed, he didn't hear the sounds so familiar to his routine. There was no singing, no clamoring, no swearing. All he heard, if he strained his ears, was a low mumbling, like a radio turned down to an impractical volume. But he knew it wasn't the radio. He knew it was Tess.

He stood in the doorway of the kitchen, surveying its contents. Tess was wearing her old turquoise terry-cloth bathrobe, tied with a frayed ribbon and pulling at the seams. He admired her lack of regard for her appearance. He interpreted it as a sense of security rather than slovenliness. She sat with arms crossed over her stomach, a relatively new habit. After her first miscarriage she had adopted that posture, as if to protect her abdomen, not from internal pain but from hostile invasion. She had had three miscarriages altogether, two in the last year, and her struggle to keep her spirits up was taking a toll. She looked tired these days but no less pretty. She had the kind of face that was at its best when left alone. Her skin was the color of rich buttermilk, a pale golden tone which she hated but he found enticing. Her eyes were stained-glass green, her teeth small and straight, her face a perfect oval. Her hair was ash blond and she wore it in an unimaginative blunt cut below her chin. It was reasonably cared for, yet purposely unattended, as if to say, it's only hair, after all.

Joe stared at his wife for a long moment, feeling all the things he always felt for her, trying to absorb them completely so that he wouldn't become annoyed by the mess in the kitchen. It looked as if they had entertained a party of twelve the night before, even though they had eaten out.

"Somebody better call the Red Cross," he said.

Tess didn't answer, and it was then that he noticed she wasn't alone. Sitting across from her at the table, behind a pyramid of magazines and general clutter, was her best friend, Mary Grace Reynolds. Although Mary Grace's presence before breakfast was highly unusual, Joe was relieved to see her. Until then, he was afraid Tess had been speaking in those low, conspiratorial tones to herself.

"Well, M.G.," he said, "to what do we owe this extraordinary pleasure?"

"You don't owe me anything, Joe. Just pull up a chair and enjoy my company."

"Don't you have to work?"

"I do, but Dr. Powell doesn't have a patient until ten o'clock, so he told me to take the early morning off. I don't know what's going on with everybody's teeth these days. I know there's a recession, but folks still get cavities, don't they?"

"People let their health go in a recession. They consider it a luxury," Joe said, with nothing to support this except for a gut feeling.

"Speaking of health, we're out of Special K," his wife informed him. "You'll have to eat Raisin Bran."

"Just as well. My colon is smiling."

"This is what I like. An early-morning discussion of bowel activity," Mary Grace said. "Makes me wonder what you two talk about when I'm not here."

"We talk about you," Joe said, pausing by his wife for a kiss.

He sat down and poured milk on his cereal. Tess moved languidly to the counter and fixed him a cup of coffee. Mary Grace smiled at him across the table and he felt uneasy. He had known her nearly a decade, and most of that time she had been at least fifty pounds overweight. She had lost it all in the last year, and now it was confusing to look at her. He kept wanting to bend and pull her into the woman he used to know, fat and jolly, rather than sharp and aggressively attractive. Her face had always been pretty—a cliché about overweight people, he knew, but it was especially true with her. She had big brown eyes and thick brown curls, and it used to be easy to look at her from the neck up and imagine the beauty she could be. It was easy because no one had ever had to contend with that beauty. Now they did, and it was nothing less than scary.

Tess treated her old friend as if nothing were different. Women had that ability; they took change under their wing like stray pets or orphaned children. Your modification is safe with us, they seemed to say. We won't talk about it again.

He envied this quality. He spent a great deal of his time envying his wife's qualities.

"Good coffee," Joe said to Tess as he sipped it.

"She makes the best," Mary Grace enthused. "Isn't she something, Joe? I can't get over the things she can do. She reupholstered that couch all by herself? It's not easy to do that."

"You don't have to sell me on Tess. I married her."

Mary Grace shrugged and lit a cigarette. Joe waved the smoke away, feeling more irritable than he wanted to be.

"Do you have to smoke, Mary Grace?"

"Of course I don't. I probably shouldn't."

"Then why don't you stop?"

"Scared I'll gain the weight back," she answered honestly.

"You'd rather be dead than fat?" he challenged.

"Let me get back to you on that one, Joe."

"I don't know why he's being this way," Tess apologized, then shot a look at her husband.

Joe shrugged, unsure himself.

"I get the feeling something's going on," he finally answered. "And that makes me edgy."

Tess and Mary Grace exchanged glances.

"What's going on?" he pressed.

Mary Grace took a puff of her cigarette and seemed about to say something, but Tess intervened.

"Nothing's going on. Eat your cereal or you're going to be late. You know how the Glasses are about punctuality."

"The Glasses are hardly ever on time themselves," Joe said defensively. He didn't like to think of himself as being manipulated by a couple of balding guys who seemed to have forgotten everything they ever knew about the law. Glass and Glass was actually the town's oldest law firm, having been passed down by generations of Glasses, and people kept coming to them more out of habit than anything else. New lawyers set up shop, but people were suspicious of them. Their fathers and their fathers' fathers had used Glass and Glass (Glass, Glass, and Glass, back when the eldest Glass was alive), so they couldn't see any reason to change the pattern, even though Joe didn't think they were a very competent firm. He was one of two new lawyers they had taken on to handle the workload and "introduce modern and innovative ideas" into the company. So far the most modern and innovative contribution he had made was persuading them to invest in a fax machine. Most of the time it sat unused in the corner of the coffee room, as the old partners were wary of it.

Joe didn't have the impassioned devotion to the law that he saw in some of his former schoolmates, but he did believe that there were sensible and efficient ways of getting the job done, none of which were practiced at Glass and Glass. However, when he tried to make suggestions, one of the balding Glasses would chuckle condescendingly and say something beginning with, "Son, when you've been an attorney for as long as I have . . ." Eventually Joe gave up and concentrated on the tedious, unchallenging tasks they assigned to him: reading contracts, writing briefs, having dinner with clients.

He had never really wanted to be a lawyer, though this was something he only confronted during his long walks home in the evening. It had been an idea put into his head for reasons long gone, and before he knew it he was stuck with a profession he had given precious little consideration to.

Tess was not impressed with his career, although she wasn't critical of it either. She had just always made it clear that she would have loved him every bit as much if he had chosen to dig ditches for a living. Since he had always harbored a notion that a job was something you did to make a woman happy, her lack of interest left him feeling a bit disoriented.

In fact, Tess enjoyed making light of his job. She thought Hayward and Leon Glass were comical characters who belonged more in the produce department at Kroger's than in a legal office. It was true that they were short and stout and usually dressed badly, and that they were both more interested in college basketball than the judicial system, but occasionally Joe sensed that they were shrewd businessmen. They could be demanding when it came to the performance of their workers, and had been known to dock people for being late. So he realized that Tess's warning had some validity, even though she was joking.

"What do you do in that office all day?" Mary Grace asked.

"I write a lot of briefs."

"Do you get paid much?"

"Not yet."

"I thought lawyers were all rich."

"I thought so, too. I was misinformed."

"Do you wish you could do something different?"

Joe hesitated before answering, pausing to look at his wife. It was occasionally a touchy subject between them, because Tess knew only too well why her husband was a lawyer.

Tess didn't seem to have heard the question. She was sipping her coffee thoughtfully.

Joe said, "Wish in one hand, spit in the other, and see which one fills up first."

Mary Grace rolled her eyes. "You two are really disgusting in the morning. All you talk about is body functions. Speaking of which, when are you going to fix me up with some eligible bachelor?"

"When have you seen one around Maddock?"

"There have to be a few. No town can be completely devoid of interesting men. I figure I'm looking in the wrong places. Either that, or the ones around here still think of me as fat."

Joe started to deny that but found he couldn't, since he still thought of her as fat. It was as if the fat person had gone away on vacation but would probably be back soon.

"I'll keep my eyes and ears open," Joe said. "On one condition."

"Name it."

"Tell me what's going on."

This snared Tess's attention. She put her coffee mug down with a thud and looked at him. Her face was as serious as he had ever seen it.

"What?" he implored. "Is somebody dying?"

Tess bit her lip until it turned pale.

Mary Grace stubbed out her cigarette and sighed the smoke in his direction.

"Valerie Caldwell is back in town."

Joe resisted a laugh. The somber expression on his wife's face told him that such an outburst would have serious repercussions. Still, he could not resist expressing his relief.

"Is that it? I thought somebody's life was in danger."

"Well," Mary Grace said, "you could be right."

He did not take her invitation to debate the seriousness of the situation. Instead he asked, "How did we come by this highly classified information?"

"My mother," Tess answered. "She talked to Helen this morning."

"It gets worse. She's left her husband," Mary Grace said. "And Helen thinks it's for good."

"Well, at the risk of sounding glib, I have to ask the burning question 'So what?' "

Tess's eyes narrowed and she pinched her bottom lip with her thumb and forefinger. It was one of the nervous gestures she had developed in recent months. Only this specific gesture was new. His wife had always clutched at herself. When he first met her she clutched her face, squeezing her cheeks in her fingers until they turned a bright pink. When she walked she clutched her elbows; when she sat she sometimes clutched a knee between her hands. It was as if she felt herself in danger of falling apart, as if her limbs might go floating out to space. It would be fair, he thought, to call his wife a nervous person.

Mary Grace said, "The big deal is she wants your ass."

"That's ridiculous. I haven't spoken to her in—what—*ten* years? I have no interest in her whatsoever, and I'd be willing to bet she feels the same way about me."

"Good thing you're not a stockbroker," Mary Grace said.

Tess leaned across the table. Her hand searched for his and fell on it. Her fingers felt small and soft, like a child's.

"You know how she is," Tess said. "She wants everything, especially something she feels she has a right to. She owned you once, and I know she'd like to do it again."

"She never owned me."

"Well."

It was first rate, her "well," the kind of "well" that women spent a lifetime perfecting. Short, clipped, suggesting volumes in a single syllable.

Joe fought another temptation to defend himself. He couldn't bear to think of Valerie owning him or even having any influence over the way he lived his life. When he thought back on the days when he was involved with her, he liked to believe that he still maintained some sense of autonomy. But in the moments when he dared to be honest with himself, he knew that this retrospective wasn't entirely accurate. Valerie was the reason he was a lawyer. She had envisioned him as one, and her visions had soon become demands, and since they were still involved when he entered college, he then thought of himself as the suitable mate for Valerie Caldwell. She wasted no time in letting him know what that vision entailed.

Valerie had always threatened him, but she threatened his wife more. He and Tess had begun their affair while he was still picking up the pieces of his broken relationship with Valerie, and Tess had never overcome the insecurity of being something he settled for on the rebound. She thought she was a consolation prize. The thing he could never make Tess understand was that disentangling himself from Valerie Caldwell was much more a liberation than a defeat.

Now, if their information was correct, Valerie was back in town, and he didn't know how to begin reassuring his wife. He could have told her that Valerie's proximity made no difference. If she had wanted him she would have pursued him from any distance. But he didn't think Tess would take comfort in that.

So he said, "I can't believe you two are still obsessed with her after all this time."

"We're not obsessed, Joe," Tess claimed.

"Yes, we are," Mary Grace said. "That girl made me miserable my whole young adult life. I swear to God she's the reason I was fat. You notice I lost it all after she left."

"Not right after she left."

"Well, it took me a while to bounce back. Joe, she's poison. She's a goddamn walking disaster."

Having said that, Mary Grace moved to the counter to refill her coffee. She lumbered like a heavy person. Joe wondered if she could still feel the weight, the way amputees often claimed to still feel their missing limbs.

"My God, Mary Grace, the three of you were best friends," he said.

"That was years ago," Mary Grace said.

"So what? You can't rewrite history. You can't pretend the three of you weren't constant companions."

"Not constant," Tess said weakly, but now she would not look at him. She knew perfectly well that the first time Joe met any of them was at a Millburn dance, and they were all sitting together at the same table. He knew they were the kind of friends where one would not go to the bathroom without taking the other two along. Sometimes Joe felt his wife's impatience with him stemmed from the fact that he knew too much about her past.

"We were friends then," Mary Grace finally admitted, "because we didn't know better. We didn't realize what she was doing to us."

"And what was that?"

"We were her puppets. Her slaves. She said jump, we said 'How high?' on the way up."

"You two have nothing to worry about," Joe said, hoping to make that the last of it.

"When Valerie's in town, there's always something to worry about."

Joe pushed his bowl of cereal away and stood, putting his jacket on in an authoritative manner. Tess watched him, pinching her lip.

"I don't want to hear any more talk about her. Just what do you think is going to happen even if she is back? Will you tell me that?"

Tess smiled. "I'd tell you, except you don't want to hear any more talk about it."

Joe smiled back, relieved to see her sense of humor returning. He knew that sarcasm was a balm to her, a way of making things all right.

"I'll probably be late tonight," he said, kissing his wife.

"I'm probably not surprised."

On impulse he went to Mary Grace and kissed her on the cheek. She didn't seem to think this was extraordinary, though he couldn't remember having done it before.

"You two do something constructive while I'm gone."

"We had planned to put a new roof on the house. Maybe rewire the electrical system," said Tess.

He went out of his good but plain two-bedroom house, and began his pleasant walk to work. He tried to deny it, but the fact was, the typically jubilant mood with which he began each day had been usurped and supplanted by a dull, nagging worry he could not name.

All he knew was that his days tended to get worse as they wore on, which did not bode well for the coming evening.

4

"*Rufus Batterman* shot himself," Lana Brumfield said as she walked into her daughter's house.

Tess looked up from the book she was reading.

"Intentionally?"

"What other way is there?"

"Accidentally."

"Oh, well, *that*," Lana said, as if the idea somehow disgusted her. "No, it was intentional all right. He shot himself on purpose."

Tess turned a page.

"Where?"

"In the bathroom."

"No, I meant what part of his body?"

"He blew his brains out."

Tess tried to picture the scene, though she doubted its accuracy. In Maddock, it seemed that certain scenarios were always described the same way, regardless of how they actually might have transpired. People always "blew their brains out," no matter where they aimed the gun. They always "dropped dead," even if they went peacefully in their sleep. And married men always "ran off" with another woman, even if they simply moved their belongings across town.

Tess couldn't drum up much emotion about Rufus Batterman's death. She hardly knew him. He was a mechanic at the Ford place,

and she and Joe drove a Toyota, so they hadn't had much occasion
to socialize with him. Her parents knew him somewhat better, as
they had driven a Lincoln for years. She knew that her mother had
never cared much for him because of the gap in his front teeth and
the lisp that it provoked.

"I have to ask him everything twice," she often complained, as if
Rufus lisped just to annoy her.

But as Lana lowered herself onto the couch, trembling while she
lit a cigarette, one might have guessed she loved and admired the
man.

"Lord, what a day I have had," she said. "First I heard about Rufus. That made me so nervous, I dropped a jar of pickles I was making and it broke and juice went flying. Louisa licked it up and then
she got sick and vomited in the living room."

"Poor Louisa."

"Well, she's got a sensitive digesting system," Lana said defensively. "All Yorkies do."

"Then what happened?"

"Well, I went to garden club and had it out with Eileen Burke,
once and for all. She got up in front of the group in that prissy, put-
on way she has and told us we couldn't use Styrofoam in our
arrangements anymore out of concern for the environment. Have
you ever heard anything so stupid? Saving the world has come to
Maddock!"

"What was her reasoning?" Tess asked, turning another page before she was completely finished with it.

"Styrofoam takes forty-some years to biodegrade and I said,
'What difference does it make? We'll all be dead by then.' Everybody laughed."

"And what did Eileen say?"

Lana puckered her mouth, as she always did when impersonat-
ing anyone who annoyed her, including her husband.

"She said, 'Lana, I wish you would try to think of the future generations of Maddock.' I said, 'Eileen, I got enough trouble thinking
of my own generation. And besides, I don't think the world is going
to hell in a handbasket because I use one clump of Styrofoam in my
flower arrangement.' "

"And what did she say?"

"Nothing."

This signified the ultimate victory in Lana's mind—reducing people to speechlessness. She took a nourishing drag on her cigarette.

"I declare, I have had my fill of Maddock. I am not used to this behavior. I was raised in a city. It was your father who had to live here because he couldn't be two blocks away from his mother."

"I know, Mama," Tess said indulgently. The city her mother claimed to be from was Lynchburg, whose somewhat unsettling name was about the only interesting thing it had to offer. It was small as actual cities went, but it had half a dozen factory outlets, which to Lana was always a sure sign of civilization.

"And to top it all off, that mess Valerie Caldwell is back in town," Lana said.

"You told me."

"I love Helen like a sister, but I don't trust her daughter further than I could throw a brick. She's like that girl in the movie *The Bad Seed*."

Tess said nothing. She turned another page.

Lana sat for a moment, gazing around the living room, her eyes moving back and forth in thought, as if perusing an invisible file to find the next complaint she wanted to air.

But apparently she had actually been thinking about the room because she said, "Tess, I swear, this house looks like the wreck of the *Hespus*."

"*Hesperus*, Mother."

"I don't know what in the world Joe must think."

"He doesn't care," Tess said doubtfully. In fact, now that her mother had pointed it out, she began to worry that she was letting things go. The idea of Valerie being back in town made her especially sensitive to her own shortcomings, and suddenly she had a need bordering on panic to set things right.

She said, "I should vacuum. I'm going to do that."

Lana said, "You should get a cleaning crew in."

"I might do that, too."

Lana said, "I don't see any reason you can't keep this house clean, now that you're not working anymore. What excuse do you have?"

Tess said, "I'm trying to have a baby."

"Oh shit," Lana said skeptically. Though she had the appearance of a proper Southern matriarch, she often had the mouth of a Marine. "You aren't trying to have one twenty-four hours a day."

"But I'm . . ." Tess stopped at the edge of what she wanted to say, what Mary Grace always said, that she was a "bottomless pit of hormones." Mary Grace said it kindly, as a means of excusing Tess for her mood swings and prolonged bouts of insecurity. She believed it when Mary Grace said it, and was able to forgive herself for feeling like a speeding car with a loose wheel. Somehow, she knew she could not share it with her mother. Lana had no patience with anything as nebulous as hormones.

"I'm going to clean up," Tess said at last.

"Good. I would help but I've got to drive your grandmother to the doctor. That woman isn't happy unless she's got a pain."

"What is it this time?"

"Corns."

"On her feet?"

"Where else? I swear, Tess, sometimes you make me nervous."

Lana extinguished her cigarette and went to the door, giving her daughter what was meant to be a caring look.

"I can't help worrying," Lana said.

"About what?"

"That girl."

"Joe says he couldn't care less about Valerie, Mama."

"Let me tell you a little something about men, young lady. They don't always mean what they say."

On that sagacious note she exited, giving a dramatic slam of the door. Tess stood at the window and watched her mother walk away. It was hard to believe that the short, gray-haired woman with the skinny legs and generous behind and carnation pink Reeboks could know anything at all about men.

But Tess was superstitious about her mother and she couldn't help thinking that anything Lana foretold, however vaguely, was destined to come true.

She shuddered, then went for the vacuum cleaner.

5

Valerie awoke in her old bed, the white eyelet bedspread tucked under her chin, and lemon-colored patches of sunlight spread across the eggshell carpet. For a brief and wonderful moment she thought she might be sixteen and late for school, only a matter of seconds before Helen's stern but caring voice urged her to get moving. Even after the moment passed she tried to keep the fantasy alive. It wasn't difficult; her room was exactly as she had left it, with pictures of horses and Williamsburg scenes on the wall, her bulletin board covered with invitations, football programs, and dried corsages; there was even an old picture of her and Joe on the dresser. It was the one from the Military Ball their senior year. That annual affair was the most important occasion Millburn had to offer, a grand, old-fashioned ball, where the cadets wore their full-dress uniforms and their dates wore formal gowns, the kind which required a special trip to Lynchburg, Richmond, or even Greensboro, North Carolina, to acquire. The gym was converted into a ballroom, full of flowers and crepe paper and colored lights. People came from all over town, all over the state in fact, to witness it. And for the senior cadets, the officers, there was a ceremony called "the figure" during which the cadets paraded their dates across the floor, all of whom were dressed in white gowns and carrying a half-dozen red roses. (She understood the girls now carried carnations, a sign that the finances as well as the standards at Millburn were deteriorating.) A panel of judges eyed them carefully, smiling with admiration and a distant sense of envy, and voted on the most beautiful, the most graceful, the queen of the ball.

This was Valerie's most difficult memory about Millburn, the fact that she had not won the figure. Strangely enough, it hadn't mattered to her then. A rather plain out-of-town girl with mousy hair and slumped shoulders had taken the honor, and the miscarriage of justice had been so obvious to her (as well as to her friends) that she had to believe the judges' criteria included something ulterior and untoward.

"They always give it to out-of-towners," her mother had said. "Just to prove they aren't partial."

Joe had claimed it was because the girl's date, Alvin Carpenter, had a higher rank than he did. But Valerie did not bother to make excuses. She was secure in her own beauty, and besides, she knew that greater things were awaiting her.

Suddenly, as she stared at the picture of her younger self in the white lace gown (much grander than her wedding dress), she felt the first full stab of disappointment. Because she ought to have won, because she needed such a memory, and because greater things had not, after all, been awaiting her.

She sat on the edge of her bed, bracing herself for the sting of loneliness when she remembered that she really had left Jason. The awareness came, but nothing new came with it. More often than not she woke up alone. Jason went for a run on the beach at dawn, then drove down to a local restaurant for a business meeting—a power breakfast, as they were known. By the time he and Valerie met up again at lunchtime, he had lived out the adventures of an entire day, while she had only poured her second cup of coffee. Now she was saddened by the fact that she had no strangeness to confront, no otherness to adjust to, after making the biggest decision of her life.

The sadness only lasted a second, like an annoying cramp in a neglected muscle. She had things to do, people to see, plans to make. She was starting over. She got out of bed and slid into her old white candlewick bathrobe. Her mother had kept it in pristine condition. Gone were the stains, the tiny frays, and all that remained was the provocative smell of her youth.

The scene in the kitchen was achingly familiar. Her mother cooked, while her father sat at the table in his corduroy trousers and tweed jacket, gazing distractedly at the paper. Ingrid, the family mutt, whined futilely at his feet.

There was a substantial amount of gray in her father's hair, but it had not receded at all; his figure was still trim, his jaw still somewhat slack, suggesting a lack of concern, or even understanding of anything outside the most earth-shattering catastrophe. The fact that his daughter had come home did not qualify. He glanced up at her as casually as if she had never left, or as if her return were so predictable he felt no obligation to respond to it.

He was still a professor of general math at Redhill College, a private school for girls some twenty miles out of town, but had cut down his workload in recent years. He only went in three days a week and no longer taught night school or summer sessions. This did not seem to affect him in any discernible way. He still maintained a stern preoccupation with his work and a phlegmatic detachment from his home life. Frank Caldwell habitually employed the posture of a visitor, poised for a polite escape at any given moment, attuned to the events around him as one would be to the drama of some place like South Africa—they interested him, but didn't seem to have much to do with his life.

"Your mother told me you were coming home," he said proudly, as if to demonstrate his grasp of current events.

"Yes, Daddy. Here I am."

She kissed him and told herself he had not flinched.

"I hope it's not serious," he said.

"What's not serious?"

"This business with Jason. I like him. He's a fine boy."

Helen clucked her tongue, then pretended she was talking to the coffeemaker.

"Well, Daddy, it would have to be pretty serious to make me come home, wouldn't it?"

Frank didn't answer. He had journeyed as far as he cared to go into family matters, and now he preferred to retreat into the business pages. Valerie let him. She and her mother had developed a policy of laissez-faire with Frank, and through the years it had worked out well for all involved.

"What do you want for breakfast?" Helen asked.

"Something familiar."

"How about cornflakes?" Frank asked, shoving the open box toward her. "Can't get any more familiar than that."

"I know what I'd like. Some angel biscuits with redeye gravy," Valerie said.

"What?" her mother asked, apparently taken aback.

"You know, we used to have it all the time. Those light biscuits you used to make, with that thin salt gravy. I could die for that. I'll die if I don't get it. Ingrid would like it, too," she said.

Ingrid looked confused, hearing her name so early in the day, and having attention focused on her before she needed to relieve herself.

"Whatever made you think of redeye gravy?" Helen asked.

"What do you mean? We used to have it all the time, remember?"

Helen shook her head. "Occasionally, at Christmas."

"Mama, it was a staple of our diet. It's a classic Southern breakfast."

"I guess we aren't all that classically Southern," Frank said in a smug, self-amused tone.

"Honey, you're wrong," Helen persisted. "We have some grits, though."

"No, Mama. Don't fight me on this. It's my homecoming. I'll make it myself. What do we need?"

"Well, for one thing you need an entire ham, which I don't happen to have at the moment."

"We could go out and kill a pig, I suppose," Frank said.

"Daddy, don't you think you've contributed enough?"

"And those biscuits take all day to make," Helen continued. "Honey, I'm sorry, but if you'd given me a little warning . . ."

"Oh, never mind."

Frank turned a page of the paper, rattling it decisively.

"We've got some frozen French toast," he said. "Tastes like the real thing."

"Aren't you late for work?" Helen implored her husband.

"I am," he agreed cheerfully, folding the paper neatly before setting it aside. He was careful to preserve it for the rest of the family, never noticing that when he came home in the evenings it was right where he had left it, undisturbed.

"Goodbye, dear," he said to his wife, who only nodded in his direction. She was still baffled over the angel biscuits and redeye-gravy issue.

"What is wrong with him?" Valerie asked her mother when Frank had left.

"Nothing, sweetheart, he's old."

"He doesn't look that old."

"It isn't how you look, it's how you feel. Besides, he isn't all that different. Won't you let me fix you an egg?"

"Runny in the middle?"

"Only a little, the way you like it."

"Okay, but I want redeye gravy before I leave here."

During breakfast Helen and Valerie discussed their plan for the day. Valerie insisted on going into town and shopping at all her favorite places, including the Fashion Hamlet and the Gift Cove.

Helen acquiesced, though not without warning her that things in Maddock weren't exactly as she remembered.

"The selection hasn't been all that good since the economy took a downturn."

"When was that?"

"Well, you know. Everything is slow lately, and especially since the enrollment in Millburn has gone down."

"That's only temporary, Mama. I saw on the news last week that military schools were coming back into fashion."

"Well, that news hasn't hit Maddock."

"It will," Valerie said confidently, though she couldn't be sure if she was actually quoting a news show or just something she had said to Jason during an argument about her so-called love affair with Maddock.

As Valerie was scraping up the last bit of her egg with a piece of toast, Helen peered through the smoke from her cigarette and asked, "Are you going back to him?"

"No," Valerie said, surprised at her lack of hesitation.

"What about your career?"

"Oh, that," Valerie said.

When she was in Los Angeles, what Valerie did with her days was more like an eclectic mix of opportunities than a career—an unexpected audition for a wine cooler commercial, filling in for a friend as an extra on a horror movie, parading evening wear through the restaurant of a department store at lunchtime. At one time she thought it was all leading somewhere, that she might actually distinguish herself as the Wine Cooler Girl, or give an outstanding performance as a slain body on the beach, and that things would spiral upward from there. That was what everyone in Hollywood believed—that the next phone call could be the one to change your life. And it might be true. But sitting by the phone hoping for some nebulous big break did not seem to constitute a career, at least not to her.

Still, she felt a stab of sadness at the loss of her ambition. For years it had been like a friend to her, accompanying her in the darkest moments of her life. When she was living in a studio apartment in a crime-ridden area of Hollywood, when she sat in traffic on the freeway in the boiling heat, breathing in exhaust fumes, her ambition sat beside her; it was palpable, it had a voice. It said, *You are here for a purpose.* But the voice had grown weaker with each day she spent with Jason. His career had taken over, and his ambition was nothing like a friend. It was a loud, intrusive houseguest she felt obligated to entertain.

Among the many things she hoped to find in Maddock was that sense of purpose, a desire so strong it might send her packing again. But it would take time, and she was prepared to wait.

"My career is on hold, Mama. I need to sort my life out."

Helen looked at her, those penciled eyebrows moving into a stern question. Her mother was a hard, weathered beauty. Her hair was as blond as Valerie's, her eyes just as blue. Lines had attacked her mouth but left the rest of her face alone. Of all the people Valerie had met in her travels, Helen remained the most poised, the most unperturbed by her surroundings.

"I know you find this hard to believe," Valerie said, her voice tight and defensive, "but there was a time when I truly loved Jason. I still think he's a better person than you give him credit for."

"I only thought he could stand to dress a little better, pay a little more attention to his manners. I never commented on his worth as a human being."

"It's one and the same with you, Mother. Be honest."

Valerie pushed her plate away and swirled her orange juice around in the glass. She stared at the pulp and thought of the surfers bobbing in the Pacific Ocean.

Finally she said, "I never asked you . . . did you go to Tess's wedding?"

Valerie still could not call it Joe's wedding, for reasons she elected not to examine.

Helen said, "I did."

"Well?"

Helen took a long drag from her cigarette and released the smoke slowly, as if reluctant to part with it.

"Her bridesmaids wore lavender," Helen said.

Mother and daughter smiled independently of one another. As was often the case after all these years, there was no need to elaborate.

6

The streets of Maddock at lunchtime were lively yet civilized, people moving with fixity of purpose but without much urgency. Valerie disliked urgency; it was one of the things she disliked most about L.A., and one of the reasons she had never really contemplated living in New York. She thought it cast people in a vulgar light, all that hurrying, the frantic chasing of opportunity. People in Maddock were content to let opportunity find them, and if it never came, at least they had spared themselves the indignity of hunting for it.

The town was just as she remembered it, barring a few cosmetic changes. The discount store had changed its name from Sav-Mor to Save More, finally giving in to those vowels that the town council had been pressuring it to employ for years. Friends of her family stopped her on the street and expressed gleeful surprise at seeing her in town. Only Gertie from the jewelry store was presumptuous enough to ask outright what had brought her back to Maddock.

"She just needed a little break," Helen told her discreetly. Gertie smiled, her suspicions confirmed.

"It'll be all over town by five o'clock," Helen said, watching her walk away.

"Oh, who cares, Mama? There's no shame in divorce anymore."

"But you know how people in this town thrive on other people's misfortunes. That just gets my goat. Gertie practically glowed when I told her."

"She did not, Mama. You're too sensitive."

"I guess that's true."

They took a turn through the Fashion Hamlet, and though Valerie was disappointed at the selection—plain cotton shifts, elasticized floral skirts, espadrilles in every color—she searched until she found an inoffensive cream silk blouse with tiny shell buttons, and allowed Helen to buy it for her. It wasn't expensive, and she knew how much her mother enjoyed treating her to clothes.

"You always looked good in the white family," Helen declared as they walked toward the Gift Cove.

"You think I look good in anything."

"No, I don't. Yellow makes you pasty."

"Mustard yellow does. I can wear canary, as long as it's not next to my face."

They walked in silence for a moment. Helen seemed to be pondering something substantial. Valerie hoped the look would pass, but it didn't, and she was forced to question it.

"Well, honey, I guess it's your hair. I know it's beautiful, it's your pride and joy, but the fact is, I think you're getting a little mature for long hair."

"Mature?"

"You know what I mean. I've always thought women over thirty looked a little bit silly with long hair, like they were trying to stay teenagers."

"Mama, no one in Los Angeles considers people over thirty 'mature.' A woman in my acting class had her first baby at forty-three. And she has thighs so firm you could bounce a quarter on them."

"I wish I hadn't brought it up."

"I do, too," Valerie said. She hated being thirty-four. She hated being old enough that age-related rules of fashion applied to her. But there was no denying the years. Signs of them had cropped up seemingly overnight, attacking her in the most sensitive areas. There were tiny lines at the corners of her eyes. Her cheekbones were less defined. Her breasts were still firm, but occasionally when she power-walked she could feel her buttocks moving a bit too freely, a little farther south than they used to be.

She recalled the way Jason used to slap her there, affectionately he claimed, sometimes in front of large groups of people. Once he did it in a four-star restaurant. She had gone numb with rage, and when she later castigated him, he acted genuinely surprised.

"It's an erotic gesture. You can be sure that Henry Miller could be seen doing that and worse in the finest restaurants in Paris."

"Henry Miller can rot, for all I care."

"He's in the process of doing just that."

"I know that," she declared recklessly, though she had no idea Henry Miller was dead, and Jason could be testing her. He did this from time to time, trying to catch her pretending to know more than she did. He was often successful.

It infuriated her the way Jason could use her complaint to his own advantage. He thought Henry Miller was some kind of intellectual heavyweight (Valerie knew nothing of Henry Miller except that Jason talked about him all the time), and he was making the point that geniuses, such as Henry and himself, were obligated to live outside the constraints of socially acceptable behavior.

"I don't care what Henry Miller did in Paris. I hate being slapped and pinched like a cocktail waitress."

"You *were* a cocktail waitress," he quickly pointed out.

"For six months when I first got here. And I quit because it was so demeaning. I didn't expect to put up with the same kind of treatment from my husband."

He laughed in that superior way that he had, which was thrilling except when it was directed at her. "Sometimes I wonder," he said, "exactly who you think you are."

Valerie remembered that moment because she was so tempted to answer him, to tell him once and for all who she thought she was, and the word was on the tip of her tongue. The word was "gentlewoman."

But suddenly she heard the sound of it in her head and she thought, No, that's preposterous. I'm not even sure it's a real word. And anyway, if I say it, I could sound foolish.

This touched off in her a terrible realization that she had no idea who she thought she was. She was Valerie Caldwell, which meant something in Maddock, Virginia, and even at the University of Richmond, but in Los Angeles it fell flat on the ground, as unremarkable as a cigarette butt. The city required more of a person than a distinguished past.

These thoughts about age and purpose and Jason upset her considerably, and she found herself wanting some kind of reassurance.

"Mama, let's go in here," she said as they passed Rowland's Pharmacy. "I need some hair treatment."

"Honey, I've got a bushel of it at home."

"I don't use your kind. Don't fight me on this. I want to go in there."

"Well, all right, but Rowland has gotten so expensive, everybody in town drives to Lynchburg to the Rexall . . ."

She left her mother's voice behind her as she pushed open the heavy glass door. Once inside she inhaled the familiar smells of soap and perfume, chewing gum, room fresheners, and newspapers. She looked around at the greeting-card rack (where she made many purchases in her day), and gazed at the towers of lip glosses and mascaras on the glass counter, under which sat a selection of Monet jewelry and Timex watches. The piped-in music was still on the same loop it had been on in her day—instrumental versions of Jerome Kern and Cole Porter songs, the odd modern classic mixed in ("Listen to the Rhythm of the Falling Rain," "Close to You," "Rhinestone Cowboy").

She located the hair treatment she used, then wandered up and down the aisles, eventually working her way to the magazine rack, which was still located by the sandwich bar. Turning her head as subtly as possible, she saw what she expected to see—a counter lined with gray-uniformed Millburn boys.

They all huddled over their burgers and fries and sundaes, speaking to each other in deep, masculine tones, kept at a respectable volume. When one of them let out a quick burst of laughter, two others punched him admonishingly and he bowed his head and muffled the rest of his laugh with his fist.

They all looked the same, except for varying hair color and height, but Valerie knew that this look was deceiving. They were all different, all individual and unique, each with a different story to tell about how he had ended up in a steel-gray uniform, with close-cropped hair, shiny shoes and belt buckle, and an untimely knowledge of military commands. They wore their last names pinned to their left shirt-pocket, and their Christian names were comprehensively abandoned. Jacks and Steves and Kevins were swept away with the hair on the barbershop floor.

But they were handsome, Valerie thought, without bothering to conceal her stare. And surprisingly, they did not look all that young. Or perhaps it was just that she did not feel all that old. She felt she should be right there among them.

Suddenly her eye struck a booth occupied by a half-dozen teenage girls, all giggling excessively, flipping their hair, shrieking each other's names, and pretending not to notice the cadets. Before the afternoon was over they would be passing out phone numbers scribbled on napkins, and a girl who lived in town might even be accompanied home by a cadet or two. And she would lie awake wondering which one she liked the best, or if either of them would call.

They would. They always did.

"Valerie!" came her mother's voice.

Valerie cringed, as she might have done at sixteen, reluctant to acknowledge that she actually had a mother. At the sound of her name, one of the cadets looked in her direction. He was taller than the others, with light-colored eyes and stick-straight blond hair, short in back, a concentration of it falling over his forehead. He had a strong jaw and teeth so straight she was sure they had recently been liberated from their braces.

Valerie could tell by the scarlet sash he wore that he was a senior. The two pips on his collar indicated that he was an officer. She struggled to remember what rank that represented. Colonel? Lieutenant? But before she could decide, she was distracted by the look he was giving her. He raised his eyebrows, then his shoulders, in what seemed like a questioning gesture. She could not imagine what the question might be, but her desire to answer it made her ashamed, and she looked away.

Replacing the magazine, she went in search of her mother, whose voice had gotten lost in a lively organ version of "Begin the Beguine."

7

As Joe was heading out for lunch, he was cornered by Hayward Glass, the older and more serious of the Glasses. Leon was given to chuckling at thin air, or dishing out Latin phrases unexpectedly. "*In vino veritas*," he often said during office parties. "*Sunt lacrimae rerum*," he said during somber occasions. And, whenever he took a notion, "*Mens sana in corpore sano*." Joe liked Leon better of the two, because there was less chance of being engaged in a substantial conversation with him. Hayward wanted to know things. "How are things at home?" he often asked Joe when they met at the coffee machine. Or, "Do you feel we're treating you fairly?" he'd ask in the middle of an uneventful afternoon. Joe always felt these were trick questions, and he struggled to provide the most beneficial reply.

This day Hayward gave him a penetrating stare with his pale gray eyes, and a smile in its embryonic stage.

"I need your opinion, Joe," he said.

"Yes, sir?"

"Virginia," Hayward said. "What are its chances?"

He knew Hayward was referring to the university rather than the state itself, though he often thought his boss had difficulty separating the two.

"Chances of what, sir?"

"Oh, you know. Basketball. Are we going to do it this year?"

If doing it meant winning the ACC championship, which it obviously did, Joe had very little insight into the matter. But he felt he should offer some cogent response.

"Could be, Mr. Glass. It's too early to tell."

"Well, the reason I ask is I've been offered season tickets, and I don't particularly wish to invest if it's going to be another disappointing year."

"I understand."

"Ever since Ralph Sampson, I have been disappointed and skeptical. Gravely so."

"Yes, well, he didn't fulfill his promise."

"Promise!" Hayward expostulated. "Joseph, he did not fulfill the most cynical expectations. He was a wash! An unmitigated disaster."

"That's true."

Hayward studied him for a moment. "You're not a Virginia man, are you, Joe?"

Joe sighed, a little impatiently. Hayward knew very well that he had gotten his degree from the University of Richmond, a school whose basketball team, despite an impressive showing in recent years, did not even merit a perfunctory discussion at the coffeemaker. What Hayward didn't know was that Joe had been accepted at Virginia and had wanted to go, but that he had chosen Richmond because Valerie had. She wanted to go to school there and he felt obligated to be with her. Then she had decided he should go to law school, and she had somehow convinced him that U of R's law school was light-years beyond anything else in the state. So he passed on UVA and enrolled at Richmond. Right before they were both scheduled to graduate, Valerie informed him that she was leaving him. Her drama teacher, the infamous Phil Saxon, had pointed out to her that she was destined for greater things. Hollywood was just waiting for her to arrive. So she was obligated to go to Los Angeles. Her manner made him feel that he should have seen it coming, though he couldn't remember receiving so much as a hint of it. The shock of her leaving had paralyzed him, rendered him incapable of changing his plans. She had left him at the proverbial altar of U of R's law school.

UVA had remained a touchy subject with him, and he found it difficult even to discuss it after all these years.

"No, sir, I'm not a Wahoo," Joe said.

"But surely you have an opinion on their chances this season."

"Sir, if I had to hazard a guess, I'd say their chances were as good as anyone else's in the ACC."

It was a ridiculously diplomatic remark, but Hayward seemed to give it serious consideration. After a moment he said, "Off to lunch so soon?"

"It's nearly one o'clock, sir."

Hayward nodded distractedly. "Everyone says it was his knees, but I say it was his attitude," he stated defensively, returning to Ralph Sampson without warning. Then he gave Joe a hearty slap on the shoulder. "Everything okay at home?"

"Sure," Joe said with a mild quake in his voice.

"Glad to hear it," Hayward replied, one eyebrow raised.

Joe walked out of the office, feeling as if he had been issued a warning.

•   •   •

Violet's Cafe was less crowded than usual, as Joe's exchange with Hayward had caused him to be later than normal. The bell tinkled as he walked in, and he saw only three or four people at the counter, a couple more occupying a booth in the corner. Violet was leaning against the milkshake machine, listening to Tom Turville tell a story. Tom was the policeman whose sole assignment seemed to be the main street of Maddock. He spent most of his time at Violet's, as it allowed him an unobstructed view of the street, as well as unlimited cups of coffee.

Tom had been a policeman for over twenty years and had been involved in a number of high-speed chases and countless arrests. He had talked people out of killing themselves or members of their family, had even been roughed up and shot at by assailants. Yet he never told those stories. He preferred instead to recount the ways in which he had handled rude store clerks, apathetic restaurant managers, and (his personal favorite) hostile postal workers. He was halfway through one such account when Joe took a seat beside him.

"So I says to him, I says, 'Listen, Wilf, there's nothing in this fruit salad but apples. If I'd wanted a apple salad, that's what I would've ordered.' "

"What'd he say?" Violet asked, glancing at the window air-conditioning unit, which was issuing an ominous rattle.

"He said, 'Oh, you know how it is. Summer's gone and it's hard to get fresh fruit anymore.' "

"He can still get cantaloupe, can't he? And grapes. Any fool can get grapes."

"Well, try telling him that. Anyhow, we went round and round, and finally he knocked off fifty cents."

"I don't know why you waste your money out at the Oaks," Violet said. She couldn't understand why anybody wasted their money anywhere besides her cafe.

"It was a family occasion," Tom said, as if that somehow excused him.

"Joseph," Violet said. "I just about run out of fried chicken. I thought you wasn't coming."

"Here I am. Give me a breast."

Tom gave a raspy smoker's chuckle and said, "You could get in real trouble saying that in some places."

Joe straddled a bar stool and watched as Violet plucked a fried chicken breast from a platter and slapped it on a plate. She put a mound of mashed potatoes beside it with a thud, and sprinkled the whole thing with overdone string beans and lumpy gravy.

"You just missed Mary Grace," Violet said, setting his plate down in front of him, as a mother might do, propping her chin on her fist to watch him eat. "She came in for her plain salad and hard-boiled eggs. I swear, that girl is so skinny a strong wind might carry her away."

"Mmm," Joe said, tucking into his food.

"Too skinny, if you ask me."

"Fat people usually gain it back and then some," Tom said in a tone that suggested he considered it a criminal offense.

"Their bodies get used to being fat," Violet agreed, "and they'll do anything to get the weight back on."

"I think we should wish her well," Joe said, surprised at the sanctimonious tone of his voice.

"I do wish her well. I wish everybody well. I'm just saying how the body works," said Violet, who looked as if she had assumed the extra weight Mary Grace had lost. Her dingy apron strained across her stomach, and her face was so full it had lost anything resembling a bone structure.

Tom gazed out the window and said, "There's Milton Thornberg parking in a red zone."

"You better go give him a ticket," Violet urged.

"What for? He's a Jew—he's got the best lawyers money can buy. Lawyers from Washington he has. He'd have the whole thing thrown out of court before I could finish writing his name."

"I don't see why Jews get to rule the world," Violet said.

"Because they have money, that's why."

"Well, that's true," Violet said.

"How's business, Tom?" Joe asked, eager to get off the subject of Jews. Any conversation bordering on ethnic stereotypes made him nervous, as he was still in the grip of a liberal bent he had picked up at college. Social consciousness had been going around like a virus; he caught it and had yet to shake it. But in the absence of his progressive-thinking friends, he found it difficult to remember the root of his convictions, or how strongly he was committed to them. He couldn't be sure he was supposed to challenge Tom and Violet, couldn't even be sure they had said anything terribly negative. Until he figured it out, he thought it would be best to avoid the matter.

Tom lit a cigarette and said, "Rufus Batterman killed himself. Blew his brains out."

"So I heard. That's terrible," Joe said, though he never could remember if Rufus was the Ford mechanic with the gap in his teeth or the one with the lazy eye. He couldn't see any tactful way of inquiring, so he said, "I wonder why he'd do something like that."

"Well, it's dog days," Tom said.

"What do you mean? Dog days are in August," Joe said.

"No, sir. They last clean through September, and everybody and everything is just as crazy as it can be. You might notice, flies get blind and start bumping into windows."

"Snakes get blind," Violet said. "Flies get stupid."

"Either way, the animal kingdom is affected," Tom said. "And folks are more proned to accidents, and proned to doing stupid things."

"Is that so?"

"Yes, sir. You know Earl Gravis, lives out by the Texaco? He shot up his whole farm last year during dog days, killed a whole herd of cattle, six pigs, and I don't know how many chickens."

"Thank God he didn't go for his family," Violet said.

"He did," Tom said emphatically. "But fortunately, he run out of bullets."

"Thank God for small favors."

"Small is about all you get these days," Tom said with inexplicable stoicism.

Joe was starting to be amused by the conversation around him when the door tinkled and two women walked in. He gazed at them briefly, then looked back down at his mashed potatoes, which seemed to be expanding spontaneously. Just as he was calculating how to integrate the rest of his gravy into them, the familiarity of the face he had seen struck him like a bolt of lightning.

"Lord above, it's Valerie Caldwell," said Violet.

"Hi, Violet. Do you still make the best chicken in town?"

Her voice was frighteningly familiar. Joe could have sworn it was only yesterday that it was repeating in his ear, alternating between declarations of love and harsh demands. He wanted more than anything to assume another identity, become Tom Turville or even Violet, someone who had no significant past with Valerie Caldwell or her mother.

But it would not happen, and his attempt to avoid her gaze was becoming silly and self-indulgent. He raised his eyes to hers and a look passed between them, one that made him so uncomfortable that he had to resist every urge to dart out of the restaurant without paying. Here you are, the look said, right where I left you.

"Hi, Valerie," Joe said in a tremulous voice. "Hi, Mrs. Caldwell."

"Joseph Deacon," Valerie said in a slower tone, deliberate and self-assured. "You haven't changed a speck."

He wanted to deny that, to assure her that he had changed in every way imaginable. But he knew any effort to do so would make him appear laughable in the eyes of his audience.

So he said, "Neither have you."

It was true. She still had the same waist-length blond hair and cobalt-blue eyes. Her lips were still wide and pink and dangerous.

"How in the world is your wife?" Valerie asked.

"She's fine. She's the same as ever." He hesitated, noticing that that sounded like an insult. To his discomfort, Valerie seemed to interpret it as one. She issued a derisive chuckle and sat down beside him.

"Violet, give me a piece of ham before I scream," she said.

"Honey, we haven't had ham since December."

"Chicken, then, but dark meat and well done."

"Only way I do it," Violet said.

Joe sat for an uncomfortable moment beside Valerie, feeling her mother presiding over them like the patron saint of fortuitous encounters. He thought of Tom's description of dog days and felt very apprehensive. He wanted to light a candle, say a chant, repeat somebody's name backward.

"I'm dying to get together with Tess," Valerie said, placing a cool, slender hand on his arm. "Will you tell her I said so?"

"I will," Joe said, standing, as if this were somehow his permission to leave.

Valerie squeezed his forearm.

"It's so good to see you."

"You, too," he said.

He walked out without paying, fearing for a moment that Tom might follow and arrest him. But the most horrifying thing was that he wouldn't, because Tom understood, and Violet understood, the reasons he needed to evacuate the building, as if fleeing a toxic substance to which only he had been exposed.

8

In keeping with the pattern, Joe always found his house much less appealing in the evening than in the morning. When he set out for work, it always struck him as being a good-sized, sturdy structure on a nice street with an ample lot. In the evenings, it appeared to be the smallest house in the neighborhood, with sagging gutters, faded paint, and a badly neglected lawn. It was a simple white frame house with forest-green trim and a columned porch. But the trim seemed to be always peeling, no matter how many times he touched it up, and the columns were an austere, rectangular shape, lacking the Victorian charm of the ones on the nicer houses in town. There was a rusty porch swing in the right corner, painted the same peeling forest-green. Tonight it seemed every bit as much an eyesore as a broken refrigerator parked out front. No one ever used the damn swing anyway, he thought testily, choosing not to remember that Tess was always enthusiastic about the swing in the early days of spring, and that she and Mary Grace could sit there for hours, laughing and gossiping like teenagers.

As he came up the walk, feeling dandelions and other unidentifiable weeds brushing his ankles, he thought, I have to do something with this house.

But what? He had painted the exterior just last spring, had touched up the trim over the summer, had mowed the lawn a mere three days ago. He had bought a decorative screen door at Lowe's, but Tess had made him take it back because it was too "ornate." They had dragged rocking chairs and antique milk cans and ceramic umbrella stands and colorful mats onto the porch. They planted seasonal flowers around the boxwoods. They had done everything humanly possible to make the place look presentable, yet every afternoon it disappointed him.

Part of his disappointment lay in the knowledge that when he opened the door to his house, the situation only got worse. But this particular evening, he encountered a completely different atmosphere. The house was so free of clutter it seemed almost empty. He was greeted by an aroma of Pledge and Pine-Sol, and the pneumatic smell of freshly vacuumed carpets. The house was not just straight, it was clean. He stared at the furniture as if he had never seen it before. Olive green and pale pink? he thought, gazing at the couch.

But before he could think further, his wife was bounding out of the kitchen, wearing an apron over a floral cotton shift and waving an oven mitt in the shape of a lobster claw.

"I'm making your favorite," she said.

"Oh, really?" he questioned, sweeping her into his arms. "Pork chops?"

She drew back slightly. "Lasagna."

"Oh, my other favorite."

He kissed her full on the lips. She smelled of baby powder, Pledge, and tomato sauce.

"How was your day?" he asked, a question he never asked, and immediately wondered why he had asked it today.

But Tess was distracted.

"Lasagna is your favorite."

"Of course it is."

"You never even ask for pork chops."

"I know. I was just caught off guard."

This took her attention away from what might have evolved into a full-scale discussion.

"Oh yeah. I cleaned up. What do you think?"

"It's fabulous."

"Yeah, it's not that bad once you get into it. Cleaning, I mean. You get into this rhythm, and then you want to do the whole house, and then you want to cook some impossible meal, and then you think, God, I'm unstoppable."

"You are," he agreed, kissing her neck. "How long does the lasagna take?"

"It's got another thirty minutes."

"Great."

She interpreted his smile.

"Joe, come on. Before supper? We haven't done it before supper since . . ."

"Since before we were married."

"Please."

Still a closet puritan, Tess disliked being reminded that they had done anything substantial before they were married.

"Besides," she said, giggling, her breath coming faster, "we've only got thirty minutes, and I worked on that lasagna all day."

"If it takes longer than thirty minutes, I'd say you've got a high-class problem."

Twelve minutes later they lay in bed, stuck together with sweat, their eyes roaming aimlessly across the room. The smell of lasagna had overpowered that of the cleaning solutions, and Joe could imagine himself in an Italian pensione, tucked away with a fisherman's daughter, getting ready to ship out to sea himself in just a few short hours. Where did such ruminations come from, he wondered. He'd never even been to Italy, nor harbored any desire to go to sea.

Tess said, "How was your day?"

"The usual," he answered, which was blatantly dishonest. He had seen Valerie Caldwell, had locked eyes with her, had been touched on the arm by her. Yet he felt no desire, or even a compulsion, to tell his wife. He was going to keep it a secret. It was for Tess's protection, he told himself. It would only upset her, and there was no reason to do that. She had had enough upsets in the last year, with her three miscarriages, not to mention her nervousness when she learned of Valerie's return. Why add fuel to a fire which, if left alone, would certainly burn itself out?

Tess smiled up at him, and planted a kiss just below his jaw.

"I have to check on dinner," she said.

"Okay."

"But you're happy, right?"

"Of course."

She crawled out of bed, oblivious to her nakedness, as if she had no idea that her body could ever arouse him. She had lost the sense of modesty she had when she first started sleeping with him, and now she paraded around him as if in the act of giving herself to him she had eliminated all his desire. She thought that he had grown used to her body and now regarded it as part of the scenery, like the radiator in the corner, or the nightstand that wobbled, or the chest of drawers that collected dust. Perhaps women like Tess would never understand how men quaked at the realization of what those bodies could do. They could grow life and deliver it and feed it, again and again. A man's body by comparison could do nothing but satisfy its own desire.

How little Tess understood of men, Joe thought, watching her struggle into her bathrobe. And how grateful he was for it.

She flashed a smile at him and disappeared in the direction of the kitchen. A violent fear surged through him, as he thought of Valerie and the way her sudden appearance had startled him and caused him to circumnavigate his own intentions. He had lied to his wife, without wanting or meaning to, without even understanding why.

In a moment he heard the clamor in the kitchen—a pot lid clanging on the counter, a fork skidding across the linoleum. But even these familiar sounds failed to comfort him, and for the first time since his marriage, he felt at risk.

9

The reunion luncheon was held on the screened veranda of the Caldwell home, overlooking the hilly and heavily landscaped backyard. Though a spell of cold nights had turned a few leaves red and gold, most of the foliage was as lush and dense as midsummer.

Tess watched as Valerie served triangles of quiche onto Wedgwood china plates. Her hands were slender and white, her nails perfectly formed and polished. A gold bracelet dangled from her wrist. It made Tess shiver to watch it, so delicate was its motion. Valerie smelled like gardenias. Her soft blond hair swung carelessly beneath her chin. She wore white Levi's and a pale pink sleeveless sweater, a thin strand of pearls and earrings to match.

Of course Joe fell in love with Valerie, Tess thought. How could he not?

Then a thought, equally disturbing, occurred to her. I loved her, too. It might have been a perverse love, desperate and insecure, but it was love nonetheless. She remembered the days when they were very young, the three of them playing games in this very backyard. They would create their personas. Valerie would be sixteen, with hair down to her "kneepits," a wardrobe from Neiman Marcus, a red Corvette, and she was related to the Firestone family. Billionaires, she informed them. Tess and Mary Grace only nodded in awe, as if in saying so she had actually become these things. It never occurred to Tess to make her character related to billionaires. She was just Ginger, a stewardess. Mary Grace was Shannon, a secretary. Valerie outscored them on every level, even in her childhood fantasies.

In later years the competition grew more substantial. Her superior awareness of the world and what it took to succeed in it began to dominate their relationship. Tess and Mary Grace ended up trailing after her like docile pets. Even as she bossed them around, purloined their boyfriends, generally overshadowed them, they could not leave her. Her friendship seemed to hold out the promise of something rewarding. If they stayed around her long enough, they were bound to absorb some of her brilliance. And so they clung to their friendship, content to pay court, craving her attention when it came, pouncing on it like stray crumbs from the dinner table.

It seemed to Tess that she always came home from Valerie's house in tears over some remark Valerie had made, or smarting from some way she had made her or Mary Grace feel inferior. Her mother, who harbored an irrational objection to tears, would declare, "That is the last time you're going to that girl's house and I mean it. She makes you miserable!" But two days later the tears would be forgotten, and Tess would be begging to go back there. The misery seemed a small price to pay.

On reflection, Tess now understood that part of the attraction, perhaps the whole attraction, was that Valerie did not need them. And because of that, they desperately needed her.

The effect had not entirely worn off. Even now, Tess wanted to apologize for marrying Joe. She wanted Valerie to forgive her, approve of her. She looked to Mary Grace to see if she might be feeling the same way. But her friend was revealing nothing. She sat with her legs crossed tight, one hand wedged between her knees, the other supporting a cigarette.

"I love this yard," Valerie said. "I used to sit for hours under that magnolia tree and try to picture the man I'd marry."

Tess thought of Joe, and a net of panic descended on her, complete with visions of dirty dishes and unironed shirts, the lasagna that was burned on top and cold in the middle. And those pregnancy tests. All those pregnancy tests she had taken in the last year—some positive, some negative, some inconclusive. Test tubes full of powder, plastic cups full of urine, the egg timer dinging at all hours of the day and night.

The last time she held the little plastic test in front of Joe's face he shook his head and said, "I just don't know pink from white anymore."

And the miscarriages, always at night it seemed, the cramping that went all the way to her toes, that horrible, hollow feeling of her body letting go of its charge.

"So you limited yourself to one," Mary Grace said.

Valerie looked at her. "What?"

"One man that you'd marry."

Valerie smiled tensely. "I don't think anyone pictures getting married more than once. I mean, from the time we're little, there's all that talk about The One."

"Was he what you imagined?" Mary Grace asked.

"Who?"

"The guy you married."

"Oh, him." Valerie thought for a moment. "I never could have imagined Jason."

"Why not?"

She shrugged, then smiled.

"I think when we get older we realize there isn't a One. Marriage is more like musical chairs. The music stops, and the chairs are all being taken, and you settle for what's in front of you."

"Really," Mary Grace said, running a thumb across her lip. "Is that how marriage works?"

"Well, no," Valerie admitted. "Not for everyone, I guess."

"There's some truth to it, though," Tess volunteered.

"Oh, really," Mary Grace said, her eyes landing hard on her friend.

"Mary Grace, I swear, I will not live long enough to get over how skinny you are," Valerie suddenly observed.

"I won't be much longer if you keep heaping quiche on me," Mary Grace said.

"One little piece isn't going to kill you."

"That's how it always starts. One little piece."

Valerie didn't reply. She took a noiseless sip of iced tea and looked back out at the yard.

"What's Hollywood like?" Mary Grace asked, lighting another cigarette, taking a bite of quiche between puffs. "Do you see stars and stuff? I mean, are they just walking around buying groceries and having their cars worked on and shit?"

Valerie smiled.

"They're just ordinary people. So, yes, they do ordinary things."

Tess said, "I always heard Harrison Ford was a nice man."

"What do you mean they're like ordinary people? Do they stand in line at the DMV? I can't see that. I can't see Arnold Schwarzenegger at the DMV."

"Anyone want more tea?" Valerie asked. No one answered.

"You ended up living in Malibu, right?" Mary Grace asked.

"In the hills above Malibu. Not on the beach."

"But pretty close."

"Close only counts in horseshoes." Valerie smiled tightly.

"What does it take to get on the beach?"

Valerie shrugged. "I guess I never figured that out."

"Correct me if I'm wrong," Mary Grace persisted, "but when we were young you kept saying, 'You can stay here if you want, but I'm going to live in Malibu one day.'"

"Yes, I probably did say that. Anyone want more salad?"

Tess shook her head and tried to think of a new topic. But Mary Grace was on a roll.

"So after all that talk, you finally got to Malibu. So it was only the hills, big deal. You got there, and now you're back in Maddock. What's the story?"

"The story is," Valerie said evenly, "that a child of sixteen believes anything is possible."

"*I* didn't," Mary Grace retorted.

"You must miss it," Tess said quickly, hearing that combative tone creeping into Mary Grace's voice. The last thing Tess wanted now was a confrontation. Coming to this luncheon had created enough tension—whether or not to go, whether or not to tell Joe, what to wear, what to bring. It had kept her awake for an entire night after she got Valerie's phone call. She had lain in bed, listening to Joe's steady breathing, holding her secret inside like some insidious illness that had been recently diagnosed. She knew she was going and she knew she wouldn't tell him. What she didn't know was what this all meant.

But no confrontations, not now. She was not ready to slam headfirst into her past.

Valerie contemplated Tess's remark, her head cocked to one side, her hair falling across one cheek.

"No. You don't miss L.A. You go to L.A. to miss other places."

"What the hell does that mean?" Mary Grace asked.

"Everyone comes there from somewhere else. And they all walk around looking sad because they aren't somewhere else. They talk about getting out. It's almost like they come there so they can have a place to dream of escaping. It's very strange."

"Was your husband like that?"

"No, Jason actually likes L.A. He's not dead, by the way."

Tess issued a stiff laugh, hoping to lighten the tone. Mary Grace was moving in for the kill.

"Did you miss Maddock when you were there?"

"Oh yes. I mean, that's what happens to you. You get homesick for places you once hated. And I think you tend to forgive your hometown its imperfections in a way you'd never forgive a place you've moved to."

"Is that so?" Mary Grace challenged.

"I guess you'd have to leave here at some point to understand," Valerie replied.

"You know," Tess said, struggling to introduce another subject, "we never got to meet your husband. You never brought him to Maddock, did you?"

"No. He won't come to the South. He thinks it's still the way Sherman left it. Burned out and defeated. I couldn't sell him on the good points."

"Which are?"

Valerie looked at her.

"Mary Grace, it's obvious you're frustrated with Maddock for some reason. But is there any point in pretending there's nothing to recommend it? We all had a good life here. As far as I can see, most people still do."

"What people have here is a lack of options," Mary Grace said.

"Well, that's probably true," Valerie said, "if you believe it." Her voice was quiet and strong, and it hung powerfully in the air. It was the last word.

Mary Grace took a drag on her cigarette, squinting at Valerie through the smoke. Tess stared at her fingernails and thought, *Nothing has changed.*

Valerie finished her quiche and wiped the corners of her mouth with a white linen napkin.

"Anyhow, I don't suppose my husband will ever get to see Maddock. I think it's over between us."

Tess and Mary Grace bowed their heads, not out of embarrassment but out of reverence for her words. It felt like a serious moment, one worthy of silence and contemplation, like the end of a war. Or rather, the beginning.

"But don't you have a job back there?" Mary Grace asked. "Somebody told me they saw you on some game show, wearing an evening dress and pointing at cars."

"Oh, that." Valerie laughed. "I'm not sure you can call that a job."

"Getting paid to wear evening dresses and smile? Sounds like a great deal to me."

"I want to act," Valerie said, "and the business is in a recession right now. Even Jason is suffering from it, and he's one of the most sought-after writers in Hollywood. He's on the A list, as they say."

Tess let herself look at Mary Grace and detected the beginnings of an eye-roll. Quickly she looked out at the backyard, as if to give serious consideration to Valerie's comment, or the rhododendrons that lined the walk.

"Why are we talking about me, though?" Valerie asked. "This is a reunion. Let's talk about us."

"What us?" Mary Grace asked.

"Us," Valerie emphasized, drawing an invisible, all-encompassing circle with her forefinger.

Tess and Mary Grace had very little to say on the subject of "us." They stared at their hostess, waiting.

"I was thinking," Valerie said, giggling into her fist, then placing her palm on her chest. "I was remembering those dances we used to go to at Millburn. Not the big ones, like the Military Ball, but those little monthly things they threw together. Remember those songs, 'Freebird,' and 'Colour My World,' and 'Stairway to Heaven'? We would cry when we heard them. We'd dance with anything that moved."

She laughed harder. Tess and Mary Grace smiled distantly.

Valerie caught her breath and sighed. "Sometimes I just think about the way they smelled. They all wore Brut. Just one big moving gray cloud of Brut. Their breath smelled like Wrigley's Spearmint. I remember their bleached white fingernails, and the short, prickly hair at the back of their necks, and those crisp, starched shirts that smelled like . . . I don't know . . . steam and heaven."

Tess stared at her. She barely remembered those details. Her adolescence seemed to consist only of the struggle to get Joe to notice her. She knew that took up no time at all—it only began in her junior year, shortly before he and Valerie got together. But all she could remember of those dances was sitting by some date whose face she had already forgotten, watching Valerie and Joe moving in circles under the colored lights. Joe's face always seemed so pinched and anxious. Tess used to think of how happy she could make him, if only he would let her.

"Oh, Tess," Valerie said, "do you remember Dan Rausseo, that really good-looking Italian who danced in a square, like he was marching tours? You said he kissed like a commode plunger."

"I don't recall kissing anyone named Dan Rausseo."

"Oh. Maybe it was Mary Grace."

"I don't recall kissing anyone good-looking," Mary Grace said.

"Well, maybe it was me."

"That's more likely," Mary Grace agreed.

There was a moment of silence. Tess stared out at the trees and tried to remember Dan Rausseo and all the boys who must have come before Joe. She must have had a life before him. But where was it?

"Let's go for a walk," Valerie said.

"In this heat?" Mary Grace grumbled.

"Especially in this heat. There's nothing like it in the West."

Mary Grace gave her another skeptical frown. "The sun is always out in L.A."

"Yes, but it's different. It's aggressive and dry. Here, it's a gentler heat."

"A gentler heat," Mary Grace intoned. "Well, of course. It's amazing everyone doesn't move here. How do we manage to keep the population to a mere two thousand?"

Tess looked away. Mary Grace no longer amused her. She was trying so hard to outdistance Valerie. After all this time, she still couldn't see how impossible that was. Once Valerie had imagined more of the world than they had; now she had seen it. Trying to deny it made them both look ridiculous and even more provincial than they already were. Being with Valerie was like being in the grip of an undertow; they were powerless. Their only hope of survival was to swim with it.

"Shall we go?" Valerie asked. "Mama will clear the dishes."

Tess and Mary Grace slid their chairs back, resigned. They were going to have to endure this—Valerie's rediscovery of a place which to them had become tiresome and predictable.

They walked past brick and white frame houses, sprinklers hurling water onto what was left of the grass, radio stations battling each other through open windows, a phone ringing, the clink of dishes, a piano note.

As they topped the hill, Valerie suddenly stopped talking and slowed her pace. She stared respectfully at the brick-and-marble sign, which was so much bigger in her memory but still impressive in its own quiet way.

"Let's take a stroll around, shall we? For old times' sake."

"Around Millburn? It's not a visiting day," Tess said. "Girls aren't allowed."

"Well, we aren't girls," Valerie said.

It was a hard point to argue, and so they followed.

10

Nothing about the grounds had changed. The lawn still sloped away from the street, giving it a sunken quality, and even in autumn the grass was a cool pistachio green. The swimming pool was drained and starting to collect crisp brown leaves, making it look like a large bowl of cereal. Valerie stared at it, thinking of the times they had snuck into the pool, pretending they were taking swimming lessons. Sometimes they could get away with it for hours, mingling among the housewives with children, before a teacher or the nosy commandant's wife would discover them and make them leave. That was always part of the thrill of Millburn— the fact that they shouldn't be there. And even when they were allowed, there was always someplace they shouldn't be, some corner they shouldn't turn, or some door they shouldn't open. In those days, Valerie had never met a door she couldn't open.

Now she felt her fearlessness escaping her. In fact, halfway down the drive, she wanted to turn back. She was not prepared for the effect these grounds would have on her, the rate at which the memories would assault her. They rushed at her, one after another, like bullets. The rosebush beside which Pat Casey kissed her the first time. The oak tree where she and Marshall Burton met, left each other notes, and hid from the watchful eye of the school commandant, Colonel Fullham. The steps leading down to the football field, where she told Gary DePaul she didn't want to go steady with him. He stood at the top and hurled his class ring down to the fifty-yard line. And then there were the memories of Joe, but for the moment she refused to let those in.

Her brain was jammed with thoughts, none of them particularly welcome. How lost those days were to her, how old she had become, how little she had appreciated her charmed life, how few of her dreams had been realized. She remembered how strongly she felt her ambitions, and now she was forced to confront the fact that she had done nothing with them. She had squandered so much of her promise.

Millburn Academy suddenly rose up before them, the brick buildings looking stately and imposing, yet somehow inviting. A few yards in front of the breezeway stood a cannon, pointing at the clouds as if they, with their unpredictable patterns and surreptitious moves, were the enemy.

"Remember the Military Ball?" Tess suddenly said. It must have been the sight of the new gym, the big one with the white Doric columns and gables, that made her think of it.

"Which one?" Valerie asked.

"All of them. The whole spectacle. All those girls decked out in white, like sacrificial virgins. Remember how we planned for it and talked about it, and somehow the ball itself was always a letdown? We enjoyed the anticipation more than the event."

"Oh, I don't know," Valerie said, feeling encouraged that Tess wanted to discuss it. "I enjoyed the ball. I just remember feeling hideously depressed the next day. It was always in February, and there was nothing to look forward to except the rest of a long winter."

"I remember one ball in particular," Mary Grace said to Valerie. "I remember the one that Bobby Durham took you to."

"Oh yes. Sophomore year."

"I didn't go," Mary Grace said.

"Didn't you?"

"No. Because Bobby Durham was the love of my life. You knew it, Tess knew it, everybody, including Bobby Durham, knew it. You said you were going to persuade him to ask me to the ball. And the next thing I knew you were going with him, and I was sitting at home watching television. You went with him just for spite—you never liked him. You dropped him like a hot potato right after that. Then he died in a motorcycle accident, and I never even got to dance with him."

Valerie stared at her friend, too surprised to reply. It had never occurred to her that such a shallow grudge could still be smoldering. What was more, Valerie could barely remember Bobby Durham, let alone the fact that Mary Grace had liked him first.

"Mary Grace, I'm sorry. I never realized . . ."

"The hell you didn't."

"He died?"

"Summer before his senior year. His motorcycle went up under a furniture truck."

"I never heard about that."

"Well, you were with Joe then. You didn't care about anything but getting his class ring around your neck."

Now Valerie's mind moved on, trying to recall wearing Joe's class ring around her neck. It seemed such an antiquated notion, though something about it now struck her memory, in the form of a rash on her chest.

"I'm sorry, Mary Grace," Valerie said, dazed and distracted. "I didn't mean to hurt you. And I have to say, I can't believe it still means anything to you."

"How could it not? That haunted me my whole life. It's probably the reason I was fat."

"Mary Grace, be fair," Tess said in a low voice.

"What? You're gonna defend her, after she took Joe from you?"

"Excuse me?" Valerie interjected. "How is it that I stole Joseph?"

"Tess liked him first and you know it. She told you at the first fall dance, and the next thing anybody knew, you and Joe were inseparable."

"I don't remember that," Valerie said.

"Well, you seem to have a very selective memory," Mary Grace observed.

"Yes," Valerie said slowly, feeling a dark, quiet anger settling on her like soot. "Here's something I remember. I seem to recall Tess paying visits to Joe behind my back. Writing letters to him, all through high school and college, swearing to wait for him, pledging her undying love."

Valerie caught Tess's look.

"Of course I knew. You always thought I didn't."

"How?" Tess whispered.

"Joseph told me."

Tess turned pale. Valerie felt the old familiar annoyance, wanting her friend to fight back, defend herself. But in that regard, nothing had changed.

"Tess, don't look so stricken. Joe and I were in love. We couldn't keep anything from each other. Just as I'm sure he couldn't keep anything from you now."

Tess looked down at the asphalt, shaking her head, pinching her lip.

"Valerie, nothing ever happened between us. Not while you two were together."

"Oh, I know that."

Valerie felt disgusted with herself. She had not really meant to attack Tess, just when things were going so well. But the memories were weighing on her, like a heavy meal, making her feel bloated. She wanted to strike out, and as always, Tess was the easiest target.

"Why are you apologizing to her, Tess?" Mary Grace demanded. "My God, all the men she stole from us, you owed her at least one."

Almost without knowing it, the three of them had stopped walking. Now they stood in front of the chapel, in front of the alabaster soldier caught forever in a solemn salute.

"Look, are we really having this conversation?" Valerie said. "We're in our thirties, aren't we? We're beyond this. It's over."

Mary Grace said, "It's only over for the person who won. For the rest of us, it just keeps going."

"So you're telling me that for the rest of my life I'm going to be held accountable for what I did as a teenager," Valerie said.

"Yes," Mary Grace answered. "Did you think you could come back here and wipe the slate clean?"

"Well, to start with I didn't even know that there was a slate. I didn't imagine anyone was keeping score. I was hoping I could come back here and find my friends, and we could all find a way to concentrate on the good times."

"What good times? I don't remember any."

"Now who's got a selective memory?"

"Valerie's right," Tess said softly. "The three of us were inseparable. You can't spend that much time together and not have good times."

Mary Grace turned on her.

"Whose side are you on? You act like you don't have these feelings, too."

Tess ducked her head.

"Sides? What sides?" Valerie expostulated, fighting back tears. "This isn't a volleyball game. It's life, and it's short, and this is all a waste of time."

"Don't talk to *me* about wasted time." Mary Grace yelled. Her voice carried, and Tess recoiled. "The whole first part of my life was a vacuum. It's lost to me. I don't even have a past. Don't you see a pattern here? All your memories are happy ones, and all of ours aren't."

"I have some happy memories," Tess said weakly.

Valerie took a second to catch her breath and gather her thoughts. "Mary Grace, can I say something to you?" she asked. "It will probably hurt you, but I have to say it anyway."

"That's never stopped you before."

Valerie looked at her a moment, then said, "You're still acting like a fat person."

Mary Grace's eyes widened. It was hard to surprise her, but Valerie could see she had done it.

"You're still bitter, mad at the world for not allowing you into the inner circle. That's how you acted in high school. That's the reason men weren't attracted to you, not because of your weight. But look at you now. You're thinner than I am. You're beautiful. You're inside, with everyone else. It's time to let it go. So you didn't have your moment back then. Have it now. Nothing is stopping you."

Mary Grace looked as if she had been socked in the stomach. Her eyes never left Valerie's face. Everything suddenly seemed to go still; even the leaves seemed to stop moving in the wind.

Tess said, "Well. Isn't that enough for one day?"

"Oh, that's always your answer, isn't it, Tess? Don't look at it. Maybe it will go away," Mary Grace snapped.

"Well, Valerie's right. I mean, Joe and I are married. You've lost the weight. Everything has changed."

"Except one thing," Mary Grace said softly. "I'm still alone."

"But it doesn't have to be that way," Valerie said. "You could have anyone."

"This is Maddock, Valerie. There isn't anyone. I'm too old for Millburn boys."

"Well, what makes you think the man of your dreams can only exist in a ten-mile radius? I don't know a lot about the world, but I know you can't find the love of your life until you go looking for him."

"But why?" Mary Grace challenged, tears rising to her dark eyes. "Why can't he come looking for me?"

The moment was rescued by a cadet moving toward them with the confident gait of a mature teen. He was dressed in his casual uniform, day gear, with his hat pushed back on his head to reveal a hank of stone-blond hair.

"Well, hello again," he said with a toothy smile.

Valerie stared at him and recognized him as the cadet she had made eye contact with in Rowland's Pharmacy.

"Hello," Valerie said, flattered that he remembered her.

He gave Valerie a brief glance, then looked at Tess.

"Hello, Becker," Tess said.

They smiled warmly at each other. Becker saluted her, then reached for her hand. Tess blushed as he kissed it quietly.

"This is Brett Becker," Tess said to her friends. "An old friend."

"She's known me since I was a sophomore," Becker said with an air of gravity.

"I used to work in the library here," Tess explained to Valerie. "He used to hate to read, but I finally got him interested in some Hemingway."

"I like him. He's brief," Becker admitted.

"These are my friends Mary Grace Reynolds and Valerie Caldwell."

"Rutter," Valerie corrected her, then wished she hadn't. Rutter had a distinguished sound in Hollywood, where there was always the chance that someone would recognize Jason's name. In Maddock, however, it sounded like someone who moved large appliances for a living.

There was an awkward lull, which Tess took as an opportunity to announce their departure. However, no one moved.

Becker let his eyes float until they connected with Valerie's.

"I have seen you before, though."

"I don't think so," Valerie said.

"Oh yes. In town."

"No, I don't live in town."

"I know I've seen you."

"Tess is right. We have to go."

"Goodbye, Becker," Tess said.

She and Mary Grace began to walk away. Valerie hesitated, then joined them. When she looked back she saw his retreating figure, passing beneath the breezeway. He was going back to his barracks to do his homework or shine his belt buckle for inspection or write a letter to his mother. He could have been any cadet, any day, any year.

The walk back to the Caldwell home was quiet. The air around them had thickened as the sun started its descent. Valerie remembered this about the South—sometimes the evenings were actually closer than the days. Or maybe it just seemed that way because one came to expect relief and was inevitably disappointed.

Mary Grace left as soon as they got back. She kissed Tess on the cheek and gave Valerie a cool, perfunctory wave, but not without thanking her for the lunch. Manners, Valerie thought. They persisted in the face of all adversity.

Tess spent a few minutes with her, sitting on the front porch steps. They talked about gardening and weather and the new mall over in Danville, which Valerie had yet to visit. Valerie finally worked up the nerve to ask about Joe.

"He's fine," Tess said shortly, hesitant to reveal more than that.

"Happy with his job?"

"Oh yes."

"I always said he'd make a great lawyer."

"Oh," Tess said with an uncharacteristic snort, "I guess."

"And what about kids?"

At this Tess seemed to turn rigid, keeping her eyes fixed on the ground.

"What about them?"

"I assume you're going to have them?"

"I don't know."

"Well, you have to. The two of you were born to be parents."

Tess said nothing.

"It's strange," Valerie said. "I was always the one who talked about having children. Remember? I had their names picked out. I wanted twelve of them."

Tess said, "You wanted everything."

It was true. Valerie had no interest in denying it, yet she felt that she was admitting to something shameful. Wanting everything in Los Angeles was such a common condition, it didn't merit a moment's worth of analysis. The same affliction here seemed to promise a violent, biblical fate.

"So you were a librarian at Millburn," Valerie said, considering this a safe subject. "Imagine that. Working there after all those years."

Tess nodded with a smile.

"Why'd you quit?"

"I don't know."

Valerie smiled. So like Tess. She thought if Tess's picture were on a piece of currency, the underlying motto would be: "I don't know."

"Will you ever go back?"

"Maybe," Tess said. "I like to think it's there if I want to."

"Yes, it's nice to have something to fall back on."

They sat on the steps for a few minutes longer, listening to the be-

ginnings of the evening sounds—a few stray crickets, the distant
hum of the television news, the paper boy cycling along his route—
the hollow, thunking sound of papers missing their target. Mrs.
Perry, the Baptist minister's wife, wandered by, being walked by her
cocker spaniel, Echo. The dog had to be fifteen years old, Valerie
thought.

"Hello," Mrs. Perry called out casually, as if it were only yesterday that she had seen Valerie and Tess sitting like teenagers on the
front step.

"Hello, Mrs. Perry. Hello, Echo," Valerie said.

"Oh no! Echo's long dead. This is her pup, Jeremiah."

"Really? He's the spitting image!"

Mrs. Perry only smiled and shrugged and declared, "This
weather!"

"I know," Tess answered.

"It's so nice to hear people talking about the weather," Valerie
said. "In L.A., what can a person say? Looks like sun again!"

Valerie laughed, and Tess chuckled politely. They watched Mrs.
Perry going along her way, her sneakers making sucking noises on
the sidewalk.

"My life is a mess," Valerie said.

"Oh no," Tess answered with a degree of urgency.

"But it is. I haven't done anything. My marriage is over. Nothing
turned out the way I thought it would."

"You're still young," Tess said hopefully.

Valerie just looked at her. "Does Mary Grace really hate me?"
she asked.

Tess shook her head, laughing nervously. "Mary Grace just wants
something she can never have."

"What's that?"

"A happy childhood."

Valerie remembered a T-shirt she had seen several times in L.A.
which claimed, "It's never too late to have a happy childhood." She
was on the verge of mentioning it when it occurred to her that there
was something pathetic about quoting T-shirts. Finally Tess stood
and announced her departure.

"Let's get together again soon," Valerie said. "You name the
time."

Tess nodded.

"We should have a party, you know? For old times' sake," Valerie
suggested.

"That would be fun."

"Well, we'll work around your schedule. Since I don't have one."

Tess gave her a quick kiss on the cheek, then walked out to the faded blue Toyota waiting in the driveway. Valerie watched her slim, apologetic figure and thought, Joe married her. He married her. Till death do they part.

The Millburn chimes started, announcing the dinner hour. Shortly after, Valerie heard the sound of drums, as the cadets fell into formation, then marched into Mess. The dull, staccato rhythm was soothing to her, and she listened until the last drumbeat had faded.

Then she went inside, eager to feel the cool rush of central air-conditioning on her face. But even after she was inside, the sense of deflation did not leave her. She often felt that way after any sort of get-together. Perhaps it was the prospect of facing all those dirty dishes, although in this instance her mother had cleared them all and put them in the dishwasher. So perhaps it was the thick, deafening silence that invaded the room.

Or perhaps it was the residue of her own chatter, echoing in her brain, making her feel ridiculous.

11

On Sundays Tess and Joe went to the Methodist church, one of four Protestant churches located at respectful intervals along Main Street. They varied little in architecture or philosophy, so families often chose their denomination based on proximity to their homes. When Tess and Joe first moved across town, there was some danger that they would go with the Presbyterians, but tradition won out over location, and they stayed with the Methodists, much to Lana Brumfield's relief.

During the ten years they had been married, Tess and Joe had rarely missed a Sunday lunch at the Brumfields', much to Joe's dismay, since he harbored an intense dislike for Tess's mother. He had never admitted this to Tess. He supposed he would in years to come, when they had run out of things to discuss and worry about. But lately they had had their hands full with their attempts to start a family. And now there was the return of Valerie Caldwell.

Joe tried to endure the Sunday lunches by positioning himself beside Ray, Tess's father, a perfectly innocuous fellow who only wanted to discuss lawn care, a subject that seemed to interest him beyond reason. Though he tried to lose himself in discussions of crabgrass and hydrangeas, Joe couldn't escape the knowledge that Lana was always somewhere nearby, peering at him and smoking. Many times Joe had tried to recall what he had learned in Psych 101 long enough to analyze his mother-in-law, but try as he might, the only diagnosis he could come up with was that she was mean. There was mischief in her eyes, intrigue in her face, ill will in her voice.

On this particular Sunday Lana served an overdone roast, mashed potatoes, and peas and had initiated a discussion about anyone who had behaved inappropriately at church.

"I thought Marsha Walford's outfit was in bad taste. As much money as she has, she can afford to wear a dress to church. An old pantsuit, like she didn't have anything better. If you ask me, that's a form of showing off."

"I liked that hymn we closed with, 'Oh, for a Thousand Tongues to Sing,'" Tess said, looking a little dreamy.

Ray chuckled. "When I was a boy, I thought they were saying, 'Oh for a thousand donkey strings.'"

Joe was conscious of laughing too loudly. He felt Lana peering at him as she plopped a charred piece of roast on his plate.

"It's the preacher's fault this roast got too done. If he'd preach a normal sermon like anybody else, instead of acting like he's running for office."

"It's his moment in the spotlight," Ray said. "It's his one day to shine."

"Can't he shine for twenty minutes, like everybody else?"

Joe couldn't imagine how Ray remained the sanguine creature that he was, in the constant company of Lana.

He stole a glance at his own wife and wondered if there was any chance Tess would turn into her mother. It seemed highly unlikely. They didn't resemble one another physically and were poles apart in personality. Lana the stirrer-up, the cynic, always expecting the worst and hoping to find it. And Tess, always wanting things to be right and good, willing to do all the work to make it that way. The things she sometimes refused to see frustrated him.

Like what you've been up to.

He sat up, looking around, as if someone else might have heard. It was annoying, that little voice in the back of his brain, struggling through his preoccupation with Lana and his attempts to listen to Ray's instructions for transplanting dogwoods. He felt guilt surrounding him like a nimbus that only the pure of heart could see. This was why he avoided Tess's eyes.

She didn't suspect anything, of course. She wouldn't, even if she had the opportunity. She'd battle it, rail against it, and go on believing in him. Initially she had been worried about Valerie, he knew that. But he had put her fears to rest and she never mentioned it again. You only had to tell Tess something once. Her faith would take her the rest of the way.

"Mama, we should ask Mary Grace to lunch some Sunday. Since her mother moved to Florida, she doesn't have anybody to spend weekends with."

"She should come to church. That's a start," Lana observed.

"Well, it's hard for her to do things alone," Tess said.

"Nobody's alone at church. If she came, she might meet some nice man to go out with."

Tess said, "She was born and raised in Maddock. She's already met everyone here."

Lana thought about responding to this, and instead turned her attention to Joe's plate.

"Joseph, you haven't touched your food. You're going to be skinny as a rail."

She slapped him on the back and gave him a warm, accepting smile. He was overcome with guilt. Despite his dislike of Lana, which he felt was not too cleverly hidden, he knew that she admired and respected him. In moments such as this, he felt tempted to return her feelings and wasn't sure why he couldn't. After all, he had been in search of a family, and here he was given one. Ray was an unobjectionable father-in-law, and Lana had every intention of treating him like her own son. But he resisted, and sometimes he felt it was some deep-rooted flaw in his character that made him reject it.

"Besides," Lana went on, "if I invited Mary Grace, I'd have to invite that mess, Valerie Caldwell."

"No, you wouldn't," Tess said quickly, avoiding Joe's eyes.

Joe thought, She knows. She must. She'd have to be dense not to know. He felt hollow with fear for a moment as he wondered if he had married a simple, incurious woman. And if so, how had he allowed it to go on, and how could he amend it?

The moment passed, and Tess's profile suddenly looked familiar and serene. It calmed and thrilled him, as the sight of his bed did on evenings when he was especially tired.

"Well, that's the way it always was in high school," Lana said. "If one came the other one had to. Y'all were the three musketeers. I kept saying, 'Leave that girl alone, she's trouble.' But you and Mary Grace thought she was the cat's pajamas. And every single evening, somebody would end up crying over something Miss Valerie Priss Pants had done."

"We didn't think she was anybody's pajamas," Tess said. "In a town this size, you hang around with whoever's available."

"Huh," Lana said skeptically.

Joe felt his insides corroding with frustration, watching Lana's rejection of Tess's generosity. This was the reason he disliked Lana so. It was the way she talked to her daughter, so swiftly denouncing those good intentions. Lana wanted her daughter to be cynical, suspicious of others, unwilling to trust their motives, just as she was. She saw her daughter's goodheartedness as a weakness. And Joe realized that in his worst moments, he felt the same way.

It's wrong, he thought, glaring at his mother-in-law. We should envy her this characteristic and aspire to it. But we can't, we won't. And why not?

His eyes met with Lana's and he tried to say, I don't want to agree with you. But he did agree, and she saw it. He looked away, but felt it was too late.

"Lana, I don't see why you have to go dragging up things that happened years ago," Joe finally managed to say. "Everybody seems to have moved on. I for one am tired of discussing Valerie as if she were some kind of plague."

"I never said she was a plague. I just said she's trouble, and God strike me dead if I've told a lie."

"Don't tempt the Lord, Lana," Ray said and laughed heartily. He never seemed to know when a crisis was at hand.

"Joe's defending her because she had him wrapped around her finger for all those years."

"Lana, for Christ's sake, I didn't marry her. I married Tess."

"Well," Lana said. She was the queen of the one-word answers. Tess had obviously learned this at her mother's knee.

This time the word hung over Joe like a cloud—the way cartoon characters were often followed by little animated manifestations of weather.

Tess refilled her iced-tea glass. Lana cut into her meat and inspected it for doneness. Ray speared one pea at a time and smiled distantly at nothing.

This is a crazy family, Joe thought. How did I end up in it? But he knew how. And he knew how he had become involved with Valerie, and how he had settled in a place as unlikely as Maddock. It was all because his parents had not approved of any of the schools in Chesterfield and had insisted on sending him to Millburn Academy. Then they had the nerve to die before he could hold them accountable.

They had died his first year in law school, during a trip to the

South of France. His father, a terrible driver in the best of circumstances, had had too much to drink and took an incautious turn on one of those twisting roads carved into a hillside. Joe had felt it was a sort of natural conclusion to his youth. His parents had always been distant—which explained how he ended up at Maddock—and once he was grown they simply disappeared. Rode off into the sunset in the truest sense.

Looking around after graduation, he realized he needed a home, a family. Maddock and its inhabitants were the closest thing he had ever had to that. His years at Millburn represented the longest time he had ever stayed in one place. The smallness of it, the lack of possibilities, soothed him.

Sometimes, such as now, he found himself looking at Tess and wondering if his mother would have loved her. He couldn't imagine, since he was never quite sure if his mother loved *him*. He thought she would find Tess quaint. His mother found everything quaint. Sometimes at night he could picture her in one of her Armani suits, her black hair wound neatly into a twist, her fingernails perfectly sculpted, her drop pearl earrings swaying gently as the car plunged over the hills of Antibes toward the Riviera, and he wondered if in those last few seconds, she found even her own death quaint.

But he knew he wasn't really wondering what his mother would have thought of Tess. He was wondering what he thought, if he could possibly love her, considering the way he had been treating her.

He had seen Valerie twice during the last two weeks, talked to her on the phone once, and thus far had neglected to tell his wife. The first sighting was innocent enough. That time at Violet's was a pure accident; he had even run from her. The second time was somewhat less fortuitous. He had spotted her coming out of the post office as he was leaving work. He had frozen on the step and the moment of decision pressed down on him. He could have turned and gone in the opposite direction, toward home.

But he decided to check his mailbox. As he walked that way he tried to convince himself that this was a perfectly justifiable action, even though he no longer rented a mailbox in the post office. Occasionally a stray letter would find its way there, and it was better to be safe than sorry. It could be a bill or something from the government.

He never made it to the mailbox. Valerie stopped him in front of Leggett's, where they had a lengthy discussion about her reunion luncheon with Tess and how well it had gone. He merely smiled and nodded, trying to disguise his bewilderment, as Tess had mentioned nothing about a reunion luncheon. In any case, he was glad it had gone well and told her so.

Then there was the phone message. She had called him at work and his secretary had taken the message. He had kept the slip of paper, staring at it occasionally to remind himself that he had resisted her. He could call at any time, but he hadn't, and he wouldn't.

"I'm tired, Joe. Can we skip dessert and go home?"

It was Tess's voice, breaking into his thoughts like a breeze. He struggled to smile.

"Go home?" he repeated.

Somehow the afternoon had dissolved. His food was eaten, Lana was smoking a cigarette, Ray was rattling the paper and sipping coffee.

"Yes, let's," he said.

"Don't y'all be strangers," Lana called out as they said their goodbyes.

Tess hummed a hymn as they walked down Main Street toward Church Lane.

"Sundays make me gloomy," she said. "It's a gloomy kind of day."

Joe kissed the back of her hand. His lips felt coarse against the smoothness of it, like a fine piece of glass he had carelessly scratched.

"Joe," she said, "I want to have a baby."

His eyes felt entangled by the leaves overhead. He couldn't look away.

"I know you do."

"Well, I think we should do something about it."

"I thought we were."

"No, I mean . . . something else."

Now he looked at her. He sensed something troublesome coming, something he'd want to rebel against.

"Obviously, things aren't working," she explained.

"I don't think that's obvious at all. We've only been trying for a few months."

"Years," she said.

"One year, maybe. And we haven't really been concentrating."

"We shouldn't have to concentrate. That's the point. It should just happen."

"Let's give it more time."

"How much more?" she demanded.

He looked at her. It wasn't like her to demand.

"Suddenly we're old, and it's too late to give it more time. I want to do something now."

"You're only thirty-four."

"Three," she said. "Thirty-three. Valerie is thirty-four. Remember?"

He said nothing. He thought the remark was uncalled for.

"I want to go to a doctor," she said.

"You've seen Dr. Stephens. He says you're fine."

"He's a G.P. I want to go to a gynecologist. An infertility specialist, even. They have them in Danville."

"They have psychics in Danville. Doesn't mean they know anything."

"It's not like you to be so narrow-minded."

"Yes, it is. It's exactly like me."

A stiff silence followed. He could see their house in the distance. He felt if he could just make it there, everything would be all right. All of this would go away.

"Don't you want a baby?"

"Yes, I said I did. Go to a doctor. Do whatever you want. Have yourself x-rayed. I'll jerk off into a little cup. Whatever you want. Let's just make sure we continue the line. It's done so well thus far."

It didn't even sound like his voice, and it just kept going. He could see the muscles in her face tightening. She began to pinch her bottom lip. He was going to have to pay for this later. It wasn't like the old days, back when he and Valerie used to fight, walking down this very street as he headed toward Millburn. Then he was only in this town on a temporary basis. Everything could be sidestepped, overcome. At the very least, in those days, he could rush back to the stark, masculine environment of the barracks. He could wrap himself in gray, making himself like hundreds of other cadets. The sameness. The dullness. The lack of emotion. No, the absolute denial of it.

He had no such luxury now. And he knew, looking at the boxy white house he owned, that he was no longer protected. Emotion lived in that house, as it lived outside it, and there was nowhere he could go to be safe.

12

Joe arranged to meet Valerie at the Oaks Cafe out on Highway 29. He couldn't risk seeing her at Violet's. Everyone he knew went there for lunch, and there was even a chance that Tess would show up. While the Oaks wasn't exactly a hideaway, it wasn't quite as bold as meeting his ex-girlfriend in the heart of town.

"Right there for the world to behold," he could hear Violet saying. "Like we didn't have eyes nor ears."

"People do funny things in dog days," Tom Turville would hasten to add. "They don't even act like theirselves."

As he drove out to the Oaks, his hands sweating on the steering wheel, Joe wondered if he was in the grip of dog days. It would explain a lot about his behavior—the way he jumped every time the phone rang at work. The way he had become so short-tempered with Tess, particularly on the subject of having a baby. The way he threw himself into yard work and household chores, obsessed with improving the appearance of his home. And, most recently, the way he had begun flinching at Tess's every comment.

"Your white dress shirts sure are wearing out fast," Tess had said to him that very morning. "What are you doing in them?"

"What kind of ridiculous question is that?"

She stared at him, open-mouthed, holding the shirt next to her chest like a wounded animal.

"I'm not doing anything in my shirts I haven't always done. It's the weather. Clothes don't hold up in the heat."

Wordlessly, she turned back to the laundry basket, fishing out another shirt and spreading it across the ironing board. Watching her at this task, he felt a stab of regret replace the joy he usually felt. He wanted to snatch the iron out of her hand and advise her to stop pampering him; he wasn't worth it.

"I'm a lousy adulterer," he wanted to say, and when he'd remembered that he was no such thing, he felt even worse. He had the will but not the courage to cheat on his wife. And that made him less than an adulterer.

He spent part of the drive to the Oaks wondering why that word had come to haunt him. He wasn't really a believer. He went to church because Tess seemed to enjoy it, and because his not going to church would have created a controversy far stronger than his lack of belief. He did not feel up to the challenge of defying religion. Let someone with more (or less, as the case might be) conviction than he take care of that.

He did not put a lot of stock in the Ten Commandments, yet he was willing to label himself an adulterer. Perhaps it sounded more substantial than the other options—cheater, infidel, two-timer, deceiver. If and when he took some action in the direction he was headed, he did not want a dime-store denouncement of his behavior. He wanted the real thing.

You are not going to cheat on your wife, he reminded himself as he pulled into a parking space. You simply are not.

The Oaks was not crowded, but right away Joe saw two businessmen from town he knew well enough to nod to. Their presence made him feel less guilty somehow. He had been spotted, so he must proceed as if he had nothing to hide.

Valerie was sitting at a table in a corner, sipping iced tea through a straw and tossing her long blond hair over her shoulder. From a distance she looked sixteen. Joe's palms would not stop sweating. He rubbed them against his trousers, then shoved them inside his pockets.

"Joseph," she called out, waving to him, as if he might have overlooked her.

"How long have you been here?" he asked as he approached the table.

"A while. But you know me, always early."

He smiled. He didn't remember that about her.

"You look absolutely wonderful," she said.

He sat across from her and slid his chair noisily up to the table.

"You don't look so bad yourself."

"Oh well, women don't hold up as well as men. I might look as young as you do, but you can be sure I've worked harder at it."

He stared at her eyes and wondered if she had taken advantage of any cosmetic surgery in Los Angeles. Everyone there did it, he was told, like going to the dentist. He wanted to look at her breasts and ponder the same question, but he was too scared to glance. If he remembered correctly, and if all had remained the same, Valerie's breasts were perfect.

She was wearing a black sleeveless dress with pearl buttons. Her earrings were medallions of gold with appendages that jangled whenever her head moved. She always jangled; that he did remember.

She smelled of gardenias, her favorite flower.

"Joe, I had the strangest sensation when you walked in, that absolutely nothing had changed."

Joe swallowed. "What do you mean?"

"Oh," she said, smiling and tucking a piece of hair behind her ear, "that you were going to sit down and talk to me like you used to, about love and marriage and children, and all those things. It sounded so easy then, didn't it?"

Joe swallowed. "What became of that feeling?"

She smiled at him. "It went away, of course. It was just a feeling."

He nodded and opened his menu, just to have something to look at.

"You have no idea what coming to this place does to me," Valerie went on. "Do you know how many birthdays I spent out here? How many milestones we celebrated—cheerleading tryouts, graduation . . . any major event ended up here. In fact, do you remember the last time we were here together?"

He glanced up. "No. When?"

"Military Ball. Your parents took us here the day before. Your mother sat there staring at me. It was like some kind of political torture, like she was waiting for me to break down and confess."

"Confess what?" he asked, troubled by that portrayal of his mother, which he knew to be more than accurate.

"A desire to steal her precious son and corrupt him? I don't know. You tell me what crime your mother suspected me of."

"She liked you," Joe said weakly.

At this Valerie threw her head back and laughed.

"Oh, Joseph," she said with a hint of pity.

"Do y'all want to order now?"

The waitress was a thin, almost consumptive type with a pile of dyed brunette hair. Joe wondered what kind of woman would dye her hair that color. He felt, staring at the daisy pendant around her neck, that he understood absolutely nothing about women.

"The chicken salad for me, Doris," Valerie said. "And I'm willing to bet Joe's going to want roast beef."

"That sounds good," he said, though every instinct in his body told him to order something different. Defy her. Don't let her do this again. But he was too tired, and he wanted the waitress to go away.

"You know her?" Joe asked when she had gone.

"Sure, Doris Pickerel. She was in my class. We were cheerleaders together."

"But that Doris was . . ." He struggled for the word.

"Beautiful," Valerie said. "We all used to be."

"You still are," he said before he knew it.

Valerie smiled and looked into her iced tea.

"Doris has had three children and two divorces. That can take a toll. And I have had an easy life."

"I never thought of life in L.A. as being easy," he said. "And you're on the verge of a divorce yourself."

"Yes," she said, looking up at him. "That's what I wanted to talk to you about."

Joe felt his throat tighten.

"Why me?" he asked.

She shrugged. "I thought it was obvious."

He reached for his fork and turned it over nervously, making impressions on the white linen tablecloth. He constructed a tower of dots and stared intently at them.

"Tell me anyway," he said.

"Because you're a lawyer."

"I see," Joe said, hoping his voice didn't betray something—relief? disappointment?—some emotion he didn't want her to recognize.

"I need your legal advice, Joseph. I'd be willing to pay you for your time, of course."

Before he could respond, Doris approached, her stockings singing as she moved across the floor.

"One chicken salad and one roast beef." She leaned over, and the daisy pendant swung in Joe's face. A plate of gray roast beef, lumpy potatoes, and fat green peas appeared before him.

"That was fast," Valerie said.

"Can I get y'all anything else?"

"More tea for me, please, Doris. And Joseph would probably like some water."

"No water," he said.

"Are you just going to choke?" Valerie asked.

"No water," he repeated.

Doris went away, taking the smell of hairspray and nail varnish with her.

Finally Joe looked up. Valerie was preoccupied with her chicken salad. She was rearranging it on its bed of lettuce, delicately picking out the parts she didn't care for—the oversized chunks of celery and onion. She salted, then peppered it, then stirred it around, then put a minuscule portion atop a saltine.

"You cannot get food like this in Los Angeles," she declared.

"You can't get chicken salad in Los Angeles?"

"Not like this. I mean, out there they use yogurt instead of mayonnaise and they put in water chestnuts and cilantro and all these things which should not get anywhere near chicken salad."

She smiled and bit into her cracker.

"Joseph, I swear, I don't think I had a pleasant meal the entire time I was there. My husband was into haute cuisine. Goat cheese and quail and balsamic vinegar. He'd send his Ahi tuna back if it wasn't pink in the middle. And I'd always want to say, 'Tuna's supposed to be cooked. In fact, it's supposed to come in a can!' "

She laughed. Joe tried to, but it wasn't in him. She didn't seem to notice. She just sighed and said, "Funny, when you leave, you don't miss goat cheese."

Joe cleared his throat, wishing he had some water.

"I don't want you to pay me for having lunch with you," he said.

"Oh, it wouldn't be for that. It would be for legal advice. I have no earthly idea how to go about getting a divorce."

"Well, you can't use me as your lawyer. It's an entirely different state."

"I know you can't represent me. But you can advise me. Divorces are pretty universal. You've handled a few, haven't you?"

"Yes."

"They must have some similar characteristics? I mean, is there some kind of pattern to them?"

He shrugged, sawing into his meat. "Well, there is, in terms of years. How long have you been married?"

"Four years."

"Well, that defies the pattern somewhat. The popular years are two, seven, and fifteen."

"Really? Why?"

"Two years seems to account for those people who are infatuated, addicted to love. The passion wears off, the marriage goes with it. Seven is the old seven-year itch. Fifteen is when the kids are old enough to bear the separation."

"Interesting," she said, nodding, impressed with his knowledge. He hated himself for feeling pleased.

"Well, that's pretty typical of me," she added. "I can't even get divorced like a normal person."

"Let me ask you a question—what grounds are you citing?"

She shrugged. "Irreconcilable differences. Or is that too common? Maybe you could help me come up with something original."

"I once represented a woman who cited irreconcilable driving."

"Really?"

"She claimed her husband was such a bad driver that she could no longer subject herself and her children to the dangers involved."

"What happened?"

"The judge recommended counseling. They ended up hiring a chauffeur."

Valerie laughed. "You're making this up."

"Only partly. It was something I read."

Valerie smiled and touched his arm. "I've missed you."

He squirmed and reached for his napkin, which had fallen on the floor.

"Seriously," he said, once he had regained his composure, "are the differences really irreconcilable?"

"I suppose. I don't think I love him anymore."

"Well. It's hard to argue with that."

"Is it? I mean, is love essential to a happy marriage?"

Joe looked at her. "Depends on who you ask, I guess."

"I'm asking you. You've got a happy marriage."

He swallowed hard.

"I assume you're still in love," she said.

"Yes."

She waited, and after a protracted moment he realized he had answered only part of her question.

"And, yes, I suppose some degree of love is essential to a happy marriage."

"Well, there you go," she said. "So should I talk to him first, or is it better just to let my lawyer contact his lawyer? And do I want a separation first, and if so for how long, and should I ask for money, and if so how much? These are all complicated questions, and maybe it's my Southern upbringing, but I don't feel comfortable inflicting them on a stranger."

Joe struggled to chew another piece of roast beef. The restaurant suddenly seemed like an echo chamber. The noises from the kitchen bounced off the walls, the snippets of conversation traveled along the bare wood floor. Somewhere a car horn was blowing intermittently.

Joe put his fork down. He couldn't pretend to be interested in food anymore.

"If you want my unprofessional opinion," he said, "I don't think marriage is a perfect concept. The modern version of it is fairly untested. As little as a hundred years ago, men and women were content to live separate lives. They rarely interacted with their children, let alone each other. One could argue this was the only means of keeping a union together. One could argue that expecting complete and satisfactory companionship from a single person is unrealistic. And one could make a further argument that we should just do the best we can and learn to settle for less."

Valerie was staring at him as if he'd just spontaneously removed all his clothing. "It's amazing to hear you say that."

"I'm just putting forth a theory."

"But when we were together, you believed the opposite. You had complete faith in relationships. If I recall, you said that people should find a partner in life before they pursued anything else."

Joe had no memory of saying any such thing, yet somehow it did not surprise him. He did recall a time when he might have believed it. But one of the problems with mating for life was that people's beliefs changed, and changed drastically, no matter how staunchly they were once committed to them.

"Don't pretend you still know me, Valerie," he said. "Fourteen years of my life have escaped you. A lot can happen in that time."

"But I do know you. And you know me better than anyone on earth. Don't you see, the past is more resilient than anything. I can sit here and tell you things about you that your own wife probably doesn't know. I can remember how the small of your back feels against my palm. It's that clear to me."

Joe shifted in his seat. He couldn't recall how the small of her back felt. But for that matter, he couldn't recall how his wife's felt. He gave precious little consideration to the smalls of backs.

"Valerie," he said, "the reality is, we broke up. And we married other people."

Valerie waited, as if she didn't quite get the point. Joe pushed his nearly full plate away. Finally her expression changed and she propped her chin on her fist.

"Tell me something, Joseph. How did you feel about Millburn?"

"What about it?"

"Were you happy there?"

He shrugged. "Sometimes."

"What times?"

"I don't know."

"What didn't you like about it?"

"I was alone."

She sat up, staring at him as if he had just struck her.

"Oh, I'm not talking about you," he said quickly.

"Then what are you talking about?"

"My family," he said. "I was away from them."

"But you hated your family," she said.

"No, you hated my family."

"Only your mother. And that was because she hated me first."

It was true Joe's mother had taken an almost immediate dislike to Valerie. But she was not the kind of woman who would state such a fact plainly. His mother was taut—everything about her, from her hair to her clothes to the lines around her eyes, to the emotions she let escape her lips. And though her eyes nearly burned with disapproval when she looked at Valerie, the most she would ever say to him was, "She's a bit obvious, isn't she?"

Less critical remarks than that had caused him to abandon his love interests before. He couldn't bear his mother's disapproval, mainly because he always had a nagging suspicion that she was right. But Valerie was the only woman who could cast a shadow on his mother's opinion. She was, in many ways, superior to his mother. She was more beautiful, more demanding, better at getting what she wanted.

Now, as he sat across from her, trying to avoid her eyes, Joe saw the situation with even more clarity. Valerie was the only woman who had ever frightened him more than his mother.

Valerie shook her head slowly and said, "You never uttered a word about missing your family. You always made it sound as if you never cared to see them again."

"Teenagers say things like that, Valerie. And any family is better than none."

"Oh, really?"

"Listen, you don't understand what Millburn was really about. We had reasons to hate our families. We'd all been gotten rid of, like excess baggage. No—worse, like difficult excess baggage. We needed to be watched as well as stored away. None of us had anything in common except that. And we all claimed to hate our families, and we all wished like hell our families would come and get us. That knowledge was what kept us together. That was the unspoken bond."

Valerie pushed her own plate away and looked off to the side, pressing her fingertips to her lips. He wondered if she might cry. Though her posture suggested it, her eyes remained as dry and cool as ever.

"You never told me this," she said.

"I never knew it. You can't see a situation when you're in it. Especially at that age. Now I know it, and now it's all too late. That's how life works. It's some kind of cosmic scheme. You can only fix something when the fact that it's broken doesn't matter anymore."

"I had no idea," she said quietly, shaking her head.

Joe let a moment pass before getting back to the only subject that interested him.

"Are you sure you want to leave him?" he asked.

She looked up, and he added, "Your husband."

Valerie shook her head.

"No, Joseph. I'm not sure. I haven't been sure of anything since . . ."

"Since what?" he asked.

"Since Millburn," she said.

Her hand was right there on the table, unguarded, alone. He could have touched it. It would have been so easy. The fact that he didn't he decided to interpret as a victory, a show of strength.

But driving home, he faced the real reason he had not touched her. He knew she did not want him to and that she had, for that moment, forgotten he was there.

13

Dr. Vincent Ross's office was on the third floor of the medical center, right next to the Danville hospital. Floors and floors of doctors' offices, people milling in the lobby with varying afflictions. People in casts, women with protruding bellies, old people shuffling, eyes on the ground, children crying and struggling to escape their mothers' grasp, healthy middle-aged people who looked tense or tired or frightened. It was all a bit overwhelming to Tess, whose only experience with doctors had been Dr. Stephens's waiting room, which was filled with people she saw daily in the grocery store. They had usually only dropped in for some nose spray or a tetanus shot, or just to pay their respects to Gil, as they hadn't seen him since the Christmas party. No one in Dr. Stephens's waiting room had anything dire; but here, in the hospital lobby, all manner of problems could exist, and Tess felt herself turning into a hypochondriac. Maybe I can't get pregnant because I've got leukemia, she thought, looking at a youngster with a shaved head as she herded into the elevator with the others. Anything's possible.

Dr. Ross's waiting room was full, but there were two other doctors in the practice. Maybe she wouldn't have to wait long. She was starting to feel faint. Had she eaten? It was hard to remember, but she didn't think so.

She was taking her fourth *Cosmopolitan* quiz when a nurse

called out her name. The sound of it startled her, and she jumped a little. An enormously pregnant woman watched her as she moved across the room. Could she sense that Tess was infertile? Tess smiled at her, even though in her heart she despised her, willing her to have a long, hideous labor.

I'm going to hell, she thought after the door had closed behind her.

The nurse weighed her, took her blood pressure, and made her pee in a bottle. When this was finished she led her into a room and asked her questions while she undressed.

"Three miscarriages?"

"That's right," Tess said, ripping the paper robe a little in her haste to get it on.

"Are you sure they were all miscarriages?"

"Yes."

"How do you know?"

"I just do."

"Did any doctor confirm it?"

"Only one. The one where I was three and a half months."

"Did he give you a D and C?"

"Yes."

"Did you save the specimen?"

"What specimen?"

"The fetus."

"No. Why would I?"

"Because sometimes they can determine the cause of the miscarriage by looking at the aborted fetus."

"What was I supposed to do? Fish it out of the toilet?"

"Yes."

Tess shook her head. "I opted not to do that."

The nurse finished writing and clicked her pen loudly. She was tall, thin, red-haired. She looked like a person they might cast as a nurse on a soap opera, the kind who was having an affair with the doctor and blackmailing him at the same time.

"You're officially difficult," she announced with a smile.

"Excuse me?"

"Three miscarriages. That makes you a difficult case. Pregnancy-wise. They can run tests."

Tess stared blankly.

"That's good news," the nurse said, squeezing her arm.

She went out without telling Tess what to do or expect, so she sat on the edge of the examining table and looked at the magazines available to her. *Parenting. Child. Babies USA.* As she stared at the pudgy, smiling faces, she could not locate any sense of desire. Nothing overwhelmed her; a maternal swoon did not descend. Perhaps it was only in that moment that she realized she had given very little thought to anything beyond a pregnancy. Getting pregnant had become the ultimate goal; the inevitable result was so remote it didn't speak to her at all. And if it did, it only served to alienate her. The baby faces in the magazines seemed devilish and demanding. They looked as if they knew something she did not want them to know, and she couldn't be sure she wanted that kind of presence around her on a permanent basis.

She finally discovered a *Reader's Digest* and was reading about "Life in These United States" when she heard a quick rap on the door. The doctor entered in a rush, a flurry of white, a stethoscope banging against his chest.

"Hello. Mrs. Deacon. You're new, right? What can I do for you? I'm Dr. Ross."

His accent was distinctly Northern. Without even focusing on him, she knew his look was, too.

"Oh . . . well . . ."

His hand was on her throat, kneading her glands.

"I'm not really sure."

"Well, if you're not, who is?"

He had finished with her throat and had moved on to her eyes, shining a light into them. He looked up her nostrils after that. She felt embarrassed. Should she have blown her nose before she came in?

"Okay, let's get the pap smear over with."

She lay back, her feet in the stirrups. Dr. Ross sat on a stool and wheeled himself between her legs. It was only then that she got a good look at him. He was short with a round face, small dark eyes, and a five o'clock shadow. Even though his hair was starting to gray, she sensed he was younger than he looked. She wouldn't have called him handsome, but there was something captivating about his face. It was fierce. She couldn't look away from it. He turned on a light, aiming it between her legs. She heard the clink of metal, and felt something cold inside her.

"A little pressure," he said.

She flinched. He didn't seem to notice. He threw the metal contraption into the sink with a clatter.

"I'll just check your uterus now," he said.

"Oh, go ahead. Everyone else does."

She was surprised at herself. Maybe it was having a strange man's hand inside her that made her feel so reckless. He laughed but didn't even pause in the process of exploring her. He rummaged, as if he might have left his car keys in there. Finally he finished, turned off the light, and pulled off the rubber gloves with a snap.

"You're fine," he said. "What seems to be the problem?"

He hadn't checked her breasts, but she was afraid to ask why. A ridiculous part of her felt that he simply wasn't interested in them.

He leaned against the sink, his arms crossed, fixing those small dark eyes on her. His mouth and eyes had a natural downturn to them, which made him look sad and angry. She could picture him flying into a rage for no reason. His hands were small, his fingers chubby. He wasn't wearing any rings.

"I want to have a baby," she said.

"Why?"

"Excuse me?"

"Why do you want to have a baby?"

"I . . . I just do." It never occurred to her to justify it to anyone, let alone to an obstetrician.

"So what's the problem?"

"I can't get pregnant. Well, that is, I can't stay pregnant."

"Uh-huh. Have you eaten?"

"I'm sorry?"

It sounded as if he were on the verge of asking her out to lunch.

"Have you eaten today?"

"No."

"I thought so. It showed in your urine."

She looked away from him, uncomfortable. It seemed perverse that a stranger could glance at her urine and tell she had neglected to eat breakfast.

"Do you have an eating disorder?" he persisted.

"No. Of course not."

"You don't skip meals?"

"Well, when I'm busy . . ."

"Binge and purge?"

"No."

"Happily married?"

This, she felt, was going too far, even in the interest of medicine.

"That's personal," she said, sounding like Geraldine Neal, the church secretary. She suddenly felt older than her years.

Dr. Ross sighed. Tess looked at him. He had a fascinating face, with a varied terrain—smooth forehead, lined mouth, cavernous eyes, sharp nose, wide lips, eyebrows raised in a permanent question. He had a smart face. And that face deserved a taller body.

"Mrs. Deacon," he said, "I am not in the business of spreading gossip or feasting on other people's problems. I don't personally care about the quality of your marriage. I'm not going to race out of the office shouting, 'Mrs. Deacon and her husband haven't had sex since St. Crispin's Day.' "

"I know that," she said, now sounding like a twelve-year-old.

"But the fact is, I can't talk to you about getting pregnant without getting into some rather personal areas. Bottom line, we're talking about copulation. Sperm, penis, vagina, so on."

"Do you have to be so condescending?"

"Do you want to get pregnant?"

"Yes."

"Then talk to me. Mrs. Deacon, are you and your husband having sex, and if so, how often?"

"Yes. Every week, I guess."

"Really?" he asked, sounding impressed. Or maybe he knew she was lying.

"Well, it varies."

"And do you understand the times of the month you're most likely to get pregnant?"

"Yes."

"You've been pregnant three times, I see. All three were spontaneous abortions?"

"Miscarriages."

"That's what we mean."

"I know, but it sounds horrible that way. Like I chose it somehow. I didn't. Joe was right. I shouldn't have come here."

"Joe's your husband?"

"Can I get dressed now? I'd like to leave."

"Of course. This isn't a jail."

He closed the chart and tucked it under his arm. Then he offered his hand to her. She shook it. It felt warm and smooth.

"Nice to have met you." On the way to the door he added, "You probably just have a hormone imbalance."

"Excuse me?"

"That's the most common cause for multiple miscarriages. It's easy to treat, so I wouldn't worry. Good luck."

The door closed and she was alone, wearing a paper robe, staring at the smiling faces of cherubic babies. They knew something, but for the life of her, she couldn't figure out what.

14

"*So*, was Thomas Wolfe right?"

When Valerie heard a male voice on the phone, she assumed, for no good reason, that it would be Joe. She was so sure of it, in fact, that she found herself hopelessly confused. Joe wouldn't talk about Thomas Wolfe. Besides, Joe had a Southern accent, and this man didn't.

"Was he right? Can you go home again?"

"I'm sorry," she said, "with whom did you wish to speak?"

"Oh my God! The South isn't a myth. Faulkner didn't exaggerate. I have a whole new lease on life."

The voice was coming back to her, fighting its way through the fog.

"Jason?"

"Don't sound so surprised. You didn't think I'd just let you go, did you? I wanted to let you sweat a little. Of course, I'm the one who ended up sweating. I'm not supposed to tell you that. I'm supposed to be oblique. The hell with it. I miss you."

She felt breathless and confused. She reached for her iced tea and noticed her mother standing in the doorway, eyebrows raised, waiting for information.

"Mother, can you excuse me?"

"I thought this was my kitchen."

"Please."

Helen moved to the counter and put her cigarette out, taking her time, letting the smoke drift out of her nostrils. Then she walked slowly out of the room, and Valerie wouldn't have put it past her to be hovering on the other side of the door.

"What do you want, Jason?" she asked, pressing her palm to her chest. Her heart was racing.

"So many things. But most of all, my wife back."

"Are you all right?"

He never talked this way. In fact, this was the most he'd said about their relationship in all the time they'd been married. He usually regarded her as a place to put his eyes while he was thinking about his next screenplay. At least, that had been her sense of things.

Suppose he was dying? Would she be obligated to go back to him and nurse him through the darkness?

"No, I'm not all right," he said. "I'm lonely."

"You've never been lonely."

"I don't know how you can say that. A writer exists in a perpetual state of loneliness."

"Then you ought to be used to it."

He laughed; for some reason she felt proud.

"How's your work going?" she asked.

"Paramount's nibbling."

"What?"

"My latest movie. It's on a higher somebody's desk. And the lower somebody loved it."

"That's great."

She couldn't remember how many of these stories she'd endured, how many times she'd gotten her hopes up, only to find herself weeks later consoling him in a bar as he downed Stoli martinis. He'd go on endlessly about the seventies movies he'd fallen in love with—*The Godfather, One Flew Over the Cuckoo's Nest, Midnight Cowboy, Chinatown*—and about how he'd been misled into thinking he'd be able to make those films one day. But no more. There was no such thing as selling anyone in Hollywood on a film of substance, something character-driven, with a depressing ending. He'd pursued a dream that no longer existed and that was being systematically destroyed by the same industry he'd sacrificed his youth to belong to. Now he belonged, and he had never felt less at home or less valued.

She recalled that diatribe almost word for word, and now she found herself feeling almost homesick for it.

"So, seriously," he said, "when are you coming home?"

"Seriously, I'm not."

"You have to."

"Why, is the laundry piling up?"

She knew her comment was unfair. He did the laundry just as often as she did. He cooked twice as often. And he was better at cleaning. The only thing she had really deprived him of by leaving him was regular sex, and that was something he gave every indication he could do without.

He sighed. "Val, look, you know how L.A. is. It's the loneliest place on earth, even when you're in a crowd. How can I come home to this empty house every night?"

"I did."

"What?"

"You were always writing the next big unproduced screenplay. I sat in the den and watched *Jeopardy*. I can do that here, and I have more friends."

"Why didn't you ever say anything?"

"How could I? You never left your computer. I'd have to get a modem to tell you anything."

"That's funny," he said seriously. "That's good."

She could almost see him writing it down and filing it in his index cards, the section marked "Comebacks—Comedy."

"Jason, I have to go."

"Val, you're not thinking about divorce or anything? I mean, you can't be planning to stay there."

"Why not?"

She waited. She wanted to be swayed.

"Call me when this passes," he finally said. "I've got work to do."

"I've got work to do, too," she said irrationally.

The dial tone was her answer.

●　●　●

Mrs. Fullham, the commandant's wife, was in charge of the library at Millburn Academy. Oddly enough, she looked terribly ill at ease inside it, as if its staunchness offended her. She was a tall, curvaceous woman who always dressed as if in anticipation of an emergency dinner party. Colorful suits, opaque stockings and heels, heavy, dangling earrings, eyeliner that looked tattooed on. She smelled like the cosmetics section of a department store.

"I have old-fashioned ideas about the way a library should be run," she told Valerie as she showed her around. "I think it should be as quiet as humanly possible. No whispering, no sliding chairs across the floor, no coughing or sneezing if it can be avoided. A library should be a little haven from the madness of the outside world."

Valerie looked at the view of the grounds from the window, and wondered what madness Mrs. Fullham (Madeleine, she'd been instructed to call her) could be referring to. The leaves seemed reluctant to sway in the breeze, lest they disturb the peace.

"You'll find in some of your more modern libraries a tendency to tolerate talking, even smoking, if you can believe that. Of course, the boys here are only allowed to smoke in the snack bar, so that shouldn't be a problem."

There were no boys in the library at the moment. It was a Wednesday evening, and they were all at vespers. Valerie could hear the solemn strains of the organ, and the distant hum of hymns being indifferently sung. She knew what the boys were thinking of. After vespers they were allowed an hour for phone calls. They'd all rush to the booths, like newspaper reporters in forties movies. Most of them would call their girlfriends, in or out of town, and even the ones with no one to call would think of someone, just to enjoy the luxury of a line to the outside world.

Joe had called her every Wednesday at 7:05. He'd devised a scheme—he'd put an OUT OF ORDER sign on one of the phones before he went to chapel. Even after the cadets had figured it out, they wouldn't disturb his phone. He was an officer, after all, and they were just a bit afraid of him.

"The most important task you'll have," said Mrs. Fullham, "besides advising them on what to read, is to check them when they leave, make sure they aren't pilfering any books. They are especially prone to sticky fingers around midterm, when they have research papers due. But occasionally they'll try to lift some novels with lurid accounts of . . . well, you know, the adventurous ones. For example, we are unable to keep Henry Miller's novels in stock."

Valerie nodded, thinking immediately of Jason and his references to Henry Miller swatting women's behinds in Paris.

"Tess Deacon was very good at this job," Mrs. Fullham said, as they made their way out of the reference section, toward the card catalogue. "She had a way of keeping the boys in line without alienating them. They respected her. She has such a high regard for literature. And such a gentle nature."

Valerie nodded, hesitant to comment.

"I'm a little reluctant to replace her," Mrs. Fullham said. "She made it sound as if she might want to come back. But I need help here, and she does want to start a family."

"Yes, I know."

Mrs. Fullham looked at her. "You've spoken to her?"

"Yes, of course. She's one of my oldest friends."

"I know, but . . ."

She stopped, checking the positioning of her sculpted hair.

"Well, I mean . . ."

"You mean, she married Joseph."

Mrs. Fullham blushed, or seemed to—it was hard to tell, beneath the generous amount of powdered blush already in place.

Valerie smiled, hoping to reassure her.

"I know it's silly," Mrs. Fullham said, "but while the rest of you move on, we seem to be stopped in time here at Millburn. I always think of you as Joe's girlfriend. I picture all of the cadets with the girls they dated during their days at Millburn, long after they've married and had children. Isn't it silly? Some of the boys have their own children enrolled at Millburn. And I just keep picturing them with their date from the Military Ball." She laughed, a deep, masculine laugh. "It's especially silly with you. I mean, you moved on to Hollywood and married a famous writer. How could I picture you with Joe Deacon?"

"I know what you mean," Valerie said.

"Do you? I thought it was just us. Cloistered as we are within these brick walls. We tend to think the world begins and ends here."

"I understand completely," Valerie said.

Mrs. Fullham showed her the basics of the card catalogue, and asked if she was familiar with the Dewey decimal system.

"Well, I did go to college," Valerie said evasively, because she'd never been able to make heads or tails out of any numerical system.

"Yes, of course," said Mrs. Fullham, who seemed equally uninterested in the subject. She then took Valerie on a quick turn through the music room. The albums they had to offer were limited—a few gospel records, some Shakespeare read by unheard-of actors, and a battered collection of Gilbert and Sullivan. They all looked as if they hadn't been touched in years. Finally she showed Valerie the list of boys who were on the delinquent list—those in possession of books overdue or unaccounted for.

"Be hard on these boys. Hound them. If Tess had one failing, that was it. She had a difficult time intimidating anyone. They thought of her as their friend. Which is good, but only up to a point."

"You can count on me," Valerie assured her.

They left the library together, Mrs. Fullham smiling as she locked the door, showing Valerie how it had a tendency to stick in hot weather. Valerie couldn't resist questioning her smile.

"Oh, it's just such an odd thing. Valerie Caldwell working in the library. My husband used to say you were the terror of the campus."

Valerie felt offended, irrationally so, and found it hard to smile in response. Mrs. Fullham must have interpreted her response.

"Oh, you know how Howard is. He thinks young girls are a plague waiting to happen. You remember, all the boys were so taken with you. And if I may say so, you did nothing to dissuade them."

Valerie started to protest.

"I know, they're so irresistible. It's hard to put them off. But Howard used to come home so worked up. 'I chased Valerie Caldwell off the campus again,' he'd say. 'Next thing you know, I'll be chasing her out of the barracks.' "

Mrs. Fullham laughed. Valerie struggled to smile.

"Well, you must admit you were quite a temptation. Before Joe, of course. We were so relieved when you started going with him. We thought you two would eventually settle down."

Valerie wondered who this "we" was—the commandant and his wife, the Academy, or the town at large?

"We did settle down," Valerie said stiffly. "But with different people."

"Yes, that's true. I said to Howard the other day, 'Think how much trouble Valerie Caldwell was, and look how well she's turned out.' And do you know what Howard said? 'A leopard can't change his spots.' "

"Colonel Fullham was always so clever."

"Clever to a fault," Mrs. Fullham said. She gave Valerie's arm a warm squeeze. "Anyway, we're glad to have you."

They parted beneath the breezeway, Mrs. Fullham heading to her husband's quarters behind the old gym, Valerie starting down the hill toward home. She passed the chapel as vespers were ending. A battalion of gray-suited men was heading in her direction. Even though she was well into her thirties and had mingled with the most famous in Hollywood, she was still overcome by the thrill of being on the Millburn campus after hours, right in the midst of the student body. It seemed an elite position. She smiled at the boys and felt their heads turning to follow her.

Just as she was about to round the corner toward the hill, she caught sight of a familiar face. It wasn't the face that she spotted first, though. It was the hair, so blond it shone in the fading sunlight. There were the perfect teeth too, white as the moon, though she was probably imagining the clarity of them. She wasn't close enough to see that well.

But this she did see—Brett Becker made a slight bow in her direction. She hesitated, then froze, unsure of how to respond. What would she have done in days gone by? How did she react to such an acknowledgment?

She turned on her heel and acted as if she hadn't seen him.

Long after she reached the bottom of the hill, she could hear the excited chatter of boys released from their obligations, and she could almost picture them racing to the phone booths. Except now none of the calls would be to her.

Perhaps this was the most depressing part of growing old—the realization that going home was just going home, that nothing new and exciting would be waiting for her. When she left Hollywood she had given up the notion that a single phone call could change her life. Milestones did not come in the form of phone calls anymore. If they came at all.

15

Tess was crying when the phone rang. She was standing at the window, staring out at the backyard and replaying mental movies of her life. She often did that—creating montages of the most salient moments.

There was the time she and Joe had raked leaves all afternoon, and when all their work was done she'd been overtaken by an impulse and jumped into the biggest pile, scattering them to kingdom come. Joe had just stood there, too stunned to be angry, and then finally he jumped in along with her. She remembered the smoky smell of dried leaves; she could hear the rush and crackle of them, and the way they muffled all other sounds. She remembered his arms around her and his breath on her neck, and the sensation that here in their bed of leaves they were protected; no one could find them because no one would think of looking there.

Then there was the time they put up a bird feeder and watched as the grateful birds swooped down on it. She remembered how rapaciously they ate, and how a squirrel had attempted to invade their territory by climbing down a weak limb, lunging fruitlessly, then scrambling to safety. She and Joe stood and laughed, until all the food was gone—a matter of seconds, it seemed. Then Joe moved on to some other chore and she stood and watched the empty bird feeder, feeling a little sickened. She had been laughing, amused by the greed of the animal kingdom, and that amusement now made her ashamed. It threatened her belief in God. If animals are simply greedy by nature, all we have done is train ourselves to be polite. There is no such thing as goodwill or selflessness—only manners.

These thoughts had shaken her. It was not like her to question something so small, so elemental. It had scared her, and a mild depression had stayed with her for days.

Her movie stopped short, and she was alarmed that after all these years with Joe, she really only had a couple of memories set in their backyard. No, only a couple that were carefree, frolicking, and happy. What was the rest of the movie?

The phone rang. She looked at it, swiping at her tears. The reason she had come into the kitchen was to get away from her mother, who was still sitting in the living room, lighting another cigarette. She supposed her mother meant well, but why did she always bring unpleasant news? And why did she seem to delight in it?

"I'm only telling you what I heard," Lana had said. "I'm not saying it's true."

"What, Mother? What?"

"Well, Nelson Gray was having a business lunch out at the Oaks, and he saw them come in together. No, I think he said Valerie was already there, and Joe came in. Looking real sheepish, he said, though he did nod hello."

"That doesn't mean anything."

"No, it doesn't."

Just as it hadn't meant anything that Joe had confessed to Valerie, all those years ago, about his secret meetings with Tess. She had trusted him not to tell and he had. But he was seventeen. So how much could it matter?

And how much could this matter? She felt she had lost all perspective, all ability to judge. This could be insignificant or of colossal importance, and she felt incapable of making that distinction right now. Had there been a time in her life when she would have known?

"I don't want to say I told you so," Lana had said in a soothing tone.

"Then don't," Tess snapped.

"Well," Lana said, pressing her lips shut and looking away. She only opened her mouth again to put a cigarette in it. That was when Tess had risen and gone into the kitchen, afraid of the things she might have said to her mother. Who only wanted to help, after all.

The phone continued ringing. Any sane person would have given up.

"Are you gonna get that?" Lana called from the den.

Tess picked up the phone but didn't say anything.

"Hello?" came a male voice. "Anyone there? Mrs. Deacon?"

The voice was vaguely familiar but out of place, as if it belonged to someone in a movie.

"Yes," she said.

"Oh, you *are* there. This is Vince Ross. Listen, I felt bad about my behavior the other day. I hope you'll understand that I was just coming off of a difficult case. . . ."

"Who is this?" she asked, bewildered.

"Dr. Vincent Ross."

"Oh," she said. "Oh."

"Tess, is that Joe?" Lana called from the den. "Don't tell him what I said!"

"Anyway," he continued, "I was just coming off a difficult case. A woman we spent three years trying to get pregnant, and her amnio had come back . . . not good. Unfortunately, I took some of that emotional baggage into the examining room with me, which I've vowed never to do, and I don't know how to tell you how sorry I am."

"All right," Tess said, feeling as if this were somehow a clandestine conversation.

"I'd like to ask you to come back in for another checkup."

"I don't think that will be necessary."

"Excuse me? Why not?" She didn't answer. "Are you pregnant?"

"No, it's not that."

"Then why can't you come back?"

"I'm afraid I can't really discuss it."

"Why do I feel like I'm in an Ian Fleming novel?"

"I appreciate the call."

"Please, I really think we can help you. Let me make you an appointment for next week. How's Tuesday?"

She hesitated. She looked out at the backyard again, at the tree where the bird feeder once had hung. Where did they go now that there was no food for them? How did they survive?

"All right," she said.

"Ten o'clock. I'll see you then."

Tess hung up without saying goodbye.

Lana awaited her with questioning eyes.

"It wasn't Joe, Mama."

"I wouldn't want you to tell him for anything in the world."

"Then why did you bring it up?"

Lana looked momentarily surprised, then rebounded.

"It's just something I thought you should know about."

"What do you think I should do? Just stew about it? Be sullen and withdrawn for a few days, hoping Joe will take a hint? Maybe hold out on sex until he gets the picture?"

"Now you're just being ornery," Lana said, stubbing out her cigarette.

"There has to be a reason you told me. If you don't want me to confront Joe about it, I'm left with nothing but gossip."

"Someday you may be glad you found out about it."

"Oh, I see. I hoard up all this information until the day I really want something. Then I spring it on Joe—Oh, so you don't want to get me that new Broyhill dining room set? Well, it just so happens, twenty-three years ago, a friend of my mother's saw you out at the Oaks with Valerie Caldwell. Yes, I know Valerie's dead now, but in those days . . .'"

"Fine," Lana said, getting to her feet. She was dressed in a pale yellow-and-blue jogging suit, canary-yellow Reeboks to match, and Tess thought, This is how we all end up, the easiest possible route to sophistication.

"How's Daddy, by the way?" Tess asked.

"Don't ask me questions you don't want to know the answer to."

"Who says I don't?"

"He's killing himself, if you must know. Smoking cigars in the basement till all hours of the night, taping television shows and editing the commercials out, pasting all his golf scorecards in a scrapbook, making gardening charts. Does that sound like a man who has any interest in living with the rest of us?"

Tess shrugged. "If it interests him."

"Sleeping all day interests me. That doesn't mean I should do it."

"What is it you think he should be doing?"

Lana moved to the front door without answering.

"Who was on the phone, anyway?" she asked.

"A friend."

"A man?"

"Mother."

"Things certainly have gotten secretive around here."

Tess leaned her head against a column and stared out at the grass with its dried brown patches like eczema on the healthy skin of the lawn.

Lana squeezed her daughter's arm. The hand was bony, marked with age, and Tess stared at it, wondering if had ever been soft and warm, or full of good intentions.

"I just want you to protect what's yours," Lana said.

"And what's that, Mother?"

"If you don't know, I can't tell you."

But she told her anyway: "I want you to have more than I had."

"I have a husband who eats lunch in secret with his old girlfriend. I don't have a job. I don't have a child. What am I protecting?"

"You could get your job back," Lana said.

"You don't think I could have a child?"

"I don't think it would solve your problems."

"Why? Because it didn't solve yours?"

Lana gave up and headed down the walk with intensity of purpose, toward her next task.

•   •   •

I have to be better, Tess thought, staring at a neglected pile of newspapers on the back porch sitting next to a flowerpot filled with stagnant rainwater. She stirred the mashed potatoes and thought, If I can be better, everything will work itself out.

Behind her she could hear Joe at the kitchen table, flipping through the pages of *Sports Illustrated*. As usual, he had come home in a quiet, sullen mood, as if something had gone terribly wrong at work. But nothing had. At least, he said nothing had.

I'll be a better person, she told herself. I'll clean more and cook more, and I won't be jealous of Valerie. She thought of the luncheon in Valerie's backyard, and how they had sat on the front stoop talking like old friends. It was true Tess harbored resentments toward Valerie, but Valerie didn't seem to be aware of them. Was it fair to blame Valerie for crimes she didn't even know she had committed? It was possible that Valerie had changed, and that she only wanted to rebuild their friendship. Maybe Tess was obligated to give Valerie the benefit of the doubt.

In the years following Valerie's departure, Tess and Mary Grace had reconstructed a past that was not entirely accurate. They painted themselves as innocent, unsuspecting victims on whose deepest feelings Valerie had trod without a trace of conscience. Valerie had everything; they had nothing. They surrendered; she possessed. They trusted; she betrayed. This was a version of the story that they had grown comfortable with; but in her darkest hours, Tess had her own transgressions to confront.

It was true that Tess had pursued Joe behind Valerie's back. It was his senior year at Millburn, and nearly every Saturday night Joe had sneaked over to Tess's house and complained to her about his relationship with Valerie, how he wished it would all end, how he longed to be free so that he could have a healthier, more nurturing relationship with Tess. She was sixteen, and such claims impressed her and rang true. Somehow, she excused him when he kissed her briefly on the cheek and went off to keep his standing appointment with Valerie. After all, Valerie needed him. He could not abandon her yet. It seemed impossible now that she could have bought the image of Valerie as such a fragile figure, someone who had to be handled delicately and who might shatter at the prospect of rejection.

The whole scenario seemed perverse to her now that she was exhuming it. She had actually considered Joe's actions to be noble. She respected him for being unable to leave Valerie. And she grew comfortable with her position as the long-suffering other woman. No, "comfortable" was too kind a word. She had become a martyr to it.

"Everything okay in there?" Joe called out, suddenly intruding on her thoughts. She realized, with a sinking feeling, that her ruminations had caused her to forget the pork chops, which were now overdone. They looked okay, but they would be dry.

Tess served Joe his pork chops and mashed potatoes, and watched as his nose wrinkled in confusion—obviously, these foods did not belong together, but it was all the meat she had in the freezer. And somehow getting to the grocery store seemed an insurmountable task.

But I will be better, she thought. She made a tentative decision that she would make more of an effort with Valerie. Maybe she would throw a party for her, to welcome her home, and to prove that the past was behind them.

Please, let it be behind us, she prayed to some undefined presence as she watched Joe sawing into his meat. He speared a rectangle of it, and slipped it between his teeth, all without taking his eyes off his magazine. Is this what my mother wants me to protect? she wondered. She wants me to have a better life than she had. That was the typical hope of the average American parent. Everyone living contentedly inside their little shells, hoping for their children to do even better. But if everyone was so happy, why did they dream of something else?

And what kind of life was based on the next generation doing better?

She pondered this as she watched Joe chewing, his jaws moving up and down like pistons in an engine.

"How's the food?" she asked.

He looked up. "It's good, really. I'm just so beat tonight. Sorry I'm not much of a conversationalist."

"Why?"

"Why what?"

"Why are you so beat?"

He just shrugged.

"Is the meat overcooked?"

"Not really."

"You think it's strange—pork chops and potatoes."

He shrugged again.

"Are you sure everything's all right at work?"

"Did you ask me that already?"

"Yes, but . . . I don't feel like I got an answer."

"Everything's fine, Tess," he said, trying to be sweet, but there was an edge to his voice.

She let a bit of silence go by, but something had taken over her, like a seizure, and she could not control her tongue.

"The doctor called me today. The infertility one. He wants me to come back."

"For what?"

"Hormone treatments."

"Shots?"

"I suppose. Maybe pills."

"What do you know about this doctor?"

Tess shrugged. The truth was she didn't know anything, but for some reason she wanted to trust him.

"He seems to know what he's talking about."

"I'd get a second opinion," Joe advised.

"It's not that big a deal. It's not like surgery."

"Why are you obsessing about this?" he asked after a long sip of water.

"I'm not. I'm pursuing it." He didn't respond.

"Or I could go back to work."

"Instead of having a baby?"

"I suppose."

"Do you want to do that?"

She shrugged. "I always loved that job. Being around books and encouraging the boys to read. It made me feel like I was accomplishing something."

"So why did you quit?"

"You know why. To have a baby. All I'm saying is, if that's not happening, maybe I should go back. Madeleine said I could anytime."

"You never used to be like this," he said abruptly.

His remark caught her off guard. She could only stare at him.

"Indecisive," he explained. "Unsure, questioning everything. When I met you, it was like you knew exactly what you wanted."

"When I met you, you were all I wanted."

This was the truth, and she thought it might soften him. But it seemed to have the opposite effect. He slammed his cutlery down and hurled his napkin toward the floor. As if to defy him, it floated down and landed softly like a flower petal. Tess stared at it.

"I'm finished," Joe said.

"With what?"

"Dinner. I'm going out."

"Where?"

"For a walk. I want some fresh air."

She followed him to the door, feeling frantic and out of control. She stood in the hallway as he put on his jacket.

"You never go out for a walk. You never mention fresh air."

"Maybe it's time I got some."

She followed him out onto the front porch, every instinct in her body telling her to go back. Your dignity is all you have left, don't sell it down the river.

"Joe, stay and talk to me," she said.

He turned suddenly and said, "Everything's different."

"Different? How?"

"It used to be when I came home I'd find peace. I could relax, there were no demands. You accepted me. Now it's all this talk, all these questions. You want me to give you answers, about babies and jobs, and I don't know what. Did you marry me because you thought I had answers?"

"No, of course not—"

"Because if you did, you were misinformed. I don't have any answers. I don't even know what I'm doing half the time."

"Joe, I don't want any answers. I just want to talk."

He took a deep breath.

"So talk," he said.

They were standing on the porch, the night sounds conspiring around them—crickets, frogs, the distant sputtering of traffic from Main Street, the sporadic buzz from a nearby transmitter.

Tess was aware of this small window of time, this reprieve, during which she was obligated to submit some convincing evidence.

She touched his arm. "Remember back during the Millburn days, when you'd come to visit me? You said you thought marriage was less about passion and more about who you wanted to sit down at the breakfast table and eat cornflakes with. Do you remember that?"

The slightest smile twitched at his lips. "Yes. I think."

"And you said you could see yourself eating cornflakes with me."

He nodded. "And I have."

"Yes," she said. She had proven her point, and now she stood wondering how far that point had taken them.

"Tess, listen. There comes a day when you're through with the cornflakes and you say, 'What next?' "

"Is that where you are?" she asked, her knees feeling weak.

"That's where we both are. You've finished your cornflakes and you're saying you want a baby. I've finished mine, and all I'm saying is, I don't know what I want."

A long moment of silence followed. Even the night sounds seemed to recede. She longed for some big commotion—an unexpected thunderstorm, an earthquake. Something to shake them out of this moment.

"I'm going for a walk, that's all," he said. "It's not the end of the world."

He turned and started walking. She watched until he disappeared down Church Lane, into the darkness that led in a million different directions, all away from her.

16

Valerie had always possessed some kind of telepathic ability, or so Joe had believed. That was why he wanted to tell her everything—he knew she would find out eventually, just from looking in his eyes, and he couldn't stand being caught in a lie to her. He would far rather be caught lying to the IRS or the FBI. They were just government flunkies. At least they had no direct line to his soul.

Valerie saw things he did not see. Like when she told him not to go to the University of Virginia.

"UVA's greatest claims to fame are its failures. Ted Kennedy, for example. Edgar Allan Poe. Do you want to be just another guy who failed to live up to Thomas Jefferson's standards?"

And he didn't want to be a failure or to be perceived as one. She had made it sound that if he just rejected the easy choice, success would fall into his lap. And perhaps if she had stayed with him, it would have. But she left, and now he just seemed like a guy who couldn't get into UVA. That was how the Glasses saw him. And, strangely, that was how he saw himself.

A small, humiliating part of himself believed that if she had become famous, his failures would be perceived as respectable. If the world knew who she was, then he could proudly announce, "I didn't go to the university of my choice because Valerie Caldwell, the movie star, talked me out of it." It didn't mean as much to the world to say that the woman who pointed to cars on game shows had heavily influenced his life.

As he approached from a distance, he could see her on her porch. It seemed as if she knew he was coming, and would have sat there until her premonition came true.

"Joseph," she said.

That was all.

He sat beside her on the stoop. The frogs croaked, obscenely loud, as if they were mocking him. Crickets buzzed in the yard like a live wire. He could hear the pat-pat of moths hitting the porch light.

"Do you know what my husband told me once?" she said.

"No." In fact, most times he managed to forget about her husband.

"He said, 'Valerie, the reason you're not happy is that you believe your life should have a story to it. But most people's lives don't have a story. Most people's lives meander. The struggle to turn it into a story is your greatest source of misery.' That's what he said to me."

Joe wasn't sure how to respond. He'd never heard of anyone talking to his wife that way. He tried to picture the setting: A candlelit dinner? Driving in a car? In bed? Where would one feel inspired to launch into such a diatribe?

"He sounds pretty smart," Joe said. "Well, he sounds like he thinks he's smart."

"He does. He is."

Joe didn't add that this sounded like bullshit to him, because he couldn't be sure how she felt about her husband. And he couldn't be sure he wasn't speaking out of envy or insecurity.

"Do you think that's true?" Joe asked.

"Oh, probably. Who wouldn't want their lives to be a story? But I think my real source of misery is that I keep looking for somebody to tell it to."

Joe's hands turned into fists inside his pockets. His fingernails bit into his palms.

"You can tell it to me," he said.

She gave him a slow smile.

"The parts you don't already know."

"Those parts, yes."

She looked out at the road. He followed her gaze. Something scurried across it—a possum or a raccoon. Something that didn't want to be seen, frantic to get back in the shadows.

"What are you doing wandering the streets?" she asked, as if she saw some kind of connection.

"Oh, I don't know. I like to walk at night."

"Joseph," she said in a low voice. She had not lost her ability to catch him in a lie.

"Tess and I had a fight. It was stupid, really." He laughed, but it sounded false. She was waiting, and he knew he had to say more.

"It's my fault. I'm going through something. I don't know what it is. I'm frustrated at work, and I'm short-tempered with my wife. Maybe one of your California psychologists would have a name for it."

"Well, they would, but it would just be an upscale synonym for everyday emotions. Like restlessness. Or boredom."

Joe looked at her. His stomach tightened. He could feel tough shreds of pork lodged between his teeth.

"Take me for a ride, Joseph," she said.

"I don't have a car."

"I do."

*   *   *

The golf course was flat and wide, sliding off in the darkness like eternity on the ground. He felt as if they were parked at the edge of the universe, the only two people inhabiting an airless planet. This was how he used to feel way back when. He used to imagine that if he opened the door, and let the outside in, they would not be able to survive.

Joe found it discomfiting to acknowledge that being with Valerie always made him think of death, or at the very least, alienation. But it did seem they could exist as a couple only by shutting everyone else out. When they were together, they had no friends. He was never close to anyone at Millburn, anyway, and Valerie's friends always seemed more like minions. That was his first impression of Tess, that she was just a satellite of Valerie.

Now here they were again, cut off from the world, primarily because they should not be together.

They sat still, staring at the night as if watching a drive-in movie.

"You do love Tess, don't you?" Valerie asked suddenly.

Joe looked at her. He was sure the panic showed on his face.

"Of course," he said. "You know Tess. It's impossible not to love her."

Valerie was quiet, so he elaborated.

"She's so patient and loyal. Sturdy."

"Yes, I know. Tess was always so content to be the support beam. It was impossible to get her to see the whole structure, let alone be the architect." Valerie laughed, then waved her hand in a dismissive gesture. "Never mind me," she said. "I've had a couple of glasses of wine."

"But it's true," Joe said quietly.

"Why did you choose her?" Valerie asked.

"Because you were gone," he answered without hesitation.

"No, not then. Before. When we were still together."

He looked at her, flushed with guilt.

"I didn't choose her," he said. "I never made love to her. I mean, while you and I were together."

"But you confided in her. You'd go see her and not tell me. What did you talk about?"

He didn't want to tell her. He wanted out of this. He wanted to throw the car in reverse and keep reversing until something stopped them.

"How did you know?" he asked.

"She told me. Well, I made the suggestion and she confirmed it. But I knew, even back then. I could see looks passing between the two of you. It was like you wanted me to know."

"I always loved you."

"Then why did you go to her?"

"Because of how much I loved you. And I knew you were going to let me go, and I wanted her to catch me when that happened."

He couldn't stand what he was saying, and he hated it even more because it made almost no impression on her. She listened, her face completely still, computing this information as if it were pure scientific theory.

"Well, how does it feel being caught?" she asked.

He stared out at the black landscape, and he felt that something terrible was about to happen.

"I love Tess. I do."

"Yes, we've established that. She's impossible not to love. But isn't that a curious goal, to be the kind of person people can't help but love? Isn't it a little bit dishonest?"

Joe couldn't help bristling in his wife's defense, and it made him feel hopeful.

"How is that dishonest?" he asked.

Valerie sighed, and after a moment she said, "Did you ever see the movie *Citizen Kane*?"

"What? Yes, I suppose. Orson Welles had a sled called Rosebud or something."

"Yes. It's my husband's favorite movie. I can't tell you how many times I suffered through it for his sake. But there's one line in it that I liked. Some character says, 'Money's not hard to get, if that's all you want.' Well, I feel the same way about love. It's not hard to get if it's all you want."

"It's an admirable thing to want, isn't it?"

"Not if you're willing to sacrifice everything for it."

Joe felt disoriented. He knew that later he'd be able to form some cogent defense, but at the moment he was lost. For all his experience as a lawyer, he simply could not produce a decent rebuttal in her presence.

"Well, isn't that what you were looking for when you went to Hollywood?" he finally asked, violating the first rule of law: Never ask a question you don't know the answer to.

"Oh no. Not at all," she answered. "What you're looking for out there is people who will love you in spite of yourself. What difference does it make if you're rude or abrasive or inconsiderate? They'll love you anyway if you're good at what you do. It's love based on perception, not substance. Believe me, Joseph, it's liberating. You can be a total shit and still have people falling all over you."

"Then why didn't you stay there?"

She shrugged. "Because I couldn't be a total shit. It wasn't for lack of trying."

"I don't know what you're talking about."

"Love on your own terms, that's what. I'm talking about the dishonesty of a person who sets out to be loved at any cost. They're always hiding the real stuff. Because, Joseph, there's always more to a person than the part that wants to be loved."

"What other parts?" he asked.

"Well, the part that wants to be angry or jealous or selfish. The part that wants to be powerful, or do something important. You can't leave a mark on the world without making some people hate you."

"I'm not sure that's true."

"Of course it is. At the very least, you have to risk people hating you. Risk, Joseph. That's what we're really talking about. Has Tess led a life of risk? Have you?"

Joe squirmed, tapping his fingers on the steering wheel.

"I'm not sure we understand each other anymore."

"Of course we do. You're just like me, Joseph. You want your life to have a story. But you want it to be quiet and simple, without conflict, yet full of longing. You want the hero to suffer in silence. You want the hero to do the right thing."

He gripped the steering wheel. The seat whispered as she slid across it.

"But let me tell you something else my husband always says. A story has to have drama. And there's no drama without conflict."

"Oh, really," he said, hoping to sound defiant. "Where would we be without your husband's wisdom?"

"It's so strange to see you in civilian clothes," she said, her fingers brushing against his sleeve. "Even in college, I couldn't think of you as a civilian. But I suppose you are one now."

"Valerie, I always was. Millburn isn't the military. It's some make-believe thing."

"What do you mean?"

"The whole school is somebody's dream of where adolescent boys belong. Away from their parents, forced to face the cold, cruel world. It's a rite of manhood. But because nothing in it is real, the man never emerges."

"Why was it any less real than the life we're living now? Me running from some film writer, and you in that never-never land you call a marriage."

"Well, to use your own analogy, we were just a bunch of boys looking to be loved."

"No," she said, "looking to be recognized. The gray uniforms, the rank, the short haircuts. Inside your world, you might have all looked the same, but to others you were different. Remember how the town boys made fun of you? Or the people in your hometown? It was an escape from the sameness of the world. You were trying to distinguish yourself at the risk of being ridiculed. Don't you see that?"

"No, I don't."

"Oh, Joseph, you must. I never would have loved you if you had tried to fit in. I loved you because you were trying to be different."

Joe shook his head. Had he ever really wanted to be different? He could not recognize such an instinct in himself.

"You had the wrong idea about me," he said.

"Maybe you've got the wrong idea about you. Maybe you just got tired of fighting."

He wanted to deny it, but he did feel so very tired. He couldn't remember the starting point of the argument anymore.

"I've told you before, I love Tess," he said.

"You keep saying that."

"Because it's true."

"The truth doesn't have to be told more than once. Lies get told over and over."

He looked at her. She gave him a penetrating stare, a smile playing on her lips. He could have sworn there was a nimbus forming around her face, a faint reflection of light illuminating the cold blue of her eyes. That was when he heard the tapping on the window, and he realized the light was real.

The hunched-over form of Tom Turville was outlined against the window, shining a flashlight beam into the car.

"Okay, boys and girls, the fun's over," he said, his voice muffled, as if under water. His police badge flashed in the light.

Joe felt consumed by panic. Part of him believed he could and should start the engine and drive away, taking a chance that Tom never saw him and wouldn't follow. When he realized how ridiculous that was, despair descended on him like a fog.

Valerie seemed oblivious to the implications.

"Joseph, look, it's Tom Turville."

"I know who it is."

"Roll down the window."

He looked at her and she smiled, making a rolling motion with her hand. Joe rolled down the window.

"Just what do y'all kids think you're doing?" Tom insisted. "You think this is a public park? It's a private golf course, and the shareholders, all decent churchgoers, wouldn't appreciate you necking on the premises."

A beam of light fell on Joe's face.

"Joe Deacon? That you?"

"Yes," he said.

"Well, why didn't you speak up? I declare. That Tess?"

"No," Valerie said. "It's me."

"Valerie Caldwell? Now, that's a combination I haven't seen in a while."

"We just came out here to have a talk," Joe said.

"Course you did. And it's a nice place to talk. Only if I was you, I'd be careful. Dog days and all, never know what kind of lunatics are lurking around."

"Don't worry, Tom, we're careful," Valerie said. "Joe's the most careful person I know."

"Well, I'm not saying he ain't. I'm just saying it's dog days and anything can happen."

Tom turned off the flashlight, and Joe felt a little relieved, as if somehow the darkness might make him forget who they were. He heard Tom spit on the gravel. The world suddenly felt incredibly small, shrinking in on him, and Joe wondered again how he had ended up here.

"Really, now, when you've finished talking, y'all run on home. Give my best to the wife."

"I will," Joe said.

Tom lingered a bit, as if he wanted to issue them just one more dire warning about dog days, then decided against it. They sat and listened to his footsteps diminishing.

"Well, that's that," Joe sighed. "By tomorrow it'll be fodder for lunchtime conversation."

"What will?" She put a hand on his shoulder. "Joe, nothing has happened."

He started the car and, at last, put it into reverse.

17

Valerie had trouble sleeping that night and many
nights afterward. Small sounds woke her—moths bumping into the
window screen, the walls popping and shifting in the change of
weather, the refrigerator, way in the distance, shuddering on and
off.

Once she was awake, her mind became a playground for anxi-
eties and failures, past and not quite past, leaping ahead to catas-
trophes that had yet to befall her. It was odd. She never used to
worry about things. She always slept soundly, with some unidenti-
fied assurance that everything would be fine. Was that God, she
wondered. She didn't remember being religious in her youth. But
perhaps she had been without knowing it. And if God had been
looking out for her, had He abandoned her? Was she supposed to
go seeking Him out again, like a spurned lover, and apologize?
That hardly seemed fitting. Yet from what she remembered from
her days in church, that was the deal. If you ignore Him for too
long, you're supposed to go find Him again and convince Him you
really do love Him, and maybe you should try again. So He says
okay, and then you take Him for granted once more, and the whole
cycle starts again.

Ridiculous, she thought these long nights, turning under her
crisp white sheets, that such notions could occupy her thoughts for
so long, until the train whistled—always around 3:00 A.M., but

what train? Where was it going? In all her life, she had never asked. She imagined being on it sometimes when it awakened her, but in the morning, a train passing through Maddock seemed like a dream. At 6:00 A.M. she heard reveille, and the Millburn boys marching into Mess I. An hour later the town hall clock chimed, and shortly after that, her mother would call for her to get up or she'd be late for school.

These mornings no one called her. Helen gave her worried looks when she came drifting in to breakfast at eleven. She didn't confide in her mother about the sleepless nights; Helen would immediately have assumed it had to do with Jason, with saving her marriage or the pain of letting it go. She could not turn to her mother and say, "It's about my disappointment in Joe." She could hardly say it to herself.

This was the most ridiculous part of all, using Joseph to reconstruct some love story she had idealized over the years. She didn't want him anymore; she didn't even find him all that attractive. How could she have believed this man would change her life? He wasn't even interested in changing his own life.

She was starting to believe that Jason was right. In the time she'd been away, she had romanticized Maddock and given its inhabitants powers that they never possessed. Her memory had failed her; her history was fiction.

This made her think of some story she had read (or more likely, Jason had told her) about a group of people who had some specific mental disorder in which their memory did not extend beyond four or five minutes. They were thinking, functioning human beings, but they had no past. And because of that, they had no character. It was not the past but the memory of that past which formed and substantiated the individual.

She did not want Joseph to offer her a future. What she wanted was the confirmation of their past. She wanted him to see the same picture she saw and to invest it with just as much meaning. It didn't seem like much to ask; yet, once again, he had failed her. These were thoughts that would keep anyone awake, and it was no wonder that she could not rest, could not look ahead or plan her own future.

Some days, when the humidity was not especially bad, or if she had been arguing with her mother, she sat out on the veranda and stared at the lawn, sipping glasses of Chardonnay long after they had ceased to taste good. She felt the acidic trail they left in her throat, and the dizziness they caused afforded her no real pleasure.

In fact, she had a hard time remembering pleasure. It seemed to have something to do with uniforms and the smell of Brut, the girlish giggles of her friends. Lip gloss and corsages and backseats and the hum of the cicadas and the future all blending together and promising more of what made her feel blessed. But it was all so vague now, and getting vaguer by the minute.

On the days when she did not sit on the veranda, she went to work in the Millburn library. And those days were always better.

The job made her feel adequate. It made her feel indispensable. This was nonsense, she knew, because the fact was the cadets mainly used her as something to look at while daydreaming. Rarely did they ask her advice on what to read, and when they did, they didn't hear her answer. They were too busy trying to look down her blouse or brush against her or, in the case of one bold cadet, letting a hand drift over to her knee. She let these things go, and after a while it became clear she wasn't responsive. Soon the boys were content to keep their distance, to smile and stare and whisper, but never approach unless they needed her help.

She stamped their books, putting tiny numbers into little boxed columns, and the neatness of it made her feel competent and controlled. Not like acting, which always made her feel slightly crazy— stepping outside herself, going beyond whatever made her feel comfortable, restrained. Acting was the total denial of self, while most jobs were the constant affirmation of it. I am the person who stamps books, and I'll do it again tomorrow, and the next day, and the act of stamping books gives order to the world. Everything she had ever counted on might be changing, but when she stamped those books, the sameness lulled her into believing that familiarity could be resurrected.

Maybe it just felt more like a job than any she had ever had. It felt like work rather than opportunity. Somehow she had the notion it was lending legitimacy to her position in Maddock. She had been here nearly a month, and she wanted to believe that the town was accepting her as part of the scenery.

But Los Angeles never went away. People would not let it. They seemed to think she had been touched by magic. And perhaps, if they talked to her long enough, got close enough, they could believe in magic, too.

• • •

"Paul Newman," said a boy with recent razor burns and an unfortunate arrangement of teeth. "Ever seen him?"

Puryear, his name tag said. He smelled of aftershave, but not Brut. Polo, maybe.

"Only in the movies," she said, taking his books, checking the date. "This one's a little overdue."

"Tom Cruise?"

She had actually seen Tom Cruise once, had ridden up the escalator in front of him at the Beverly Center.

"That's going to be fifteen cents."

"Julia Roberts?"

She smiled tensely. "Mr. Puryear, did you want to check any more books out?"

"My mother saw Lorne Greene once. I mean, when he was alive."

"I'm sure he looked much better then."

"He was in the Chicago airport. She said he was looking around, like he was lost. He had Samsonite luggage, just like my father's."

"It's very popular luggage."

"I heard you were a movie star in Hollywood."

Valerie smiled. "People exaggerate in a small town."

"Were you in any movies?"

"A couple," she admitted. "And come to think of it, I did eat in Paul Newman's restaurant a couple of times. But I never saw him."

"He runs a restaurant?"

"He owns it. But he's not in there every day testing the potato salad, if that's what you mean."

"I have an uncle who went to high school with Warren Beatty."

A cadet at a nearby table cleared his throat. He gave Valerie a look as if to say he didn't care where she was from, he had a calculus exam on Monday. She tried to apologize with a smile, but he looked away.

"Do you want another book, Puryear? I have to close up soon."

"Yeah, but I don't care what the book is. Something short. I have to do a report so I won't have to walk tours. See, Mr. Webb, my Bible teacher, caught me eating a Little Debbie Swiss roll in class, and he stuck me. But I had a free weekend coming up, my mom and stepfather coming all the way from Raleigh, taking me to Danville to the Western Sizzlin' and all, so I did not want to walk tours this weekend, so I went to him and asked could I do something else, so he said yeah, I could write a book report."

Valerie stared at him. Perhaps the school really was lowering its standards in these bad economic times.

"What about *The Old Man and the Sea*?"

"Read it."

"Well, let's see. Edgar Allan Poe? He was from Virginia."

"I think Ellen Barkin is sexy. You look like her, kind of. Is that really her body in *Sea of Love*?"

A cadet approached the counter with a small stack of books.

"You want to check those out?"

"No, I'm returning them."

"Who you really look like is Meg Ryan," Puryear said.

"Can I help you find something else, Mr. . . ."

She glanced at the name tag, then looked up to see Becker smiling at her, revealing those straight white teeth. His hair needed cutting. She wondered why someone hadn't mentioned it to him.

"I've found what I'm looking for," he said.

"What have you been reading?" she asked, concentrating on the books. "*The Brothers Karamazov, The Magic Mountain, Death on the Installment Plan*. Impressive titles. Doing a research paper?"

He shrugged. "Just reading for pleasure."

She smiled. "Really? Because Tess—Mrs. Deacon told me you weren't a big reader."

"Mrs. Deacon doesn't know me that well."

"My father shook hands with Jerry Lewis at a celebrity golf tournament," Puryear persisted.

"You know what, Puryear?" Becker said. "You're chewing gum in the library and you failed to salute an officer. So what'll it be? Fifteen tours or your butt in a chair?"

Puryear slid away from the counter, annoyed, but aware that this was no idle threat. Becker turned back to Valerie with a satisfied smile.

She said, "In my day, an officer who stuck other cadets was considered a rat."

"I didn't stick him, did I?"

There was something disarming about his smile. Valerie found it hard to look away.

"You don't owe on these. And you're not looking for anything else. So I guess you're free to go."

"I didn't say I wasn't looking for anything else."

"Mr. Becker," she said, "the library closes at five. It's close to that time now, and I'm sure you have things to do before Mess III."

"Nope."

"Nothing at all to do, no calls to make, no shoes to shine?"

"Do I look like somebody who's interested in shining his shoes?"

"I don't know you well enough to make that kind of judgment."

She picked up the bell on the counter and gave it a quick, sharp ring to indicate that the library was about to close.

"Come have some coffee with me," he said.

"When?"

"Now. We've got an hour free before Mess."

"Thank you, but I don't think so."

"Why not?"

"It's inappropriate, Mr. Becker."

"It's inappropriate to have coffee with a cadet? Geez, what did you think I was suggesting?"

Valerie looked away, embarrassed.

"Miss Caldwell, I'm sorry if you took what I said the wrong way."

"It's Mrs. Rutter."

"So you'll have coffee with me?"

She mustered a smile.

"You just don't give up, do you?"

"Not yet."

She considered the alternative—going home, sitting on the veranda with some tea—or white wine, which she was relying on more and more these days—and turning over disturbing thoughts, hoping Jason wouldn't call and wondering why he didn't.

"I'll have one cup of coffee with you," she said.

"That's all I'm asking," he said, wide-eyed, hands spread to convey his innocence.

They went out together after all the cadets had left, and she locked the door. When she turned she saw Puryear lurking in a corner, watching, not smiling.

•   •   •

"My parents should have got divorced but didn't. They fought all the time. You know, family vacations were my idea of hell. Stuck in the car, those two and my little asthmatic brother. They'd start fighting before we passed the first exit on the highway, and my brother'd start crying and then wheezing, and we'd have to pull off into some godforsaken town and find a doctor."

Becker took a drag on his cigarette and shot the smoke into the air with force and decisiveness. It was mildly exotic, watching him smoke, because in L.A. she rarely saw anyone with a cigarette. Cocaine she had seen, and marijuana, and speed and Valium being ingested like candy, and martinis sipped and smacked over like lemonade. But smoking was taboo, the vilest of drugs, or perhaps the crassest. It simply wasn't tolerated. In fact, it was hard for her to believe that it was permitted here at Millburn. But looking around the snack bar, she didn't notice anyone taking exception to it, or even paying attention to it. No doubt such acceptance had a lot to do with the fact that the local economy still depended to a great extent on the fortunes of the tobacco farms that surrounded Maddock.

The room was full of cadets, filling up on grilled cheese sandwiches and hot dogs before facing the horrors of Mess. A big-screen TV displayed a football game, though no one appeared to be watching it. A couple of teachers sat nearby, also smoking, oblivious to any activity around them. No one cared that she was having coffee with a man fifteen years younger than herself.

"Is he all right now?" Valerie asked. "Your brother, that is."

"Sure. He grew out of his asthma. He'll be coming here next year, in fact."

"And are your parents still married?"

"No. My dad killed himself. Four years ago. Almost five."

Valerie felt embarrassed and wanted to look away.

"Is that why you were sent here?" she asked, feeling obligated to respond in some way.

"Yeah. But I wanted to come. I begged my mother to send me. I knew I'd like it."

"How? How did you know?"

"Because my dad went here, and he liked it."

She wondered if it was wise for him to follow in his father's footsteps.

"He was an orphan, and he was raised by this aunt and uncle who didn't care what he did. So he liked the rules."

"I see."

"That's what the world is all about, he told me. Without them, everything falls apart. So the more, the better."

She felt he might be teasing her, though nothing in his face suggested it.

"Maybe that's what happened to him in the end. He ran out of rules," Becker said.

Valerie could not shake the feeling of embarrassment, though she realized it was inappropriate.

"How did he do it?" she asked.

"Car in the garage thing. Carbon monoxide."

"Oh."

"Except we didn't have a garage, so he had to go to a friend's house."

"I see."

"But it's weird, because the woman used to be my mom's best friend and now they don't talk. I guess that's an impolite thing to do, kill yourself in somebody else's garage. It made everybody look bad."

"Well, I don't think that would be my first concern. What things looked like."

"Oh yeah. It would. It's everybody's first concern, deep down."

Staring at Becker, she wondered if his stoicism was genuine. If so, was it a sign of maturity or the lack of it? She knew women who left work early when they broke a nail, who wept on their shrink's couch if a man didn't call. And then there was Jason, who plummeted to the depths of despair when some faceless person called his writing "soft."

Perhaps outside of L.A. people didn't devote so much attention to their feelings. It was hard to remember.

"How long have you been married?" he asked her.

"Four years."

"And?"

"And what?"

He put his cigarette out, watching the motion.

"Well, married people usually live together."

She smiled but didn't say anything.

A bell rang. She could not look away from his ice-blue eyes. They reminded her of someone's she had seen before. In a split second, she realized she was thinking of her own.

"I guess you should get going."

"I guess so," he admitted. "I'll walk you out to the breezeway."

They moved through the swarm of boys heading up to the barracks to prepare for Mess. They skidded around corners, thundered up the stairs, burst through the doors, like soldiers scrambling to respond to a surprise attack. Becker guided her through the bedlam, a strong hand cupping her elbow.

All was calm under the breezeway. Evening light cut underneath the arch. Becker looked like something from mythology in that golden light, something she might have dreamed, Valerie thought.

"Can I see you again?" he asked.

"I'm in the library Monday, Wednesday, and Friday, come rain or shine."

Becker shook his head. "That's not what I mean."

She smiled. "I know it's not. But I was trying to spare your feelings."

"Look, I know you're married, and I know you're a lot older than I am."

"Well, not that much older."

"It's just, I like talking to you."

"I like talking to you, too."

Another bell sounded.

"You're going to be late," she said.

"Can I have your phone number?"

"No, Becker, you can't."

He gave her an impish grin.

"Can't blame a guy for trying."

He disappeared around the corner to join the ranks, the rituals, the rules he claimed to admire. She smiled and walked off into the coming evening.

18

When the doorbell rang, Tess thought it was Mary Grace. She was expecting her. They were going to plan the welcome home party for Valerie. At first Mary Grace thought the idea was pathological, and then the idea that it was pathological began to appeal to her. Tess insisted she was doing it to be nice, but Mary Grace wouldn't believe it. She focused on how much fun it would be to watch Valerie squirm in Joe's presence, looking around her at the home he had made with Tess. But Tess knew there would be no squirming. Her life with Joe seemed so small and pallid. Valerie might pity them, but Valerie did not envy.

"This is pure altruism," Tess had told her best friend.

"Yeah, and I'm gonna join the Peace Corps," Mary Grace had replied. "This is pure gloating, and I think it's great."

It wasn't gloating, but it wasn't altruism, either. Altruism did not ask for any sort of reward. The reward Tess sought was Joe's appreciation of her.

Tess went to the door wearing her old jeans and Joe's old University of Richmond T-shirt. He had given them all to her but complained when she wore them, so she would have to change before he came home. Her hair had not been brushed since morning. Her face was devoid of makeup. None of this occurred to her until she saw that her visitor was not Mary Grace, but a perfect stranger. A male stranger.

"May I help you?" she asked through the screen door.

He turned to her. He was short, with graying hair and strong features. His head seemed disproportionately large, but she realized it was only because his features were so pronounced. Where had she seen him before? He wore a blue oxford cloth shirt and khakis. Black loafers, white crew socks.

"Mrs. Deacon?"

"Yes."

"Vince Ross. You're probably busy."

"Excuse me?"

"Dr. Ross."

"Oh my God," she said. Fear gripped her throat. "What is it?"

"What's what?"

"Was there something in the tests?"

He seemed genuinely confused. "What tests? You mean the pap smear? That was fine."

"Then what are you doing here?"

"I know, it's strange. I don't make house calls as a general rule. I was over here on business, and I thought I'd stop by."

"Business?"

"Can I come in?"

She opened the door. Her fear had not entirely dissolved. His presence made her feel disoriented. Entering, he snagged his sleeve on the screen-door catch. A small rip sounded in the silence.

"Shit, fuck, goddammit!"

"Oh no, I'm sorry!" She was surprised at the urgency in her voice. It was the swearing that did it; she associated it, particularly the f-word, with extreme catastrophe.

"Goddammit. Brand-new Brooks fucking Brothers shirt."

"I'm sorry."

"Don't worry about it. Are you okay? You look pale."

"I need to sit down," she said, putting her palm to her chest. Her heart was racing.

He helped her to the couch.

"What's wrong? Have you eaten today?"

"Why do you keep asking me that?" she snapped.

He stared at her, surprised. "I don't know."

"I'm okay. I'm just kind of shaken up."

"I guess that's my fault," he admitted. "Let's start over. Nice place you've got here."

"This?" she asked, following his gaze. For some reason, she wanted to contradict everything he said. "No, it isn't."

"It is if you live in a one-bedroom apartment."

"You're a doctor. You can't afford better than that?"

"Well, you know. Divorce."

"Oh."

He stuffed his hands in his pockets, seemingly very much at ease with all that had transpired. Tess's heart had slowed down to a normal pace and she felt some of her social graces returning.

"Can I get you some coffee?"

He laughed. "Southerners. When in doubt, make coffee. Coffee and iced tea are the solution to any social dilemma."

He made her uneasy, yet she couldn't take her eyes off him. He was so odd-looking, with that dramatic face and that small, unassuming body. His fingernails were cut off to the quick. The hair on his arms looked soft. She suddenly wanted to touch it. She wanted to touch his face, which was charcoaled with beard.

"I don't care for coffee, thanks. I just wanted to see why you missed your appointment last week."

"Oh." She had completely forgotten about it, she had been so busy preparing for Valerie's party. She didn't want to tell him that, but before she could formulate an excuse, he guessed it.

"Slipped your mind, huh?"

"I suppose so. I've been very busy. And I'm terrible at stuff like that."

"Stuff like what?"

"Remembering dates."

"Hmm," he said.

She felt accused. "What?"

"Well, it's just that women who are desperate to have a baby don't usually forget about their OB-GYN appointments."

"Nobody used the word 'desperate.' "

"So you just kinda want a baby."

"No, I do. I really do." She shifted on her feet. The room felt hot.

"You really want a baby."

She wondered why he intimidated her so, this small man with his receding hairline and grayish complexion and his sleeve in tatters. She felt he had come here to expose her, or to extract something from her, and somehow, without her knowing it, he had succeeded. She wanted him out, but he was resisting it.

"I guess I will have some coffee," he said.

He followed her into the kitchen. This was a Northern custom; it had to be. Southerners knew to keep out of someone's kitchen unless invited.

"How long have you been divorced?" she asked. If he was going to violate common etiquette, then she could, too.

"Almost a year. It wasn't my idea. It was hers."

"Oh."

"The thing is, I had this great job in the city."

"What city?"

"New York. I forget, it's not just the city around here, is it?"

"We have so many cities to choose from," she said, and he laughed.

"Anyway, she wanted to live in this rural environment, and she'd read in some paper about Danville. Actually, she'd read about Maddock, but there were no openings for an OB. She loved the whole idea of Maddock, this place with less than two thousand people, and an actual military academy and everything. She could picture us having a son and sending him there, of all things."

Tess smiled. Sometimes she imagined sending her own son to Millburn. Though she had to admit, she couldn't picture that son. Having a baby was still an abstract plan.

"You don't have any children?" she asked.

He shook his head.

"That's odd."

"What?"

"An obstetrician not having children."

"Actually I think it's beneficial. All the doctors I've worked with before have had them, and they want to transfer their successes or failures onto their patients. 'We breast-fed and we loved it,' they'll tell them. Or, 'We had an epidural and we regretted it.' 'We,' as if they had anything to do with the birth of a child. Regardless of our whole rosy view of the thing, doctors don't deliver children. Women do. We're spectators. Childbirth is a painful and exhausting experience, and the best thing about it is it's not happening to us."

Tess handed him his coffee and stared at him as he sipped it.

"Dr. Ross, do you normally say this kind of thing to your patients?"

"God, no," he said, laughing.

"Then why are you saying it to me?"

He stared into his cup. It was obvious he did not want to answer.

"Tell me why you really came here," she said.

"Because I couldn't stop thinking about you."

She felt a jolt of surprise.

"Why?"

He shrugged. "It was that look you had. Scared and defensive at the same time. And the way you were hesitant to answer my questions. And that remark about the uterus."

He laughed and she felt wildly embarrassed.

"And those beautiful green eyes," he added softly, looking right at her.

She wanted to tell him to leave, but she was afraid to reveal her panic. She tried to act as if this were all perfectly normal, having a man she had met only once, but who had actually palpated her ovaries, standing in her kitchen drinking coffee and complimenting her eyes.

He said, "I guess I recognized something you were going through. Some fear, some desperation, some lost feeling. A need to go through the motions even though you don't really understand the motions anymore."

"You certainly saw a lot for a five-minute office visit."

He shrugged. This was obviously a habit, a mannerism. "In all honesty, I think I saw some of myself."

"Yourself? In me?" He nodded and she rolled her eyes. "I love that. My mother sees herself in me, too. That's how she always knows what's best for me. I don't seem to have a personality at all. I just seem to be an amalgam of all the people around me, including a doctor I've only met once."

He looked at her with surprise and a little bit of concern. "I didn't mean it as an insult."

"Then maybe you should know that everything you say sounds like an insult. How dare you come in here and tell me I don't really want a baby?"

"I said no such thing."

"Everybody has my problem figured out. Valerie and Tess, and Joe. Especially Joe. He says I used to know what I wanted and now I don't, and because I don't, he doesn't. I don't want people seeing themselves in me, get it? If you want to see yourself, go look in a mirror."

"Tess . . ."

"You don't know how I feel. Nobody knows how I feel because they're too busy telling me how I feel to listen. And don't call me Tess."

He stood still for a moment, then slowly emptied his coffee into the sink.

"All right, Mrs. Deacon," he said.

She desperately fought a desire to apologize. There was no taking it back, and anyway, she didn't feel sorry. She felt oddly happy. But as she followed him to the door, she did find herself saying, "I can fix your shirt."

He turned. "What?"

"I can sew it."

"No. It's ruined."

"So, what, you're just going to throw it away?"

He shrugged. "I'll get a new one."

"Just like that?"

"Not everything can be fixed, you know. People come in my office, they want me to fix it. That's all they want. Fix this, I don't care how, I don't care how much it costs. Just fix it. Make it right again. Maybe I get tired of fixing things. Maybe sometimes I just want to throw something out!"

Tess stared at him, resisting a smile. But the smile was stronger, and it won. Vince Ross smiled back.

Mary Grace appeared in the doorway at that moment with an armful of recipe books. Tess felt her stare and was immediately defensive.

"Oh, hi," she said, trying to sound casual. "Mary Grace, this is my doctor, Dr. Ross."

"Vince," he said, offering a hand.

"Vince," she said, shaking it. "Italian?"

"Sure," he said with a smile. "It was Rossini before Ellis Island."

"You're not from around here, are you?"

"He works in Danville," Tess said. "And I'm sure he wants to get going."

She felt a need to rescue him from Mary Grace.

"Looks like you two are about to do some cooking," he said, nodding at the books.

"Well, we're trying to get a party together. Tess's idea. I'm not very domestic myself. But I happen to love parties."

"Really? I hate them myself."

"You're welcome to come," Mary Grace said, losing the usual edge in her voice. Tess felt she was watching a character transformation take place.

"Well, like I said, I hate them."

"Mary Grace, Vince is a doctor. He has better things to do with his time."

"I'm also divorced," he said, "which means I have less to do with my time than I used to."

"Well, at least you managed to get married," Mary Grace said, "which is more than some of us can do."

"Thank you for coming, Dr. Ross," Tess said.

"Call me Vince."

He smiled at her, then went out.

"Call me anytime," Mary Grace said, watching him walk to his car.

"Don't say that," Tess snapped.

"What? Why?"

"If you knew him, you wouldn't. That's all."

"Why?"

Tess shrugged, and nearly shuddered when she realized the shrug was something she had picked up from him. Something he had left behind.

19

Later, when he'd had time to reflect, he would say that none of it would have happened if it weren't for the party. That wasn't true, of course, but he needed a moment to pin it on, a catalyst.

Joe did not like parties, did not make any bones about disliking parties, and until now had never allowed one in his house. He thought it went back to his childhood. His parents would entertain once a month, and he would lie in bed listening to the benign chatter filtering under the door. The sounds began softly, got louder as the evening went on, and by midnight there were usually one or two raucous voices rising above the monotone of the music. There were small scandals. People were drunk and had to be talked out of driving, or stuffed into a cab. Sometimes there were loud arguments. Sometimes his father's voice was the loudest, the angriest. And Joe lay in bed wondering where that anger came from and where it went.

In the morning his parents would act as though nothing had happened. They would butter their English muffins and sip coffee at the table. Occasionally they would complain about their friends, but they did that on a regular basis anyway. So these parties began to signify in Joe's mind a sort of secret ritual, where alternate personalities emerged for a night, then were tucked away again. He was afraid that if he ever crept out of his room, his parents wouldn't even be recognizable to him.

One of the things he had liked most about Millburn was the absence of parties. The dances didn't count. They were structured, and the options were limited. To dance or not to dance, to take a girl's phone number or not, to get her a glass of punch or take her outside for a breath of air. Later, after he'd met Valerie, the dances just became a reason for her to dress up, and for him to parade her around, drawing looks of envy from the other cadets.

He had not attended parties in college or in law school, and he had no intention of allowing one in his own home. Yet when he came home from work that day, Tess and Mary Grace were sitting at the kitchen table, with the menu planned out.

"What's the occasion?" he asked, his voice tight with anger.

Tess heard it and understood it, but Mary Grace charged on.

"A welcome home party for Valerie Caldwell. Is your wife a genius, or what?"

"She's something else," he said, his eyes fixed on Tess.

She looked away from him, pretending to write.

"Joe, you have to be a woman to appreciate the beauty of a plan like this," Mary Grace continued. "It's a generous act, but at the same time, we'll be rubbing her face in the facts."

"That's not it," Tess said.

"What? Oh, come on. You can't keep anything from Joe. You want him to believe this is genuine and heartfelt?"

"Yes, do you want me to believe that, Tess?" Joe asked.

"He can believe what he wants. I can't control his thoughts."

Tess stood and went to the counter, as if on a sudden impulse to wash the dishes. Joe stayed put, unsettled by the accusation in her voice.

Mary Grace watched, her head turning back and forth between them.

"Uh-oh. I sense a little hiccup in the domestic bliss."

"Mary Grace, for God's sake, shut up," Joe snapped.

Tess wheeled on him.

"Leave her alone. If you've got something to say, say it to me. Get it out instead of sniping at me the way you have been. For once in your life, say what you want!"

Joe felt stunned at her tone, and shocked at the rage flaring in her eyes. He had never seen this before. Rage was something he could have sworn was alien to Tess. She might have read about it, or observed it in others, or even imagined it. But she had never, as far as he knew, possessed it.

Yet there it was, in those cool green eyes, the kind of rage that caused people to do dangerous things. The sight of it made him feel crazy. He threw his briefcase on the table. It knocked over glasses and dirty dishes and a saltshaker. Shards of glass lay at Tess's feet, but she didn't care about that. He knew what she cared about—the salt, spilled unluckily across the linoleum. She wanted to throw a pinch over her shoulder; he knew that, and it angered him even more.

"If you go through with this party, then I'm leaving," he said.

Tess kept staring at the salt.

Mary Grace said, "Don't you even want to hear about the hot hors d'oeuvres first?"

"Get out of my house," Joe said.

To his surprise Tess said softly, "Yes, you should go, Mary Grace."

"Hey, you don't have to tell me twice. I'll do something pleasant, like clean my toilet," she said, standing.

Her voice was weak, quavering, like someone who knew she was in a corner and could think of no graceful way out. Suddenly, Mary Grace looked ugly to Joe. Her sharp chin, the tight skin around her neck, her angry black eyes. She gave him a small, mocking smile as she brushed past him. He wanted something bad to happen to her.

As for Tess, he just wanted her to disappear. He wanted to blink and find her gone without a trace. He turned and walked back to the bedroom.

He lay down on the bed with his clothes on and shut his eyes. The next time he opened them he sensed it was late. The light on his side of the bed was off, but Tess's was on. She was nowhere in sight. The house felt empty, hollow, but for some distant roar he couldn't name.

When the roar finally stopped he realized it was the water in the bathroom. He stood and went in there, expecting something horrible, final. All he saw was Tess sitting in the tub with a book. He stared down at her but could not see her body for all the soap bubbles. He knew this was a habit of hers. She did this whenever she wanted to mourn or escape. She did it after every miscarriage.

She looked up at him, her eyes big, but not pleading as they often were, and not combative as they had been in the kitchen. Just clear, and seeing, and resigned.

"You can have the party if you want," he said.

"I don't want to."

"You can."

She shook her head. "Forget about it." She turned a page, leaving a damp fingerprint on it.

"Look, I just had a bad day at the office."

"No," she said, "you didn't."

He walked over to her. She looked at her book.

"What are you reading?"

She showed him the front. *A Tale of Two Cities.*

"You've read that before, haven't you?" he asked. Please, he was asking of this sentence. Take us to another place.

"I've done a lot of things before," she said. "I just seem to keep doing things over and over."

He touched her hair. She stared at the words in front of her. Her eyes traveled; she really was reading. This scared him more than anything else. Finally she looked up at him.

"What's happening?" she asked.

He could have lied, could have moved past it, could have soothed her fears as he had done so many times before. The question was an invitation for him to do just that. And he was prepared to oblige her, to make some elaborate excuse and restore the calm of their marriage.

Then she closed her book and he realized the question required an answer. And it required the truth.

"I don't know," he said.

"But it's happening, isn't it?"

He swallowed.

"Yes."

She opened the book again. The bubbles moved and rustled, like paper, like fire.

20

Gymnasiums always smelled the same. For the life of her, Valerie could not determine the source of that smell. Was it the polish on the floor, or the unfinished concrete walls, or the varnish on the bleachers? Or could it be the lingering smell of rubber and sweat and too many bodies and too much enthusiasm seeping into the skin of the room? She'd often heard that unlike sounds and sights, it was impossible to conjure a smell in one's memory. If there was an exception on earth, it had to be this smell, which she could and did recall at will.

The familiar aroma assaulted her the minute she opened the door. She was surprised that it was unlocked. Maybe no one had ever imagined a person wanting to go into the old Millburn gym at one o'clock in the morning. There was nothing to steal, no reason to linger, nothing of interest to look at, let alone take. The sports equipment was all safely secured in the new gym. The old gym probably wasn't even used anymore except for phys ed class, and then only for the lowerclassmen.

Her footsteps echoed across the floor. The room was illuminated by some distant source of light—a full moon through the window, perhaps, but more likely from a lit backroom someone had neglected to check. She moved through the shadows like a swimmer parting the waters with her arms.

A single chair stood near the center of the court, as if it had been waiting for her to come and sit on it. She did. And she stared up at the netted hoops, at the blank scoreboards, which in fact probably no longer functioned, and at the huge clock hanging down from center court. It said five minutes to twelve, as if it had stopped on that significant number years ago. She stared at it, mesmerized. She could have sworn the strains of "Freebird" played somewhere in the distance.

"Miss Valerie Helen Caldwell, escorted by Lieutenant Joseph Michael Deacon."

The voice was anonymous and surreal, but for Valerie it was so distinct it nearly made her head turn. She saw herself and Joe moving to the center of the papier-mâché arch. She could see her white dress and the red roses, and she could see the panel of judges staring at her. They made her so nervous she had been unable to look them in the eye, and instead stared intently at the ground. That could have been the fatal mistake.

When the name of the winner had been announced, she could not look at Joe, and she could not look out into the audience, where her parents (and Joe's parents, though she tried not to think of that) had been sitting. Again, she looked at the ground, until the dark lines and planks of wood ran together. It was suddenly so clear, the crashing disappointment, the shame of it. If she could not be the queen of the figure, how could she go on to greater things? Somehow, she must have rationalized it all away. But now, staring at the moment as clearly as if she had been hypnotized, she could not imagine how she got past it.

Was that the moment Joe lost interest and began courting Tess? Was that the beginning of the end, the moment that broke the spell?

She put her head in her hands. Her long hair fell around her face and onto her arms. Her thoughts were scattered like marbles, years and years of them, rolling around. Her mother telling her to cut her hair. Joe saying he loved Tess. Mary Grace making all those terrible accusations. Becker's father lying lifeless in a car, dead of carbon monoxide poisoning in a friend's garage. Jason saying she was not cut out for hard times. It descended on her and she felt exposed and accused and suddenly, unexpectedly, guilty.

Had she really made so many people unhappy? It had not occurred to her that way. Her memory was only of trying to make herself happy, but maybe it was not possible to have one without the other. She thought of L.A., where every person on the street thought it was his or her birthright to be happy or to extract happiness from the universe, or to steal happiness, or buy it or befriend someone who had it. Any way of getting it was fair game, because no other emotion was worth having.

But here, that sublime condition seemed tied into some moral equation, where one could only win if someone else lost.

She did not want others to lose, but she wanted to win. And here, now, as she stared at the empty spot on the gym floor where she had lost a contest larger and more consequential than she understood at the time, she knew there was no such thing as having one without the other. Someone else had won, so she had lost. And now, she knew it was not possible to be both kind and important. Gentle and powerful. Good and right.

Jason had an explanation for all this. She had only listened to it with one ear at the time, but now she struggled to recall it. He was always saying something about the cult of happiness, how someone once said that in Hollywood, every ounce of energy is put into proving that life is not tragic. Back then she couldn't imagine what was wrong with such an effort, but now she wanted to understand what Jason seemed to know, in fact what he seemed perfectly comfortable with—that happiness isn't all there is to life.

The memory of her attraction to Jason came back to her, almost stealing her breath. All that knowledge, all those things he had thought about and worked into his philosophy of life. It scared her and thrilled her, and now she missed its presence. His presence.

To her surprise, she also missed Los Angeles, and that crazy, frenetic feeling that anything was possible. The police helicopters hovering over their roof at night reminded her that chaos was all around and might encroach on her at any moment. But the other side of that unease was the excitement, the life-altering events that could travel through something as delicate as a telephone wire.

Jason had not called since that one awkward time. Obviously, he had pushed her out of his mind. And Joe had not pursued her since that night at the golf course. It seemed she was left alone, unfollowed. Never in her life had she been unfollowed. She always left a room with the sound of her name echoing.

A sense of danger descended and she stood abruptly. If she sat here much longer, her past might unravel completely and leave her defenseless. In a split second of lucidity she was able to see herself, a nearly middle-aged woman sacrificing her future in an effort to romanticize her past. She began to walk, and her footsteps rattled off the walls; the smell was now nearly overwhelming. She could not come back to the gym again. Hollywood had encouraged her

not to believe in last chances or final moments, but this was undeniably one. What Hollywood could not accept was the lack of resolution. The story that just ended and did not live on, did not carry
a promise or possibility. The story that simply died.

She walked out of the gym, preoccupied by these thoughts, down
the curved driveway toward the street that led to her house. She was
eager, almost panicked to get back home. She felt sixteen again,
and the idea of sneaking out of her parents' house seemed extreme
and unforgivable.

"Valerie!" came a voice out of the darkness.

She turned. Brett Becker was running after her.

"I saw you," he said, gasping as he reached her. Even in the dull
light she could see that his face was pink. "I was lying in my bed,
staring out the window, and I saw you."

"You have amazing vision," she said.

"Not really. It was you, your hair, shining under the light. You
were alive, it was like you glowed. What's that word they use for an-
gels? Gossamer."

Valerie laughed. "Becker, in all my life, I've never been gossamer."

Her laughter seemed to make him grow. He stood tall, and in the
dim glow of the streetlight he seemed bigger and older than he was.

"I haven't thought of anything else since I met you," he said.

She laughed again. "Oh, you know that can't be true."

"Why can't it?"

She sighed. "Because, Becker, I remember saying that when I was
your age."

She did remember it. Well. But she knew there was always something else to think of. Making good grades, and graduating, and
keeping her parents happy, and in her case, getting out of Maddock
and doing something important.

She said, "You mean to tell me you haven't thought of your
mother, and of your future, and of the days after Millburn?"

"That's just filler in my brain. Confetti," he said.

His voice was smooth and certain. She wanted to believe it. But
she knew better. She knew because of all the times she had stood
here on the twisting drive underneath the thick awning of leaves.
She believed it then, but she couldn't anymore.

"You are sweet," she said. "You are every girl's dream."

"Then let me," he pleaded. "Let me be what you dream about."

He moved forward to kiss her. She pushed him away.

"I've ruined enough lives," she said.

"Ruined?"

"Go back to bed."

She started walking away.

"It takes a lot of work to ruin a life," he called after her.

"Good night, Becker."

"You haven't ruined anybody's life. Not yet."

It was the last thing she needed, a reminder that she had not quite done enough.

She was tired by the time she reached her house and the whole episode with Becker seemed remote and silly. To be dismissed. But for one important fact which she had hoped to ignore.

As she lay awake, she found she could not ignore it. The train whistled near morning and she was still thinking of it.

He did what no one had done in so long.

He saw her, he wanted her, he came after her.

She had walked down that long drive with the sound of her name echoing through the trees.

Part Two

1

"*How are things* at home, Joseph?"

Hayward caught him as he was pouring a cup of coffee. He had successfully avoided his bosses all morning by sending his secretary for coffee, but by the fifth cup he was starting to feel ridiculous, so he went for the sixth one himself. It was a mistake.

"Going very well," he lied, though not effortlessly.

"Really?"

Joe smiled.

"You know, I remember the early days of our marriage," Hayward said, which was unsettling because he rarely talked about his family, unless it was in relation to basketball. "Etta was homesick for Durham. You know, that's where she's from. And all she talked about was going back. Well, I knew that wasn't possible, given my obligations here. So every day I came to work pretending all was well, and every evening I came home to a woman holding her Siamese cat on her lap and crying."

He chuckled, gazing over Joe's shoulder with a dreamy look.

"Even now, I can't abide the very sight of a Siamese cat."

Joe said, "I'm not a big cat fan myself."

Hayward studied Joe's face.

"Let's go into my office," he said.

Joe followed, his hand shaking enough to send splashes of coffee onto the dull gray carpet. He wasn't sure why he was so nervous.

He could imagine worse things than losing a job he never really cared for. It was the fear of discipline, he supposed, going all the way back to Millburn. Getting in trouble. He hated that idea more than almost anything—the idea that his failure could leak out, could become common knowledge overnight, could be talked about the next day.

He sat across from Hayward's imposing, immaculately kept desk. Pictures of his extended family adorned the room. Joe could never keep Hayward's and Leon's children straight. One had all sons, the other all daughters, and all had married and multiplied. He often wanted to inquire after them but he feared making a blunder. People could be sensitive about their children.

Hayward loosened his tie and leaned back in his leather chair, still studying Joe. Joe sipped his coffee, waiting.

"I have a friend," Hayward said, "a lawyer in Roanoke, who is very well connected."

Joe nodded uncertainly.

"He knows a lot of people in Richmond. A lot of senators and such. Senator Kruger? One of his best friends."

"Really," Joe said.

"This friend of mine can arrange almost anything. Anything legal, that is."

Joe felt his head swimming; he was hoping that any minute, the point would come clear, and he wouldn't have to carry on nodding with the dull-witted smile locked in place.

"And though what we're talking about isn't strictly aboveboard, it certainly isn't illegal."

Joe blinked, waiting for the rest. When it was obvious Hayward wasn't going to continue, he asked, "What are we talking about, exactly?"

"Getting you and your wife a child."

Joe squirmed. So many emotions assaulted him at once, it was hard to know which one to address first. Humiliation was the most immediate. He sat up straight, cleared his throat, and gave Hayward a level stare.

"I'm sorry, Mr. Glass, but that's a personal matter."

"I know it is, Joe, and I'm not going to discuss it with anyone else other than this lawyer friend of mine."

"I don't know how this lawyer friend is supposed to help us have a child."

"Adoption, Joseph. You can't go through the regular channels anymore. Just signing a list at social services? Could take years.

Years, if ever, for a healthy, white, drug-free newborn. Now, this lawyer friend of mine says that the way it's done these days is to advertise for a birth mother. You can't actually pay her for her child, but you can 'cover her expenses' while she's waiting to have the child. You simply interview the young lady. . . ."

"Mr. Glass, we aren't in the market for a baby."

"It's nothing to be ashamed of. Plenty of couples are infertile. Our own brother, Melvin, the one who chose not to join the firm? He and his wife were not blessed, as they say."

Hayward's tone made it sound as if not entering the firm and being infertile were directly connected.

"So they adopted a boy. Granted, they had some troubles with him as a teenager, but he seems to have settled down now."

Joe swallowed, trying to suppress the anger pulling at his throat.

"I didn't realize I'd ever discussed this matter with you before," he said, his voice taut.

"Well, Joseph, this is a small town."

"Does that give people license to pry into their neighbors' personal lives? The fact that there aren't many of us here means we have to use each other's problems as a form of entertainment?"

"I suppose not," Hayward said with a chuckle, impervious to Joe's tone. "It's just a hard thing to avoid, all of us living right up under each other as we do. It was Etta who told me that she heard Tess had gone to that new gynecologist in Danville. She'd heard about it in church, I believe, from Margaret Perry, who goes over to Danville Medical Center every week for arthritis treatments. Or is it gout?"

"Tess went to see him once. It doesn't mean she's infertile."

"No, of course not. But he did make that house call, and we figured it has to be a serious matter when a doctor actually leaves his office to go anywhere but the golf course."

Again Hayward chuckled. Joe could only stare at him, unable to do anything about the surprise he was certain had registered on his face.

Hayward saw it.

"Joseph," he said, "perhaps Tess isn't telling you everything."

After he swallowed, Joe managed to reply, "Obviously she doesn't need to tell me everything. She'd be right in assuming it would get around to me eventually."

Again Hayward chuckled, but this was different. His look was knowing, his smirk accusing.

"Well, Joseph, I can see you aren't ready to discuss this yet.

When you are, let me know. In the meantime, I'll let you get back to work. A man who's trying to start a family doesn't need any more distractions in his life."

Joe was at the door before he deciphered the tone of this last sentence. He turned to see if he might be imagining things.

Hayward's smirk was gone. He gave Joe the stern look of a father, or a battalion adjutant.

"Isn't that right, Joseph? All of us want to be distracted, from time to time, but we've eventually got to face the music."

Joe looked at him, his mind spinning. He felt disconnected, as though he were losing a sense of himself, his ability to interpret others.

"I suppose."

"Well, you think about it."

And he did, for the rest of the afternoon, unable to tear his gaze away from the dirty window in his office.

2

Valerie's day had started out so well. Tess had called to tell her about the welcome home party, which excited her and made her feel hopeful. Maybe she'd been wrong about Tess and Mary Grace. Maybe they valued the friendship as much as she did and it had just taken some time to overcome their defensiveness. People in Maddock were always suspicious of newcomers—even if they were former citizens. Change startled them and made them do strange things.

Maybe this was a sign that things would get back to normal. Her friends could sit on the veranda with her in the evenings, sipping iced tea and reminiscing about the Millburn years. She and Tess could drive to Burlington and go to the factory outlets. She could meet Mary Grace at Violet's for lunch. They could start a bridge club. She'd make those blondie squares for refreshments. And fresh fruit for anyone who was dieting.

She was getting way ahead of herself, she realized. The important thing was that she was moving closer to the reasons she had come back to Maddock in the first place. The thought soothed her. That evening she did not have any wine before bed and slept better than she had in weeks.

The first person to chip away at her optimism was her mother. When she told her about the party the next day at breakfast, Helen tightened her lips and glanced down at her fingernails.

"What, Mother?"

"You can go if you want," she said.

"Of course I'm going. It's a welcome home party in my honor. You're invited, too."

"Well, I'm not so sure."

"Why? Why aren't you sure?"

"It makes me a little uncomfortable. All those people staring and whispering, wondering what's going on."

"What do you mean? Who's whispering?"

"Everyone, Valerie," she said flatly, as if her daughter were being willfully obtuse. "You've been here over a month. People have started speculating. Even Lana has been cold to me lately. She hasn't called me in three days."

"I have no idea what you're talking about."

Stubbing out her cigarette, Helen said, "I'm talking about the way it looks. A thirty-five-year-old woman leaving her husband and moving in with her parents."

"Thirty-four. Do you want me to leave? Is that what you're saying?"

"I'm not talking about me. I'm talking about everyone else. What they think. What they'll say."

"Mother, since when are you so concerned with what other people say?"

Helen gazed up at her.

"Always," she said. "I've always been concerned. And you should be, too. That's been your problem since you were a child. You just didn't care what people thought."

"I tend to look at that as a strength, Mother."

"Well, maybe it's a strength in Los Angeles. But it certainly isn't here," Helen said.

"What is so shameful about a woman leaving her husband and moving in with her parents?"

As a reply, Helen said, "Louise Henderson told me she'd heard that your husband was an alcoholic who beat you, and that he started stalking you and threatening you, and that's why you had to come here."

Valerie considered this for a moment, then said, "Louise Henderson had better worry about her own alcoholic husband who tried to put his hand down my shirt every time he drove me home from babysitting."

Helen didn't seem surprised by this information. She lit another cigarette and stared at the window as she exhaled.

"Mother, I haven't hurt anybody. I haven't broken any laws. I haven't done anything wrong."

Helen trained her cool blue eyes on her daughter's face and let them stay there, as if to teach her a lesson.

"You keep talking about right and wrong, Valerie. This is something else. It's about the way things seem. Don't you know that's what life is all about here? It's about how people interpret things. What people think is what you have to live with."

"I don't have to live with other people's opinions."

"Well, I do."

Their eyes locked. Helen was making a choice, establishing her priorities. She had taken all the grief she intended to take from Valerie. Now she wanted comfort. In short, she did not want her daughter anymore.

Valerie was so shaken by this realization that she could not possibly pursue it. Instead she went into her father's study in search of a phone. She wanted to talk to Jason. She wasn't sure why; maybe it was a reflex. Back in Los Angeles, she would always call him after a bad audition or an argument with her agent. He had a way of rationalizing things, and making her feel that nothing was ever her fault. He always absolved her, placing the blame on someone else, and even when she didn't quite believe him, she loved him for it.

Could she really ask Jason to absolve her now? She had left him, after all. Maybe they could talk about it more rationally, now that some time had passed. She had been so caught up in her homecoming that she had neglected to think of the hurt she might have caused him. She hadn't thought she was capable of hurting Jason, but he *had* called her and had claimed to be suffering. Maybe she should have taken that call more seriously.

Sitting down at the desk, she realized it was the first time she had been in her father's office since her return. Perhaps it was the first time since she was a teenager. It was the one demand her father had made all his life. He wanted no one to disturb this room, the one thing in the house which was undeniably his, uninvaded by his family.

It was a simple, no-nonsense room, like the man himself. The desk was mahogany but other than that, basic. Papers were symmetrically stacked on one side, a collection of writing utensils neatly arranged on the other. In between were three black-and-white photographs. One of Helen on her wedding day. Another of Valerie at about two months. And a third of Valerie sitting in Helen's lap in the backyard. Nothing in the picture indicated it, but Valerie knew it was her fifth birthday. These pictures had been on his desk for as long as she could remember, and it gave her pause to realize that Frank had not bothered to update them. Was he just lazy? Was this the point in their lives at which he lost interest? Or was it that he just preferred to remember his family this way—young, unspoiled, and uncomplicated?

She studied the pictures. Helen was beautiful, almost breathtaking, but Valerie's own young, chubby face made her feel embarrassed and inadequate. There was no reason to think that child would ever be exceptional. Perhaps that was what her father liked about those pictures, even more than his wife's former beauty. The dimpled, unremarkable child, a force he could handle in those days.

Perhaps her father could see what Valerie couldn't and what her mother had chosen to forget—that their daughter was nothing special. She had grown into a kind of beauty, a golden girl, but they had seen her in her rawest condition—as a baby. And they had looked into that pudgy countenance and known that it would never change the world.

The possibility stared her in the face, but she did not want to accept it: Valerie had grown into her glory, but she had not been born to it. Over the years she had convinced herself that she had come into the world destined for greatness. Maybe, like everyone else who ever left home, she was simply chasing it.

Valerie picked up the phone to dial her number in Los Angeles but had to stop midway—already it was becoming a little vague. When it started ringing, her heart began to speed up. The sound of Jason's voice might put all of these concerns away.

She was trying to formulate a sophisticated first sentence when a woman said, "Hello?"

She sat perfectly still, paralyzed with confusion.

"Hello?" the voice came again. It was a young voice, and in her mind it was connected to a face which was equally attractive.

Valerie slammed the phone down, breathing hard. She flipped through her father's Rolodex until she located her own number. She read her father's neatly printed notation: Rutter, Valerie Helen Caldwell (daughter).

As if he might forget? she pondered, then dialed the number he had written.

The same woman answered. Valerie couldn't speak, and the "Hello" came again, a little annoyed this time.

"Jason, I don't get it," the woman said. "Somebody calls but doesn't say anything."

There was a muffled fumbling and finally Jason's voice.

"Hello? Who is this? Identify yourself. Pant. Do something."

Valerie did something. She hung up and immediately dialed Joe's number.

His secretary said he was in a meeting. Valerie hung up and left her hand on the receiver, as if in anticipation of another call, or the inspiration to make one.

Quite some time passed before she realized she had done nothing but stare at the photo of her own young, unremarkable face.

·   ·   ·

Sometime in the late afternoon Valerie became bored with sitting on the veranda—bored with her own depression. She decided to go outside and prune the roses. She put on her jeans and an oversized T-shirt and rummaged up her mother's gardening gloves and pruning shears. As she headed out into the oppressive September sunlight, she wished for a wide-brimmed straw hat. But for that missing element the day was perfect—sweet and close and pleasant. The ripe smell of roses hung in the air. Crickets were already starting to complain, though it was not close to dusk.

She approached the rosebush, which was covered with shaggy yellow blooms, most of them past their peak, their petals fallen like trash to the ground. For the longest time she just stood there, wondering what to do. She had some vague memory of pruning, but it refused to come back to her.

After a moment she began to snip. She snipped at anything that looked as if it had worn out its welcome. Soon the roses were whittled down to tiny buds, and the bush looked young and hopeful.

She was caught up in the task, unsure of its purpose but grateful for the business of it, when she heard soft footsteps behind her.

"So you've got a green thumb, along with everything else."

She turned. Becker stood behind her, dressed in full day gear, his hat pulled down over his forehead, obscuring his hair, making his teeth seem bigger and brighter than ever. His thumbs were tucked inside his belt, and one knee was bent in a familiar teenage athletic stance.

"Well, Becker. What a nice surprise. What brings you out into the world?"

He shrugged. "It's Thursday."

Thursday afternoons were free days for the cadets. That she remembered. She and Tess and Mary Grace used to organize their calendars around Thursdays.

"No, I don't have much of a green thumb. I'm just pretending," she said.

"Well, I could have guessed that. It's a little late for pruning roses," he informed her.

"Oh, is it?" she asked.

"They're pretty much finished by September."

"I see. And where do you get your information?"

"Life," he said with a shrug. "My father was a botanist."

"Really."

It was hard to imagine a botanist killing himself. It seemed that was reserved for classically troubled souls—writers, artists, psychiatrists. Scientists occasionally, but usually those who dealt with the complexities of the human condition. She couldn't imagine anyone despairing over plant life. What sent him over the edge? His inability to grow the perfect orchid? The fact that there seemed to be no real meaning in cross-germination? No altruism among organic matter? The cruel indifference of frost? Weeds? Weeds eventually won out.

She was annoyed with herself for wanting to smile at these thoughts.

Becker didn't seem to notice.

"Want to go into town and get a Coke?" he asked.

"No, thank you. I'm busy."

"You're not busy. You're finished. Come on. You've got time."

She sighed. "Yes, Becker, I do have the time. But I don't want to. I'm tired."

"What are you tired of?"

She smiled. "You wouldn't understand."

"Try me."

"You are sweet, Becker."

"I'm not sweet. Stop saying I'm sweet."

"You're persistent, too."

He pushed his hat back, liberating some of his hair. Valerie stared at him. His face was perfectly smooth and square—all the bones and tissue in the right place. Nothing had shifted. Nothing on his entire person was where it shouldn't be.

"Please come have a Coke with me."

"Becker, I can't." After a pause she said, "I'll walk you to the corner though."

He smiled. This seemed to placate him.

The walk soothed her a bit. She forgot the pruning, and she forgot the strange woman's voice, and she forgot the fact that Joe had not returned her call, even though she had left word it was urgent. She watched Becker's shiny shoes moving along the sidewalk. She smelled the aftershave and the gum. She could almost feel the strength of his arm muscles—firm, veins running across them like roads across a map.

She stopped at the corner, but he didn't. She watched him go, wondering what to do. After a second he stopped and turned.

"We're halfway to town now. Might as well finish the walk."

"Becker, it's been nice talking to you."

She turned away. She heard him running after her, and then she felt his fingers closing around her arm. He had followed her. Again.

"I know you don't take me seriously," he said.

"I do take you seriously. I just don't take us seriously."

"Why not? Is it the age thing? Because, you know, a lot of people get around that. I think I care more about you than any men your age. Your jerk of a husband hasn't even come after you. I mean, if I were married to you, I'd track you down."

She smiled, shaking her head slowly. It was hard for her to fathom this youthful confidence, this unwillingness to see the way things were. Of course, she had had that quality at one time, too. It was what had driven her to Los Angeles. Back then, she would not believe she could not have anything she wanted. It was a faith in her own uniqueness that drove her in those days and made her oblivious to obstacles. She wondered if that faith still existed in any degree. If not, she was afraid to imagine what would become of her.

She did not mention this to Becker. She knew Becker would not understand such a fear. Want was what he understood. Want was what moved him like a motor. And he did not yet recognize impossibility.

"I love you," he said.

"Oh, Becker," she said wearily.

"I do. I can't think what else to call it. I lie in my bed and I think about you, and I try to figure out what else it can be. Nothing else fits."

"Lust," she said. "Lust fits."

"Well, that too," he said, grinning, as if he'd been caught.

She should have said goodbye then, but he was hard to leave. His face was so appealing, and his presence oddly comforting. As reluctant as she might be to admit it, his desire for her was reassuring.

It felt familiar, like old clothes, and like rich, starchy foods, and all the things she had come rushing back to Maddock hoping to find. Standing there, watching him scraping the toe of his shoe along the heat-baked sidewalk, listening to the chorus of the crickets in the grass, she felt more comfortable and sure of herself than she had in a very long time. The confusion of Los Angeles, and the disappointments of her homecoming receded, and all the missing pieces of her memories fell into place. Loitering on a corner with a Millburn boy she felt right, she felt whole.

She stared at Becker, open-mouthed, as this awareness settled on her. The only thing that made her feel complete was no longer available to her. Because the only thing that Valerie Caldwell could ever be, and still be content, was sixteen.

Was this possible? Could it be that at her age the best was already behind her? Could the rest of her life consist of nothing more important than breathing and reminiscing?

She thought of all the people closest to her. Joe, Tess, Mary Grace, her mother and father—they all seemed to expect nothing, no recognition, no rewards for their efforts. They had all settled with their reality; they did not rage against it. Is this where she was headed? If she stayed in Maddock long enough, would she become equally undemanding?

She had more than half her life to live knowing that the pinnacle had come and gone. Perhaps other people could live with such awareness, but the thought of it filled her with cold terror.

These thoughts flashed through her brain in what seemed like a short time, but when she looked at Becker she could tell that it hadn't happened all that quickly. Though he hadn't moved, his face had started to turn pink from the sun, and sweat grew like a row of peas along his brow.

When her eyes met with his, he smiled inquisitively.

"You okay?"

She nodded.

"Here's the thing," he said, as if finishing an earlier thought. She wondered if he'd been talking the whole time and she hadn't heard. "The other night, when I saw you coming out of the gym, I thought to myself, Something's dogging her. Something's haunting her, making her miserable. It's the same with me. With me it's just I get lonely over there. I get to feeling dried up. We're just being shoved around by all these bullies, and we're supposed to forget about being individuals. Do you know, they won't even let us put pictures on the walls? They say it's to save the plaster, but I know. They don't want us to do anything to make ourselves feel in any way different from the hundred other guys on our hall. What if we started feeling special? We might start wanting stuff. We might start reaching out and demanding and getting mad. God forbid we get mad. We're just robots, following orders."

"Becker, listen to me," she said, but there was no stopping him.

"And love? Well, forget it. That's the last thing you're supposed to feel. It makes you wild. It makes you want to do desperate things. Valerie, when I look at you, I start to feel desperate. And I miss that. I think we're all supposed to feel that. It's what gets people going. It's what got Columbus on a boat. It's what got Pilgrims to the New World. It's what got pioneers on a wagon."

"It's what got Joan of Arc burned at the stake," Valerie said.

He shook his head. "You don't take me seriously."

"I do, Becker, really. And God knows, I'm flattered, but you're so young and I'm . . . well, I've got a lot on my mind right now."

"You're so beautiful. It's like you're not of this earth. I want to take you away to the moon or somewhere and save you from being spoiled by it. Really. I was reading about global warming in *Newsweek*. And my first thought was, I have to save Valerie from that."

She said, "Well, on the moon I wouldn't even be able to breathe, so I think I'll take my chances here."

"See what I mean?" he said. "You think I'm a joke."

"No, I honestly don't, but, Becker . . ." She paused, wondering if she should burden him with her ruminations. Maybe she should just take them back home, to the veranda and the glasses of Chardonnay. But Becker waited, and so she spoke.

"You don't know it yet, but wanting something is not enough. Neither is faith. Neither is beauty. None of it gets you where you want to be."

"Well, what does?"

She shook her head. "That's not the question. The question is, where do you want to be?"

"With you," he said, gazing into her eyes.

"I have to go now," she said.

"I can make you happy," he promised.

She walked away, glad that her back was to him so he couldn't see the panic on her face.

3

The cafe was crowded, and before Tess went inside she wanted to get out. She didn't feel like seeing or talking to anyone, didn't feel like being seen, and especially didn't feel like eating. But Lana had dropped by the house saying she felt blue, and Tess immediately felt responsible for her blueness and obligated to relieve her of it. It was only after she was halfway to town that it occurred to her she had her own mood to contend with, her own problems to brood about, and that she had somehow allowed her mother's concerns to take over. But it was too late. She couldn't suddenly turn to Lana and say, "Hold on, I'm more depressed than you are."

So she just fell in step with her mother and listened to her chatter about all her dramas, her little meatballs, as Joe sometimes said. She smiled, remembering. "That's what your mother's doing in life. She's making little meatballs."

Joe tried to pretend he liked Lana. He only let a comment like that slip occasionally. But Tess knew better, and for a long time she put it down to the fact that men never liked their mothers-in-law. But lately, spending this time with her mother, she began to wonder if he wasn't onto something.

"Let's get a booth," Lana said. "I can't stand sitting at that counter. I always feel like my butt's spilling over."

Normally, Tess would have laughed or reassured her mother

about her butt dimensions, but today she didn't feel like taking her mother's bait at any level.

When they had settled in the booth, said hellos to Violet and Tom Turville and Geraldine Neal (who had recently quit as church secretary over what the pastor had only referred to as a "financial issue") and Boots Palmer (who was in between affairs and didn't have any wives to avoid) and Gertie from the jewelry store, Lana began to list all her reasons for being blue. She began laying the meatballs out, one by one.

"Louisa has got kennel cough," was the first one. "From when I took her to get a bath at the vet? I said to Sheryl, Marvin's assistant, I said I'd rather her have fleas than the croup. She tried to tell me that kennel cough isn't serious, but I know. Eunice Fuller's cocker spaniel died of it."

"Eunice's cocker spaniel was thirteen years old, Mama."

"And then your father and I aren't speaking to each other. I wanted a parquet floor for the dining room, and he knows I have always wanted parquet for the dining room. Before we even got married I told him I wanted parquet for the dining room. And we finally have enough money saved up, and what does he spend it on? Without telling me? A riding lawn mower! So I told him he was greedy-gutted and always had been. Which is the gospel truth."

Tess sipped her iced tea and wondered if she should have chicken or minced barbecue.

"Then, you knew about Rufus Batterman's wife."

"No. What about her?"

"She's engaged, that's what. Her husband's body isn't cold in the grave, and she's engaged to Ham Edwards. I talked to Helen this morning, and she said that romance was going on a long time, and it's probably the reason Rufus shot himself."

As if to give the story emphasis, or perhaps closure, Lana lit a cigarette and took a couple of leisurely puffs, leaving Tess time to digest the information. Tess knew that some kind of reaction was expected of her, probably one of anger and outrage, but she found it was hard even to pretend to be interested.

"You're upset about that?" Tess asked.

"A woman is the cause of her own husband's suicide? And she just goes right on about her business for all the world to see? Yes, I'm upset about that."

"Well, I just can't see how it matters."

Lana's eyes narrowed. "You can't? Then I'd say you've got a problem."

"I mean it matters somewhere to somebody, I suppose, but not to me. I didn't know Rufus. You hardly knew him yourself. I don't see how it affects your life."

"I didn't say it affected my life."

"But you're depressed about it."

"That's just one of the things I'm depressed about."

"Don't y'all know it's too hot to eat?" Violet said, approaching the table at a slow, lumbering pace.

"Lord, I was saying to Helen this morning, if it don't cool off soon I might have to kill somebody," Lana said, her blues as well as her indignation suddenly receding. "It's supposed to be fall, isn't it? I've never seen a summer go on so long. I can't even catch a good breath in this humidity."

"My air-conditioning's acting like it might go," Violet said. "And if it does, I'm going home and y'all can all make your own lunch. What can I get you?"

"Minced barbecue," Tess said.

"In this heat?" Violet questioned, shaking her head. "All right."

"Give me a chicken leg. Are your butter beans fresh?"

"Jolly Green Giant."

"Then slice me up a tomato."

Violet collected their menus, and Tess's eyes connected with hers for a moment. She couldn't mistake Violet's expression—one of curiosity and sympathy, a look that Tess accepted as appropriate, until she realized that Violet couldn't really know about her problems. This look was something else, something from the outside. Violet knew something she didn't. Just like those babies.

She was still analyzing the look when her mother's voice picked up again where it left off, bemoaning Rufus Batterman's plight, and vilifying Marlene's behavior.

"And do you know, she showed up at church Sunday morning as if nothing had happened? I couldn't believe my eyes. I told your father, that's the same as blasphemy."

"I thought you weren't speaking to Daddy."

"This was before the lawn mower. I said to him, 'What does she take the Lord for, a fool? Doesn't she think He knows what she's been up to?'"

Tess said, "Maybe she's under the impression that the Lord is merciful and forgiving."

Lana's lips bunched together. "Well, He might be merciful and forgiving, but He's not an idiot."

Lana smoked, staring at her daughter, her eyes cold and steely. Tess found it hard to face them.

"Mama," she said, "I understand what you're saying. I do. But first of all, I think it's wrong to enjoy discussing other people's misfortunes."

"I'm just repeating what I heard."

"And second of all, you don't know the whole story. Maybe there were other problems. Maybe they had some kind of agreement. Maybe Rufus Batterman slapped his wife around or cheated on her."

Lana looked shocked.

"I don't know how you can say that. He was the nicest, sweetest man I ever met."

"He changed your oil and your spark plugs. How much could that tell you about his character?"

"I won't hear a word against him."

"But you'll hear as many as possible against her."

"I don't know what in the world has gotten into you," Lana said, shaking her head. "I really don't."

Rubbing her head, Tess said, "Mama, I'm tired and I've got a lot on my mind."

"What? Has something happened?"

Tess considered telling her about her problems with Joe. But Lana looked so eager for more drama that Tess felt determined not to give it to her.

"No, nothing's happened."

Tom Turville slid off his stool and headed in their direction. Tess suddenly felt like crying. It was a bad day, a lost day, and she didn't want to be in it anymore.

"How are y'all doing? Keeping out of trouble?"

"Best we can," Lana said, smiling, though Tess knew that she disliked Tom and wasn't terribly good at hiding it. Tom had given Lana a ticket once for double-parking and she had never forgiven him. "Too hot, though. Hard to even breathe out there."

"Dog days," he offered as an explanation. Tom pushed his hat back. His face was dry, lined, like cracked pavement. His teeth were crooked, and his eyes a dull, rain-cloud blue. His fingers were yellow from nicotine.

"Saw your husband the other night," he said to Tess.

"Oh, really? Where?"

"Out to the golf course. Just sitting in his car. I thought he was some teenager up to no good."

Tess felt herself turning cold from head to foot. She could feel her mother's eyes bearing down on her, but she wouldn't surrender to them.

"You're sure it was Joe?"

"Yeah, I talked to him. First I thought you was in there with him."

"I can't breathe," Lana said.

"Mama," Tess snapped, annoyed. It was no time to hear her moaning about the heat.

"So I shined my light in there," Tom went on.

"I can't breathe," Lana repeated, and her tone made them turn their heads. She had dropped her cigarette on the table. It rolled like a smoldering log. Tom Turville grabbed it, then looked at Lana.

"You okay, Mrs. Brumfield?"

She didn't answer. Instead she grabbed her chest, uttered a sputtering sound, and fell face first onto the table. Tess shot up from her seat, sending silverware in every direction. She felt people's heads turning.

"Mama," she said, more calmly than she felt. "Mama, talk to me."

But Lana was out. Her skin looked bone white.

"Good God," was all Tom Turville could say.

Violet attempted to run to them.

"Call an ambulance," Tess said.

Tom was frozen, as if he'd never seen anything quite so unsettling. Tess moved over to her mother, lifting her off the table. Her head drooped to one side, spittle forming at the corner of her mouth.

Don't die here, Tess was thinking. Don't die here. And every time that thought went through her brain, the "here" was attached to it.

Tom ran off, toward some unseen goal, and his keys and change and handcuffs jangled urgently as he went.

4

Tess sat in the waiting room, remembering.

She was surrounded by other people, each one alone, each one staring at the floor, lost in thought. Magazines littered every surface, though it was hard to imagine that anyone in that room could think about fifty fast pasta recipes. One man fingered a Styrofoam coffee cup. Tess found the squeaking sound soothing. Every now and then a door would burst open and the heads would shoot up, and a doctor or nurse would breeze past them chattering about something unrelated to medicine.

But in between, she remembered.

There was the time she and her parents were at Cherry Grove Beach in South Carolina. She couldn't have been more than five. She was standing on the sand, crying because she wanted to go back to the hotel. And her mother kept saying, no, they should stay, she'd be bored at the hotel. But she kept on, and finally her parents gave in, and they went back to the room. She remembered standing in the doorway, looking at the small, airless room, thinking, No, I don't want this, either. And her lip went out and she began to cry. The next thing she knew, her mother had wheeled around and was heading for her with something like fury in her eyes. In her memory, those eyes were actually incandescent. And her mother's mouth was tight, her teeth clenched, air rushing through them like steam from an iron. She stood in the doorway and waited for her wrath.

Tess was certain the wrath had come—blows to the legs, maybe even the face, her arm tugging on its socket as she was dragged across the room, the skin burning under her mother's fingers. Her mother was never one to spare the rod, and she had so many memories of being hit it was sometimes hard to sort them out. For some reason, though, this particular memory of the beach had always stayed with her, and it was hard to know why.

But while it still hurt to recall it, she understood her mother's anger. She could imagine all that had come before that moment. The loading up of toys and towels and swimming apparel into the car. The drive to the beach from the hotel. The unloading, the settling down, the countless efforts to entertain. Then the whining to go back, then the disappointment, just as her mother had predicted. In short, Tess had been a brat and her mother had responded appropriately. But two things stayed with her. First the degree of her mother's anger—that obsidian rage in her eyes that reached much farther back than the day at the beach. Often she wondered how far back, and where it came from.

Then there was that disappointment she had felt standing in the doorway. She remembered that feeling more acutely than any other in her life. No, this isn't it either. This isn't where I want to be.

It was a feeling she hadn't had very often, which was probably the reason it had stayed with her. And because it had frightened her more than anything she could remember. That sense that no place could make her happy.

The door burst open and she jumped. A doctor came over and talked to the man with the Styrofoam cup.

Their tones were low, solemn, and all she could hear was the man saying, "Five or six?"

The doctor nodded.

"But not seven."

"No, not yet," said the doctor, and walked away.

What could that mean? She wondered about it for a while, and about the fact that the news, whatever it was, hadn't seemed to alter the man's mood in any way. He just went on fingering the cup.

Another memory came to her. She was older now, in her teens, and she was sitting on her front porch with Mary Grace. They were listening to the radio and Tess was crying. Mary Grace had just told her that Pat Casey, a Millburn boy that Tess had been dating, was taking Valerie Caldwell to the spring dance. Tess was trying hard not to believe it, because Pat had been declaring his devotion to her a mere two weeks ago. But then she had introduced him to Valerie one Thursday in the drugstore, and she couldn't mistake the look in his eyes, the way they followed Valerie around, the way he kept asking her questions, and the way he had kept so quiet during their walk back to Millburn. After that his calls had come less frequently. Then he said he wasn't sure he could come to see her that weekend. And then Mary Grace had broken the news.

Tess recalled feeling that her heart really might break—that it would cease to function normally, and that she would become an invalid. Because she honestly didn't know how she could bear this.

Her mother had walked out on the porch and found her that way, and after she dragged the story out of Mary Grace (Tess herself had been too busy sobbing to talk), that same look of rage had accumulated in her mother's eyes.

"That's it," Lana had said. "That is the last you are seeing of that girl. She's nothing but trouble. She's the bad seed."

Then Lana marched into the house, and Tess flew inside after her. She was too late. Lana was already on the phone, saying, "Get this straight right now, Valerie Caldwell. You are not welcome in my home. Or on my porch or in my yard. Don't call Tess again, don't speak to her. When you see her on the street, act like you don't know her. Because people like you we don't need. You're rotten to the core."

Tess stood in horror and amazement, listening to the words spewing from her mother's mouth, once again wondering where the anger came from, this anger on her behalf. In fact, her mother actually sounded more upset than she herself felt. (Even if her heart was breaking, it was only because of a boy. Valerie hadn't killed anyone. And really, a lot, if not all, was fair in love.) Maybe the worst part of all was that she was now losing not only Pat Casey, but Valerie, too. And she couldn't do without both of them.

After she hung up the phone, Lana had turned to her daughter with a look of satisfaction and accomplishment. There, the look said. See what I've done for you. Tess wanted to tell her she didn't want that; she'd never wanted her mother to fight her battles for her. She just wanted to be held, coddled, comforted. But Lana didn't have that in her. Anger was all she had to offer. She gave it like a gift.

Tess felt exhausted by these memories and struggled to find a more pleasant one. Something jolly, something of her mother playing with her, some picture of her mother smiling. It wouldn't come.

Surely such a picture existed, but Tess felt too tired now to find it.

The door burst open and another doctor came out. He was wearing scrubs, a mask dangling under his chin, a stethoscope slung over his shoulder. She must have stared at his face a full five seconds without recognizing him.

"Tess?" he said, moving toward her as their eyes met.

"Oh God," she said, without meaning to.

"Vince . . ."

"I know," she said wearily. She swiped at her eyes and said, "What are you doing here?"

She was too disoriented to be embarrassed by the remark.

"Emergency C-section," he said. "What are you doing here?"

"My mother's sick."

"I'm sorry." He sat beside her on the couch. He smelled like soap.

"What's wrong with her?" he asked in that indelicate way that only a doctor could get away with.

"Heart attack."

"Jesus. When?"

"About an hour ago. Maybe two. I can't remember."

"You're all alone?"

"I guess. I mean, I am. I should call my father. I haven't done that yet."

"What about your husband?"

At first it seemed an odd question, and, indeed, it had never occurred to her to call Joe. She couldn't imagine him being interested in her mother's health. It was only now that Vince mentioned it that the idea of her husband being by her side seemed normal, let alone inevitable.

"Yes, I should call him, too."

He put his hand on her arm. A tingle shot through her and she felt embarrassed. His arm and hand seemed impossibly clean and white. She tried to picture where it had just been—inside a woman's pelvic cavity, extracting a baby.

"Have you heard anything?" he asked. "Maybe I could round up some information."

"The doctor came out once. He said it looked like a mild attack. But they're moving her into intensive care right now."

"They have to do that," he said, "regardless of how mild the attack was. Just for the night, anyway. But if he said it was mild, it was. They don't spread that information around lightly."

She nodded, wanting to be reassured. But his presence had a different effect on her. She felt more agitated, jumpier, and much more on the verge of something. His hand on her arm was uncomfortable, disproportionately heavy. Yet she dreaded the moment when he would take it away.

"Try not to worry," he said. "The cardiac unit is good here. She's in capable hands."

"Okay."

"Want me to make those calls for you?"

"What calls?"

He smiled and patted her arm. Then he took his hand away and she felt overwhelmingly depressed, as though she wouldn't make it. Suddenly he put an arm around her and she collapsed against him, crying into his green shirt. The antiseptic smell of him filled her nostrils and she felt almost high.

"It'll be all right," he said.

That only made her cry harder because he didn't understand, and she wanted to tell him. She wasn't crying because of her mother—at least, not because of her mother's condition. She cried because all her memories of her mother were so dark, so disturbing. Because she wanted a different mother, a different past. Because she had forgotten to call Joe, because she did not associate him with comfort. And because she realized that the moment in the doorway at Cherry Grove Beach had come back to her, and had not left, and might never leave. The moment of knowing: No, this isn't it. This isn't where I want to be.

5

Joe had to work very hard to stop himself from believing that Lana had somehow contrived her heart attack to interfere with his plans. She had known, in that evil, omniscient way of hers, that he was dangerously close to cheating on her daughter. So she had engineered the only thing that could have prevented it. In fact, if he hadn't heard the doctor's report with his own ears, he would have thought she'd made the whole thing up.

The doctor told them the excellent prognosis as they all gathered around her hospital bed. He said there was very little scar tissue on the heart. He said she'd have to watch what she ate, she'd have to give up smoking, exercise moderately, and avoid stress. Other than that, she'd live a normal life.

"Hell," Lana said, "what kind of normal life is *that*?"

"You have to do it, Mama. You know you do," Tess told her.

"It'll be fun," Ray said, smiling, as if he saw this as a new, exciting prospect, like remodeling the house. "We'll take long walks in the evening, and eat frozen yogurt instead of ice cream, and whenever you want a cigarette I'll pinch you!"

"I can hardly wait to be released," Lana said.

"Mama, now listen to reason," Tess urged.

"I haven't heard any reason yet. Joe, how about you? Got any advice to offer?"

Joe felt turned upon. He could swear the gleam in her eyes was one of suspicion, and that crooked smile was trying to break him.

"I don't give out advice, Lana. Not for free, anyhow."

"Ha, ha," she laughed, throwing her head back. "That's a lawyer for you."

During the drive home Tess was silent. But Joe recognized that it wasn't the usual kind of silence. It wasn't the baiting kind, waiting to be broken. It wasn't trying to extract something—some argument or apology. Glancing at Tess, he could see she was intent upon the silence, comfortable with it, and that scared him more than anything.

"Tess," he said, "I'm really sorry about this."

She looked at him, her eyes swimming a little, coming out of a spell of thought. "What?"

"Your mother. I'm sorry."

"Why are you sorry?"

He shrugged. "That's what people say."

"But it's not like you caused it."

"I know," he said irritably. "But it's what people say."

She shook her head. "I never understood that."

He was worried about her. This flightiness couldn't be real. At least, it couldn't be coming from something as unremarkable as her mother's illness. So she, too, might be trying to break him.

What if he turned to her and said, "You know, you were right about Valerie. She does have that effect on me. And no matter how hard I try, I can't stop thinking about her. I have always loved her."

The impulse was so strong he wasn't sure he could control it. He clenched his jaw until it hurt.

He glanced at his wife again and saw that profile, so peaceful, so sure of itself. She watched the surroundings shoot past as if she understood the universe completely. For that second, he fell in love with her again.

But when he looked away, at the road stretching enticingly before him, like a promise, as simple and elemental as air, urging him onward, it was Valerie's face he saw, and Tess disappeared.

Is she thinking of me now, he wondered. Does she ever?

"Watch that pothole," Tess advised.

He swerved and for one delicious moment the car skidded, seemed to lift up, as on an air cushion, and only for that split second it was out of control. There was never any real danger, but even the hint of it was enough to jar him and make him look at his wife for reassurance.

But she did not seem to notice. She was intent on watching the universe.

6

The knock came late, and Valerie was the only one still up. Her parents had gone to bed early, though she knew they hadn't gone straight to sleep. They devoted at least an hour each night to discussing their dilemma—having their grown daughter living at home with them. She heard them through the walls, and not in particularly hushed tones, as if they wanted her to hear.

At first it was unsettling to think that her parents could be disturbed by her presence. Then it began to dawn on her that people never intended for their children always to be in their charge. They merely wanted to raise them to a certain age, a certain level of accomplishment, and let them go, get back to the life they had been leading before. Children were an interlude, not a lifetime commitment.

This realization disturbed her because she had not abandoned the notion that if all else failed, her parents would take care of her. They would be waiting with open arms, blank checks, and unconditional love. Where else on earth could she find an offer like that? To discover that the offer was for a limited time only made her feel devalued—like one of the excess of unwanted things piled up at a pre-inventory sale. The realization added to her fear that the only time she had ever been special was when she was young. Whatever it was that had made her desirable as a child was gone for good.

These thoughts kept her awake. They kept her eating diet popcorn and diet Cheez Doodles and diet Ruffles potato chips until midnight. Then they had her drinking diet beer, which made her feel more bloated than relaxed. Finally she went back to Chardonnay and ignored the six extra pounds that had settled on her hips. The problem was, she did not know how to have a genuine crisis. Her life had not prepared her for it.

The knock came as she was watching the end of *Mildred Pierce* and starting on her third glass of wine. She thought she had imagined it and hoped to ignore it, until it came again, louder, and something made her think it might be Joe. But when she opened the door, Becker was standing there in his fatigues, out of breath, his forehead beaded with sweat. His face was a discolored, splotchy pink, like the skin of a newborn.

He was breathing too hard to speak. She stood waiting, wondering if she should let him in. It didn't seem right, yet nothing else made sense.

"Help me," he finally said between gasps. "Please."

"Come in, Becker." She pulled him in. He still smelled like aftershave through all the sweat. "Do you know what time it is?"

He shook his head.

"You're going to get in a lot of trouble."

He nodded, wiping his mouth with the back of his hand.

"I'm AWOL."

Thinking, she said, "That's right. You are. You can get busted for that. Do you want to lose your rank, right here before the Military Ball?"

He looked confused. "I wasn't really thinking about the Military Ball."

"No," she said, "I guess you weren't. Come in and sit down. Do you want something to drink?"

He followed her, as if in a daze. His eyes fell on her glass of wine.

"Some of that. Or a beer."

"I'm not giving you any alcohol. You're in enough trouble as it is."

He stood by the couch, watching her, and it took her a few seconds to realize that he wouldn't sit until she did.

"At ease, Becker. I'm going to get you some coffee."

While they waited for the kettle to boil she sat beside him and listened as his story unfolded.

"It all started when I called home. My mother's been in France, I knew that. But she was supposed to be home, and the housekeeper kept hedging, saying she wasn't sure where she was. So I smelled a rat, and I called the apartment she's renting in Paris. Some man answers the phone, some strange man with an accent. Not French. Something else—Scandinavian. And he said yes, my mother lives there, but she's out shopping. Only she's not renting the place, she owns it. Turns out she has no intention of going home, she's gotten a job in an art gallery, and she's already enrolled my little brother in some English boarding school."

He took a breath, wiping his brow, which continued to bead with sweat.

"Do you get it? She's not coming home. She's moved over there."

Valerie nodded sympathetically. Though obviously not sympathetically enough. He seemed frustrated with her response.

"She's abandoned me. Do you get it?"

"I get it, Becker."

To her surprise he put his face in his hands and began to cry. The kettle whistled. Valerie sat for a moment, wondering if she would add the last straw by getting up to turn it off. Finally the fear of disturbing her parents took over, and she got up. Becker never moved. He didn't move, in fact, till long after she'd put the coffee cup in front of him.

After a while he said, "I didn't know what to do. I mean, I wrote an essay for history and I shined my belt buckle, and I went on with business as usual. Then it was lights-out, and I just lay there in my bunk, staring into nothing, and I realized I'm all alone. I'm stuck here. Nobody's coming for me."

Valerie let a respectable second or two pass, then said, "It's not a Turkish prison, Becker."

He looked at her, his eyes red and swollen, tears rimming the bottom. He looked so young and raw. She wanted to tell him to grow up, and yet that was the last thing she wanted him to do. That naive belief, now betrayed, was what made him so appealing. Nothing was small in a young life. Everything was the most important thing that had ever happened.

"You don't understand," he said, pulling out a starched white handkerchief to wipe his eyes and his forehead. "Your parents want you."

She shook her head slowly, recalling with a smile the thoughts she had been struggling with before he came.

"No," she said. "Nobody's parents want them forever. For a spell, maybe. Parents are people, and they just want their own lives. Nobody's really invested in anyone else's life."

"Oh, great. So what are you saying? We're all on our own?"

"Yes. That's what I'm saying."

He shook his head. "I don't believe it."

"Then what do you believe, Becker?"

"I believe in love," he said. "Eternal and everlasting."

"Are you talking about God?"

"No. People. People fall in love. They do that so they won't be alone. People don't want to be alone."

"People don't want to die," she said, "but they're going to."

"Is this what you learned in Hollywood?" he asked bitterly.

She laughed, even though she knew it was inappropriate. She thought for a moment, staring into his untouched coffee.

"No," she finally answered. "I think I had to come back here to learn that."

"You didn't realize you were going to die, in Hollywood?"

"Nobody in Hollywood thinks they're going to die. You learn to seek immortality one way or the other. Through fame and fortune, mostly, but if that fails, through a life devoted to good health." She slid the coffee cup toward him. "Drink."

He picked up the cup but only stared into it, swirling the liquid around, as if he thought it might be poisoned.

She said, "Look, I'm not trying to depress you. In a way, I'm trying to reassure you. Everybody's unwanted, really. How many times have you looked around and wished a certain number of people would disappear, just to make more room for yourself? I know I wished that all the time on the freeway."

"But not your family, and not the people you love," he insisted. "You don't want them to disappear."

"No," she admitted. "You want them around so they can appreciate you."

He finally sipped the coffee, and after the initial sip he began to gulp it. It was half empty when he put it down again.

"We're all alone and we're all replaceable," Valerie said.

"I don't believe that."

"Well, no one does. Until they've been replaced."

He turned to her and raised his eyebrows, wanting more. She smiled.

"I called my husband the other day, and a woman answered the phone."

He waited for more. She didn't think she should have to elaborate, but she did.

"We've been married for four years. I've been gone barely a month, and already there's a woman in our house, answering our phone."

At last, he seemed to get it. He said, "Do you know her?"

"I didn't recognize the voice. I can't imagine who it would be. I mean, Jason's somewhat asocial. There are women in and out of his life, actresses and agents and stuff. But he can barely remember their names. I mean, Jason hardly had time to pay attention to me, let alone find someone else."

It was quiet for a moment. She stared at the carpet, trying again to imagine who the woman might be. It couldn't be any of their friends, because they didn't have a lot of friends, and the ones they did have, according to Jason, had insurmountable character defects.

"Well, he's getting a dose of his own medicine," Becker observed, suddenly sounding very chipper. "I mean, you're sitting here with another man in your house."

"Yes," she said, smiling. "I suppose I am."

"And besides, you left him, didn't you? So why do you care that he took up with somebody else?"

"Because you care. You never stop caring. This whole business about becoming adults, learning and growing and maturing—it's bullshit. Nobody grows or learns anything. You're jealous when you're five, you're jealous when you're fifty. You think about rivals and old flames and you carry grudges around, and if they start to weaken, you nurse them back to health. You get older, but the only thing you learn is better manners. Better ways of camouflaging."

He listened to all this with rapt attention, nodding, stroking his chin. "I know what you mean. I do. Like, last year I was all hung up about making the soccer team, and I got cut in the last round. So I say, well, I've done that now, I've learned something from it. And this year I won't give a shit. So I don't try out, but I just sit around getting all pissed off when I see guys who aren't as good as I am making all-regional and all-state." He shook his head. "It's like, you can't get over it and you can't get around it."

Valerie smiled patiently.

"And, you know, Latin," he went on. "There's a great example of not learning anything. I've been taking it for three years now, and I keep getting an A in the class, 'cause I keep memorizing stuff for the tests. But I can't remember anything. So I haven't really learned anything. I mean, if you pointed a gun at me right now, I couldn't say a whole sentence in Latin. Except *caveat emptor.*"

"*Per ardua ad astra,*" she said.

He looked at her. "What's that?"

"The motto of the Royal Air Force. 'Through hardship to the stars.' "

Nothing dawned on him. "What does that mean?"

"It's something Jason used to always say when I complained about things. Not getting anywhere, missing my home, missing my friends. '*Per ardua ad astra*, Valerie,' he'd declare. 'What do you think hard times are for?' "

"What are they for?"

"I guess they get you to a better place. I guess they lead you to glory in some way. That's what Jason wanted me to believe."

"Did you?"

"Sometimes," she said, suddenly aware of a tightening in her throat. "Whenever he said it."

She felt Becker moving closer to her and intentionally kept her eyes on the rug. If she saw him, or acknowledged that she saw him, she'd have to tell him to stop. And at the moment, she didn't feel up to it.

He slipped his arm around her shoulders.

"Becker," she said evenly.

"Listen to me. Just listen."

She looked at him, but he didn't speak. He stared at her, his face as still as a photograph. The sinking feeling of ridiculousness came over Valerie again. How could she have let this happen? If she did intend for her life to be a story, how could she let it go in this direction? How could she let it be a sad, unsatisfying, pathetic tale?

Becker's gray wool trousers scratched against her leg. Somehow her skirt had traveled above her knee. She pulled it down and it traveled again, guided by Becker's index finger. Valerie felt doomed by her own weakness, and in that doomed state of mind she began to wonder, What difference does it make? People do desperate things all the time. The soul needs a little desperation. To be valued and appreciated, even a bit desired—these things are important to the human condition, regardless of the source.

A decisive rap on the door interrupted her thoughts and Becker's actions.

"Damn," he said, looking stricken.

She felt chilled all over, yet she was conscious of sweating.

"Who could that be?" she asked, standing, checking her watch.

"I've got some idea," Becker said, looking frantically around the room. "Can I hide in your bathroom?"

"No, Becker, you can't. Do you think you can run from this forever?"

"I can give it a shot."

She shook her head. "I hate to do it, but I've got to answer that door."

"Why?" he asked desperately, looking as if he might cry again. "I thought you cared about me."

Valerie had no answer; she hadn't recalled telling him that. She hadn't even recalled thinking it. But she realized that she did care, and because she did she had to send him back to his world as soon as possible.

"Do you want to be like your mother?" she asked. "You can't run off to Paris. You can't take a vacation from the world, Becker. You know they'll find you and you know they'll make you face it."

"How can you say not to run? What are you doing?"

Valerie stared at him.

"This is my home," she said.

"Well, Millburn is not my home. And I'm not going back."

"No, it isn't home," she said, putting a hand on his arm. "But at least it's a place where people care about what you do."

Her tone seemed to calm him and he stood very still, the pink-ness draining out of his face. She touched his arm, and a kind of calm passed over him. He managed a weak smile.

"Colonel Fullham, hello," she said, even before the front door was fully open.

He stood before her, her old nemesis, looking every bit the way he had all those years ago. Stout, straight, his face pinched in a sour frown, expecting the worst and always ready to welcome it. His nose was comically sharp amid an otherwise fleshy arrangement of features. He had not one strand of hair left, or so it seemed under the amber porch light.

"Please, come in," she said, after he was several steps inside.

He stopped and turned to her.

"Valerie Caldwell. You're up to your old tricks, I see."

"No, you don't see, I'm afraid."

"When my wife told me you were back in town I first got a chill, and then I figured, Well, she's too old to cause any trouble. I see I was wrong. Where is he?"

"Well, the fact is . . . may I call you Howard?"

"No."

"The fact is, Colonel, that Lieutenant Becker is going through a rough time. As you know, his father is deceased, and his mother has just moved to Paris without telling him. I hope you're going to take that into consideration. I hope you're not going to treat him like just another soldier. Because your boys aren't soldiers."

His jaw tightened and his cheeks turned an unhealthy rose color.

"I hope you're not telling me how to run my academy."

"I'd never presume."

"Good."

"They're children, really. And they all end up at Millburn for very special and specific reasons. What they need more than anything is understanding. I'm just asking you to keep that in mind."

"Where is he?"

She led him into the living room where Becker was standing as still as the alabaster statue in front of the chapel. When he saw Colonel Fullham he gave a sharp salute, even though the colonel was in civilian attire.

"At ease, Becker." After Becker's arm had dropped the commandant took a moment to scrutinize him, then asked, "Are you finished? Is the fun over?"

"It was never any fun, sir," Becker answered in a monotone.

"Well, whatever it was, is it over?"

"Yes, sir. Sir."

"Then let's go."

In the same monotone Becker asked, "May I ask how you found me, sir?"

"People had seen you conversing in the snack bar with Miss Caldwell . . ."

"Mrs. Rutter," she interjected.

". . . and I made the appropriate assumption."

"And may I ask what will happen to me, sir?"

"That will be answered later, in detail, Lieutenant Becker."

Becker, who seemed completely devoid of will, let alone youthful defiance, followed his commandant to the door. He didn't even dare to look back at Valerie. It was only as they were leaving that she took a chance and spoke.

"Becker," she said. In spite of the circumstances, he turned to her. "*Per ardua ad astra.*"

He smiled, though she wasn't sure he remembered what it meant.

But she was confident that sometime in the night it would come to him, and perhaps it would provide him with some small comfort. As on many nights, in times past, it had comforted her.

7

"*I guess* we should still have the party," Tess said.

"What party?" The word itself surprised Joe, since there seemed so little to celebrate. Tess's mother was still bedridden, though there was not much evidence for the necessity of it. She was as outspoken as ever, and as resistant to her recovery as most people were to their death. Tess spent most of her afternoons tending her, and came home as exhausted as if she'd minded a kindergarten class for eight hours.

There hadn't been much party talk around the house. By the same token, there had been very little Valerie Caldwell talk, either. Though Joe had often thought of her, he had seen very little of her. Phone messages from her littered his desk. He kept pushing them aside, too guilty to call her, too guilty to throw them away.

"I've already sent out the invitations," Tess explained. "People will be coming on Friday unless I call them."

"So call them."

"Forty people?"

"We don't have forty friends in Maddock. Even if we did, they wouldn't come. They'd have read about your mother."

"And they'd take the party as a sign that everything was all right."

Joe sighed. "Look, the whole thing is your idea. I don't know why you're asking me.

"Because I care about what you think." She paused, twisting a thin strand of hair before saying, "You're my husband. I love you."

He shot up from his chair and paced away from her. She stayed in her seat, watching him, undeterred by his anger.

"Look," she said. "I know it's been hard lately. But nothing has changed how I feel. I lie in bed at night and I stare at you. I look at your face, and I just want to crawl inside and find the person I knew. The guy who used to sit on my porch and tell me he loved me. You could talk to me then. You wanted to eat cornflakes with me."

"Will you stop with the cornflakes?" he asked, turning on her. "I was a kid, for God's sake. When will people stop holding that part of my life up to me as evidence? Everyone else on the planet gets some sort of dispensation for their adolescence. But me, I seem to be held accountable for every word, and I just don't understand it."

Tess stared at him, not hurt, not even very resigned. She tucked a piece of hair behind her ear.

"Who else is holding you accountable?"

He felt tempted to answer. But it was late, and the Glasses would be waiting for him in the morning, looking for signs of disruption in his personal life.

"I'm going to bed," he said. "Have the party."

"Fine," she said to his back.

Later, in the middle of the night, he awoke and stared at the creamy curve of her back. Her breathing was sweet and uneven, like a baby's.

He remembered their honeymoon in Myrtle Beach. The Myrtle Beach Hilton, probably the nicest hotel Tess had ever been to. Even then, all he could think of was how Valerie would have enjoyed it. She so appreciated nice things. But most of it was lost on Tess. She merely laughed when the poolside Jamaican waiters brought her drinks, saying, "They must be thinking, 'For this, I got on a boat?' " As the waiter in the four-star restaurant was unfolding the napkin and placing it in her lap she said, "Well, thank goodness. One more drink, and I wouldn't have been able to find it."

Joe had laughed at the time and even now he found it endearing in a distant way. But he knew what his mother would say—that Tess was uncomfortable with her own place, which made her a kind of outsider in her own skin. Valerie would never have made fun of a grand occasion. She would have accepted it without comment, made the most of it, and never would have denied her entitlement to it. His mother would have respected her for that.

But then, it was futile to pretend he had any idea how his mother would behave, how she would interpret things. His parents were strangers to him then and were growing less defined by the year. He sometimes thought he was re-creating them, giving them fictional characteristics. He was rewriting his parents from memory and improving them where he could.

His parents had let him drift along without any ability to make judgments. They had allowed him to pick up all his understanding of the world from a military academy. Nothing mattered there but courage and perseverance. He did not know how to demand or request. He only knew how to accept his surroundings. It was no wonder that he felt drawn to Valerie—she was the most decisive person he knew. Tess had once possessed some of that trait, but he felt it leaking away.

He slid closer to his wife, hoping to recapture some of what once made him feel secure with her. He felt her body next to his, and he wanted to make love to her. But he couldn't imagine how to tell her. Stroking her skin did nothing. Whispering next to her ear did less. Finally, after what seemed like hours of eliciting a response, she moved.

She turned to him, her face so close to his own it was like looking in a mirror.

He thought of kissing her, but something else happened.

"Who is he?" he asked.

"Who?"

"The doctor. I heard a doctor came here."

There was a long silence. "Who told you that?"

"Someone. But why did he come?"

"Because," she said softly, sleepily. "He knew what I wanted."

"What was that?" he asked, worried, desperate for her response but dreading it.

Nothing came but the soft sound of breathing in his ear.

8

Valerie spent far too much time thinking about the welcome home party. While she was working in the library, she found herself writing down possible outfits:

> Black button front dress
> Drop pearl earrings
> Single strand pearl necklace
> Black pumps

Then she would scratch it all out and start again:

> Navy silk pantsuit
> Cream shell
> Ruby earrings
> Navy low heels

These lists began to accumulate. Then she became embarrassed by her efforts to decide and, in an effort to undermine her own intentions, she wrote:

> Red strapless sequined evening gown
> Diamond tiara
> Glass slippers

It was hard to believe she could take such an occasion so seriously. When she had accompanied Jason to industry events, she hadn't worried much about what she wore. She was confident that whatever she put together would be successful, and even if it weren't, nothing catastrophic would happen. She would look fine. No one would be embarrassed.

What exactly did she think might result from the welcome home party? That the man of her dreams, the one to make all her insecurities dissolve, would suddenly appear in Maddock, Virginia? Or did she think that she could make such a perfect impression on the people who already knew her that their complete faith in her as the golden girl would be renewed?

In her more honest moments, Valerie feared that none of her friends had ever perceived her as a golden girl. They considered her claims to greatness to be part of her general eccentricity, the same odd impulse that made her want to leave a perfectly good place like Maddock to begin with. She knew that any effort to impress them might well be met with ridicule or contempt. Maybe the best thing to do would be to show up in jeans and a sweatshirt. Such thoughts preoccupied her as she stared at the dull blue walls of the library.

To her genuine surprise and disappointment, she had lost interest in her job. She was not at all concerned about what books she recommended for the cadets to read. She knew they cared even less than she did about books. She recited, by rote, the books that would be simultaneously respectable and painless: *The Old Man and the Sea, The Catcher in the Rye, A Separate Peace*. Once, devilishly, she had recommended *Sons and Lovers*. When the cadet balked at the length of it she said reassuringly, "It's about incest," and watched as he wandered away, flipping frantically through the pages.

The only thing that kept her mildly interested in her job was the possibility of seeing Becker again. She knew he must have suffered some punishment after the night he showed up at her house. She found herself wondering, far beyond the bounds of natural curiosity, what had become of him, but would have felt embarrassed to ask any of the cadets except for Puryear, whom she considered too dull-witted to draw any assumptions from her inquiry.

"He's around," Puryear said. "I think I saw him at formation the other morning."

"Does he appear to be doing okay?"

"He's kind of a dick," was Puryear's reply.

"I'm not really asking for a character analysis," Valerie said, but he could not be deterred.

"Last month he stuck a guy for talking during vespers. I mean, everybody talks during vespers. You couldn't survive if you didn't. And I've seen him chewing the fat right in the middle of the Apostles' Creed. He's a total hypocrite."

"But he's still here," Valerie persisted.

"Oh sure. Can't you smell?" Puryear thought this was an invaluable joke and laughed uncontrollably.

"Please take a seat and be quiet," Valerie demanded.

"My cousin Jeffrey, in Maine? He lives three blocks from Stephen King."

"Puryear, sit down before I send you to the commandant."

"God," he moaned. "You're like so different."

She knew she was like so different. Her own inconsistencies had her baffled. She never knew what she might say or think or do. She felt disconnected, free-floating. She sat and wondered where all the helium balloons that ever escaped a child's grasp ever ended up. Was there a balloon junkyard somewhere, next to an odd-sock junkyard—a place where all disconnected things went to die?

The library usually protected her from such disjointed thoughts, but no longer. And because it didn't, she often thought of quitting. If she was going to torture herself with irrational contemplations, she might as well do it at home, in the company of Ingrid the mutt and a glass of wine. She might as well be close to a phone, where she still irrationally thought Jason might try to reach her and explain the unfamiliar female voice.

She didn't quit the library job, though, out of a concern that doing so might force her to move on. She could not think of moving on. All she wanted to do was sit still, as still as the universe would allow.

On the afternoon before the welcome home party, Valerie was flipping distractedly through *Southern Living*, when the library door opened and Becker came in. Neither his gait nor his posture seemed to have changed at all. He walked confidently into the room, looking around for someone he might want to confront. After a second he went directly to the music room. Valerie waited for her heart to slow down. Illogically, she was afraid he might see the rate at which it was beating.

Finally, when several of the cadets had cleared out to get ready for Mess, she headed toward the music room with a couple of Richard Pryor albums to file away. She found Becker gazing disconsolately at the Beethoven collection, concentrating, yet not really seeing it.

He heard the door close behind her and looked up.

"Hi," she said.

"What's the Eroica?" he asked.

"What?"

"I'm supposed to listen to the Eroica and describe the ways it defies traditional rules of classical music."

"Oh," she said.

"I think it's Beethoven."

"What class is this for?"

"It's not. It's for me."

"Really?"

He shrugged. "It's for my mother."

"Your mother?"

"I don't know. She thinks the reason she and I haven't gotten along in the past is we don't have enough similar interests. Her new boyfriend, Bjorn, says I don't pay enough attention to the arts."

"I see," Valerie said quietly.

"You see what?" Becker challenged.

"Well, I see that you're now trying to please your mother's boyfriend."

"And?"

"That's not good."

"I suppose you know what's good. Your husband shacked up with somebody else. Is that good?"

Anger flooded her; she felt her face flush. She was about to set him straight when her eyes fell on his collar. His vacant collar. Nothing but empty pinholes where his rank had once been displayed. He followed her gaze, then stared evenly at her.

"Oh, Becker," she said.

"Private Becker to you, ma'am."

She sank into a wobbly chair next to him. It groaned in complaint.

"They busted you," she said.

"That's what you get for going AWOL."

"But you weren't really AWOL. I thought Colonel Fullham would understand that."

"You actually thought Colonel Fullham would understand something? What universe are you from?"

"I tried," she said quietly. "I did what I could."

"Well, thanks," he said sardonically.

For a long moment they sat in silence, staring at all the aged, warped album covers of various nondescript Beethoven recordings.

There was nothing here to help him, nothing in the classical world that had kept up with progress. Millburn was no longer keeping up. It was simply trying to survive.

"Becker," she said. "I really am sorry. I tried to help. I thought I could. And I don't understand what you're blaming me for."

"You made me go back," he said.

"I was trying to do you a favor."

"You wanna do me a favor? Kiss me."

She sighed and looked away.

"Why can't you do that?" he demanded. "Why can't you take a chance on me?"

"Because I'm older than you. I've been there and I know what you're feeling, and I know how fast it goes away. I've seen the future, Becker, and it's not kind to passion."

Becker smiled a sad, mature smile at the floor.

After a while he said, "When I was about nine years old I broke a neighbor's window with a baseball. Not on purpose. I just threw the ball and it went wild and broke a window. Know what my father said to me?"

"No," Valerie answered, feeling a little impatient.

"He said, 'Never mind. Glass is meant to be broken. That's what it's for. If people never meant to have something broken, they'd build their houses out of concrete. In the end, they can't resist putting glass in. They know it's risky. But people put glass in their houses because they want to look out on the world. And the chance they take is that while they're looking, something is going to fly right back at them. Something is going to smash. Something is going to break.' "

He pushed the records away from him and looked directly at her.

"That's how desperate they are to see what's coming."

Valerie stared at him, wondering if he was finished, if everything should make sense to her now.

Then Becker added, "I thought my father was the biggest weirdo for saying that. But what I couldn't know was that he was just a few years away from offing himself. Why? Because he could see what was coming."

"I think that's oversimplifying it a bit," Valerie said cautiously.

"Really? Well, look at you. You spend a lot of time looking ahead, and you're not too happy."

"That's not why I'm unhappy," she said, her throat tight with frustration. "I'm unhappy for the very same reason you are. Because I want things. Because I can't accept the way things are. People who accept their circumstances are the ones who hold the world together. People like us, who are always demanding . . . well, I'm just not sure what we're here for. We're like a fly in the cosmic ointment."

He nodded slowly. "That's good. Fly in the cosmic ointment. You oughta be on MTV."

"Stop it," she said bitterly. It was bad enough to have her husband ridicule her. Hearing it from an adolescent was more than she could take.

She stood, prepared to walk out, even though she was a long way from having the last word.

"No, you stop it," he said to her back. "Stop worrying about what's coming. Just do what you want."

"That's an immature attitude."

"So what? Be immature. Make a mistake. The world's not gonna end. And who knows, maybe you'll get away with it. Maybe nobody will ever know about it."

She turned, unashamed of her lip quivering with anger.

"I'll know about it," she said. "And you don't understand my problem, anyway. It's not that I look ahead, it's that I look back. I know where I've been. And it's a lot farther than you. I'm not going to kiss you or sleep with you or fall in love with you just because your father's dead and my husband's with another woman. These are not good reasons."

He stared at her for a moment. Then he said, "If I come up with a good reason, will you sleep with me?"

"Goodbye, Becker," she said, turning away.

"No, wait. Just help me, then. Isn't that your job? Help me. Please?"

She turned back and sighed, feeling exhausted. "Help you what?"

"Find Beethoven."

She hesitated, caught between her obligation and her need to escape. Becker turned back to the albums, shuffling through them, the smell of aged cardboard and vinyl wafting up.

"I'm pretty sure it's Beethoven. The Eroica. It's a symphony. I don't know which number."

Valerie stood there, stranded, while Becker kept flipping the pieces of cardboard. The albums created a breeze on her face as they slapped together, each impact accompanied by a whisper of stale air.

9

The party happened like a tornado. Joe watched it drawing closer and knew he should run for cover, but he wasn't sure what would protect him. Maddock had actually had a tornado watch once, right after he and Tess were married. He remembered her looking at him in that critical moment, pale and concerned, asking where they should go if one actually materialized.

"I don't know," he'd replied.

"What do you mean you don't know?"

"I grew up in Richmond, not Kansas. I don't know where to go."

"Yes, but you're . . ."

He knew what she was trying to say. He was the man, he should know. He was the rock she was counting on. Here was the first threat to their physical well-being and he had no more to offer than an adolescent. Get down, go up, get under, climb over—he didn't know where to start. Finally he led them into the bathroom because he'd heard once on a news program that bathrooms were the only rooms ever left standing in homes that were demolished by tornadoes. They also said that the best thing to do was lie in the bathtub and pull a mattress over you. So this they did, lugging the mattress from the double bed into their tiny bathroom (they lived in an apartment then), then lay down in the bathtub and, after much difficulty and a great deal of nervous laughter, managed to enclose themselves in this porcelain can. After a few moments of lying together like that, their breath warm on each other's necks, waiting for death or destruction, they both began to feel excited. They struggled valiantly to find a way to make love, but it proved to be impossible. In the meantime, they grew closer, their chests pressed together like those of Siamese twins, and for the first time since he was promised such a phenomenon in his wedding ceremony, he felt as if they were indeed one person.

The tornado had never come, of course. The next morning as they dragged the mattress away and pulled themselves out of their cocoon, they felt slightly ridiculous to find that the sun was up, and the morning news was on, and they had to go to work. Tess poured Cheerios and made coffee, Joe read the paper, and neither of them mentioned their extreme reaction to something that had never been a real threat. But the event had tied them together as surely as if they had shared some dark secret.

And now, years later, as the party approached, Joe longed for some resurrection of that feeling, even for some potential catastrophe such as a tornado. He wanted to feel that anything was endurable as long as he and his wife were together, and no event could take one without the other. But nothing came, and Joe was sorely reminded of the fact that most people did not find themselves pressed together in a bathtub beneath a mattress, but instead spent their days sadly and strangely disconnected, like bees gathering and stinging randomly, full of unquestioning purpose.

•   •   •

Max Burgess was the first to arrive, a former Millburn day student (his parents were locals) who had exhibited some evidence of genius early on, and reminded everyone of it ever after. He went to Harvard, then inexplicably came back to Maddock to teach English in public high school. But Max was not the least bit diminished by this perceived failure and acted as though it were the most natural career move that a genius from Harvard could make. Joe had been so convinced Max was destined for greatness that he still found it strange to see him on the streets of Maddock, tall, oversized, lumbering around in his rumpled suit, pushing his glasses back on his nose, his tattered briefcase bumping against his thigh.

Max had never married, and he was always the first to arrive at any social event and the first to start eating the hors d'oeuvres.

Tess left Max and Joe alone in the den as she continued the party preparations. Mary Grace was in the kitchen with her, and Joe found himself occasionally straining to hear what they were saying in their mumbling, mysterious tones. Tess was in a black mood, this he knew. She had been since her mother's heart attack. And Mary Grace was like a bloated rain cloud, threatening to ruin anybody's day. She had put on a good ten pounds since Valerie's return, and much more of her old surliness had come back with them.

Max pushed a cracker into the shrimp dip and said, "You know, ever since I received the invitation, I've been thinking about parties. Why we don't have more of them. They satisfy some basic, primitive need, don't you think? You can date them back to, oh, I don't know, at least ancient Greece. Bacchanalian orgies and so on. And the Romans were notorious for them. Literature is full of them, of course. *Tom Jones. Barry Lyndon. Gatsby.* Not to mention film. Remember that Buñuel film *The Exterminating Angel*? Where no one could leave the dinner party? And then there was that big ostrich head at the end?"

He threw back his head and laughed.

"No, I don't think I've seen that one," Joe admitted.

"It's brilliant." Max chomped on his cracker and said, "I suppose parties have often been used as a sort of sedative—calming the masses. Like in big business, where everyone feels so disenfranchised. Yet every year there is the Christmas do, just to bring people together and stuff them with starchy food, and make them believe all their sacrifices have been worthwhile, and that management gives a fig about their well-being."

Joe suppressed a yawn.

"Well, think of Millburn," Max went on. "The way they'd give us an asinine little dance every month to make the place feel less like a prison. The Military Ball, for God's sake. Did that really fool anybody?"

Joe said nothing. He was thinking of Valerie and how proudly he had escorted her across the floor beneath the colored lights, his back perfectly straight and his saber singing quietly next to his knee, while her white gown rustled like a waterfall.

"No, I guess not," he said insincerely.

Tess came in with a plate of stuffed mushrooms.

"Tess, this shrimp dip is exquisite," Max proclaimed. "There's something about it almost Proustian. One bite and I'm transported back to my childhood. Do you know what I mean?"

"Not really. I've never tasted a dip that transported me anywhere," Tess said.

Mary Grace, who had followed Tess, carrying the rumaki, did not resist a giggle.

Max, who should have been offended, threw his head back and laughed too. Joe looked at his watch. It was barely eight o'clock.

The room seemed to fill gradually, yet all at once it was full. Joe was able to escape Max only to find himself in more dubious company—married couples from the church who only wanted to talk about their children, upcoming potluck suppers, the softball league, or whether or not this summer was more humid than the last. Joe felt dazed, sleepwalking through the event, and only two things were capable of prodding him back to some state of awareness—his wife's dark looks across the room, and the knowledge that any moment Valerie would arrive.

Tess looked beautiful tonight, he could not deny it. She wore a black dress, sleeveless and seductively loose, hanging almost to her ankles, just above flat black sandals. A gold locket fell in the hollow of her throat. Joe watched her from a distance, feeling the way he must have at so many Millburn dances, looking at the girls and thinking they would never notice him. Oddly enough, Tess had seemed so much more available back then, as an awkward teenager eating popcorn at the refreshment table, than she did now as his wife of over a decade. Tonight, especially, he wasn't sure he could even get a smile from her, let alone a dance or a kiss. There was a distance between them, and it was a distance he had willfully created.

He was drinking too much; he recognized that. Valerie, the guest of honor, had not yet arrived and already he felt the room swirling a little. His tongue seemed loose, his brain wild, and he was afraid of talking. He had already admitted to one of the churchgoers that he thought the idea of a personal God was ludicrous—some intelligent being who let an entire plane go down just because one person's number was up, or who allowed some guy to get leukemia because he forgot to give thanks for a meal.

Every time this sense of alienation descended on him, he poured another scotch, a strategy that did not help matters.

He was sitting by himself in the corner rocking chair when he noticed a complete stranger in the room. This man was more than unfamiliar—he was obviously out of place. His clothes were expensive but uncared for. His hair, graying and swept back, did not look right at all, though Joe wasn't sure why. For one thing, the stranger's head was too big. His body was short and compact. He kept one hand casually in his pocket while the other held a beer, and he gazed around the room with a gleam of curiosity.

After a few minutes of staring at him, Joe decided that the scotch was distorting his perception, and that the stranger wasn't really freakish. He was just different, a new face in a crowd of people Joe was far too accustomed to seeing. He finally found the will to move across the room.

"Joe Deacon," he said, offering a hand to the stranger.

"Oh," the stranger said, switching his beer to the left hand so he could shake. "Vince Ross. Nice to meet you."

Joe was trying to think of some discreet way of asking who he was, when Vince Ross said, "I'm your wife's physician."

"Really? You work in Gil Stephens' office?"

"No, in Danville. I'm her gynecologist."

Joe nodded stiffly. Could this be the man? It was hard to imagine being threatened by this character, yet something in his eyes said that if they were ever engaged in a battle of wits, Joe would find himself bleeding on the floor.

Joe's pride kicked in and he refused to be intimidated by this man simply because he had a medical degree. Doctors were all cut from the same cloth as far as he was concerned. Out to rob people, using their specific knowledge as a means of blackmail. Give them money, they'd tell you what to do to stay alive.

It also did not escape Joe's limited awareness that this man had seen his wife naked.

"Are you here on business?" Joe asked.

Vince laughed. "Not at all. To tell you the truth, I think your wife was taking pity on me when she extended the invitation. It's obvious that my social life is fairly nonexistent."

Joe couldn't think of a response, so he pointed his chin in the direction of the hors d'oeuvres table. "Help yourself."

"I will, thank you."

A pregnant pause ensued.

Joe said, "Well, I don't know how much this party is going to enhance your social life. Are you looking for women?"

Vince didn't seem surprised by the question, but calmly answered, "No, that's not my primary agenda."

Joe wondered if the man was gay. In a way, that would make him feel much more at ease, though his dealings with the gay community were as nonexistent as Vince claimed his social life was.

Joe looked around the room and suddenly felt very dizzy and confused. "Disenfranchised" was the word Max had used, and now it settled into his brain and would not leave. His friends, who were not his friends but people he had happened to know for several years, looked ridiculous to him. They moved around the room like the bees he had imagined earlier, bumping into each other, questioning nothing. Even his wife seemed like a bee, the queen, he supposed, around whom all the drones circulated. His eyes burned. He rubbed them. When he looked, Vince Ross had moved away.

Then there was a voice, as clear and inspiring and faith-enhancing as a rainbow.

"I can't apologize enough. Late for my own party."

All heads turned to Valerie Caldwell, who had just made her entrance, a vision in white, who with her golden hair and blue eyes looked like a figure in a stained-glass church window to which all eyes were drawn and which caused all minds to ponder the possibility of perfection.

10

As parties went, this was not a spectacular one. Valerie had been to parties at the homes of movie stars and agents and studio executives. She had gone to galas and openings and screenings and awards banquets. She'd seen gravlax and caviar and quail eggs passed around like Fritos. She'd seen hundred-dollar bottles of champagne opened and left to go flat on somebody's coffee table. She was once at a dinner party where the main course was lamb embryo. Yet as she looked around the small, undecorated room, with trays of rumaki, egg rolls, cheese cubes, and raw vegetables, the large bottle of Gallo wine and the cooler of beer, she was deeply moved by the amount of effort that had gone into this event. No catering company had moved in and thrown it together. This was the result of Tess's working all day in her own kitchen, all on behalf of her friend.

The guests were mostly people Valerie had known in high school. There were a few people she didn't know at all but who seemed vaguely familiar, mainly because they possessed that Maddock look. She felt disoriented as she studied the faces. It occurred to her she had experienced her high school days in a kind of dream state, aware of people but not involved with them, either thinking of Millburn or thinking ahead. There was no one in the room she wanted to hug, no one whose life she had ever once wondered about since she'd been away. There was Kathy Snyder, with whom

she once had been fairly close—they had done science projects together, anyway. Yet she had not given her the briefest thought in fifteen years. Then there was Henry Lawson who had asked her out
and been refused on so many occasions she still felt ashamed to
look at him. Derek Miles was there, the one town boy she had
dated. He had taken her to the high school prom when she was a
sophomore (he'd been a senior), and had been a great basketball
star and had even gotten a scholarship to Duke. They had spent a
whole evening together, an important one at that, but she was
damned if she could remember any details about him. What did
they talk about then? What songs did he like? What color were his
eyes?

He was the first guest she talked to, as they sipped their wine,
and he introduced her to his wife, also a classmate, who seemed as
unfamiliar to her as a foreign diplomat. Her name was Claire. Valerie would have sworn on a witness stand that she'd never met a
person named Claire. And yet this woman, toothy, hippy, wearing
a tight sundress, swore that they had lockers side by side in gym
class.

"Remember O.C.?" Claire asked her, giggling into her fist.

"No. What was that?"

"O.C. In gym class, if you didn't want to take a shower with
everyone else you said 'O.C.' to the teacher. It meant 'on cycle.' I
mean, how stupid. Why didn't we just say, 'I've got my period.' Was
that ridiculous?"

"Yes, very," Valerie said. Her smile felt painful.

"You girls probably have a lot to catch up on," Henry said, and
left them alone.

Claire proceeded to tell Valerie all about their three-year-old
daughter, who liked to approach strangers and tell them, "I'm
wearing big-girl panties!" Valerie laughed. She was starting to feel
a little sick to her stomach; she had not eaten all day. Finally she
managed to escape to the kitchen.

She found Tess in there, mixing up another batch of onion dip.

"I can't believe you did all this," she said to Tess, hugging her.
Their chins bumped. "I mean, after your mother's illness, I was
fully expecting you to cancel. You know I would have understood."

"There was no need," Tess insisted. "My mother's recovering
well."

"I'm so glad. Helen has been beside herself. I think she's been at
your mother's house every single day."

Tess nodded, turning her attention back to the onion dip.

"I'm having a really good time. It's so nice seeing all these people," Valerie said, glad when she was finally finished with the sentence. She hoped she was hiding her disappointment, because it wasn't Tess's fault. She wasn't sure whose fault it was that she no longer felt connected to these people, if she ever had, and could not find a place among them.

"Good," Tess said. "I'm glad."

Valerie stared at her friend and noticed a kind of dourness about her. The corners of her mouth turned down. Her skin looked taut, pulled across her cheekbones like ill-fitting clothes. She had always been pretty, in an unthreatening way, but Valerie had never once seen Tess looking severe. She decided to blame it on the unforgiving fluorescent light.

Mary Grace breezed into the kitchen then, carrying an empty bowl. "The shrimp dip's going over like gangbusters."

Mary Grace's dimpled smile faded when she saw Valerie.

"Hope I'm not interrupting," she said curtly.

"Don't be silly," Valerie said.

"The party's a success," Mary Grace said, then to Valerie, "I hope you're enjoying it."

"Of course I am."

"I can't believe he showed up," Mary Grace said to Tess.

"Who?"

"The doctor. Vince, is it? He's pretty cute."

"He's not cute," Tess snapped. "He's a grown man."

"Okay, he's handsome."

"He's not even that. He's losing his hair, and he swears too much. He's socially retarded."

"Whoa, apply the brakes. What's the matter?"

"Nothing's the matter," Tess said, clutching a bowl of onion dip. "It's ridiculous for the three of us to be congregating in the kitchen. There's a party going on."

With this, Tess breezed out, and for the first time Mary Grace and Valerie looked at each other with a kind of mutual questioning.

"Think she's nervous?" Mary Grace asked.

"It seems that way," Valerie said, hoping to convey her gratitude for this moment of connection.

Mary Grace stared at her for a moment.

"Who can blame her?" she finally asked and tried to walk away, but Valerie stopped her.

"What does that mean?"

"I think you know."

"Tell me anyway."

Mary Grace turned her cold black eyes on Valerie. "The entire town knows about you and Joe."

"Knows what about us?"

"Please."

"I have a right to know what the entire town is saying."

"You were out at the golf course with him! Tom Turville saw you!"

"Yes," Valerie said calmly. "And?"

"Oh yes, that's it. Butter wouldn't melt in your mouth. I suppose you were discussing politics."

"No, not politics. I can't really remember what. But nothing happened."

Mary Grace shook her head slowly. "You still don't get it, after all this time. You *make* things happen, Valerie, without even trying. That's why you're so dangerous. You've worked it out so you'll never have to take the blame."

Valerie shook her head with a smile. "You've always given me powers that I just don't possess."

Mary Grace glared, unable to respond.

Finally she blurted out, on the verge of tears, "If you're a friend, why did you let me be fat? Why did any of you? Why didn't you just tell me, Mary Grace, you're a blimp, you're letting the best part of your life go down the drain, get a grip!"

Valerie shook her head. "But the best part of your life isn't down the drain. Mine is. Yours is still waiting."

Mary Grace stared at her, open-mouthed; then she turned and walked slowly out of the room, unaware of her surroundings, like someone who had been told of a death.

• • •

Valerie returned to the party, approaching a small knot of women who were clutching wineglasses and giggling like schoolgirls. She hoped to join in their mirth, but they didn't make much of an effort to talk to her. She wondered if they were genuinely disinterested— in which case, why had they bothered to come? Perhaps they were feigning disinterest, which was equally illogical. Maybe they'd all come to get a look at her, like some exotic zoo creature. None of them asked her about Hollywood, as if to deny the fact that she'd ever been there. She didn't mind if they were jealous or intimidated or disinterested. What worried her was that all of these people had resented her then, and had come to the party not to hail the conquering hero, but to gape with satisfaction at one who had dared to try something better and had failed.

The women talked among themselves as Valerie looked around the room. Her eyes fell on the doctor, who had returned and settled himself among a group of familiar men, among them Joe and Max Burgess, the person she remembered as Maddock's one true genius. She recalled having senior English class with him, but could not place him elsewhere in her life. Why had they never gotten acquainted? It would seem she should have been interested in someone who, like herself, thought of moving beyond the limits of Maddock, Virginia. Certainly Max had wanted to see more of the world and had a greater claim to it as he proved himself suitable for Harvard University. The world had validated his suspicion that he was bound for some special place. Valerie had made her move on faith and had yet to receive such a validation.

Now, they were both back in Maddock.

"Excuse me, ladies," Valerie said to the women. They didn't seem to notice when she left.

"I don't know," Max Burgess was saying as Valerie approached their little circle. "I'm sure this is an unpopular stand for a Presbyterian to take, but I am an existentialist through and through. Nothing else makes sense. Predestination seems to negate the entire purpose of the universe."

"In what way?" Joe asked.

"I know I'm speaking to a churchgoer, but the fact is, if we are all cursed or blessed the moment we are born, then there can hardly be any point to getting up in the morning."

"Suppose there isn't any point," Joe argued. "Wouldn't we all get up, just the same, simply for lack of a desirable alternative?"

"I'm sorry for you if that's how you live your life. And I know it can't be, with that lovely wife of yours. Valerie Caldwell, please pull up a chair. You're as radiant as a dream," Max said. "Now, if there were ever any reason to get up in the morning, gentlemen, I offer exhibit A."

He made a motion to Valerie, and the men smiled at her. Valerie felt self-conscious, though she wasn't sure why. She usually handled compliments gracefully. Then her eyes met the doctor's and she realized he was making her nervous.

"Don't let me interrupt this fascinating discussion," Valerie said.

Dr. Vince Ross had been silent to this point, stroking his unshaven chin. His eyes stayed on Valerie, studying her with curiosity—or so she thought. After a second she realized he wasn't seeing her at all, but staring just past her shoulder.

"It's not how I live my life necessarily. I'm just saying it's the old Sisyphean thing," Joe replied. "We keep doing it for the sake of doing it."

"People are driven by hope," Max insisted. "Without it, we'd all take five hundred Seconal and end it. Am I right, Dr. Ross?"

Dr. Ross took a sip of his beer, thumbed the corner of the label, then shrugged. " 'What drives people' is a loaded statement. It presupposes that all people are driven, when the fact is, most are not. There are basically two kinds of people in the world—those who act, and those who do not act. And the latter make up the majority."

A ponderous silence ensued. Max Burgess twisted his brow. "You're not talking about acting in the professional sense."

"I'm talking about action—effecting changes in your life. Choosing a course and pursuing it. Most people don't act—they react. They're acted upon."

"Do you put yourself in that category?" Joe asked, his eyes widening. He seemed to take an excessive interest in this conversation.

"No, not at all," the doctor answered honestly. "I do feel driven. Which is not to say that I always act in the appropriate manner. I fuck up, plenty. Excuse me," he said with a glance to Valerie. She felt herself blush. "But that's the penalty of being someone who acts. You're going to make mistakes, sometimes fairly sizable ones."

Max Burgess was twisting his lip, looking deeply perplexed. "Well, couldn't one say that choosing not to act is in itself an action?"

"One could," the doctor replied, "but one would be guilty of wishful thinking. Look, it's just easier not to *do* anything. It's safer. But I happen to think it's ultimately very destructive."

"What makes you an expert on this subject?" Joe asked in an agitated tone.

"I never claimed that," Dr. Ross admitted. "But every day of my life, I have to deal with infidelity. And what I see . . ."

"Infidelity?" Max questioned. "Lucky you. What profession are you in?"

"Infertility, I said."

"No sir! Infidelity. I know I'm not hearing things, am I, Joe?"

Joe shook his head slowly. "You said infidelity."

"Then I misspoke."

Tess approached the table with a bowl of shrimp dip.

"How's everyone doing here?"

"Splendid," said Max. "We're discussing infidelity."

"Oh?"

She put the bowl down and lingered, looking at the doctor. Joe stared intently at his wife. Valerie examined the triangle and wondered about the significance of these looks.

"Actually, I said infertility."

"What about it?" Tess challenged.

"Well, just that sometimes the reason people are driven to conceive is fear. They fear a life without children, because such a life is unstructured, free-floating. It's undefined. People come from families and they seek to repeat what they've come from. Without that kind of definition, they really don't know what to do with their lives, or with each other. So, you see, there's a case where a single act can save you from more complicated action down the road."

No one spoke. Tess kept staring at the doctor, her mouth slightly parted, as if she were on the verge of a comeback that never materialized. The doctor continued.

"Because, you see, children prevent you from doing anything. They completely occupy your time and attention. You can't address your concerns and desires because you're so wrapped up in the children. And they also provide a very nice reason to think in simplistic terms. How many times have you heard people say, 'I didn't believe in the death penalty until I had children'? They have the right, now, to believe in retribution and bloodletting because it's all wrapped in this sacramental blanket called children. Children make it easier for us to be less questioning, less demanding of ourselves intellectually. Passing out clean hypodermics to drug addicts? Sorry, can't think about it. I've got the children. Poverty, world hunger? Sorry, children. And the more children you've got, the less you have to apply yourself to any other question."

Joe shook his head, staring hard at the doctor. "You're a pretty bitter man," he said.

"No, I'm not," the doctor responded quickly, as if he'd heard the charge before. "I'm an angry man. There's a difference."

"Are you saying that people shouldn't have children?" Valerie asked.

"No. But *some* people shouldn't. And some people can't. And I think we have to stop behaving as if the people who can't or don't procreate have nothing else to offer society. There are other things to be done here. And maybe the people who can't have children, instead of spending ten thousand bucks a pop on infertility procedures that rarely work, or trying to buy other people's babies for the price of a luxury sedan, should think about applying themselves to other, equally important issues."

He said all this directly to Valerie, but she knew he wasn't speaking to her. His comments seemed directed to someone else in the circle or the room.

"Wow," Valerie said. "You're probably not very popular with the AMA. An obstetrician who talks people out of having children."

"I've never held the belief that life is a popularity contest."

"Well, it is in these parts, mister," said Max Burgess and followed with a hearty, self-satisfied laugh.

Valerie looked at the doctor for longer than she wanted to. Then she turned and saw Tess staring hard at the floor, and she knew that all of this talk, this whole performance, had been for Tess's benefit.

"Tess! Tess, you'd better come here!"

Mary Grace was waving from across the room, gesturing toward the doorway leading to the bathroom.

"What is it?"

"Just come and see."

"I'm in the middle of a conversation, Mary Grace."

"Well, your bathroom floor is covered in shit."

The men scrambled, elbowing each other, trying to be first on the scene. Only the doctor assumed the position of a spectator, standing but remaining in the living room. Valerie found herself alone with him, but the awkwardness of it made her abandon any effort to talk to him. She wandered in the direction of the guests huddled outside the bathroom door.

"Do you have a plunger?" Mary Grace kept repeating.

"A plunger won't do a lot of good, Mary Grace," Joe said. "It's already overflowed. We don't need to bring anything else up."

Tess brought an armful of towels out of the linen closet and stood there with them. Valerie wondered what purpose they would serve, what purpose anything would serve at this point. The smell was drifting out into the living room. She noticed a few guests sneaking out.

"Is there anyone we can call?" Valerie suggested. "Surely there must be people who deal with this kind of thing."

Max said, "I doubt there is any service which will put shit back into the sewer line."

"I meant a plumber," Valerie said with forced patience. She remembered now that she had always hated Max Burgess. He was a smart-ass jerk back then, and he was a smart-ass jerk now.

Tess began to spread the towels on the bathroom floor. They quickly turned a murky brown. Mary Grace started to giggle, and soon was breathless. Joe glared at her.

"Are you enjoying this?"

Mary Grace shook her head, but kept on giggling.

"I'll call a plumber," Valerie said, turning to leave. As she did, she found herself face to face with the doctor.

"I've already called one," he said. "It'll take him three or four hours to get here. And that's an optimistic estimate."

"That's just fucking great," Joe said, kicking the bathroom door. It flew back in his face, and he slugged it with his fist.

"Joe, for God's sake, what are you trying to prove?" Tess demanded.

"Get off my back. Jesus Christ, don't start on me."

"Hey," said Vince.

"What?" Joe asked, wheeling on him. His fists were clenched.

Vince raised one hand in a peacemaking gesture. Joe breathed hard. Valerie looked at Tess and thought she saw her bottom lip quivering. But it must have been her imagination, for Tess was still, her lips pressed firmly together, looking as solemn as a nun in her black dress.

Valerie said, "Well, let's just let it be for now. You've got another bathroom, don't you, Tess? You've gone to all this trouble, let's just enjoy the party."

"Exactly," Mary Grace said. "No reason the stench of human waste should put a damper on things. Let's go have some shrimp dip."

"Very fucking funny," Joe said. "You're a goddamn treasure, Mary Grace. You ought to get paid for your material."

"Joe, why don't you drop dead and put us out of your misery?"

"Stop it," Tess said. "This is Valerie's party. Let's show some consideration. This is her night."

Valerie looked at her, trying to determine if she was sincere. There was no way of telling what those cold, serious eyes had to hide. She had never seen Tess look this way, as if she were beyond caring about anything.

"Whatever you want to do, Tess."

"Let's finish the party," Tess said, without hesitation.

·   ·   ·

It didn't take long for the guests to clear out. Before Valerie knew it, the only people left at her party were Joe and Tess, Mary Grace, and the doctor. Max had finally departed, pontificating about King Arthur as he went out.

"There is a place in England he was said to have lived. Tintagel. I've seen it. Tintagel—it's like poetry, isn't it? You can visit it, you can walk where King Arthur walked. . . ."

His voice dwindled and died off in the night.

Joe sat sunken into the couch, clutching a beer. Mary Grace sat on the other end of the couch, Tess and the doctor on the floor across from them. Valerie was on the edge of a footstool, eating a cracker, marveling at how she had adjusted to the aroma. The room smelled dead, but it was appropriate, since somewhere inside her she felt the same way.

"Do you want another beer, Vince?" Mary Grace asked.

"No. I have to drive back to Danville."

"You can stay at my place if you want to."

Tess shot her a look.

"What?" Mary Grace said. "It's an innocent offer. I have a couch."

"It's very kind of you. If I have a cup of coffee, I'll be fine."

No one moved to make his coffee. They all sat in silence, except for the sound of Mary Grace finishing off a bag of Ruffles.

Suddenly, Joe said, "Welcome home, Valerie."

She looked at him.

"Nobody's said it, so I thought I would."

Valerie stared at Joe, who was slumped and sullen. She looked at Mary Grace, her plump arm disappearing into the bag of chips. She looked at Tess, sitting on the floor, chewing on a thumbnail, her other arm clutching her waist. What was lacking in them? What had made her understand, so long ago, that her future was not connected to them?

Maybe it was hope. She had once had more of it than they did. And as Valerie's hope leaked away, so did the charm, the magic of her life.

She said, "There's this bumper sticker you occasionally see in California that says, 'Welcome to Los Angeles. Now go home.' "

She laughed, though no one else did. She pinched the bridge of her nose, trying to make the tears stop. When she controlled herself and looked up, everyone was staring at her. She got to her feet.

"Good night, everyone."

"Good night," Tess said in a quiet voice.

Outside it was as dark as the dead of winter. The moon was covered with a thick skin of clouds. A few crickets chirped. She walked along, listening. She imagined a whispering sound behind her, like water rushing, and soon the sound turned into footsteps, running. She turned. Joe was following her. She stood in place and waited for him.

His arms encircled her, and she felt his breath on her neck. She arched her neck and stared up at the sky as his lips touched the hollow of her throat. For a second the clouds parted, and the moon peered down like a milky, impaired eye, straining to bear witness.

11

The plumber came and rammed a snakelike object down the toilet, brought up another bucket of sludge, left greasy footprints on the floor, and charged one hundred and seventy-five dollars. Tess paid him and avoided his efforts at small talk. ("Looks like your party ended on a bad note. You ought to get them pipes redone—you're gonna have this problem all over again. Old houses, you know. You related to the Deacons from Charlottesville?") She mopped up the mess, washed the towels out in the bathtub, cleared away the party dishes, took a shower in the spare bathroom, purposely neglected to brush her teeth, and got into bed. She read. The story moved past her like a train, fast and shiny and unclear. She had no idea where it was going. She sipped a flat diet Coke. It must have been approaching 3 A.M. when the front door closed. A silence followed, and then Joe was in the doorway, staring at her.

Finally she said, "The plumber came."

"Was it expensive?"

She told him the price. He shook his head.

"Those guys get away with murder. They've got everybody by the short hairs."

He lingered in the doorway, and the silence took over again. Tess was starting to feel ridiculous. Why should the end be so hard? Everything leading up to it had been so horribly painful and awkward, the end should be a blessing; yet it was so hard to welcome it.

"Are you going now?" she asked, and her throat felt constricted. Still, the words had come out and she was suddenly free. Free from the awkwardness, and free to grieve, where before she had only been free to dread.

"Either now or in the morning," he answered solemnly.

"Why wait?"

"Well," he said, looking around. "I wanted to make sure you were okay."

"I'm okay. The plumber came."

"I wasn't thinking about the plumber."

Slowly he moved over to the bed and sat down. She felt it sink, and she sank with it, part of her wishing it would just keep sinking into the ground. Like quicksand—what an appealing concept. Letting the earth just suck you up to your most primal form. To be swallowed, to disappear.

He said, "Tess, you know, this isn't really about Valerie."

"I didn't say it was."

"In a way this has been coming for a long time."

"Yes, it's been coming. But the coming doesn't matter. A lot of things are coming, like incontinence and death. It's the arrival that matters, and here it is."

"Yes," he said.

There was a distant gurgling sound—the pipes in the bathroom resettling, probably—but it fueled her quicksand fantasy. It was the first time in her life she really did want to die, and she figured it was because she simply had no idea how to proceed from here. People didn't kill themselves out of despair, she decided. Most people never made it to that exquisite state. It was the limbo people could not bear, the uncertainty, the not knowing. Suicide was an unwillingness to stick around and find out. Suicide was walking out on a movie, even though you had paid all that money, because the resolution seemed unworthy of the suspense.

She knew she would not kill herself, and that knowledge made her feel weak. She would not kill herself because she wasn't up to it, and to her dull surprise, Joe wasn't up to it. He wasn't worth it.

Joe said, "You know, I loved you when we got married. I loved what you had to offer. I never lied to you about that."

"What did I have to offer?"

The question stumped him momentarily. "Well, you were devoted to me."

She smiled, looking away. "From the moment I met you, it was like nothing else mattered. I never had another goal."

He shook his head. "No, not from that moment. From the moment Valerie and I got together, that was when nothing else mattered to you."

She rubbed her forehead. "It's so hard to remember. It's hard to remember what came first. Valerie talks about Millburn, she remembers every detail. But it's all a fog to me. I'm aware of it all in my head, intellectually. But I can't feel it."

"I feel it sometimes," he admitted. "Now I feel it."

"But it doesn't really change anything."

He shook his head.

It seemed like a lot of time passed before he spoke again.

"I guess I'll try to get some sleep. I'll sleep on the couch," he said. "If you don't mind."

"Whatever."

She felt strangely giddy now. Now that all of this tension was out of the way, she wanted to talk the way they had in the old days. It seemed she only wanted to talk to him when something was at risk.

What she wanted to say was how oddly disappointing all of it was. How everyone seemed to spend so much time waiting for calamity, but the calamity never came. It was the quietness of life that was so debilitating, the softness of it all.

12

"*I want you* to take a look at this."

Lana opened the freezer door to reveal the small compartment packed with frozen dinners. She pulled one of the packets out and waved it in her daughter's face.

"Healthy Choice. We've got fifteen of those damn things in here, Healthy Choice chicken, steak, and pasta. No sodium, no fat, nothing but health. It makes me want to puke."

"It's good for you, Mother."

"I know that. But your father has lost his damn mind over health. He cuts out coupons for these things and goes down to Food Lion every time they have a special and stocks up on them. Then he sticks them in the microwave and brings them to me on a tray. I say, 'Ray, that goddamn microwave is gonna kill me before my heart does.'"

"The microwave is perfectly safe, Mother."

"How the hell do you know? How does anybody know? And guess where your father is right this minute? At the church, signing us up for the walking group. This bunch of old people goes walking three days a week. I'm gonna spend my final days tromping around town with a bunch of busybodies."

"You'll live a lot longer."

"Who wants to live like this?"

Louisa jumped up in Lana's lap and began to lick her face.

"Louisa's the only friend I have left in the world." Sensing for a second her daughter's feelings, she added, "Family doesn't count."

Tess struggled to smile.

"I don't intend to stay here forever, Mama. Just until Joe and I get things straightened out."

"You mean get back together."

"No," Tess said softly. "That's not what I mean."

Lana released a dramatic breath. "Well, stay as long as you like. Valerie's moved in with her parents. Why shouldn't you?"

She received some kisses from Louisa, then said, "I've been expecting this since Valerie Caldwell's plane landed."

"It doesn't have all that much to do with Valerie."

"And the earth doesn't have all that much to do with the sun. What do you think I am, a fool? It's my heart that's going, not my brain."

Tess fingered the *TV Guide*. This kitchen was the room she had spent most of her early years in, but it didn't feel all that familiar to her. Growing up, it had seemed like her room. Everything revolved around her—her toys, her Barbies, her E-Z-Bake oven. Any kind of mess she made had been tolerated. Now she was a visitor, and her presence made a mess of the unspoiled landscape.

"Mama, I'm trying to talk to you about something serious."

Lana looked at her, her eyes wide, her lips parted, as if Tess had just insulted her beyond measure. She looked downright stricken. Tess felt confused, but she knew she shouldn't—she had seen this look her whole life, every time she dared to say something like, "Mama, please listen." Or, "Mama, you don't understand." The simplest thing could paralyze Lana, especially if there was some requirement on her part to receive or reveal emotion.

Tess moved past the look and said, "I don't think Joe ever loved me. I think he wanted to, but he didn't. He just never forgot about Valerie. I couldn't make him forget."

Lana shook her head, her mouth tightening, adding to the network of wrinkles. "You always gave up so easy. You just rolled over and gave in to things. Here you are making excuses for that girl, after all she's done to you."

"I'm not making excuses for her. It's just that Valerie always made up the games, and I got too involved in playing them."

"You'd always forgive her. You'd always go running back down there. The things she did to you still curl my hair, and you went running back like a whipped dog. Now she's stolen your husband, and you're still doing it."

"But see, I don't think it was ever really about Joe. It was always about Valerie. Joe was just a small part of that."

"You talk like a train hit you," Lana said.

"Mama, don't get worked up."

She was concerned about the color of her mother's skin—rough and gray, like pumice, her lips the color of ash. It would be the limit to cause her mother to have another attack. There was only so much she could bear, only so much guilt she could drag along behind her.

"I'm not worked up, but my God, Tess, show some sense. Get mad at her, for the Lord's sake."

"It doesn't help."

"The hell it doesn't. I get mad, and I say what I think, and I feel a whole lot better."

"Mama, you're always mad. You've been mad your whole life. It's in your character. It's your perpetual state. Satisfaction, contentment, that's a departure for you."

She felt rotten, hellishly so, like something sent from the devil. It seemed wrong and unfair that now, finally grown, she could defend herself to her mother and express all the anger she'd felt as a child, anger at that wild-eyed woman who jerked her by the arm and rained blows on her face. Now, the person available to receive this anger was a shrunken, wrinkled, gray-haired old lady with a bad heart. It wasn't right; there was no satisfactory way to end this. Those moments of peacemaking, realization between mother and daughter, the mending of fences and closing of rifts—simply did not, could not, happen. People died and left wounds untreated and grudges unresolved. Life was not circular but jagged, the ends never quite meeting.

"Do you want me to die?" Lana asked. "Is that what you're hoping for? Because you're about to get your wish, and maybe you'll feel bad about the way you talked to your mother. Maybe you'll look at your own daughter and know and feel bad."

"I'm not going to have a daughter. How can you be talking about that? My husband and I have broken up, Mother. You're talking about me having a daughter. This is the worst thing that has ever happened to me."

"I thought it was no big deal."

"I never said that."

"You said it was a long time coming. You said Valerie's not to blame."

"But I never said it was no big deal."

"Well, excuse me, I must be hearing things."

Tess was wondering if she should pursue this, should accuse her mother of not listening, if that road would lead anywhere at all, when she heard the front door open and her father's cheerful voice ringing out through the hall:

"Hello, anybody home?"

The next sound they heard was something heavy being dragged across the floor. Tess and her mother exchanged a look.

"What in God's name is that?" Lana asked.

"Now, don't move. Just wait there," Ray called out. "Wait till you see what I've got."

It seemed to take forever, the two of them sitting at the kitchen table as the dragging sound got nearer. Louisa hid under the table and quivered. Finally Ray backed into the room, pulling a stationary bicycle by its handlebars.

"Christ almighty," Lana said.

Ray was undeterred. "I was driving home past Boots Palmer's house, and she was having a yard sale. Here's this perfectly good piece of equipment sitting out there for twenty dollars. In the store they go for well over a hundred."

"The love of God," Lana said. She stared, unable to move.

Ray chuckled, as always oblivious to his wife's tone. "I knew Mama was going to resist, but she'll love it once she gets used to it. It's got a computer, Lana. It acts like it's going uphill."

"I'd rather have parquet floors," Lana said. "I've told you for twenty years I want parquet floors before I die."

"Well, you'll get them. First we have to get you well."

Lana cast a long-suffering look at her daughter. Do you see what I've got to contend with, it asked.

Ray took out his handkerchief and wiped his brow, grinning at his new acquisition. Tess felt a stab of affection for him, followed by frustration and pity. He will never learn with her, she thought. He's living in one marriage, while she exists in another. Her whole life Tess had been struggling to get them, to get all three of them in fact, to live together in the same world. But now, this moment in her parents' kitchen, she knew her efforts had been and would always be in vain. They were separate objects, connected only by blood, which was not thicker than water, not thicker than anything—in fact, was quite possibly the thinnest substance of all.

"Help me move it down to the basement, Tessie."

Lana said, "You take that thing right back where you got it."

Ray chuckled.

"I mean it, Raymond. That thing belonged to Boots Palmer? She's gone to bed with everything in town. I'm not sitting on that seat. I'll catch AIDS."

"I know just the corner for it, down in the basement, next to the fireplace. You can watch the TV from there. You can ride while you watch Oprah."

"You've plumb lost your mind," Lana said. "That's all there is to it. My entire family has lost its mind."

Ray said, "Boots had her grandfather clock out there for sale. Two hundred dollars. I told her that was a steal. I've seen them in antique stores for a thousand."

"It's a wonder you didn't buy that, too."

"We don't have any use for a grandfather clock, Lana."

"We don't have any use for a damn stationary bike neither."

For the first time, Ray showed the smallest sign of disappointment. "Mama, you've got to stay in shape. We want you around for a long time, don't we, Tessie?"

"Of course we do."

Lana started to object, but her eyes met with her daughter's and she seemed to surrender. Her mother wanted to believe that; everyone wanted to believe they were wanted. It was a hard thing to reject. Tess looked away.

"Come on now, Tessie, help me take this down."

She grabbed the handlebars, and together she and her father worked the bike (which was unexpectedly heavy) down the basement stairs, bumping against the walls as they went. Her father talked the bike down: "There, that's it, not too fast, right on target, that's the spirit, almost there." Finally they deposited it in the corner next to the fireplace, then stepped back and admired it like a painting, judging its aesthetics.

The room was quiet and cool. It was Ray's recreation room, and it reflected his personality. His gardening books lined up neatly on a bookshelf. A small television, a masculine couch, brown-and-white tweed, a lamp shaped like a golf bag, the desk where he paid his bills and filled out the tax forms. On the desk were three photographs—his and Lana's wedding, Tess's graduation, and Tess and Joe's wedding. The three most salient moments of his life captured and condensed.

Tess stared at the photographs while her father admired the bike. These were the only moments that really mattered to him, to anyone, and there was so much excess in between. In truth, life could be reduced to those moments. Life could be summed up in three photographs. Everything else was filler. How far everyone traveled to end up in a paneled room, looking at a stationary bike.

"She's a beauty, isn't she? I think that's a real bargain. I think it was my lucky day, driving by Boots's house when I did. Strange, I never take Meadow Hill, but today I did because I was thinking about your mother and missed the turn at Havenhurst. Well, that kind of makes you believe in fate."

Tess couldn't reply, even if she had wanted to. She was clutching her face in her hand, and she had started to cry. The tears seeped through her fingers. Her face felt wet and ruined. She could not look up.

"Oh, now," Ray said, his arm encircling her, his free hand patting her shoulder. "Tessie, don't. Mama's going to be fine. She'll get used to the bike. Mama's going to be just fine."

13

Nothing was as Joe had imagined it. First, there was the strangeness of Tess moving out. Somehow, he always thought he'd be the one to go. When he was much younger, a female client had informed him during a divorce settlement, "It's a fact of life. The man packs."

Now he had to reckon with the fact that he was in the familiar surroundings of his home, with the unfamiliar complication of his wife's absence. He was afraid to use any of the large appliances, because he believed they could only be controlled by his wife, that the washing machine and the oven were hostile to him and would refuse to comply with his wishes. When he thought of divorce he thought of himself in an apartment somewhere, in a place so far from here that he'd at least have a different area code. The reality was that Tess was just around the corner, living with her parents, and they faced the possibility of running into each other at any given moment. And what would they say? It seemed they were just being willful children, refusing to play in the same sandbox, and that any time now someone would call them on it.

Slowly, without his doing, the town began to find out about it. People stared at him sympathetically. People stopped asking how things were going. The Glasses called him into their office to express their sympathy and to say, in so many words, they hoped things could be settled amicably and that it wouldn't interfere with his work. Joe could tell they wanted to use harsher language—they actually wanted to threaten—but chose to let him get through the tough times first. They were probably harboring a hope that divorce was not inevitable. He could tell from the way Hayward looked at him that he suspected this all had to do with their inability to bear children.

He didn't call Valerie. He thought it was wise to give it some time. It didn't look right to jump on the phone the first night or the second or third, and call her and tell her essentially that all was clear, she could come right over. He waited until it felt right. But days passed, one after another, and the evenings grew shorter, and fall was upon them. Leaves collected on the ground and he couldn't make himself rake them. Finally a boy came around, offering to do it, and he paid him and sat on the porch watching. This used to be his job. He used to take pride in keeping his house in order. Now he felt vaguely intrigued that he could just live here, let someone else take care of it, and not allow himself to become involved.

Since his breakup, he had begun to think more and more about his parents. How would they feel about this? He tried to imagine, but the image was too pale and insubstantial. He saw his mother in a fancy, expensive suit, her hair pulled tight around her head. He saw his father with a stern, willful expression. He smelled something like furniture varnish. He heard the soft roar of an expensive engine, taking him somewhere. He could not hear a laugh or feel a touch. His parents would not come to him, so their reaction remained lost, and his reaction was lost with it.

Finally he called Valerie.

"Where have you been?" she asked.

"Here. Why?"

"Oh, I don't know. Two weeks have passed."

"I've been busy. There are a lot of things to sort out."

"Where are you living?"

"Here, in the house. Tess is at her mother's."

"I know."

"You do? How?"

"I heard. This is Maddock, Joseph."

He tried not to think of that, of having his private life being passed around the town like the collection plate in church.

"Come to dinner tomorrow night," he said. "I'll cook."

"You're going to cook, Joseph? Oh my God."

"It would just be steaks on the grill. Or hamburger," he added, as a kind of threat. "Will you come?"

"I'm practically there."

•   •   •

And so Valerie came to the empty house, wearing a sleek blue sundress, her hair in a French braid in back, a thin strand of freshwater pearls around her neck. She looked young. She was wearing less makeup than usual, and her skin was translucent, with a few fine lines that only added to her charm. Her lips were soft and pink and bare of gloss. She looked peaceful and observant and slightly melancholy.

"I need to get out of the house," she said, walking around the kitchen, her hands clutching a glass. "I'm going stir crazy."

"We can eat outside."

"I mean my house, Joseph. My parents' house. They don't want me."

"That's crazy," he said. He was tearing up bits of lettuce to put in the salad. He wasn't sure he was doing it right—they were all uneven, like shredded bits of a love letter torn up in anger and despair. He didn't know how to cut up a tomato, so he decided to put whole cherry tomatoes in, and garbanzo beans from a can. The steaks were sitting on the table, raw and exposed, doused in meat tenderizer, looking like something left over from an autopsy. He felt embarrassed seeing them sitting out there, exposed, while Valerie paced in her beautiful dress. They were drinking white wine.

"No, it's not crazy. They want to have their own lives. They don't want me around polluting it. Think about it. You live all that time trying to rid yourself of things. That's life, isn't it? You spend the youthful part acquiring things, then you start giving it away. Not building up, but whittling down. Getting rid of debt and responsibility and worry. Cleaning out the garage. Cleaning out the closets. Sending things out in the world. The last thing you want is more baggage."

"You're not baggage."

She smiled and sipped her wine. "It just seems to me that we're all going in the opposite direction. We're supposed to be going out, and instead we're coming back."

Joe looked at her. He could smell the charcoal from the grill, ready, waiting. He could hear the evening sounds filtering through the screen door. He didn't care about going out or coming back.

She was standing there. He could touch her. He didn't care.

"You're the one who came back," he said.

"I know. I may have done the wrong thing."

He moved closer to her. "Don't say that."

"Well, I don't know. I expected to know so much by this point in my life. I'm in my mid-thirties. I thought I'd be wise. I don't know a damn thing. People of our generation, we don't learn. We just remember."

She was drunk, obviously. Her words sounded lazy. But her smile was as tantalizing as ever.

"I'm hungry," she said as he approached her. "Can we eat soon?"

"There's plenty of time for that."

"Never count on time," she informed him, not resisting but not entirely accepting his arm around her waist. "This is something I learned in Los Angeles. You don't rely on time because you never know when the big one's going to come."

"Big what?"

"Earthquake, of course. That's all anyone thinks of out there. Our lives revolve around it, it's the sun of our solar system. We have earthquake kits and latches on our cabinets and extra food and water stored away. Blankets and candles and flashlights with fresh batteries. No one sleeps with a picture or a mirror over their bed. Any minute, things could fall. Any minute chaos could ensue."

Joe thought about this a second, sipping his wine. "That's true of anywhere."

"Oh, it is, but only in small doses. Any minute someone like Rufus Batterman can shoot himself. But not any minute could an entire city be demolished."

"What about ICBMs?"

"Oh, that," she said, waving a dismissive hand. "Nobody thinks about the bomb anymore. Nobody even believes it exists."

"Funny, isn't it?" he asked, tossing the salad with wooden tongs. "It was all we thought about growing up. It's how we all thought we'd die. Now we're back to worrying about stuff like strokes and cancer."

"Well, that's what I mean. Our generation is going back, not forward. Back to the days when the bomb didn't threaten us and remind us of . . . whatever it is."

"Our mortality."

"That's it. But in Los Angeles, we still have that. We live on top of the bomb. And I think that's why there's so much energy devoted to finding the good life."

"It's not a bad philosophy," Joe said. He felt alive and excited, so close to her, where anything could happen, and involving himself in an interesting conversation at the same time.

"Oh, but it is," she objected. "We've got to count on tomorrow. That's what helps us keep order, I think. The idea of tomorrow, and paying for it, and owning up. Otherwise we'd all just do whatever we pleased."

"Better than never getting what you want."

Valerie shook her head. "I'm not sure about that, Joseph. I'm really not sure."

Then what are you doing here? he wanted to ask her. But he looked at the way her eyes moved dreamily around the room, and he realized his convictions were no deeper than her attention span.

He took the steaks out to the grill. He stood over them, watching them sizzle, letting his mind race ahead to what might happen after they were done and consumed. He tried to remember what it felt like to make love to her. It was so long ago; anyway, it would be different now. They were older, had been through so much. Certainly they had learned or forgotten things.

The smoke and the smell of the steaks drifted up to his nose, and he felt intoxicated, from the wine certainly, but also from the thrill of possibility, the unknown and the known mixing together like delicate flavors. He was afraid and eager and nervous, but not tentative, which was a feeling that had dominated his life till now. He felt other hands, other forces had been pulling the strings of his life. He had given in rather than taken action, and the feel of action was a frightening and liberating thing. Staring at the steaks browning, he understood, of all things, why people went to war. Because anything could happen, certainly something would, and none of it would be boring.

"Joseph." Valerie's voice rang out. "Joseph, the phone is ringing."

"Let it ring," he called back.

"Well, I have, but it keeps ringing."

She was standing in the doorway in her blue sundress—backlit, tantalizing, and not quite real.

"Let it ring," he insisted, and turned the steaks over again.

They ate their steaks, cooked to perfection, and salad and cucumbers left over from the garden, in the living room, huddled over the coffee table, glancing at each other in candlelight. Every now and then their smiles met, touching as softly and seductively as lips, and he felt himself falling hopelessly in love. He didn't know how it was possible. Two months ago he would have sworn before a jury that he was in love with Tess. Now those feelings were gone and he felt as if his life had begun and ended right here.

The phone rang.

"My goodness," Valerie said, "you're very popular tonight."

"Let it ring."

It rang. And rang and rang.

Joe felt annoyed. He did not want the intrusion of anything, least of all real life, and his desire to make the world go away was almost stronger than his sense of responsibility to answer to it.

"Hello," he said sternly into the receiver.

He looked at Valerie, sipping her wine, smoothing a stray strand of hair back into place.

"Joe, it's Tess. I'm sorry to bother you."

"What is it?" he asked, still watching Valerie. She was touching a napkin delicately against her lips. Nothing could stop him now.

"It's my mother," Tess answered. "My mother's dead."

14

Lana's death threw everything off. Valerie had not even brought a proper black frock with her—just a taffeta minidress with puffed sleeves, and the button-front linen sundress. She didn't want to bare her arms on so somber an occasion, so she was forced to wear white wool. She considered white the next most appropriate color—the color of lilies and snow, death images—but the way she was drawing stares convinced her that no one else in Maddock interpreted it this way.

She was not prepared to feel the deep, serious sorrow that a death demanded. She had come to Maddock to explore nothing more somber than the death of her marriage, which was more like a beginning. But Lana's death was nothing like that. It was the end of so many things, not the least of which was Valerie's notion that she could control the rate at which she would receive disruptions and disappointments.

Her mother cried bitterly through the service, and what unnerved Valerie the most watching this was the realization that as much as anything, her mother was suffering from fear. Lana was Helen's best friend, but Helen was someone who did not rely heavily upon friendship. She appreciated it but did not chase it, did not treasure it, and therefore could not grieve about its loss for long. What this moment meant to Helen was that her own death was inevitable, and was closer than she cared to calculate. She was no longer getting old. She had arrived.

Valerie could not resist crying a little at the graveside ceremony, staring at the two-toned bronze coffin with the spray of flowers draped across it, although the truth was she had never liked Lana all that much. She could not forget those phone calls she'd received in high school, reprimanding her for upsetting Tess, telling her to keep her prissy butt away until she learned some manners. She never doubted Lana's distrust of her, but it was partly because of it that a lingering fondness had followed her through the years. Lana was everything Tess was not—skeptical, angry, confrontational. She respected that, though she had no real desire to be around it.

As the preacher droned on about eternal life and death having no victory, she stared at Tess and wondered what would become of her now, what would become of both of them. Ready or not, they were both being forced into the future, the next step, the next level of their lives.

Valerie stole a few glances at Joe. He sat on one side of Tess, Ray sitting on the other. They sat stiffly, like guests randomly seated side by side at a dinner table, nothing but accident connecting them. Once Joe's eyes touched briefly with Valerie's, and he looked away so quickly that his body seemed to jerk from the impact. Valerie squeezed her eyes shut. It was as hard as it had ever been to witness his lack of courage.

When the service was over and everyone began moving back toward their cars, Valerie found herself face to face with Mary Grace. She was the most difficult person to make eye contact with, because Mary Grace would never consider looking away. Staring was her specialty.

"You'll come by the house," Mary Grace said to her, more like a prediction than an invitation.

"Yes, of course," Valerie said, bristling.

The house was still and morose, people gathering in little clusters, speaking in hushed tones. Valerie struggled to catch Tess's eye, but Tess was too intent on shaking hands and appearing strong, consoling the guests rather than letting herself be consoled. Joe hovered near her, not acting as her husband, but not avoiding that role. As always, he was positioned somewhere in between.

Valerie sought sanctuary in the kitchen, where she found Mary Grace heating up casseroles.

"Life is a fucking bitch," Mary Grace said, shaking her head, looking elegant if a little portly in her black dress. The weight was creeping back, which made Valerie relax in her presence.

"This shouldn't happen to Tess," Mary Grace said. "She doesn't deserve this."

"Well, no one deserves the death of their loved ones. It just happens."

Mary Grace fixed one of her cold, black stares on her and said, "It doesn't have to happen while your marriage is in shreds, does it?"

"Shreds? Would you go that far?"

"I would. You'd probably go farther."

"Mary Grace, I'm sad about this. I've known Lana since I was a child. My mother is heartbroken. A whole era of my life has come to an end."

"So why don't you go back home?"

"I am home."

Mary Grace said nothing. She stirred a tuna casserole, then put it back in the microwave.

"Mary Grace, I'm not the reason they broke up."

"What am I, an idiot?"

"I don't want to fight with you."

"You never want to fight with anyone, Valerie. You just want to take what belongs to them and keep on being admired."

Valerie filled her glass with wine and said, "I know you find this hard to believe, but I have troubles of my own."

"I believe it. I just don't care."

"Well, all right." Valerie sipped her wine. "Tell me this, did you ever like me?"

Mary Grace actually seemed to think about this. "Maybe. Yeah, sure. When you're fifteen you kind of like everybody who likes you. You have to get older to really dislike people."

"You have to learn hate is what you're saying."

"Yeah," Mary Grace said, satisfied with that response. "I guess that's it."

"It seems a shame to spend a whole lifetime learning something like that. I mean, hate is easy. It's the easiest thing in the world."

"Yeah, but it's satisfying," Mary Grace said.

She took the tuna casserole and left Valerie standing alone, trying to remember why she had come into the kitchen in the first place. It was to wait for Joe to follow, she remembered, but suddenly she was tired of waiting for him.

Before she left, she went to Tess, who was sitting perfectly still in a red velvet wingback chair. Ray was standing off in a corner, one hand in his pocket, staring forlornly at the ground. He looked more confused than anything. Joe stood next to him, clutching a drink with both hands, taking deep breaths. The room was alive with chatter, but these three were not joining in. They were waiting for it to be over.

"Tess, I'm going," she said. "I'm so very sorry. Please…"

She couldn't finish the thought. Tess raised her eyes to Valerie and something came alive in them, if only for a second. The look was a mixture of anger and resentment and real affection. Valerie summoned her courage and hugged her friend, and though it was awkward and nothing close to warm, she felt better for it.

"Valerie," Tess said in a soft voice. "It's so strange, isn't it? How things turn out."

"Oh, it is," Valerie said, sounding even to herself much too earnest. "It really is."

She lingered, hoping they could take it somewhere from there, but nothing happened. Tess turned her attention back to Lana's much prized Persian carpet.

Joe locked eyes with Valerie again as she was going out. But all she saw in his eyes was fear.

Why in the world had she ever thought a man as spineless as Joe was going to protect her from anything? It had always been a matter of her carrying him, telling him how it was going to be, trying to make him see a picture that he just couldn't envision. He didn't want to forge anything. She wanted to be with someone who wanted to forge. She had thought Jason was such a man, and though she still wasn't sure what he was exactly, she noticed that no new trails had been blazed by him.

She remembered the days when she used to read magazines about people in Hollywood, remarkable types of people who set out to change the world, who rose from obscurity to greatness, and it had never occurred to her that any of it was luck. It was fearlessness, a knowledge of something greater and a desire to achieve it. It had been her sole intention in life to attach herself to those people. Why had it been so hard to find them? Where were they now? Certainly there were struggling Steven Spielbergs and Oliver Stones wandering around. Certainly they wanted a woman to share it all with them. But how was it possible to recognize those people in the early stages? Was it luck, or was it a special kind of insight she did not possess?

Well, it didn't matter. It was too late for her. She was almost thirty-five, and she was reaching the age where great men no longer needed her. Great men needed women in their twenties with perfect bodies and flawless skin, and a naive faith in their abilities. She was losing all of it, but most important, the latter. She thought of the story she'd always heard about how Stephen King's wife rescued his first novel from the trash can and wiped it off and made him resubmit it. That took a certain kind of innocent belief and devotion. She wasn't sure she'd rescue any man's anything from the trash.

She had already made peace with great men not needing her. She was prepared to settle for any man who needed her. Perhaps it was time to go for one who still knew how to follow his heart, without reservations, damning the consequences. Brett Becker, crying on her couch, following her, needing her.

Ridiculous, she thought. This is grief speaking. Grief and guilt. And self-pity.

But Becker would reassure her. He would tell her she had not caused Lana's death—she just happened to be on hand for it. She had not caused Tess and Joe's breakup, either. She did not cause anything, it seemed. She just arrived on the scene and observed while events unfolded.

Yet this awareness did not comfort her. In a way she wanted to be responsible for something. Effecting events would at least give her some kind of power. Instead she felt caught up, incapable. Maybe it was better to make things happen, even if the things that happened were horrific. Maybe anything on earth, actions shameful and irresponsible and even insidious were better than no actions. People who act, and people who do not act. That was what the strange doctor at the party had said.

But what could he know? Balding and pompous and angry. If Jason had taught her anything it was that she always attributed genius to the wrong people. She always imagined she saw it in unhappy people, but that couldn't be right. Geniuses would be happy, wouldn't they?—possessing the means to work everything out. Where was happiness, if not in having the answers?

Part Three

1

"*Violet*, give me a fried-chicken plate."

Violet didn't move. She stood firmly planted behind the counter, staring at Mary Grace as if she'd just asked for an order of heroin with a hypodermic on the side.

It seemed to Mary Grace that the conversations around her had come to a halt. It was just like in one of those scenes in a movie, where somebody makes an inappropriate remark and the sound-track suddenly goes dead. Looking around, however, she could see that no one was really listening, except Tom Turville, who peered at her through the smoke from his cigarette.

"Did you hear me?" she asked.

"Yeah, I heard you," Violet answered. "I just can't believe what I heard."

"I'm hungry. I'll go back on my diet tomorrow."

Violet still didn't move.

"What, are we not in America? Is free enterprise still in effect? I give you money, you give me what I ask for. That's how it works."

Tom said, "You can't argue with her there, Violet."

"I hate to see you put that weight back on."

"Five pounds, big deal. I can sweat that out in a week."

"Looks more like twenty-five to me."

"Give me a goddamn chicken breast, please."

"Hey. Hey," Tom Turville said.

Violet put a chicken breast on a plate and slid it toward her. "It's your hips."

"I want a fried-chicken plate, which includes mashed potatoes and string beans, last time I checked."

Violet shook her head and complied. "You want a milkshake too?"

"No, I don't. But by God, if I did, I'd have it."

"The Lord's name still commands some respect around here," Tom said.

"So read me my rights."

Tom said, "When your momma lived here you didn't carry on like this."

"I don't carry on, Tom. There's no one to carry on with."

Violet wiped her forehead with the back of her hand and stared mournfully as Mary Grace sawed into her chicken.

"How's Tess gettin' on?" she asked finally.

Mary Grace shrugged. "I hardly talk to her. I went around a couple of times, but she was too depressed to see anybody. She just sits in that house with her father, cooking things and watching TV."

"That's the hardest thing I've had to contend with all year," Violet said. "Her mama dying like that. You know she had her heart attack right here in my restaurant. Right at that table."

Tom nodded importantly. "I dialed 911."

"Well, that's not the attack she died of."

"No, but that's what got the ball rolling."

Mary Grace swirled the mashed potatoes around in her mouth, loving the thick, starchy feel of them, like paste, filling up the emptiness inside her, connecting all the disconnected parts.

"How's Joe gettin' on?" Tom asked.

"I know absolutely nothing about Joe Deacon."

"Who caused the breakup there?" Violet asked. "Do you know that?"

"I do," she said. "And it wasn't Tess or Joe."

"I had a feeling there was something like that to it," Tom said, shooting out a blast of smoke.

"Can I have one of those, Tom?"

He looked alarmed. "You're in the middle of eating."

"Well, I'm breathing your smoke. Might as well have my own."

He gave her a Marlboro and she lit it, took two puffs, put it in an ashtray, and went on eating.

"If you don't mind a personal observation, Mary Grace, you seem on edge," Violet said.

"Oh, really? Just because my best friend's mother died, and her marriage broke up, and my archnemesis is back in town, and I'm not married and don't have any babies and I spend my whole life sticking my fingers in people's mouths, I can't see how I have any excuse to be on edge. Can you?"

"Then, too, dog days," Tom said after a respectable pause.

"It's October, Tom."

"Well, sometimes they last clean up to Thanksgiving."

"I don't believe in dog days."

"They probably don't believe in you, neither."

The door opened with a tinkle. Madeleine Fullham, the wife of the Millburn commandant, walked in wearing a white raw silk pantsuit, a fake gardenia pinned to the lapel, and too much makeup. Her flowery scent preceded her.

"Good afternoon, Mary Grace," she said, putting a hand on her arm. It felt slightly wet. "My, that looks good."

"I was hungry," Mary Grace replied defensively.

"I wish I could eat like that. I look at something like that and I gain five pounds."

"Well, you better not look."

"How's Tess doing?" Madeleine asked, squeezing Mary Grace's arm and lowering her voice slightly.

"I don't know. But you can ask her. She does answer the phone these days."

"Well, I know, but these things can be so awkward."

"'Tess, I'm sorry your mother died. How are you doing?' Nothing awkward about that."

"Some people don't like to talk about it. I think it's wise to give grieving people some distance. But I hope you'll relay my regards to her."

Mary Grace said nothing. Her stomach was starting to feel heavy. Disgust descended on her like a sickness.

"How's Colonel Fullham doing?" Mary Grace asked, feeling a need to exonerate herself.

"Oh, he's fine. He's like that Energizer Bunny. He just keeps going and going," Madeleine said, cackling. "I tell everybody that."

"I wish I could get me some of them Energizer batteries," Violet commented.

Madeleine smiled indulgently, as if Violet had ruined her moment.

"Give her my best, won't you?" she said, squeezing Mary Grace's arm again before she moved away.

Violet clucked her tongue, watching Madeleine Fullham walk away.

"A white silk suit," she despaired, "a month and a half after Labor Day."

"Why do people keep giving me messages for Tess?" Mary Grace asked. "What am I, her answering service? I hardly ever see her anymore."

Tom said, "I'm surprised there's only been one death this summer. Hot as it's been."

"Well, there was Rufus Batterman," Violet reminded him.

"Oh, that's true," he said, and seemed cheered.

Mary Grace pushed her plate away and said, "What kind of pie have you got?"

"Oh, now," Violet said, shaking her head.

Before Mary Grace could respond the door tinkled again. She looked up on instinct. A man walked in, someone she'd never seen before, who did not look like he belonged in the state, let alone the town. He wore faded, oversized Levi's, a white T-shirt, and a neutral-colored sports jacket. His glasses were tortoiseshell, the expensive kind, and his hair curled erratically around his forehead. He wore gleaming white tennis shoes, one of them untied. He seemed disoriented and at the same time more confident than anyone she'd ever seen. They all stared at him as he lingered in front of the door, getting his boundaries. He took off his glasses, polished them on his jacket sleeve, and repositioned them.

Was he handsome? It was hard to say, Mary Grace decided, until she could determine what he did for a living. He was the kind of man whose physical appeal had everything to do with his role in life.

Finally he moved toward the counter, staring up at the clock or the blackboard specials—something on the wall seemed to fascinate him.

"Help you?" Tom asked.

"Well, let's see. I suppose that depends. Am I in Maddock?"

"Yes, you are," Violet said. "And if the questions don't get no harder than that, we're all in luck."

He laughed politely. Mary Grace studied him. His eyes, which at first had seemed cold and threatening, no longer struck her that way. There was a warmth in them, but she decided in that split second that he was simply aloof. She knew aloofness. She had seen (and admired) it in a lot of men. Her boss, Dr. Powell, was aloof. She had tried for a long time to capture Dr. Powell's attention—

wearing her white uniforms tighter and lower cut than regulations suggested. Brushing against him when she handed him instruments or vacuumed a patient's mouth. She had lingered after work, discussing root canal with him, hoping to get him to see her in a new light. The word around town was that he was gay. She didn't believe it. She believed he was aloof. Even though he did seem obsessed with cleanliness and talked about sofa fabrics and took yearly trips to the Greek islands. Well, even if he was gay, that didn't mean he wasn't aloof. Aloofness she knew like an unwanted friend.

"Well, I wasn't sure," the stranger went on. "I saw the signs that said Maddock, next three exits, and I didn't see another sign until one that said Millburn Academy, next right. So I took that."

Mary Grace tried to identify his accent. It clearly wasn't Southern, but he didn't sound like a New Yorker either. In fact, he didn't seem to have an accent at all, like someone who had not been influenced in any way by his culture or surroundings. Maybe he was from the Midwest. She'd never met anyone from there, and wasn't even sure what states it involved.

"Are you a parent?" Violet asked him.

"What?"

"A parent. Of somebody at Millburn."

"Oh no. I'm not a parent at all. Not that I know of at any rate. Actually, this is my first trip to the South. I don't even know anyone in the South."

"I'm Mary Grace Reynolds," she said, extending her hand. "Now you know one."

He shook it. His grip was strong.

Violet said, "I'm Violet Ramsey and this here is Tom Turville. Now you know three."

"Well, how fortunate," the man said, without introducing himself. He remained standing. There were no seats left at the counter.

"You hungry?" Violet asked.

"I suppose. I haven't thought about it."

"Since when do you have to think about being hungry?"

Tom said, "Some folks are that way. Just as soon take a pill to keep theirselves alive. My wife was like that, God rest her soul. Thin as a flute, her whole short life."

"Take a seat in the booth," Violet said. "I'll bring you some chicken."

"Well . . ." The man hesitated, looking around.

"I'll sit with you," Mary Grace said.

"Want me to bring your pie over there?" Violet asked.

"Forget the pie. Just coffee."

The man followed her to the booth, seemingly for want of other options, and still seemed poised to dart away after they'd settled in.

"Where are you from?" Mary Grace asked.

"California. Jersey, originally. I thought it would be colder here. I thought it got cold in the fall."

"Well, it's Indian summer."

"Dog days," Tom said from the counter, still listening.

"What's that?"

"It's kind of a superstition around here. Dog days. When it's hot and it seems like the order of the universe is messed up. Accidents happen. People drown. They die. They change their lives in some drastic way."

"Wow," the man said, genuinely impressed. "And this phenomenon occurs primarily in the South?"

"I don't know. I thought it was everywhere."

"We don't have that in Los Angeles. Well, actually I suppose we do. It's just that dog days are every day in Los Angeles. Did you ever see the film *Dr. Strangelove*?"

"Yes," Mary Grace lied.

"Well, Los Angeles is Slim Pickens, riding the bomb triumphantly, joyously greeting destruction for the sake of accomplishment. Oh Jehovah! Look at this."

Violet set a fried-chicken plate in front of him.

"My arteries are shuddering. This looks completely unforgiving."

"Eat up," Violet said, then waddled away.

"Los Angeles, you said?" Mary Grace persisted.

"That's right."

"I know somebody there. Well, sort of. What do you do there?"

"I peddle my wares."

He began peeling the skin from the chicken in a delicate manner, as if performing an autopsy. "You know, elsewhere in the civilized world, we've learned to wean ourselves from this kind of thing."

"It's good. Violet makes the best chicken in town. Course, she also makes the only chicken in town."

The man made a waving motion in front of his face and said, "I'm sorry, I hate to be anal, but do you have to smoke?"

"Of course I have to. It's a habit."

"Has no one east of the Mississippi heard of cancer?"

She knew she should have felt embarrassed, but what was the

point? She was too excited being so near someone who had come so far to be here.

"What's your name?" she asked.

"Jason," he replied. "Jason Rutter."

She caught her cigarette before it fell into her lap.

"Oh God, you saw it," he said, pinching the bridge of his nose.

"Saw what?"

"*Personal Injury.*"

She stared at him.

"The nun with amnesia and a dark past. Can't remember if she committed a murder. She falls in love with the lawyer who defends her."

She nodded, though she had no idea what he was talking about.

"I wrote that."

"Great."

"This chicken is pretty good. My nutritionist would be having convulsions right now, but invading the body is the best thing for it. The senses need assaulting."

"I know your wife," Mary Grace said in a low voice.

This stopped him. His eyes were no longer aloof.

"You know Valerie?"

"She ruined my life."

He absorbed this, then nodded, swallowing what had been stalled in his throat. "That makes two of us."

"What are you doing here?" she managed to ask.

"I guess I'm on some kind of mission. I guess I've come to get my wife back. It's like *Heart of Darkness* or something. All during the plane flight I kept thinking I should write a movie about this. A man who journeys into the darkest part of the country to retrieve his estranged wife."

He paused to extract a piece of fat from his mouth. He examined it like an archaeologist before setting it aside.

"You think this is the darkest part of the country?" she asked.

"I don't know. It's an unfair assessment. But I'm talking about poetic truth rather than real truth. The poetry is what we're interested in seeing. Everything else is what we have to endure."

"What about some more iced tea?" Violet asked, hovering over him with a pitcher, though he hadn't touched any of what was in his glass.

"Let the man eat, Violet," Mary Grace commanded. Violet waddled away again.

"So you know Valerie," Jason said, wiping his mouth with the paper napkin.

"Yes. We went to high school together. She stole every one of my boyfriends. She made me miserable."

"How did she steal them?"

"Just by being who she is."

"Well, I'm not sure you can hold her accountable for that."

"I should have figured you'd be on her side."

"I'm not. Like I said, she ruined my life, also. I only intended to be married once in my life. If I can't convince her to come back with me, I'll have to discover a whole new course of action."

"Why did you marry her?"

He chewed his chicken and thought. "She was so beautiful."

Mary Grace waited for the rest. It never came.

"That's it?"

He shrugged. "For a lot of men, that's enough."

He chewed some more, then added, "She's a throwback to something. Romance. Some kind of idyll. Maybe it's the South. I haven't been here long enough to know. But I know I've never met anyone like her. The kind that just moves in and tells you who you are."

"That's every woman," Mary Grace said.

"True. But most women I met had the wrong idea about me." He paused, staring off dreamily. "I liked who she wanted me to be."

Mary Grace felt rankled. If this was true, she had completely miscalculated Valerie's tactics. Men didn't appreciate her for who she was but for how she made them feel about themselves. Was that fair?

"Tell me, how come you didn't just call her up? How come you had to breeze into town like a knight in shining armor?"

"You know Valerie. You can't impress her with a phone call. It takes much more."

"So you're just going to show up on her doorstep?"

"I am if I can find it. I don't have her address. It's ridiculous, I know, not having your wife's address. I could call information, I suppose, but I like the challenge."

"You could ask me."

"I could, but I have the feeling you won't tell me."

She nodded slowly, sipping her coffee.

"I hate to take the challenge away."

"Well, I have to find somewhere to stay first. Where's a good hotel?"

Mary Grace laughed into her fist.

"What?"

"There aren't any hotels in Maddock. It's not exactly the tourist capital of the South."

"But what about the Millburn parents? They have to stay somewhere."

"They usually stay in Danville, the next town over."

"Shit. How do I get there?"

"You could stay with me, of course."

He looked at her, his head cocked. The idea seemed to interest him, mainly because of how inappropriate it was.

"There's the guest house," Violet piped up from the counter.

"What?"

"Nelson Gray runs a guest house over on Pearl Street. Four or five rooms. Should be empty now till Homecoming at Millburn."

"Oh, thank you. Thanks very much."

"Thanks very much," Mary Grace echoed.

2

Tess sat in the examining room, fully clothed, with the green paper robe in her lap. The nurse had told her to put it on and she had defied the order. She'd never tried anything like this. Usually it was just a race to see how fast she could get her clothes off and the gown on before the doctor tapped and breezed in. She wasn't sure why she'd always been nervous about being caught halfway through the undressing process—as if there were anything to hide from the man who put his arm halfway up her vagina. Of course, now there was never any question about undressing in front of Vincent Ross. It simply wasn't going to happen. The man who had come to her party and called the plumber and who had remembered comments she made during her last pap smear.

The gown looked smooth and symmetrical and perfect in her lap. She liked the sight of the instruments all lined up and sterilized. She liked the pamphlets and the baby magazines. She liked everything better than her parents' house, still and quiet as it was now, the smell of too many flowers lingering in the rooms long after they'd been thrown out.

Her father's nature had changed somewhat—he was no longer cheerful, but neither was he morose. He was just contemplative. For a few days he kept sifting through photograph albums, sighing. He wouldn't eat. Then he started cleaning out Lana's closets, and he began to get pleasantly nostalgic, as if he were doing research for his wife's biography.

"Oh, this pantsuit! She wore it to the New Year's party at Marge Peterson's, and I spilled a champagne cocktail on it. She bawled me out for five days."

This memory made him smile, though Tess couldn't imagine why. And all of his memories were along these lines—like the shoes he had told her were too expensive, which caused her to stop speaking to him and cooking for him for at least a week. The necklace he gave her on their anniversary, which she said was cheap and refused to wear but also refused to return. It unnerved Tess to hear these negative recollections, mainly because they were so much in line with her own. The dark moments with Lana were all either of them had left, and somehow they had talked themselves into loving them, appreciating them. It worried Tess that perhaps her father's wistful smile had more to do with the fact that his wife was gone, and that he was released from the constant threat of criticism. But it worried her more to think that he, that both of them, had grown dependent upon it and would miss it.

There was a quick rap on the door and it swung open, but Vince Ross did not breeze in. He entered cautiously, looking around the room, his eyes softening when they landed on Tess. He closed the door quietly behind him and stood in front of it.

"Tess," he said, "I'm surprised to see you."

"Oh. Well, I made an appointment."

"I know that. I'm just surprised in general."

She looked at her lap. He moved slowly toward her. He stopped close to her, his stethoscope brushing against her knees.

"What's wrong?"

"Nothing," she said. "My mother's dead."

"Oh God."

She had not intended to cry. Except for the watery eyes at the funeral, which could have been a result of her allergies, she had not shed any tears for her mother. Now they came, uninvited and unstoppable. She shed them into her palm, letting them seep through her fingers and onto the green paper gown. She was frightened. Nothing made her feel more out of control and generally crazy than crying. Especially crying in front of a virtual stranger. Fortunately, he did not touch her. It might have been her undoing.

"Was it her heart?" he finally asked when she had gained control.

She wiped her cheeks with the gown and nodded.

"It was sudden. We thought she was getting better."

"Yes, well, that's the heart for you. It's a very unpredictable muscle."

She sniffed and wiped her nose with the back of her hand. He grabbed for a box of tissues, fumbled, and knocked them into her lap. They didn't acknowledge the awkwardness, which made it worse.

"I feel like I did it to her."

"That's ridiculous," he said sternly.

"No, it isn't. I left my husband. Well, we left each other. It was embarrassing for her. She had all these people to face. I could tell it was eating at her, though she wouldn't admit it."

"You and your husband have separated?"

She nodded. "She was so sensitive about those things. How it looked, what she'd have to say to people. It's because she was such a gossip. She knew how people talked because she did it herself. She knew how malicious people could be. Oh my God. I'm saying all this terrible stuff about my dead mother."

Finally he touched her, and she was ready for it. He put his hand on her thigh. It seemed an odd choice, but she liked it. She felt comforted by it.

"Some people feel anger at their loved ones for dying. It's normal," he said.

"No, that's not it. I felt anger at her for living, too. She wasn't a very generous person. She looked for the worst in people and was only happy when she found it."

"But you loved her," he said.

"Of course I did. She was my mother. But don't you see? That's my weakness. I love the wrong people. I always have. I loved Valerie. I still do."

"Who's Valerie?"

"The woman at my party." Seeing his blank look, she said, "Don't you remember?"

"Not really."

Tess smiled, then blew her nose. A man who did not remember meeting Valerie Caldwell. Where had he been all her life?

Suddenly he asked, "Do you love me?"

She felt stranded. She was afraid to answer him, and afraid not to.

"Yes," she said quietly. "I think I do."

"I'm not the wrong person," he said.

• • •

They made love that night in Vince's two-bedroom apartment, which had no furniture except for the small double bed, a chest of drawers, and a patio table and chairs in the dining area. He had a cat named Judas who mewed incessantly and stupidly at nothing, and gnawed at the doorframe. A streetlight outside the window shone in all night—he had no curtains, and the blanket he had hoped might do the trick had long ago fallen and lay crumpled in the corner.

Danville had much more nighttime activity than Maddock; cars and trucks passed underneath their window all night. It wasn't the noise that bothered Tess so much as the knowledge that the world didn't ever really shut down. She felt agitated by this awareness; it would take some time to adjust.

Lying awake in the unseen hours of the morning, Tess looked around and thought what a perfectly impractical and childish place this apartment was, and how wonderful it made her feel. It completely undermined the importance of everyday living. It thumbed its nose at what she had come to think of as necessities. People need so little, she thought. Why do we drive ourselves crazy wanting things?

Sleep was an impossibility. Neither of them tried. Tess thought their reasons were different—he probably was unaccustomed to having someone in this small bed (she hoped, anyway—but wasn't it ridiculous to ask a doctor if he'd had an AIDS test?), and she was somewhat shell-shocked by what she had done. She never expected to sleep with any man other than Joe. She had steeled herself for that, though some small part of her realized that no one really gets through life, or should have to get through it, with only one sexual partner.

Actually, what she and Vince had done together didn't feel like sex. It felt like something crazy and delicious and wrong. It made her feel that people were meant to go about doing extreme things, that life should be lived on the edge, never in the middle. There was nothing in the middle but safety, and that safety was so much more vulnerable than anyone had ever imagined. If her old beliefs had held up at all, she would be dead by now, or hideously punished.

His chest hair tickled her face. He was barrel-chested—it was hard to get her arm around him. He was shorter than Joe, there was less of him, but so much more to contend with. When he made love to her, he had expected things from her. He had made eye contact with her and actually talked to her during the act. He'd had ideas, wanted to change positions, commented on her body, kissed her on the mouth again and again. This seemed impossible to her, as if they weren't doing it right, as if any minute someone would stop them and make them start again. And, in fact, after they'd lain awake and talked for a while, he started again. She hadn't been aware that this was even possible.

She knew she should feel giddy and alive, but all she could think was that she was going to hell and that actually she wouldn't mind.

"Is it true that doctors aren't affected by women's bodies, that they just see them from a scientific standpoint?" she asked, feeling brave enough to hear the answer.

"Of course not," he said, laughing.

"When you're examining them, I mean."

"Not really. It's just that when I'm working, I'm thinking of other things. Tonight, with you, I wasn't looking for tumors."

"What if you'd found one?"

"I'd have ignored it."

"So when you examined me that first time, other things were going through your mind?"

"Yes, but on a different level. It's hard to explain. It's like a mechanic working on a car, I guess. When you're trying to fix it, you just concentrate on the parts—are they working or not? But when you see that same car driving down the street, you can admire it and covet it."

She bought that explanation. She would have bought anything.

"You do understand I can't be your doctor anymore," he said.

"That's okay. I don't need one anymore."

They made love three times. The sun was starting to rise when she finally began to feel drowsy.

"Are you Jewish?" she asked, yawning.

"No, of course not. I'm Italian."

"But aren't there Jews in Italy?"

"I guess. I've never been to Italy."

"What are you, then? Religion, I mean."

He shrugged. "Catholic. I was raised that way."

"But you don't believe."

"Sometimes I do. When I'm on a plane."

She laughed and let her fingers travel through his hair. It was thinning. She didn't care.

"Do you believe?" he asked her.

"No. I've never said that before. Growing up here, belief is just a part of you. No one asks you, no one questions you. You go to church and nobody speaks the unspeakable. But I feel guilty now. I feel like I'm going to be punished. So I must believe something. I know I shouldn't feel guilty."

"You can't use 'shouldn't' and 'guilt' in the same sentence. Should implies guilt. Native Americans don't even have a word for should."

She thought about this for a moment, then said, "I don't understand a world without should."

"Neither do I," he admitted. "But I've never been able to settle this question. When I was an intern, I saw so much terrible stuff. I can't begin to tell you. Gunshots and stab wounds and drug overdoses, all kinds of senseless stuff—I survived that. It was just people being barbaric and ridiculous. This I understand. But it was the babies. Babies born without limbs, or with Tay-Sachs, or spina bifida, encephalitis. Not the drug-addicted ones. There was a reason, however perverse, for that. It was the fuckup of nature I couldn't handle. It was all so random, these afflictions. It was a roll of the genetic dice. But the people it affected, the mothers and fathers, there was nothing clinical about that."

"I understand," she said.

"No, you don't. It's because of this pain that I want to believe. This is no chemical reaction, this is no quirk of the brain. The pain that these people feel is sublime. This pain comes from love, and this love has to come from a higher source, doesn't it? Otherwise, we'd be like automatons bumping into each other, insensitive to our connections."

"I don't know," she admitted. "But I'm so happy to be talking about it. So happy, you can't know."

"I do know."

"I used to have this dream," she said. "It was recurring. I'd dream that I'd killed somebody. The person never had an identity—when the dream started it was just a body. I'd bury it in the backyard or somewhere and go on about my business. Then halfway through the dream I'd remember I'd killed someone, and this feeling of horror would come over me. At first I'd think about getting caught and just the threat of getting caught following me forever. Then I realized that even if I didn't get caught, my life as I knew it was over, I couldn't go back because I'd done something so far outside the rules."

Her cheek was pressed against his chest. She felt him nod against her head.

"That's how I feel now," she said.

"Oh, wonderful. I've made you feel like you committed murder. I don't think a woman's ever said that to me."

"No, not that part," she said. "The part where I can never go back."

She closed her eyes, intending to reflect, but the next thing she knew, the bright, hard mid-morning sunlight was streaming in, and Vince was standing by the bed, smiling down at her, hands in his pockets. He was wearing a white lab coat over his shirt and tie and dress pants. She could not escape the feeling he was examining her. Would she ever overcome this feeling, being involved with a doctor?

"I should go," she said, rising on her elbows.

"Stay as long as you like," he said. "There's coffee on the stove, juice in the fridge, but after that you're on your own."

"I'm not hungry."

They spent an awkward moment smiling at each other. It seemed like something should be said, but what?

"Where will you be?" he asked.

"When?"

"From now on."

She wasn't sure how to answer that. In some dark part of her brain she had let herself assume she'd be here, with him, always. Once she'd slept with a man, that seemed to be a logical assumption. But she knew that was only because the only other man she'd ever slept with was her husband.

"I don't know."

"Will you get the house?"

"What house?"

"The one you lived in with your husband."

"Oh. No. I don't want it."

"You can't go on living with your father."

She nodded, though she wanted to ask why. The way he spoke made her feel homeless, and something like panic descended on her. It was hard to recognize, since she'd never felt genuine panic. She'd always had a place to go. Suddenly she knew the meaning of being cut loose, on her own, with no one (no man, she realized) to lean on. She could not lean on Vince. Not because he wasn't strong enough, but because he was too strong, and he'd expect that kind of strength from her.

"It would do you good to get out of Maddock," he said.

She looked at him as if he'd suggested she fly to the moon. Out of Maddock? She'd never been out of Maddock. She wasn't sure she could leave, that she'd be allowed. The foolishness of that made her smile. All this time, all these years—all her life, she could have gotten out of Maddock.

"I'll find someplace," she said vaguely. "I'll call you."

He leaned over, placing his palms on the bed, making it sink as he kissed her forehead.

"Make it soon," he said.

She lay very still on his bed long after she heard the front door close, feeling like a wild animal caught in the headlights of a car, thinking what she now realized the animal must think in that split second. Anything can happen, anything. And whatever it is, I'm not ready.

3

There's a movie here, Jason thought, driving along the main street of Maddock. The traffic moved at a leisurely pace, as if the drivers were all gazing up and down the sidewalk to spot faces they recognized. It was like a sanitized version of Hollywood Boulevard, a respectable form of cruising. They honked their horns, stuck their heads out the window to speak to people, came to a dead stop whenever they felt like it. On the sidewalks were little knots of spontaneous congregations. The slowness, the lack of urgency acted as a sedative to him and he, who always found himself wanting to be somewhere else, wanting to accomplish something, suddenly wanted to do nothing in particular. The town seemed to whisper, "Stay, stay." And every minute he stayed, he could hear the whisper become a shout. It was a miracle anyone ever found enough initiative to leave. It made him see his wife in a different light. The fire that burned under her feet, that compelled her to leave in the first place, must have been stronger than anything he'd ever known. It wasn't particularly hard to leave New Jersey—the refineries, the mills (most of which were boarded up by the time he got away), the dim red-and-yellow glow of New York City just across the river promising something, anything. He had grown up in the shadow of something better. The pull to possess it was present from the cradle to the grave. New Jersey was a place to leave. But this was a place to bury yourself, to deny the existence of anything at all, let alone something superior.

Valerie had not exaggerated. This was the hardest thing for him to accept. All those years he had accused her of making her home into something it couldn't possibly have been, when the truth was that she had not even done it justice.

The residential streets were even closer to the cliché. Enormous Victorian houses that would have gone for two or three million in Los Angeles stood one right after another, belonging, he was certain, to teachers and bankers and car dealers, who probably longed to live in modern brick townhouses, who probably griped every winter about how such a barn was impossible to insulate. The flora was no less spectacular. Even though it was fall, there seemed to be flowers everywhere, in bright defiance of a winter that might never show up.

As he turned off on Military Drive, he drove past a large marble sign that said MILLBURN ACADEMY. He recalled his wife waxing poetic about Millburn Academy. Try as he might, he could not get her to understand how archaic the concept of military school was. In fact, it wasn't until this moment that he really believed such a place existed. He was tempted to investigate the grounds, but something moved him forward. He wanted to get to the story he had come here in search of, the one in the plain brick colonial with the bay windows and Doric columns.

A fiftyish woman with dyed blond hair and clunky jewelry and too much perfume opened the door. He caught his breath for several reasons, not the least of which was because he felt he was looking at Valerie in warp speed. He knew this was Helen—he had met her a couple of times in Los Angeles—but she had seeped out of his memory until she struck him as someone he had seen in some student film. The note he would have given on this character was "too on the nose."

"Hello," he said. "Hello, Helen. I don't know if you remember me. I'm your son-in-law."

"Of course I remember you, Jason. What in heaven's name are you doing here?"

"Well, I suppose I've come for my wife."

This answer seemed to alarm and please her at once. She stepped aside, adjusting her hair with one hand as she motioned him in with the other.

The house was something out of an Early American museum. A Jeffersonian air prevailed. The tables were adorned with candles and candle snuffers and hurricane lamps, as if electricity were a century away from being discovered. There was an abundance of pewter. Hunting and flowered prints, brass lamps, gilt-framed mirrors, carpet which sank under his feet.

"Is Valerie here?"

"Yes, of course she's here," came a male voice. Frank Caldwell had stepped into the hallway, hands in his pockets, reading glasses down on his nose. "Have you come for her?"

"I suppose I have."

"Well, it's about time."

"Frank. You'll have to excuse my husband."

"Why? Why does he have to excuse me? A man should go after his wife. He shouldn't just sit there and let her leave."

"I could hardly make her stay. Surely you know how hard it is to make Valerie do anything," Jason argued.

"Surely we do," Frank chuckled.

They shook hands.

Jason had the strange sensation that this was the first real man he'd shaken hands with in years. The men in Hollywood were eunuchs by comparison—their grips were softer, more tentative, carrying less meaning. Frank was a man who had worried about things other than getting his movie made, and the stress of it showed in his well-worn face and graying hair. Jason longed to look like him someday, longed to show the trial of his years in his face, but at the rate he was going it would never happen. People like himself only reflected frustration, not the accumulation of struggle, and the sense of having achieved admirable goals.

"Valerie's on the back porch," Frank said. "She sits out there a lot."

"The veranda," Helen corrected. "I think she enjoys watching the night fall. Don't you have nightfall in Los Angeles? Valerie acts like she's never seen a sunset before."

"No, night doesn't really fall. It appears. It happens. Subtlety is in short supply in California," Jason said.

"Do you want a beer?" Frank asked.

"Sure."

"We don't have any," Helen said. "We never have beer, Frank. No one drinks it."

"That's a shame. We ought to. Beer is a fine drink."

"We have iced tea and coffee and white wine. We never used to have white wine, but Valerie insists on it. I guess white wine is a Los Angeles drink."

"White wine is fine."

He stood in the den while Helen fetched his drink. He and Frank stared at the TV screen, which depicted a reality show—someone dragging a limp man out of a body of water.

Frank said, "It's something else, how they manage to save all these people."

"Well, they don't show you the ones they don't save. There are a lot more of them. People who suffer permanent brain damage and other irreversible impairment. It's extremely misleading, this kind of television. Reality programming is the death of the medium, in my opinion."

"Is that a fact," Frank said flatly, as if he just didn't want to know.

"Go on out and see her," Helen encouraged as she handed Jason his wine. "She's going to be shocked, but she'll recover."

"I've been admiring your town," Jason said, wanting to delay the moment.

"Really?" Frank asked, as if genuinely surprised.

"I've never seen anything like it."

"Maddock is a family community," Helen said, by way of an explanation.

A scraggly dog squirmed its way into the room, its tail literally tucked between its legs.

"Ingrid, go back to your bed," Helen demanded. The dog shrunk further into itself.

"What an interesting dog," Jason said, offering a finger which it immediately licked.

"*Interesting!* It needs to be put to sleep," Helen sniffed.

"Why?"

"She's getting old. And no one ever cared for her the way Valerie did. She brought Ingrid home as a stray puppy. But Valerie doesn't seem all that interested in her these days."

"Valerie doesn't seem interested in anything these days," Frank said.

"Go on out and see her," Helen said again.

The moment had come, and Jason went out, clutching his wine next to his chest like a trophy.

She was not on the veranda. The rocking chair was still swaying where she had recently vacated it. He strained his eyes and saw her wandering in the backyard, a glass of wine in her hand. Taking a breath, he approached her.

She was humming faintly, and when a twig he stepped on distracted her, she stared at him as if she needed a moment to recognize him. Then she looked away, as if struggling to get back to her previous train of thought.

"Hello," he said. "Am I interrupting anything?"

She sipped her wine.

"We used to play out here. Me and Mary Grace and Tess. We played grown-ups. We pretended we were dating and living in apartments and driving expensive cars. Well, I pretended that, and I talked them into pretending it. They wanted to be married, with babies, but I kept saying no, that's too boring. We're too important for that. We're career women. We have lives of our own. We're independently wealthy. We travel and eat in nice restaurants and spend our money any way we please. We're models, we're actresses, we own businesses, I told them. We're beautiful and independent and we don't want anything from anybody. People come around and interview us and ask to take our pictures."

She laughed, then sipped her wine.

"How did they like it?" he asked.

"They didn't, at first. But eventually they got into it."

"How did it end?"

"Oh, it didn't. That was the beauty of it. It didn't end."

Jason sipped his wine. It tasted sour and green. He'd been spoiled by good California wine.

Then, as if the thought had suddenly occurred to her, she turned to him with a surprised expression. "What are you doing here?"

"Well, I felt I should try to lure you back."

"Why?"

"Because I miss you. And you're my wife."

He wasn't sure he'd put that in the right order, but she seemed so distracted it didn't seem to matter.

"What about that woman?" she asked.

"What woman?"

"I called and a woman answered the phone."

He was stumped for a moment. He thought perhaps he'd had an affair that he'd forgotten, which suddenly seemed entirely possible. He'd had a lot to drink since she left.

"Judith?" he finally asked.

"She didn't say her name. Mistresses are funny that way."

"That wasn't a mistress. Judith Markham is the producer of my movie."

"What movie?"

"The déranged psychologist? I sold it. Judith Markham wants to turn the psychologist into a detective—one of those down-on-his-luck types who realizes all his mistakes and atones for it. Wants to make it a woman, too. Melanie Griffith, she sees. A woman who learns how to be more of a woman through violence. We've had some ferocious arguments. I lost them all, but it's a go picture. They've resurrected some action-adventure director. I'm supposed to be on my knees or something. You'd know all this if you'd stuck around."

"I stuck around," Valerie said slowly. "Until I felt in danger of becoming unstuck."

He realized that she was drunk. He didn't mind. She didn't really drink in Los Angeles, even though he encouraged it because he felt he drank too much and needed company.

"I want you to come home," he said.

"I am home."

"Valerie, do we have to go into this again? This is just the place you're from. Nobody thinks of the place they're from as home anymore. That's an antiquated notion. Everybody's looking for another place to be."

"That's a Hollywood idea. Most people never leave their homes. Jesus never went more than thirty miles away from his home."

"Well, of course not. He didn't have a car."

"I'm sorry for you that you don't have a place like this to refer to."

"I have New Jersey."

"New Jersey isn't a real place. It's not the South. No one feels rooted there."

"That's a ridiculous thing to say."

"So divorce me."

"I can't believe you want that," he said, though he'd come here fully expecting to hear the word. He hadn't, however, expected to hear it so soon, or so casually.

"I'm happy here," she said. She sipped her wine and flung her hair over her shoulder. Jason had a fleeting sense of what it must have been like to pursue Valerie as a teenager—he felt there was a long line somewhere that he needed to take a number and get at the back of. But this was what he had always felt about her, and this was what had originally attracted him to her.

"Why are you happy here? What is so fulfilling about it?"

"I feel connected. I know who I am here."

"And who is that?"

She looked resolutely at the ground and remained silent.

"The belle of the ball?" he asked.

"No. What ball? You're making some kind of generalization. You have this clichéd idea about the South."

"I think that's your problem, Valerie."

"You don't have a clue about my problem."

"I see what you're doing. You think you can come back here and reduce everything to this little microcosm. That doesn't work. You can't make your world smaller, Valerie. You can only expand it. And once you've done that, you can't go back."

"What are you talking about? You sound like you're in a pitch meeting. You can't even talk like a normal person anymore. Everything is movie jargon. Everything has some kind of tag line to it. You can't make your world smaller. You can only expand it. Coming to theaters everywhere this Christmas."

That hurt. That he did not expect. He was aware of carrying the business too far, letting it be too much with him, but he believed he could still talk like a normal person. Maybe she was right, and he wasn't even sure what that meant anymore. Obviously he was having trouble reaching her, this woman he had shared a life with for over four years, so his communication tactics certainly couldn't be applauded. But was this his problem or hers? Was she trying to speak some lost language, too . . . a language of simplicity and frankness and reducing everything to plain talk—the language of the Old South?

As if to prove his point, she said, "Most people don't have a plan. They just do what they need to do, what feels right, or even what feels wrong if it satisfies some need. This constant evaluating and summarizing, taking our emotional temperature every five minutes, that's a California thing. People here just live. Day to day, moment to moment. They don't experience life, they just live it."

Jason took a long sip of wine. It was starting to taste better; the greenness was starting to appeal to him, and his head felt lighter.

"Is there someone else?" he asked.

She looked up too quickly. "What?"

"You heard me."

"No. What someone? Who could there be?"

"Well, that's why I'm asking. Because I don't know."

"Don't be ridiculous," she said, but she sounded caught.

"Actually, if you said yes, I'd be relieved."

"Why?"

"Because I know how to take on a man. I have no idea how to take on a mythical region of the country."

"I don't know why I married you," she said.

"Well, in a moment of weakness you claimed to love me."

She threw her wine into the grass, then stared at the ground as if she deeply regretted the loss.

"What the hell took you so long?" she demanded. "I sat here and waited. I thought you'd come, or call. . . ."

"I did call."

"I thought you'd do it again and again. I thought you'd make some pitch for me, the way you do for your blessed feature scripts. I thought you'd do the hard sell, but obviously I'm not worth it."

"One minute you don't want me to act like a screenwriter, the next you do. Make up your mind."

"It was humiliating!" she shouted, in a voice so loud it would have embarrassed him in Los Angeles. Here in the silence of Maddock, it was practically obscene. "You humiliated me! At one time every man in this town wanted me, went after me—they still do, as a matter of fact. But my own husband doesn't! How should that make me feel!"

The screen door creaked. .

"Valerie," came Helen's reproachful voice.

"Mother, I am busy."

"They can hear you in the next county."

"What difference does it make?"

"I have to live here. . . ."

"I know you goddamn live here, you tell me every day!"

There was a pregnant, angry pause, then the door closed again. Jason felt unnerved and took another generous sip of wine. Something in him was enjoying this. The raised voices made his heart pound. The smell of warm, rich earth filled his nose. Crickets chirped and a dog barked somewhere far off. He felt he was in the middle of a Tennessee Williams play. Somebody named Big Daddy was bound to appear soon.

He looked at his wife, small and pale in the fading light, her blond hair falling like a veil around her shoulders, and he wanted to hold her. He wanted to take her away, but not in the conventional sense. He wanted to give her the dramatic moment to which her entire life had been dedicated.

He could imagine how it might play out—a wide master with two figures under the trees. Then a push into a medium shot. . . . He shook his head. He did not want to see the screen anymore.

"Valerie," he said quietly. "I love you very much. But you have to know this. You're the one who's caught up in the movie, not me. I may talk it all the time, but I know the difference."

She shook her head slowly. "Please go away."

He stood still, weighed down by uncertainty. He had said every-thing he'd come to say and it hadn't worked. This he had not counted on.

He finally managed to turn, but as he did she spoke:

"Is it really such a bad thing, wanting your life to be a story? What's so wrong with that?"

He stood for a long moment, remembering when he had said that to her, wondering what had prompted it, wondering now how to explain it.

"Because life just doesn't make a very good story, Valerie," he said. "You can always predict the end."

4

That night, Valerie dreamed about Al Pacino.

She'd gone to bed right after Jason left, and the unsettling nature of the visit was still with her. That explained the disturbing aspects of the dream, though not necessarily the presence of Al Pacino.

She was in a theater and got up to buy some popcorn. When she came back, he was sitting in her seat.

"Excuse me," she said, "but I was sitting there."

"Don't make a big deal out of it," he said. "You can sit with me."

He slid over and they shared a seat, and she watched the rest of the movie thinking, Al Pacino, of all people. She wasn't especially attracted to him. But he was famous and she should make an effort to impress him. She was aware of a vague sense of contempt coming from him, and she wanted to combat it, but something—intimidation, manners—kept her from speaking. After the movie he offered to drive her home. They went careening over Beverly Glen, past Mulholland Drive, in some little sports car, and she gazed at all the lights in the valley below, spreading out forever, each one representing another person who was trying to make it. Al Pacino asked her what she did, and she told him she was a television star. She had no sense of lying. In the dream, it seemed to be the truth.

"Television is the death of art," he told her.

"Oh, excuse me. *Sea of Love.* That's brilliant, I suppose. That's art."

Al Pacino only laughed, which gave her an indication that this was a dream.

When they arrived at her house (which was actually her parents' house, but situated in the Hollywood Hills), he told her to take off her clothes, which she did, and he proceeded to make hostile love to her. She felt cheated and tired, but primarily bored. When it was over he yawned and said, "I guess I love you."

And in the best moment of her dream, she turned to him with a real sense of liberation and said, "Listen, I don't need you to love me. I have a husband who loves me."

She woke up feeling satisfied and strong, but the strength diminished as the day wore on, and she became preoccupied with analyzing the dream. She'd had a few therapy sessions in Los Angeles, but she couldn't really place Al Pacino as a symbol. She'd never given him much thought. She supposed it made sense to dream about sex with a man who didn't care about her, but why the tacked-on ending where she claimed to have a husband who loved her? To make matters more complicated, it was that part of the dream which gave her the most satisfaction.

She went to work at the library, the dream still bouncing around in her brain, and for a long time she forgot to wonder where Jason was, what he was doing, whether or not he'd actually left town. It didn't really matter. The confrontation with Jason was a necessity. No one, not even Jason, could watch his marriage die without putting up something of a struggle. But as struggles went, it was a poor one. Still, there was something about the sight of him in the backyard, clutching his wine, looking so out of place in his Armani jacket and jeans and sneakers, his dull, disillusioned writer's stare moving between her face and the trees and the porch light, that made her want to protect him. She felt a tug of affection for him, but she could not allow herself to call it love. Love didn't just hover that way, like a little innocuous rain cloud, uncertain of its intentions. Love should be forceful, overwhelming, and impossible to resist.

She thought of Brett Becker going AWOL, risking everything just to be with her. It was so much more of a sacrifice than Jason had made. True, it was a young, stupid affection, but perhaps that was the very best kind. It was the kind of love that didn't let in other distractions. And it was the only kind of love that had ever mattered to her.

It was a slow day in the library. A few of the cadets tried to talk to her, but she gave them short replies. She had lost patience with them. She didn't care what they read. She didn't care if they talked and didn't bother to reprimand the ones who did. Every now and then the thought of Al Pacino came back to her and she felt agitated and restless. She felt a decision needed to be made.

It was a Friday and the library closed early so the cadets could prepare for end-of-the-week inspection. She shooed everyone out and locked the doors at four o'clock. She stood for a long time in the quiet hall, looking through the narrow rectangular window at the empty library, the spines of books, and the dingy tiles. She knew something had to be done.

She went downstairs, outside, through the breezeway, and entered the rec room. The pool tables and pinball machines were crowded with cadets trying to get in their last games before surrendering to formation. The sounds were lively and excited, with a generous amount of swearing, as if they were trying to expend their true natures before the solemn dictates of discipline were forced upon them.

She went up to the desk, where the cadet on watch was staring blankly at a thick textbook. One hand was dog-earing pages, while the other roamed across the dried acne on his chin.

"Excuse me," she said. The cadet looked at her and his eyes widened. He had big blue eyes, soft and feminine, hopeful. His mouth parted but no sound came out.

"I'd like to page someone," she said.

"Oh. Um. Well." He closed his book as if she'd caught him reading pornography. "It's kinda late."

"Formation isn't for another hour. Am I right?"

"Yeah, sure, but . . . you know." His name tag said Dix. She could imagine the ribbing he took for that.

"Who did you want to page?" he asked, as if that made all the difference.

"Lieutenant Brett Becker."

"Private Becker," he corrected her.

"Oh, right," she said and had a sinking feeling in her stomach. She wanted to abandon the whole thing, but it was too late.

"Looks like he's signed out," Dix said.

"Really?"

"It could be a mistake." Dix scratched his chin and reached for the microphone. "What do I say?"

"Just to meet me out in the breezeway."

He hesitated, sighed, shook his head, scratched some more, then spoke into the microphone.

"Lieutenant Becker," he said. "I mean, Private Becker, please report to the breezeway." He cast a glance at her, then added, "Immediately."

"Thank you, Dix."

As she paced under the breezeway, she kept having flashes of Al Pacino and she felt embarrassed all over again and had to talk to her heart to stop it from racing. Wandering cadets gave her curious glances. *I don't need you to love me. I have a husband who loves me.* This kept going through her brain. Joe flashed into her head, too. That soporific stare, those indifferent eyes. What might have happened if Tess's mother hadn't died that night? Maybe nothing, maybe everything. It seemed impossible that fate could be interfered with that way.

Her heart was leaping around erratically, like a fish trying to wriggle off a hook. Something had been decided, the minute Dix picked up that microphone. This moment could not be retreated from.

She heard the click of heels on the pavement, and she knew it was Brett even before she turned. When she did she felt a jolt of excitement. He was smiling, his white teeth gleaming, the look of joy overpowering his attempts at restraint.

"I can't believe it," he said.

"Well, believe it. How are you?"

"I'm great. You look beautiful."

"No, I don't. But thank you."

He kissed her on the cheek. Something about it made her feel unsettled.

"What are you doing here?" he asked.

"I was working. I just closed the library, and I thought I'd say hello while I'm here."

"Well, I'm glad you did."

He was smiling and holding her by the elbows. What was that new look about, that confident, impartial smile?

"I've been thinking about you," he said, and at the same time dropped his hands to his sides.

"I've been thinking about you, too."

She waited for his reaction, but it didn't come. He seemed prepared to leave it at that.

"Has it been hard?" she asked him.

"What?"

"Everything, since our talk. Getting busted. All those tours."

"Oh, that. It's okay." Grinning, he added, "*Per ardua ad astra.*"

She smiled, feeling better.

"Have you talked to your mother?" she asked.

"Yes. As a matter of fact, she's here."

Valerie stepped back. "Where?"

"Here, out front. She's waiting for me, in fact. They're visiting from France. Her and her boyfriend, Bjorn. He's a tool, but he's okay. He's taking us out to dinner, anyway."

"What, now?"

"Yeah, I got leave. Listen, can I call you later? They're waiting for me. We're going out to the Charcoal House in Danville."

"What about formation?"

"Like I said, I got leave. Colonel Fullham's been real cool about it. They might even give me my rank back."

"Really?"

"Yeah. My mom came up and made a fuss and wrote him a check. You know how it goes."

Valerie nodded, though she didn't know at all. She didn't want to believe it worked that way.

"Well," she sighed, "I won't keep you."

They stood facing each other, not wanting to move. The clock in the chapel chimed.

"My husband was here," she told him. "He came after me."

His smile didn't fade. He nodded. "Good."

"What?"

"Good. I mean, that's what husbands should do. If I was your husband, I'd come after you."

She smiled uncertainly.

"Let me walk with you," she said. "I'd like to meet your mother."

He hesitated, dragging the toe of his shiny shoe along the black-top. "Well, I don't know if that's a good idea."

"She doesn't have to make any assumptions. I'm your librarian."

"Yeah. Right," he said. "But she knows I don't read."

"Come on, Becker," she said, taking his arm.

"Brett?" came a soft, unassuming voice. Valerie turned and saw a small blond woman approaching. She looked far too young to be Becker's mother. She wore a sleeveless navy dress and white sandals. She stood under the breezeway, rubbing the back of her calf with a foot, twisting a strand of cornsilk hair between her thumb and forefinger.

"I'll be right there," Brett said.

"You have a sister?"

Brett looked at her. "No, I don't."

In the next second an older woman appeared, also blond, the

years showing on her face but not in her demeanor. She was well put together, dressed in clothes that were so obviously expensive that they looked cheap. Her gait was smooth and well bred, like Becker's. They had the same face.

At least in appearance, she was not much older than Valerie.

"Darling, please. You know how Bjorn gets when he's hungry. Once his migraines set in, there's no getting rid of them."

"Yes, Mother," he said, avoiding Valerie's eyes.

It was too late to avoid anything. Everyone had seen each other, stock had been taken, and now the dynamic was moving in. The young woman was upon them, moving next to Becker. He avoided looking at her, avoided looking at anything but his own reflection in his shoes.

"Valerie," Becker said in a somber voice, "this is Leah Morrell."

"Le-ah?" Valerie asked, as if the pronunciation of the name were the issue.

"Yes," said the girl. "And you are?"

"Valerie Rutter," Becker volunteered. "She's the librarian here."

"Well, how fortunate," Brett's mother said. "That's a good person for you to know, Brett." To Valerie she said, "My son is hopeless in the literary arena."

Valerie could not respond. She wanted to, though. She wanted to shout, in fact: "I am not a librarian! And I am certainly not a good person for your son to know!"

Fortunately for all of them, she was unable to speak.

Brett's mother said, "I know his mind is elsewhere. I know it's on Leah. It's hard to complain about that, Leah being the divine creature that she is. She's the paragon of patience. It's hard staying true to a military man. No one knows that better than I do. I was a hometown honey myself."

She chuckled, and Valerie could not take her eyes off Leah, though she knew she should be looking at Brett's mother, who had fallen in love with the sound of her own voice.

"Brett's father went here, you know, and I was the one left at home, waiting for those long weekends. Waiting for the Military Ball mostly, as I'm sure Leah is. She's already gotten her dress."

"I've just taken it out on approval," Leah said, rolling her eyes, still fingering her hair.

Valerie stared at the girl, recognizing that sense of coyness mixed with absolute confidence. Leah would pick the right dress. She would walk through the figure on the arm of the right cadet. She would expect to win the crown. Perhaps she would be disappointed, but the hope was enough. That unshakable hope would stay with her for years, and the fact that she didn't win wouldn't matter. Until the moment that it did matter, and nothing else would matter at all.

Valerie looked into the eyes of Brett's mother, who was a well-preserved older version of Leah. It was like some kind of mirror game, three women in various stages, all with disappointments either awaiting, attacking, or haunting them. Brett stood in the middle of them, the point of all this performance, receiving it like a king receiving his court. No less was expected, no more could be conjured. He was where he was born to be.

"Sweetheart," his mother said, "Bjorn is in the car with the air conditioner blasting, listening to NPR. You know if they start talking about Israel, he'll be in a foul mood and we'll never get him back."

"All right," Brett said. "Good to see you, Valerie."

He took her hand and shook it formally.

"Darling, please don't call your teachers by their Christian names. Show some respect. Don't you have enough tours?"

Brett smiled and shrugged. Leah tugged on his gray wool sleeve. Valerie stood and watched them walk away, with their arms locked, their futures connected, their dreams intact.

5

Mary Grace hurried along Church Lane, her purse feeling unnaturally heavy, bumping against her hip. She felt she was concealing a weapon, when in reality it was only a Little Debbie raisin cake. It had been there all day. She had bought it after lunch and kept it there through the afternoon. It was there when she went to the bank to withdraw money for the weekend, and while she had chatted with Valerie's mother on the sidewalk, and while she went in to Save More to buy some opaque black pantyhose and hairstyling gel. It had been there, too, as she walked up the steps to Nelson Gray's guest house and asked to see Jason Rutter. Nelson's wife, Carla, had let her go on up rather than meet him in the parlor, as was the guest house policy. Carla had known when she created that policy that she would rarely, if ever, have reason to enforce it. But Mary Grace chose to take it personally. She thought Carla had made the assumption that Mary Grace would be safe in a bedroom with any man. She still thinks I'm fat, Mary Grace thought as she felt the purse pulling on her shoulder.

Jason came to the door wearing a white oxford cloth shirt, untucked and wrinkled, over a pair of faded Levi's, and a battered pair of Nikes with lightning bolts of color on the side. He was not wearing his glasses. His face looked thin, and lines had appeared around his mouth. But his eyes were big and serious and slow, and she had trouble looking away from them.

"You don't remember me," she said.

"Of course I do. I haven't met a vast number of people in this town."

"Just think of me as the fat girl who tried to pick you up."

"You're not fat."

"Oh, please," she said, walking into his room uninvited.

"Remember this. Women who aren't really fat always speak of themselves that way. Fat women rarely mention their weight. There's no need to confirm what they already know."

"That's bullshit. When I was really fat, I talked about it all the time."

"When were you really fat?"

"Up till very recently."

"Really?"

She nodded. "All the time your wife was ruining my life."

She saw his suitcase on the bed, in the process of being packed. Other than that, nothing in the room was out of place, except for a legal pad on one of the tables, a stack of pencils next to it, and a few wadded-up pieces of yellow paper on the floor.

"Were you writing a letter?" she asked.

"What? Oh no. I'm writing a movie. I like to throw away the first few pages. I like the feeling of destroying what I've created. It's liberating. It makes me think that something better is always around the corner. Usually by the time I've completed a scene, I've got a sea of paper around my feet."

She nodded, staring at the mess. "You're probably not very easy to live with."

"Impossible, I imagine. That explains my wife's exodus."

"Well, I'm not sure Valerie can live with anybody. She just gets them started and abandons them."

She thought he might object, but he just smiled. "Maybe. But there's something to be said for getting people started."

She took a deep breath, then let her purse drop to the floor.

"Is she going back with you?" Mary Grace asked.

For the first time, he looked somewhat forlorn.

He shook his head. "No, I don't think so."

"It's probably just as well."

"Why do you say that?"

"She's not the kind of person you want to plan your future with."

He straightened up, shoving his hands in his pockets. "How can you say that? You don't even know me."

"Yes, but I know Valerie."

Mary Grace started to move around the room, then stopped when she realized there was no place to move to. There was only the bed, the reproduction antique dresser, and a rocking chair. There was a window, but no exquisite view was waiting beyond it. Just the streets of Maddock, as serene and unpromising as they ever were.

So she turned to him instead.

"Tell me something, Jason. Answer me one question."

He shrugged. "I will if I can."

"Do you find me attractive?"

The question didn't seem to surprise him.

"I don't find you unattractive," he said.

"Oh, great," she sighed. "I imagine you're very successful with women, using that kind of language."

"Well, if you want to know the truth, I find it unattractive when women say things like that."

"You mean when they're direct."

"I mean when they're needy."

"I don't need anything. I'm just asking you a straightforward question. I'm not asking you to sleep with me or anything."

"I'd sleep with you," he said.

This turned her head.

"You would?"

"Sure."

"Right now?"

He looked at his watch. "Well, I've got to make it to the airport."

"But I mean, in general. You wouldn't have any objections to sleeping with me?"

"Objections? No."

She moved closer to him. He didn't flinch, didn't look away. His eyes remained on her. Something strong emanated from him, a powerful lack of concern. This man knew he would get what he wanted; there was no point in rushing it. It was very attractive. It made anyone with the slightest degree of doubt want to latch on.

All this time Mary Grace had thought it was the fat, when really it was just the need that turned men away. She could have dispensed with the need so much more easily than the weight.

"Picture this," Mary Grace said, right next to his face. "We're all in our teens. You're a cadet at Millburn. You meet me and Valerie at the same time. We both make you feel wanted. You could have either one of us. One—let's say Valerie—makes you feel like you'll always be on edge, always guessing, always trying but never succeeding. The other—me—makes you feel like you'll always be loved and needed and cared for. Which do you go for?"

"Valerie," he said, without missing a beat.

"Why?"

"Because I'm a teenager."

"So?"

"So teenagers don't want anything permanent. They don't want to feel good. They want to feel on edge."

"Then it's not what I look like."

"I have no idea what you looked like then. I know what you look like now, and it's perfectly fine."

"But you don't want me now."

"I told you, I have to get to the airport."

"I'm talking in a general sense."

He sighed and ran his fingers through his hair. "In a general sense I'd say that most men aren't ready for what you have to offer."

"What's that?"

"Being loved to distraction. Never doubting that part of their lives again."

"Well, perfect. You're getting on to forty, aren't you?"

"Not quite."

"So when are men going to be ready for me?"

He shook his head. "I don't know if they ever will."

"Thank you, Jason. You've cleared up a lot of things."

"Look," he said, following her to the door. "It's not just men. It's people. People love doubt. They love the big question mark. That's why so many seemingly perfect marriages fail. The most well-adjusted people you know will bolt from what is best for them, because the pull of that question mark is so powerful. Mystery is the stuff of life."

"And that's what's pulling you?"

He nodded, looking at his feet. "I admit it is."

"Valerie will keep you in doubt for the rest of your life."

"If I'm lucky."

She leaned down and picked up her purse. The weight pulled on her shoulder again, but this time it was comforting.

"If circumstances were otherwise," Jason said to her, "something might have happened between us."

"That's a nice gift you've given me. Eternal doubt."

He smiled. "It's the best gift of all."

"Well, how about giving me a lousy gift?"

She threw her arms around his neck and kissed him, full and

long on the mouth. She pressed her body against his and it responded. Anything could have happened. She felt, in that second, wanted by him and by every man who had ever been sucked into Valerie's wake.

But that was just a moment, and when it was over she was right back in her life, with nothing to call her own but a Little Debbie raisin cake.

Unable to resist, she sank down on the bed next to his suitcase and started to cry. She cried for all those sad years behind her, and all the aimless ones ahead of her. She cried for Tess, the best friend who was lost to her now, wrapped up in her own drama. She cried for Lana, whose departure was so sudden she couldn't even feel it yet. But she knew that Lana had taken something with her into the grave, an era of life she felt connected to—women who accepted the lot of their life and held on to their complaints and their bitterness like a souvenir. Those days were over, she knew. Women were required to do more now than attach themselves to a man—right or wrong—and mourn their lost opportunities.

Jason was standing in the middle of the room, staring at her, his hands still stuffed in his pockets, staring thoughtfully at her as if she were a museum piece.

"It's not possible," she said. "I can't change this late. I can't be a different person."

"Of course you can. Everyone can. In fact, it's all we can do. We can't change the world. For centuries people thought they could, you know. Alexander the Great thought so, Aristotle thought so, Thomas Jefferson thought so, Stalin thought so. Even as late as Kennedy, people thought so. Not anymore. That's why there are so many support groups and books and movements devoted to self-improvement. You can't change the world, so you have to change yourself."

"Nobody told me that."

"Well, it takes a while for information to get to a place like Maddock."

"So, that's the deal," she said, wiping her face on her sleeve. "I've got to pay the price for being where I am. I didn't ask to be here, you know. I don't think it's my fault."

"It's the legacy of the South, I suppose. You've always been hesitant to let the rest of the world in down here. Which is fine, as long as you can find a place in this particular world. If you can't, you're fucked."

She laughed in spite of herself. "Jason, you're just a stream of optimism, you know that?"

"That's never been my strong suit. Some famous person once said you can't really appreciate life until you recognize how horrible it is. I'm paraphrasing, of course. But that's why I like Los Angeles. I'm reminded every day of how horrible it is. Here, a place like this, you start to believe something else. Something worse. Like life is good."

"I never really believed life was good," Mary Grace admitted. "But I've always believed it would *get* good."

Jason shrugged, as if this were just further evidence to prove his point.

She sat there for a long time, the afternoon sunlight pressing on her, making her perspire, making her hair stick to her head. She struggled to brush it away from her face, then gave up. At last she stood and moved slowly to the door.

"I've really enjoyed our talk," she said. "Men don't want me, I live in the wrong place, life is terrible and it won't get better. Actually, a poke in the eye with a sharp stick would have sufficed."

"You have what it takes," he said to her. "You'll be all right."

"What makes you think that?"

"You're angry. That's the first step toward a life with purpose."

She nodded. Nothing would surprise her now. Nothing he said sounded even remotely odd. She even managed a smile.

"Have a nice trip back," she said.

"Second step, dispense with the platitudes," he replied.

"I hope your plane crashes."

He smiled. "There are two people you seek in life. Your one true love, which is difficult, and which Valerie may have stolen from you. But the other person you seek is just as important, and that she has given you."

"Oh, really?"

He nodded.

"Your one true enemy," he said.

6

Joe paced in the house, aware of nothing outside his immediate surroundings. He had distanced himself from all that had
happened since Lana's death. He took note of Tess's absence, but
he could not wonder where she was or what she was doing. He
seemed to have lost the ability to project, to picture other people in
other places. He tried to wonder about Valerie, but he had difficulty even conjuring her face.

He ate, he was certain of that, because he never felt hungry and
he was still alive, but he couldn't remember a single meal. He saw
the dishes piling up on the kitchen table and in the sink, but he
could have sworn someone else put them there. He had some vague
memory of going to work. He remembered some unpleasant discussion in Hayward's office, where he was told that he needed to
shape up or they would have to reconsider his position. He'd have
to come in on time, he'd have to pay more attention to his briefs
and not let so many mistakes pass through. He'd have to show more
interest in his clients and stop refusing phone calls. He had a memory of listening to all this but no memory of responding to it. He
could see a scene where he told the Glasses that he didn't want to be
a lawyer, he wanted to be something else. He wanted to make
something, build something that would be there after he was gone,
like houses or bridges. But he couldn't determine if he'd actually
said those things or just thought them.

He had a sense of a lawyer calling him, talking to him about a divorce settlement. But the whole time he was on the phone, he kept thinking, Lawyer? *I'm* a lawyer. And he hadn't taken in any of what was said.

One day, when he was tired of pacing, he went for a walk and found himself staring down at the grounds of Millburn Academy. He felt slightly drugged as he looked about that place, visited by a sensation that seemed to dominate his whole life—being told what to do. He had followed the rules there. He had been promised that if he did what he was told, everything would be fine. He wouldn't get tours. He would get promoted. He'd graduate and go on to some other place where he'd be told what to do. And indeed, his life had followed this pattern. His parents had told him to go there, his teachers and commandants had told him how to behave there. Then Valerie told him to belong to her, told him to go to law school, and all questions would be answered. Before he could absorb the loss of her, Tess was there, telling him what to do. Love her, marry her, have a baby with her. She never told him what to do without her. No one had ever told him what to do in the absence of someone telling him what to do.

He eventually took a stroll around the campus and gazed distractedly at all the cadets. They'd been told to wear gray and walk at a certain gait, and report to certain places at certain times. He envied them so strongly that he began to hate them. He felt tempted to confront them and say, "Smarten up. You think this is tough? You don't know what tough is! Following orders is the easy part!"

This he did not do, because he had found it virtually impossible to speak to other people. Which was why he was refusing phone calls and clients' visits at work, and why he couldn't even say anything in his defense when the Glasses dressed him down.

He went back home and put another dish in the sink, with the memory of something he had eaten clinging to the china, and he sat in an easy chair and thought about his parents. He'd never really analyzed their deaths, never thought about what must have been going on when their car sailed over the side of a cliff. Never asked why or how. But in the back of his mind he'd always assumed they hadn't put up much of a fight because perhaps they had nothing to fight for. They'd created and sent into the world this machine who would always do what he was told, and their work was done. Maybe that was his father's thought as he'd negotiated that last corner. My work is done—*whoops*, I took that turn too fast.

Somehow, this thought made him respect them more than if their deaths had been stupid and frivolous, the result of too much good wine and a lack of interest in their surroundings. Before this moment, their deaths just seemed to stop at "*whoops.*"

He knew that Tess would not come back to him and they would never have a baby, and he felt sorry for that. It was one feeling of which he was acutely aware, even though he had no lasting memory of Tess beyond the clatter in the kitchen, and the short-haired woman chewing her nails while she read. He couldn't see the two of them together. The episodes where they had talked or held hands or made plans or made love seemed to have happened with someone who looked and sounded a lot like him, but wasn't quite him. A stand-in, a body double, as Valerie might say.

Valerie was gone. She had left him again. He was reminded of that recurring Peanuts episode, Charlie Brown and the football. Every year Lucy convinced him she'd hold the football while he kicked. He suspected she'd pull it away at the last minute, as she'd always done, but every year he allowed himself to be talked out of his doubts. And every year, without fail, she pulled the football away, and Charlie Brown fell on his back.

Why did the cartoonist keep drawing that scenario year after year? Because it was always funny to see a naive, trusting buffoon falling flat on his back.

Valerie knew that. Valerie was gone, and she was probably laughing all the way back to Los Angeles, or wherever she was headed. He had not asked. He had hung up after her opening statement, "I just called to say goodbye."

There was nothing he could do to stop it. In fact, he felt that nothing he could do would stop or start anything. He was as formless as a ghost, his presence merely passing through the actions of life, not affecting them. And sometimes he felt more ineffectual than a ghost. Ghosts were capable of frightening people, and he wasn't close to that task.

He was in this same mood when Mary Grace discovered him that evening. She had just knocked and walked in, finding him in the same easy chair with an air pistol in his lap. He had no idea what he intended to do with the air pistol. He had nothing to shoot—not that a shot from this pistol would even make any living thing nervous, let alone kill it. He wanted a gun in his lap, and this was as close as he could come.

She seemed alarmed, however, and snatched it away, clutching it to her chest.

"What in the world are you thinking of doing?" she demanded.

"Nothing," he answered honestly.

"Well, you look like you've just been knocked upside the head."

"I haven't," he said and attempted a smile, in an effort to reassure her.

She sat on the couch and stared at him. She was thinner than he remembered. Or was she fatter? He couldn't recall. Her appearance always seemed to be in a state of flux.

"What are you going to do about Tess?" she asked.

"What should I do?"

She shrugged. "Well, I can't tell you that."

"Why not?"

"You've got to make up your own mind."

"She left me. She doesn't love me anymore."

"I don't believe that. Don't you think she's worth fighting for?"

Worth fighting for? What was worth fighting for? He'd been to a military school, had been trained in the ways of the military, had been prepared to attack all his life, but he'd never once in his life met something worth fighting for.

"I guess," he said sleepily. He wanted to crawl into bed so badly he was on the verge of inviting Mary Grace to join him. She was pretty, so angry, so bitter. A night with her would ensure some kind of feeling, even if it wasn't the kind he desired.

"Should I fight for her?" he asked.

"I guess. I guess we should fight. I suppose that's our whole problem," Mary Grace said finally.

"What problem?" he asked, and his question was met with a blank, broad-faced stare.

"Don't you see there's a problem?"

"Yes, but I don't know what to do. Tell me what to do."

"I don't know."

They sat for a very long moment, as long as any he'd ever sat through. Longer than the moment when his parents' lawyers told him of their death. Longer than Tess telling him she was leaving, longer than the Glasses telling him to shape up. He felt there would be no moment longer in his life, because he would not allow it.

"Oh, Joseph," Mary Grace said, sucking in a breath. When he looked at her he managed to see the person who comforted him, Tess's fat friend, the one who'd never threatened him. She wasn't there, but he saw it anyway.

"Oh, Joseph," she repeated. "How did it happen? How is it that we're the ones who got left? What did we do wrong?"

He let the question settle in the air. He took his time over it like a delicate dilemma. But he'd known the answer since she walked in, and maybe for a long time before that.

"We didn't do anything," he answered.

7

Tess sat on the carpet in her empty apartment, staring back and forth at her two most recent acquisitions—the refrigerator and the telephone. Both excited her and made her feel hopeful. Occasionally she walked over to the refrigerator and opened it, squinting as the light from it hit her eyes. There was nothing in it, but it still pleased her. She liked the sight of it, big and important, and the soothing sound of it humming in the corner, going on and off as it was supposed to do, fully aware of its purpose. This is my refrigerator, she thought, which I picked out, which the men from Sears delivered and installed, which I share with no one.

The phone gave her just as much satisfaction. It was only a beige push-button Trimline. The phone company had turned on the line without even coming to her house. They asked her if she wanted any special features and she said she wanted Call Waiting. Anything else? No, thank you. These decisions she made without consulting another living soul. She didn't need Call Waiting, didn't really even need a phone at the moment, as she had no one to call, but choosing that feature had made her day. She wanted it just because she did, and just because she said so, it was done.

Other decisions needed to be made, like furniture and curtains and perhaps extra locks on her doors. She was in no hurry to do any of it, but at the same time, she was eager, excited, looking forward. Each decision, however small, was a declaration of self. This is what I want, and it would be done.

She picked up the receiver every now and then and listened to the reassuring buzz of the dial tone. She should call someone. She should call Mary Grace. She missed her friend and had things to tell her—they hadn't really spoken since the funeral. She knew she could tell Mary Grace all about her feelings for her mother, and her father for that matter, and Joe, and even Vince. When she was holding the receiver in her hand, she had an image, also, of telling Mary Grace exactly how she felt about her—she admired her friend's candor, her edge, her ability to cut through the bullshit. In many ways, she wanted to be more like Mary Grace. But she rejected that thought almost immediately. From this moment on, she had no intention of being more like anyone except herself.

She had not seen Vince since the night they had spent together. She had talked to him once. He was the first person she called when her phone was hooked up, under the pretext of checking out its functions.

"Where are you?" he asked. "I've been thinking about you. I've been wondering where the hell you'd gotten to."

"I have an apartment here in Danville," she told him. "Just a one bedroom, next to Dan River. I can see it from my living-room window if I crane my neck. I think I paid extra for that view."

"Are you all right there?"

"Of course I'm all right."

"How's your father taking it?"

"Daddy? He didn't even seem surprised. I think he's satisfied. He hasn't been alone since God knows when, and in a way, I think that's what he's always wanted."

"What about you?"

She hesitated for a moment. "Yes, I'm alone, too. I don't know if it's what I've always wanted. I've never known what I wanted. But at least now, I've got a shot at finding out."

A silence followed. She wondered if she sounded too cavalier.

"Don't get me wrong," she added. "He loved her. He lived with her for all those years. But Daddy's one of those people who appreciate life on its own terms. If you could see how excited he gets about his garden, about trimming his boxwoods and seeing his daffodils come up in the spring, you'd know what I mean."

"I know what you mean."

"He wants peace. He wants quiet."

"Who doesn't?"

"Some of us need the commotion."

"Is that what you need?"

"Like I said, I haven't had time to figure it out."

Another silence followed. She could hear Judas mewing in the background. She tried to picture Vince lying on his bed, one arm behind his head, his feet crossed, wearing the Brooks Brothers shirt with the tattered sleeve. A current of affection and attraction passed through her, and she shuddered.

"I miss you," she said boldly.

"Ah, Christ," he said. "I miss you, too. I hate that."

She laughed.

"No, really. I swore never to miss another woman after my wife."

"Do you still miss her?"

"Miss who?"

She laughed again.

"I've got to go. I'm on late call tonight. What's your number?"

She gave it to him.

"I'll call you soon."

"Whenever," she said.

"You don't have to play it cool, Tess. I'm smitten, I admit it."

"I'm not playing anything, honestly. I know you'll call. Why wouldn't you?"

"You're something else," he said.

She didn't add the second part of her thought, which was that even if he didn't call, she would live. She was smitten, too. She wanted him desperately, but that was fine. She appreciated the feeling of wanting him; having him was another feeling altogether.

●　　●　　●

The next morning she bought a couch (an antique she found at an estate sale—a fifties-style bamboo affair with floral upholstery), and that afternoon she had her first visitor. She wasn't expecting anyone, and actually jumped when the doorbell rang. It took her a moment to even identify the sound. She went to the door with her heart pounding.

"Who is it?" she asked, her hand on the knob.

"Valerie."

Somehow, she was still surprised when she swung the door open. She thought it might be some other Valerie, a neighbor in the complex dropping by to welcome her. But it was the Valerie she knew, looking as ravishing as ever in teal-blue leggings and a pullover in the same shade. Her hair was pulled back in a French braid. Her eyes were a clear, penetrating blue, and her lips seemed redder than was humanly possible without lipstick.

She is impossibly beautiful, was her first uncensored thought. Men like Joe did not understand, and perhaps never would, that women are just as impressed by such beauty, just as taken aback by it, just as helpless in its presence.

"Come in," Tess said, remembering her manners before anything else.

Valerie came in, inspecting and taking in the contents of her surroundings in one swift turn of the head.

"I was just eating a Lean Cuisine," Tess said. "The baked rigatoni. I've got a refrigerator. Are you hungry? I don't have a stove, but I've got a built-in microwave."

She was a little disappointed in the way she sounded. During these days of solitude, she had somehow convinced herself that she'd developed flawless social skills, that she'd never have another awkward moment in her life. It was going to be harder than she thought.

"No, I'm not hungry. I was over here doing some shopping, and I just thought I'd drop by."

"How'd you find me?"

"Well, I asked your father where you were. Do you realize he doesn't have your address or your phone number? He just happened to remember the name of the apartment complex."

"I've been bad," Tess admitted. "I've kind of let myself disappear."

In one quick second she felt all the progress she'd made start to slip away. She felt awkward and badly put together in Valerie's presence. She felt the need to apologize. She tried to think of Vince as a means of recovery, but to her horror she realized she was worried about losing him to Valerie. She could just picture that scene, introducing them and recognizing that glint in his eyes. The fact that they'd already met did nothing to reassure her.

"Oh, what a nice couch," Valerie said.

"Have a seat."

Valerie sat. Tess felt foolish sitting beside her, so she sat on the floor, facing her, pushing the Lean Cuisine plate aside.

"Why are you eating Lean Cuisine? You don't need to lose weight," Valerie said.

"I know, but I just don't know what to cook for one person. I get so confused in the grocery store. It's like I just load my cart with whatever I see."

Valerie nodded as if this made perfect sense.

Tess stared at her friend and watched her take a breath and clasp her hands together, and she was nearly astounded to see that Valerie was nervous, on edge. She could have sworn she'd never seen that before.

"Tessie," she said, "I'm leaving."

"Leaving your husband?"

"No. Leaving Maddock."

"But why?"

"Well, I don't think there's anything here for me," she answered.

"But what about Joe?"

"Joseph?"

Tess shrugged. She did not care to elaborate, but Valerie, as usual, was forcing her to give more than she wanted.

"I just thought . . . you and he. I thought that was the whole point."

"I don't think that was ever in the cards," Valerie said.

Tess couldn't think of a reply. She just sat very still and received Valerie's cool appraisal.

"I hope that's not the reason you two broke up," Valerie said.

"No. Well, not entirely. But I did think—" She couldn't finish the sentence. It seemed pointless to try. A sudden fear swept over her—the fear that she had left her husband for no reason.

"There's something else I want you to know," Valerie said. "I took your job."

"What job?"

"As librarian, at Millburn."

"Oh, I know that," Tess said. "Everybody knows it."

"Why didn't you ever say anything?"

"Well, I don't know. I was relieved for one thing. It saved me having to make a decision. And then the other thing was, you weren't any good at it."

Valerie's smile faded, but only a fraction.

"Where did you hear that?"

Tess shrugged. "All over."

"Well, now you know why I was determined to be famous. I never could do the simple stuff."

"No, that's for people like me," Tess said, though she didn't mean it to sound so cold.

Valerie looked away and rubbed her hands together. "Well, that's over. All of it's over, really. I wanted to apologize to you. I just feel like . . . I know Jason would accuse me of being narcissistic for saying this. And I know the world doesn't revolve around me or anything. But I do feel like a lot of bad things have happened since I came back. In some way, I can't help feeling responsible."

"You are responsible, Valerie. But not in the way that you think. One human being isn't capable of making people behave in a way that they weren't already inclined to behave."

"Really?"

Tess shrugged. "You are the whole reason Joe and I got together. I think we both wanted to prove we could live without you. And we did for a while, but it was no good without you around to witness it. I don't know, when you came back, I think we both realized that was no reason to stay together. And now, with his parents gone and my mother gone, and you going back, we have to start all over."

Valerie said nothing to this.

Tess went on. "It's so scary, the reasons we do things. The reasons we make our biggest decisions are so very small."

"My," Valerie said, touching her chest, "you've done a lot of thinking about this."

"Look around. What do I have to do with my time but think?"

Valerie smiled. She drummed her fingers on her bare neck. "Well, formulate all the philosophies you want. The fact is, I did instigate the breakup of your marriage."

"No. I won't give you that."

Valerie looked away.

Tess said, "You're not so bad. You want to be, but you're not. Do you want to know the worst thing you've done?"

"Probably not, but go ahead."

"You forced us—I mean me and Mary Grace—you forced us to want things. By nature we were content never to go after anything, but that wasn't possible with you around. All you did was insist that we want more than we had. I'm not making light. It's a terrible thing to do."

Valerie nodded slowly. "Can I apologize now?"

"No. I'm trying to thank you."

They stared at the carpet for a long moment.

"Tell me something," Valerie said. "What are our unresolved differences? Tell me what you're still mad about."

"For leaving," she said. "For saying that none of us mattered."

The phone rang. Tess hesitated, let four rings go by, but finally surrendered.

"I've waited as long as I can. I'm trying to be mature about this. But I need to see you," said Vince.

"I'm busy right now. Can I call you back?"

A silence, then: "Is your husband there?"

"No. Why?"

"You have this tone, like you're scared of someone."

"I'm not. I'm just busy."

"All right, call me back. But chew on this. I love you."

The dial tone buzzed in her ear. She cradled the receiver, fighting a smile.

Valerie was too polite, too knowledgeable, or too unconcerned to ask who it was. It was hard to tell the difference, Tess realized, and it really didn't matter. Valerie's opinion didn't matter to her anymore. Her husband's and her mother's opinions no longer existed. She was as loose and incalculable as a cloud.

"I'd better get going," Valerie said, standing.

Tess followed her to the door.

"Goodbye, Tessie," Valerie said with a sweet, solicitous smile.

Tess thought, I never have to see you again.

She threw her arms around her friend, in a spasm of affection—for all the lost years when they might have been real friends but for the strength they lacked. "Valerie," she said, her nose pressed against the gardenia-scented hair. "You were always the most important person in my life."

"Is that true? Tessie, if it is, I think I can survive."

Tess pulled away from her, from what she knew was her last embrace with a person whose opinion didn't matter.

"The day *you* can't survive is the day we should all give up."

8

Los Angeles had a peculiar gift of making anyone who had
ever lived there, regardless of how long they had been away, feel as
if they'd never left. The minute Valerie's rented car rolled onto the
405 freeway, the familiar landscape bloomed around her—the cars
limping along the oil-slicked blacktop, the tops of buildings peek-
ing over the overpasses, Mexican restaurants and furniture ware-
houses and condominiums with Day-Glo orange Rent Me signs,
the occasional residential neighborhood, boxy houses in every
shape and color, and beyond that all the surface streets, just as con-
gested as the freeway. People going, moving, trying to be somewhere else. Above it all the sun trying to spread its favor through
the sepia haze of smog. It was all so unapologetically ugly. It was a
city that never tried to be any better than it was, couldn't honestly
see why it should be, until its lack of aesthetics became its aesthetics, and it was perversely beautiful.

Unlike Maddock, she thought, driving along, it doesn't have its
past to protect. She'd never have to worry about Los Angeles being
despoiled. It could only improve, and perhaps that feeling was what
crept into the brain of its inhabitants, night after night—we can
only do better, and so each morning they awoke with the hope of
doing just that. She drove past all the signs announcing the next
movie, the next album, the next showcase in Vegas. Vegas, the
country cousin of L.A., was always breathing down their necks,

threatening to come here for an extended visit. Sometimes she thought of Vegas as a kind of lower circle of hell, and the signs reminded people in L.A. of where they'd all end up if they couldn't cut it here.

She was afraid she wouldn't remember the way to the house, but it came back to her like a reflex. Suddenly she was moving along Pacific Coast Highway, one in a trail of cars going dangerously fast, past the harsh gray waves banging against the rocks, past the surfers, past the homeless people picking up bottles and cans and other treasures from the sand. Already, the faces of Maddock began to recede. Tess's face had reverted to the one in high school— wide and round, passively demanding and innocently hopeful. Mary Grace was fat again, and Joe, dressed in his gray uniform, was staring up at her with hazy indecision.

Only Becker's face remained sharp, clear, full of meaning. She kept seeing him standing under the breezeway, scuffing his shoes on the ground, reluctant to expose her to the truth. The bitter and embarrassing disappointment of that moment did not, and would not for a while, recede. But the memory made her feel as if she had somehow accomplished her goal without knowing what it was. She had collected yet another unresolved moment from Millburn to put in her catalogue along with not winning the figure. This was what people needed as much as anything, she decided—the memory of not getting what was desired, what was deserved, in order to keep them surging on. The need to compensate for failure was quite possibly the motor of life.

She turned off onto a canyon road and drove up into the hills.

As she drove up the winding, barely paved path, toward all the modest Spanish and Cape Cod style houses, of which hers and Jason's was one (the mansions were all farther down the road, closer to the Colony), she was surprised to find that one other face did remain clear in her memory—the face of Dr. Ross. Even at this moment she could see that big head and those intense eyes, that beard straining to come through the dough-colored cheeks. She saw his relaxed posture, heard his low, confident voice issuing his theories like a priest issuing a benediction: people who act and people who do not act.

Maybe the desire not to act was what had drawn her back to Maddock. But it was a fleeting desire, and in the end she knew that she could never live that way. She had once claimed that comfort was something she had never wanted, but she had not counted on that part of herself, that part of everyone, she imagined, that was drawn to a world where no decisions had to be made, no steps needed to be taken. It was a dangerous desire. It was a dangerous comfort.

She pulled up in front of their house, the last one on the street, a white stucco with rust trim, its lawn sadly neglected, the plants starting to wither in the heat. She'd have to do something about that. She'd uproot all the rosebushes she had planted in an effort to make herself believe she was somewhere else. She would put in drought-resistant plants: cacti and ice plant and night-blooming jasmine. She'd embrace her home, which was finally her home, because the place she had come from no longer claimed her. She had burned her bridges, but bridges deserved to be burned when they only offered retreat.

She sat in the car, hearing the sea breeze patting against the palm trees. She saw Jason's figure pass by the large plate-glass window in his office. She took the keys out of the ignition, held them tightly, feeling their teeth digging into her palm. Then she opened the door. The hot breeze and the smell of oil and salt water assaulted her. She stepped out into the afternoon, ready to face the consequences of her actions.

● ● ●

As Valerie walked up the sidewalk, she did not know about the small gathering on the bridge just outside of Maddock, the one passing over Cherry Stone Creek that connected the town to Danville. She had passed over it many times on her dates with local boys (before she knew better) and later with Millburn cadets out on a day pass, when they'd shed their uniforms and borrow somebody's car.

But that bridge over Cherry Stone Creek never held much significance for her other than as a means of getting somewhere else. There was no reason for her to imagine the scene that was unfolding.

Three police cars—fully half of Maddock's capacity—were parked there, with flares set out on both sides to stop traffic. Tom Turville was standing at the edge of the bridge, gazing over into the murky waters, as a tow truck attempted to raise the car from its muddied bottom. An ambulance and a half-dozen volunteer paramedics stood at the scene, but as the automobile was lifted, their faces fell less from the awareness of certain tragedy as the realization that their services would not be necessary.

"It's the damnedest thing," said Jeffrey Pike, the deputy sheriff, who was barely old enough to remember to shave, let alone recall the days before the new highway was built, so that this road was now all but deserted. "Who coulda just drove off the bridge like that?"

"Anybody could," Tom replied. Then, squinting, he saw all he needed to see. "But anybody didn't."

"You know that car?"

Tom nodded, confident in his wisdom, but in this moment, saddened by it. It was hard to know so many things. It was hard to enforce the law in a town full of people he cared about.

"I know it," he said. "It's Joe Deacon's car."

"Well, I'll be damned," Jeffrey said.

"No, he'll be damned. Suicide is the one unforgivable sin."

"Suicide?" Jeffrey exclaimed, as if such a notion was as unreliable as reports of extraterrestrial sightings. "You can't think that."

"How else do you explain a man just driving himself off a bridge?"

Jeffrey shrugged. "Drunk, I figure."

"Joe wasn't a drinking man." He turned away from the scene, taking a deep breath and fishing a cigarette out of his shirt pocket. "And anyhow, it figures."

"How does it figure?"

Tom lit his cigarette and let a still moment pass, absorbing all the sounds around him—the crickets and the frogs along with the sickening whir and sucking sounds of the car being retrieved.

"If you had a few years on you, you'd know," Tom said.

"Well, tell me anyhow."

Tom sucked on his cigarette, appreciating the soothing rush of nicotine to his brain. People thought he had an easy job. That showed how much they knew. There was nothing easy about having the answers.

He stared solemnly down at the black waters.

"Dog days," he said.